D0777857

MOTHER OF PEARL

MOTHER

OF

PEARL

A Novel

Melinda Haynes

HYPERION

New York

This book is a work of fiction. Names, characters, places and incidents are either products of the author's imagination or are used fictitiously. Any resemblance to actual events or locales or persons, living or dead, is entirely coincidental.

Copyright © 1999 Melinda Haynes

All rights reserved. No part of this book may be used or reproduced in any manner whatsoever without the written permission of the Publisher. For information address Hyperion, 114 Fifth Avenue, New York, New York 10011.

ISBN 0–7868–6485–0

Haynes, Melinda.
Mother of pearl : a novel / Melinda Haynes. — 1st ed.
p.   cm.
I. Afro-American men—Mississippi—Fiction.   I. Title.
PS3558.A862M67   1999
813'.54—dc21   98-47014
                                  CIP

First Edition

Designed by C. Linda Dingler

10 9 8 7 6 5 4 3 2 1

For my husband Ray,
who told me stories and showed me Jackson

———◦◦◦———

Fate has terrible power. You cannot escape it by wealth or war. No fort will keep it out, no ships outrun it.

—Sophocles

Memory believes before knowing remembers. Believes longer than recollects, longer than knowing even wonders.

—William Faulkner

MOTHER OF PEARL

I

PETAL, MISSISSIPPI

1956

EVEN GRADE WALKED PAST THE SPOT on the bridge where Canaan caught the bottle with his head and saw the blood mark was still there, but just barely. The two-week bake of August sun beginning to mask its humiliation, blending the old man's emission to a color like that of rusted girder. On a day not spent dealing with death, Even would have stopped one more time to wonder over the bigger insult: that Canaan's middle-aged forehead got split by glass and bled out, or that the bottle bearing skin and blood soared over a rail and dropped into the water that he loved. Death or no, Even's suspicion was the same as two weeks back: both. Both were equally bad.

Patting for a shirtfront pocket that wasn't there, he fixed a mark on the sun and gauged the time later than normal by half an hour; summed the earth's indifferent swing as more proof of inconsequential man. On an ordinary day he would have stood still in the spot—left foot in Hattiesburg, right foot in Petal—and considered the river Leaf. The way the trees leaned in low as if made curious by their reflection. The way those leaning trees formed a diminishing edge that followed the water like the furrow of a snake. On a day less strained he would have made a box of his hands and peered through like a blindered horse, feeling less overwhelmed by the viewing of segments. He had never known such colors. Never dreamed brown was such a rainbow. He'd always thought of brown as brown, the color of burnt toast or worn-out shoes. But after months on end he'd learned to parcel out the values into new shades fast approaching the limit of his imagination—Ten-Minute Tea. Steeped-Too-Long Tea. Barely Tea. Wet Bark. Sun-Baked Bark. Old-as-Sin Bark. Old Soggy Leaves. Just-Dropped Leaves. Fresh Wet Leaves. And these were just the browns. He was yet to go on to green, which he was just now beginning to see.

Sniffing the air, he drew in smells of hot grease and pork. Meat grilling somewhere inside Petal's boundaries. Still on the bridge, he searched the water, hopeful for a rainbow in spite of the approach of suppertime, spying out travel-blackened logs lying like sleepers inside a purple shade, but no rainbow. Too late for that. The sun so low, brown was just plain brown again. He glanced over once, saw a vague tea-colored ripple— catfish probably—and shrugged. Willie Brackett's blood was to his undershirt, red soaking in and turning stiff in the breeze, brushing against his arm like a crusty leaf. He walked on. Glanced up once to a maroon sun. Glanced back down again.

When Even passed under the caution light at Central and Main, he saw Canaan sitting on the warm deck of the loading dock of the Feed and Seed. Leaning against the wall, his shades on his bony nose, Canaan had put aside the bandage he'd worn for two weeks. On approach, Even saw the scar was healing up to that of question mark tilted to its side and he wondered over it. Canaan didn't stop reading. Just said from behind newsprint as Even approached, "I do say, Even Grade, somebody dead? Or Hercules Powder givin' overtime to their most talkative nigger? Which is it?"

"Somebody dead."

Canaan looked up. Sometimes when he was startled he took on a resemblance to that of dried-up mummy and that's how he looked then. His mouth frozen open inside a face so lined, tears or sweat or blood would never have a choice in direction. "Thy God, who?"

"Two somebodies—Willie Brackett and James Evans. You got something cold?"

Canaan handed him a green bottle and a slice of hard cheese. Sitting down to the edge of the loading dock beside a man old enough to be his father, Even bit into the cheddar and drank deep from his Coca-Cola. Canaan folded up his newspaper, crossed his arms over his chest, waiting. Realizing nothing would be coming out quick, he pushed his glasses up on his nose and said, "I've known Willie's mama since she got that boy—she ain't gonna make it through this one. Not this time. Lord, what a mess."

"If she'd got there 'fore I picked up his face and tied it back on with my shirt, she'd be dead right now."

"That why you wanderin' around in your undershirt?"

"Yes sir, it is." Even munched on the cheese and thought how good an apple would be with it.

"You there when it happened?"

"Almost. Left the area on break five minutes earlier—"

"You know how it happened?"

"I got me a pretty good idea." Even finished his cheese.

"Well, you wanna tell me 'fore I have to read the cleaned-up union version in the *Hattiesburg American*?"

Even looked back toward the bridge wondering where to begin. Canaan knew most of it. That the "Bull Gang," a group of twenty-seven Negroes with varying degrees of mechanic skills, worked whatever the union said to work—scraping out, hosing down, tightening up, loosening what needed to be, by careful degrees. Doing during their swing every low-down shitty job that needed doing, deep down where nobody else wanted to go. He knew they did it with both eyes wide open and steady on their work buddy.

Canaan knew Even worked irregular hours. He knew it was against union regulations. He also knew it didn't matter worth a shit because the union wouldn't let in the Negro in 1956. Union needed the Bull Gang like they needed their balls, but they'd rather take a rusted knife to their own crotch than admit it. Could've used their dues, too. But that didn't matter, either. Not one little bit. Colored was Colored and that was that. No use worrying over it. Better to work at worrying over whether or not your buddy's got his head on straight and able to watch the couplings right, or if he's worried about home or his woman or the numbers he's played and lost big on again and what he's gonna say to the bookie who broke his finger last month and said, "I'm goin' lower next time, nigger—" Better to wonder if that same nigger's closed off that valve good as you would, and is standing there readin' the gauge pressure like his own mama's where you're at. Flat on your back in the mud, breathing turpentine, underneath a pipe labeled three ways in yellow on black: "Warning" and "Toxic" and "Danger." No use worrying about a union in the face of pressing matters that pressed on a body a helluva lot more. Canaan knew these things as good as Even did. Better to tell it as it happened. And so he did.

He told about the siren five minutes into break. How he knew before it quit its scream what had happened. How he knew it was Willie and James because James was horny for a woman he couldn't afford who was driving him crazier by the second. Knew Willie let him slide because he'd had one just like her a few years back and sweet was sweet, no matter the cost. Even knew these things and told them to Canaan. He finished by saying how once the air cleared in sub-level two, the crew had found them both thrown against a boiler in a heap—James still clutching his wrench, burned crisp by molten resin, and Willie splayed wide, his arms spread out like Christ, with no face.

"And that's why I'm an hour late home and shirtless." He finished the last of his Coke and set the bottle on its side, spinning it easy with his finger. He didn't tell Canaan how he couldn't help crying, Oh Jesus . . . Oh Jesus . . . Oh Jesus . . . while he picked up a sheet of skin that used to be a face and put it back on a bloody smear of a thing, or how he fought puking while he pulled off his old blue chambray and wrapped up the head before Willie's mama showed up looking for her only son and found him faceless.

The caution light at Center and Main blinked steady on and off in the middle of the empty intersection where most traveled through on a tractor or beat-up truck, but very seldom in a car. The Quarter—pronounced "niggertown" by the white folks—was still out of sight, still a mile beyond with his small house and others just like it lining red dirt streets named after flowers.

"I'm headed thataway—" Even nodded his head in a direction away from town.

"I'll be on directly. Been reading more about Arkansas and what's stirring there." Canaan tapped the newspaper, still folded in his lap.

"Well, you read then, while the light's easy, but I'm tired."

"I guess you are. After what you seen, you don't need an old man's predictions." Canaan picked up the paper and opened it to its center. Spinning the bottle one more time, Even patted his shoulder and stood up, stretching, meaning to head for home.

"When I was a boy, my daddy took me down to the train depot to see a dead whale." Canaan's low voice was behind him, feathery in the hot wind. "Cost him a quarter just so I could sit up on his shoulder and touch the side of that big ole ugly thing. Never seen so many people in all my life, all straining for a look at something big, dead and pitiful. Folks said it'd washed up in Gulfport and some bright boy thought of carting it up from Biloxi, in steamy summer, stinking to high heaven, just to make a buck or two. Gulls followed, too. Thousands and thousands of 'em. They covered the train cars in front and behind, turned 'em white and noisy. Flew over the crowd. Shit over most everbody. All those birds just sitting there staring. All I could think when I saw that whale and its tiny slitted eyes—barely open and blue-cloudy—was how ugly a thing it was for us to be standing underneath a broiling sun looking at a thing so pitiful. That's what I thought. Just seven, and I thought that. I remember thinking there weren't a tarp big enough to cover a thing of that size, but I sure wished there was." He crossed his legs and shook open the newspaper. "Shirts have been lost over lesser things, Even Grade—I'm sure sorry 'bout those two boys."

Even didn't answer, just raised his hand and waved as he walked underneath the yellow light blinking overhead. He found himself back on the sidewalk and moving past the barbershop and Owl Drug. Canaan's blood there, too. His blood pennies dribbled across half of Petal because some boy in a truck took good aim and hurled a Coke at a wobbly old Negro.

The Quarter was closer now, still not in sight, but closer. Breath came easier thinking of Bellrose Street—a strange name for a place not at all like a bell or a flower, but where his house sat with its faded front porch and the green metal chair. He passed Virginia Street with its tall trees, then on past Cedar Knot Avenue where a couple of kids were rolling a ball out into the street. By that point his neck was relaxed and in spite of things, he found himself humming.

A sea of curly dock grew wild along the clay road, standing in waist-high clusters. And though he'd never noticed the wildflowers before June, he'd met them since and been told more than once that their seeds, still white and hidden, would turn rust-colored once the weather cooled and the days shortened. He'd been told a tea could be brewed from boiling out the yellow root; a tea good enough to cure the stomach and the gums and certain cases of jaundice. He'd been told the leaves were fresher and better than the juice of a ripe lemon and that the seeds could be ground up as meal or coarse flour and baked up as bread. Thinking on it, he watched the curling leaves, caught up and moving in greenish blue waves. A month ago, the hedge was just one more patch of fast-growing green springing up wild on the side of a road he walked day in and day out. Now that patch had a name and a purpose and a deep-seated sermon. Judy had said to him sometime around the middle of June, "The language of 'dock' is patience—you remember that, Even Grade, next time you see it growin' alongside the road or in a wasted place." And while he hummed some nonsense song, he did remember and thought on the true patience of a man and what it might mean and put to sum all the other countless lessons such a woman with such a memory might equal. Stretching his neck, hearing it pop in all directions, he hummed louder, his hands swinging free.

Contrary within himself over his two-sided emotions—feeling such good, sweet relief his week's shift was over on one side, but sick to death over Willie and James on the other—he reached down and pulled off a dark green, wavy leaf and rubbed it between his hands. Waxed and cool, it felt soft and thin along its curl. Folding it up accordionlike, he put the length of it in his mouth and chewed, feeling it unfold and open against his teeth like something still living. He tasted a similarity to lemons and something deeper in that spoke of well-seasoned fish and lemon meringue pie and all those tart, clean foods of summer. Never knew patience could taste so good, was his thought as he saw his street coming at him just a hundred steps away. Knowing he'd turn in and see his porch with its single green metal chair. He liked to sit there at night, leaning back in study of the stars while his nearest neighbor, who was still back a ways reading yesterday's paper on the loading dock, yelled out his thoughts from the porch next door.

Under a hard noon sun the white water tower at the top of the hill had a way of looking like a stripped-down widow woman, all flaked-out and peeling, pale and ugly and sad, but with the sun falling and the sky near purple at the horizon, the tower seemed stately again, its weaknesses shored up and braced; covered over by the evening light. Spitting out patience to the side of his porch he climbed the steps with tired, aching feet, glad to see Saturday on its way, just behind tonight's moon now, with nothing marked down on that fresh page to do either, but whatever it was that happened to come to mind.

—*I'm goin' Lo Lo to see Lo Lo, she so Lo Lo, she need Lo Lo . . .*

At the beginning of August, Even Grade was still a happy man.

2
HALF-STATES AND CURSES

THE HOUSE OF LUVENIA KORNER on Hillcrest Loop had a bedroom at the end of its hall that had not always been a bedroom.

In the beginning, at a point between 1911 and 1912 when the house was newly built by Luvenia's father, William, the room at the end had been what was called the peeling platform. Simple, a ten-by-ten porch squared off around the back door, it was a space where as a child Luvenia had been sent to do various jobs—peel potatoes, shell beans and peas, pluck a fresh-killed chicken, and on Saturdays, wash the clothes.

"Your great-grandpa called it a platform, but I called it work."

She went on to say that she'd slept out there underneath a tent—more than once, too. Four times that she could think of right off. Usually on holidays when her daddy's folks from over in Eldorado came visiting and the only other bedroom besides her father's went to the cousins. "Aunts and uncles were spread out all over—even up and down the hall," she went on to say. Her daddy, if it was Thanksgiving or Christmas and the air chilly, would build her a fire out in the backyard, far enough away from the old pecan tree and the house to be safe, about midways back into the field by the old tractor shed. Luvenia said that she would fall asleep out on the peeling platform watching a red-orange pyramid of wood crash around itself finally until it was left only a smolder—low and gray and blue—shaped like barely anything at all.

"The tent always smelled like the ass-end of the root cellar," Luvenia had said, "and there was something moldy growing on top of the old canvas that made my nose and eyes itch, but falling asleep on the peeling platform, watching a fire while the wind rustled the leaves of the old pecan tree, is one of the best memories I own. Your great-granddaddy closed it off around 1920 and we called it the dry porch then."

It was still a place where she would be sent to peel and shell and pluck and wash. It just had a different name at that point, and a gabled roof over its top that shielded from rain, and three sides of screening that kept away the bugs and mosquitoes and the biting flies.

"It was two inches lower than the rest of the house with a slight lean toward the back because he believed more in 'eyeballin'' a thing than proper measuring. Being Methodist he thought a house 'truly plumbed' was an abomination in the eyes of God."

Luvenia explained her point by telling her granddaughter how once he was done tacking down the last screen and his saw and nail bag were hanging back on the nail in the shed, he had stood by the new door opening while she—ten-year-old Luvenia—sat at the old back door and placed her jack ball down on the floor by her feet. Knees up under her dress, she watched the ball move forward and away toward the back door, picking up speed until it went flying out the opening. Her daddy had said not a word and when the ball bounced down the steps, led there by the slope of the room, he patted the side of the enclosure like one would a respected friend, and said, "'purt'near." Tossing the ball back to her he stepped up onto the canted floor and said, "Perfection's for God, Luvenia. The rest of us got to get along with 'purt'near.'"

It became one of Luvenia's favorite sayings and the day that the workmen nailed the last of the beaded board to the wall of the used-to-be dry porch of the used-to-be peeling platform, now a fresh bedroom for Valuable, she patted the wide window where a door used to be and said, "Purt'near, Baby Girl—I'd have to say this bedroom is purt'near."

Luvenia passed the saying down to her granddaughter along with a love of wide open spaces and nighttime fires as well as the room at the end of the hall that had been other things before it became a room.

Valuable wrote carefully, her body contorted around the small notebook in the curious fashion of the left-handed—*There is a coolness in a crow's world that is hateful* and then she scratched it out with her pencil, not wanting to eat up time by using the eraser. Through the walls and door she could hear loud laughter and bottles knocking together and the thud of something heavy hitting the floor. Leaning a little, she saw the two of them chasing each other down the hall like fools. There was more sudden laughter and the clear, clean sound of bottles meeting, then falling—like a game of homemade bowling was going on up in the living room. Valuable's door was partially open, and the shotgun style of the house let her keep an eye on what they were doing, which room they were in, what they were handling out in the kitchen. They had left the hall and, she could tell by the squeaking springs, had thrown themselves down on the iron bed in what at one time had been Luvenia's room. There was baritone laughter loud enough to rattle the glass in her bedroom window and then the sound of more bottles, rolling and bumping into posts or frames or legs, which, of course, led to even louder laughter, her mother's this time.

"Well, shit then!" Valuable kicked off the covers, walked over and shut her door. Having left it open on purpose because the two in the front of the house could not be counted on to act properly, she had tracked their progress, seen the generalized theme of their roamings, and come tomorrow, when it was time to make biscuits or an apple pie, she intended to know exactly where her pastry cutter and spices had been placed, and exactly where, during some maniacal fit, they had thrown her tin measuring spoons. That had been her first intention. She hadn't counted on the level of the noise, though. And she hadn't counted on being hit by a need to write, either.

Back on her bed, she rearranged her pillows and picked up her notebook. Sucking on the end of her pencil, she shut her eyes and thought of the crow she'd seen. High up. Cold. Hateful. She searched for those words again. Rummaged for verb and noun and adjective the same way she used to search for silver buttons in the bottom of Luvenia's button tin. Seeing it finally, picking up the thread one more time, she bent again, and wrote:

From pirate perch of patient pine
 a crow can watch gray meanness plait
  long finger shadows.
Cruel shades of curving. Crouching specks
 of painful shade moving forlorn
  in gold-brown grass
And laughing—

Her thrown-open door hit the wall with a bang, and then closed halfway, carried by its own momentum into the lean of the room. It had been thrown open by Enid, who picked different times of the day or night to do it, but who always entered the same way—quick and loud and with an expression on her face that faded into slight disappointment the second she found Valuable writing or reading or drawing. As if she expected to find her daughter doing what she herself would be doing behind a closed door.

Light from the kitchen shifted halfway into Valuable's bedroom, shining on the lower half of things. Bed. Low drawers of the chest. The bottom part of the stool. Light halfway between in and out. A door, halfway between open and closed. And a woman half-dressed, inserted near the center of both. A more annoying and rude thing than a thrown-open door exposing a half-state woman Valuable could not imagine. Straightening, she hid her notebook under her legs and folded her arms across her stomach while she glared at her mother.

Years earlier, when her mother had come back to town, Valuable's first daughterly evaluation of Enid Korner had been that the woman existed in a "halfway state." Somewhere between here and there. Somewhere left of "center" and south of "whole." Luvenia was newly dead, her red grave mound barely tamped, and without her grandmother around to check her math, Valuable had given the woman a chance to pull her parts together for a year or two and then she'd quit, discovering that her math, even as a seven-year-old, had been correct, after all.

As if to prove the point Enid was wearing a red half-slip and bra and watching her with eyes half closed. Her hair was halfway between up and down. Some swept up in a sloppy knot while the remainder trailed down her back. Halfway between drunk and sober, she leaned against the doorframe for support with her arms hidden behind her, as if half her appendages were missing. Slow and easy, with half the toes on one bare foot she kicked at the door, which was steady-creeping forward toward its latch because of the way things stood.

"Whatcha doin', baby?"

Valuable looked up thinking that even her voice was half woman half child. Men liked it. Valuable had heard this latest one saying he'd give her a five-dollar bill just to say certain things while they cavorted in the room that used to belong to Luvenia.

The sound a bottle makes when it hits the floor and spills—that clunk and rush—came up the hall and Enid yelled out, "Reilly, you make a mess, you clean it up!" She kicked at the door again and whispered, "He's such a clumsy fool—" while she walked toward her daughter, not as drunk as Valuable had thought, but still stumbly. Sitting down on the side of the single bed she bent forward and said, "Whew!" Elbows to knees, she appeared to be studying the grain pattern of the pine floor. Or her red toe-nails. Or something interesting down along the low edge of the bed.

Reclaiming hair that had fallen from its knot, she swept it back away from her face and fumbled for her tit. Black bobby pins were clipped to her red bra like fork tines. For as long as Valuable had known her—seven years now—Enid had worn them there, and until growing small breasts and need-ing a brassiere of her own, Valuable thought all bras came that way, with their own supply of ten to fifteen bobby pins attached to the upper side of a cup. Enid picked one off while holding her hair back with one hand, and using fingers and teeth, pinned up her hair. Three moves. Fingers. Teeth. Fingers. Done. Watching her, Valuable couldn't help but wonder which came first— the boob or the bobby? Where had those black pins been stored before Enid had grown tits that needed support? Pinned and neat, Enid went side-down on her daughter's bed, trapping her daughter's stretched-out legs under her.

"You know what? Your hair's almost as long as mine—" Enid reached for the long strand hanging over Valuable's ear. "I bet you a ten-dollar bill if we went to that photographer over in Vicksburg, he'd think we were sis-ters. You think?" Her hand was smoothing the bed, working its way toward the hidden notebook. She pulled at its corner. "Hey, you been writing again? You gonna let your mama see?"

Valuable jerked it free and put it in her lap, hugging her knees. She kept the pencil clutched in her left hand, sharp end out as warning.

"You still not talking? Well, that's okay, I guess—I guess I talk enough for both of us. At least, that's what folks in the beauty shop say. You think I do? Reilly says I do." She was leaning against the wall wrapping a piece of her hair around her ear.

Valuable made herself sit still and stare at her mother's thin eyebrows. Crows. Why, they look just like far away, flying crows. When Enid raised them, she seemed startled and young and terribly stupid, and for one timid second Valuable felt such a truckload of pity for her, it seemed as if a hand had closed around her throat. She had to swallow hard just to make it go away.

"I bet you a hundred bucks you'll want to talk one day, though. Bet when you get serious about boys and want to learn how to do your hair up pretty, you'll want your mama then. Bet you'll talk a blue streak then."

—*Such a thick river of things halfway done between us . . .*

Enid rubbed a casual palm around her knee. Applied invisible lotion across the cusp of a bone. Watching her, Valuable felt weak and strange. Dizzy, almost. As if she were searching for leverage inside a sphere.

—*Inside this thick river she drowns me with her casualness. . .*

It was the speech avoidance game. One she'd been playing since a day six years ago when she'd asked a perfectly simple question and gotten a ridiculous answer and even though she wasn't sure "casualness" was really a word, the sound of it suited her.

—*I am a bitch of a bard,* she wrote in her head, *bold, brave, brimming with benevolences unless . . . unless . . . bothered by* (some "b" word, some word like "buffoon") . . .

Valuable stared at her mother's tits.

—*bothered by bobby pins on a brassiere.*

Bingo.

"Babydoll!" This from the front of the house. The house of Luvenia Korner. The house that would always be the house of Luvenia Korner even though she was dead now and underneath hard dirt in the cemetery at the top of the hill and two people had moved in who didn't deserve to live.

"What!" The force of it pushed Enid away from the wall.

"I only got tonight, baby—I do a run to Texas tomorrow—"

"Hold your damn horses! I'm talking to my daughter—" She smiled at Valuable. "Talk to me, baby—you can't keep this up forever." She screwed up her mouth in one corner and Valuable saw her lipstick was smeared.

"I came back, didn't I? Didn't I come back and take care of you?" She reached out as if to touch her and the hand fell short and landed on Valuable's thigh, curiously warm. Valuable pushed it aside with her pencil's eraser.

"I bet if you'd talk to me we could work this thing out. Just two girls trying to be friends. Forget about the mother part, I'm too young for that anyhow—" Her hair was falling again and she was slouched over, crimping her flawless white stomach.

Valuable clutched her pencil and with a silent prayer the woman would go away, she looked around the room.

Everything here is a day, she thought. The day the dresser had been lowered from the attic. The day the chair had been reupholstered in rose damask. The day the chifforobe had been taken apart and polished with paste wax until it gleamed like gold. Over the dresser, high up on beaded board, were her pictures of horses. Some sketched on days it rained. Others cut from magazines on days it was too cold to go outside. Equine-themed days thumbtacked and prancing around her mirror. To the left, draped over a small wooden rod, was the quilt she had begun the summer Luvenia died. Twelve squares in red and white and blue. A fledgling version of Prizewinner. Luvenia had had her copy the pattern on those days her chest hurt and her legs swelled up and she couldn't walk. With her feet propped up on three plaid pillows she had called out instructions while Valuable cut out the flag-colored cloth, making a solemn promise to show Valuable how to slip-stitch the hem when the day came for finishing. That time never showed because Luvenia was finished before the quilt got a decent start. On the dressing table Valuable saw the gift from Neva and Bea, a silver brush set sent over on the day they took Luvenia up the hill. Everything was a day: the horses, the piece of a quilt, the furniture. Even the colored ribbons that Enid slipped onto the dresser once or twice a month. Because Valuable wouldn't be caught dead wearing anything in her hair she chalked those up to days that were a waste of time. She looked around the room and blinked, tasting salt when she swallowed. *Every single thing here is a day.*

"I know you talk. Neva and Bea said you talk a blue streak ever time you visit."

Silence.

"Enid! Get your pretty tail in here, girl!" His heavy feet shuffled into the kitchen and they both heard the door open to the Hotpoint. Milk bottles chinged together like loose music. "Babydoll! You hear me calling you?!" He stopped his loud foraging and the sounds vanished to a point they could hear each other breathing. An acorn from a tall oak dropped to the tin roof of the shed halfway across the yard and they both jumped like they'd been shot.

"Enid?" He was standing in the hall, blocking the light.

"In a minute, Reilly." She sounded tired. Worn down.

Valuable watched her, thinking her mother's dark widow's peak made her heart-shaped face look like a cookie tin. Covertly she felt along her cheekbones and chin and judged her own as being less sharp, softer around the edges. The resemblances were strong, though, other than that and she knew it. The same wide-set eyes and now that it had grown out over the summer, the same hair. Valuable ran a finger along her upper lip. *But I've got a different mouth, thank God.* Enid's was wide and thin and when she smiled it disappeared into two slashing red lines that made her teeth look large and like those of a horse. But men loved it. "Smile for me, baby," Valuable had heard more than once from the bedroom and even out on the street. Valuable's mouth was smaller, fuller, and since she had never seen herself smiling she didn't have a clue what her lips turned into then. She just knew she'd never been asked to smile for anyone in particular.

"You're not gonna talk to me, are you?" It was a statement, not a question.

Silence.

Enid pushed herself off the bed and stood, smoothing down her slip. Flat and tiny and slightly sunken in around the belly button, her stomach had one lonely white stretch mark. The only proof she had ever given birth. Aware of being watched, she drummed long nails and preened, cat-like. Backlit by the hall light, Valuable could see her mother wasn't wearing her panties, and at the sight of pubis every halfway sentimental thought she'd scribbled down in her head concerning her mother disappeared. Enid, a halfway woman, but one far enough along to know when effort is wasted on a thing, sensed something and pointed a finger in her daughter's direction. It trembled like the finger of a picked-on child, too, which was a strange thing since that made Valuable the bad guy.

"One day you're gonna need me," Enid said and her voice cracked. "In spite of everything I am and everything I've done, one day you're gonna grow up and need your mama. Everybody does sooner or later—even you." She walked out not bothering to shut the door she had thrown open.

"Don't hold your breath," Valuable's mouth said to the horses on the wall. But *Dear Lord Jesus, I hope not—* was what she wrote in her head.

It took her a few minutes to recover. From what, she wasn't sure. All she knew was that she needed time and space to come back to herself, calm herself down. She was in her third day of bleeding for the fourth time in six months and looking back on the night, as well as the fight with Jackson the Sunday before, she decided her grandmother had been as right about this as she'd been about corn bread. It was harder to be female in the middle of the curse. Tears showed up out of nowhere and dependable emotions turned slick and unpredictable. Girlhood is short as summer, Valuable thought to herself, disgusted. As short as summer.

Light sifted in under the bottom of the door and she looked away, throwing her pencil to the dresser where it landed next to Luvenia's quilting scissors. Holding her legs to her chest she traced the letters imprinted in the side with her mind. She couldn't see them, but she had watched her grandmother hold the scissors so often she knew what they spelled. Weiss. Tracing the letters until they blurred and ran down to last week's wasted ribbons, she looked over at the used-to-be kitchen stool sitting in the corner like one punished. Memory was there, flat on the wood like spread-out cards. That time in the air before my feet touched down on that stool was girlhood. Brief. Barely minutes. Just a small book of seconds, she thought. "I wish I'd never touched the stool, Gran. I really do wish this thing—"

Unless the preacher was coming for a visit or maybe the insurance man was coming by to collect, Luvenia always wore her stockings rolled down around her ankles like beige tubes. Up meant formality, something special, and this is what Valuable remembered. Those tube-like beige things missing from around her grandmother's shoes while she set the stool in front of the kitchen sink and said, "Today is corn bread and a talk. You're nearly 'bout seven. I guess you're old enough now." Suspended between knowing and not, Valuable rose so high in Luvenia's arms she could see out the kitchen window. So high she saw the redbirds scrambling out on the grass. Holding her arms out like a bird, she looked down and saw the brown of the stool. Once she was there Luvenia handed her the stirring pot for making tap water corn bread and with the same attitude one would use in describing the color of a truck, told her she would bleed one day.

"Every woman does this and it ain't nothin' to worry about." Luvenia's face was wide and confident, and while she measured out her recipe, she told her all about it. "You might go to the bathroom one day and wipe your bottom and see blood, so don't you be scared by it because it's not forever. Three to six days at most. And if cramps come as part of the package, a hot water bottle'll help."

Valuable watched the wet meal turn to yellowy mush and then she looked out the window where the birds were picking at seed. "Why can't I just sit on the toilet and be done with it?" Valuable asked, alarmed as much by the three to six days of it as she was by the initial information.

"Because you'd be sitting there 'til the cows come home," was her grandmother's answer.

"I bet it skips some girls—I bet not everybody bleeds." It was a prayer.

"Yes, they do, sweetie, and by the time it rolls around, you'll be ready for it. Proud of it even, because all your girlfriends will be doing the same. Now watch that water. Turn the hot up because the temperature is crucial."

She had lied on that one. Valuable didn't have any girlfriends. "How come I have to bleed?" Her throat was closing up.

"Because the curse is a part of life, honey. A woman drops an egg inside her lower stomach and it sits there waiting and if what it's waiting for don't come, it gets washed out by the blood." Luvenia had walked over to the stove and dropped water off her finger into the grease.

"What's the egg waiting for?" They had chickens. She'd seen their eggs. They were large and came out a chicken's ass.

"The egg is waiting for the seed of a man, and if it don't show up it leaves. Washes out." Luvenia took the pot from Valuable's hands and stirred vigorously. "A full moon makes the coupling painful for the woman, too. That, and high humidity. That's why it's so darn important to consult the Almanac before setting a wedding date." She'd shoved her glasses up on her nose with a wet finger. Valuable wished her grandmother would undo her stockings and roll them back down around her ankles and talk about something simple. Like biscuits. Stranded on the stool she watched the redbirds, suddenly hating the color of them.

"Coupling's a mess, too. A good wife will think ahead and take an old hand towel with her. Maybe stick it between the mattress and springs so that once he's done she can blot herself and the sheets." She dropped more water to the grease and judged it ready.

"Is there bleeding then, too?" Valuable asked, wondering what had happened to her voice; why it sounded so high and strangled.

"No—well, maybe just a bit the first time. After that, it's just a pure-d mess."

"Oh." And this bad because pure-d in Luvenia's book was saved for things like vomit or when her dog got smashed by a car.

The cornmeal went sizzling into hot grease, splattering high and angry. Over the noise of it Luvenia said that while it was not altogether unpleasant for a wife, the man was the one who seemed to howl at the moon over the whole business of depositing the seed. "There's nothing a man loves better than emptying that old chuck wagon," she had said while she slid a spatula underneath the thin, crusty bread and flipped it onto a flowered plate. "Perfect," she said.

Valuable learned to make corn bread just as well as Luvenia. She never developed a taste for it, though, seeing how blood was as much a part of the recipe as meal and water and grease.

Her vision cleared and she saw the scissors and wondered over it all.

"I'm not dangling over the stool anymore, am I?" And she felt silly for saying it because it was almost like Judy Garland whining to her dog, "Well, Toto, we're not in Kansas anymore, are we?" But it was the truth. She still felt seven years old and suspended in the air, not knowing.

Fourteen and a half now, she stared at her wall halfway expecting it to open up into a window over a sink where she could see the redbirds.

One reason she still felt like a child was because the logic didn't work. The thing about the towels and their purpose was just part of it. The physical mechanics of the act of seedplanting was another. Where? (She had examined her body and couldn't imagine.) How? (Again, she had examined her body and couldn't imagine.) She was set on the why, though. Because more than anything else in the whole wide world, a man enjoyed emptying his chuck wagon, whatever that was.

They'd been swimming naked since they were seven years old and there wasn't a single thing on Jackson's body that came close to resembling a covered wagon. His privates were different from hers, that much was true. External and tubular with an extra pouch thrown in by God for some queer reason. But there was nothing on his body that looked like a wagon carrying seed. She'd come close to asking him about it. Where it was kept and why men enjoyed emptying it to the point they howled at the moon. But she didn't. She kept her questions to herself for the same reason she'd been burying the proof of her bleeding out in the backyard under the old pecan tree. The chuck wagon and its seed were related to her bleeding somehow, and this being the case they were too embarrassing to discuss. With anyone. Even her best friend.

Feeling steadier in the head, Valuable leaned over and slipped her notebook underneath the wooden bed slats and walked to the door and listened. Opening the door a crack, Valuable watched the images in the mirror.

The only door in or out of the house was past their room, and because Enid liked to watch herself in the oval mirror out in the hall, Valuable knew the door would be left open. Easing out into the kitchen she scooped Reilly's cigarettes off the table while she watched Enid's head off the bed, upside down. Her mouth open as well as her eyes, fingers using those bobby pins of hers to curl her hair while Reilly did whatever it was he was doing, on top of her.

Once back behind the closed door, Valuable pulled off her pajamas and pulled on a button-up shirt and a pair of pedal pushers. Frowning, she looked at herself in the mirror while she felt her crotch. The bulk of her Kotex made her feel like a giant baby with a problem. She always worried that every person she met knew exactly how cursed she was between her legs. She hated it. Hated everything about it.

Turning off her lamp, she put her ear to the door one more time and listened. She'd watched the whole show once when she went for buttermilk at midnight, so she knew the routine. How long it would last. How they both would collapse once it was over. She thought it was a shame, too. Sad as winter, almost, the way those two played circus games in Luvenia's bedroom.

"But I'm not over that stool anymore, am I?" Crossing to her window, she put her shoulder behind it and pushed up until the sashes met. Swinging over her legs she dropped out the opening of the used-to-be peeling platform, down onto the cool, dark dirt behind the camellia bush.

She had to tap on his window for fifteen minutes before he woke up.

Seeing his head through the open blinds, she stepped back where he could see and waggled the stolen cigarette pack in front of her face. He rubbed his eyes, yawned, and held up one finger in an "okay, just one minute" signal. Edging toward the flower trellis, where she'd be hidden if anybody got up to go to the kitchen or something, she waited, wishing she'd gone to the bathroom and checked on that business down there before she'd climbed out her window and walked up the hill to his house.

Droplets from Mrs. McLain's late watering dripped off the trellis onto her shoulders and across the bridge of her nose and she shivered. Chilled because the faucet at the side of Jackson's house leaked and she'd stepped into a puddle up to her ankles, she held on to her elbows while the three-quarter moon slid behind the clouds and all those shapes she knew as well as the back of her hand disappeared like ghosts. If she'd been thinking she would have brought her lighter. The four-leaf clover one Jackson lifted off his father. If she'd just had the good sense to bring it along she could snap it open and at least see the magnolia trees. Moving out from under the trellis to the side of the house where even without a steady light things seemed more familiar, she sat down on the grass holding her stomach, wishing for an aspirin.

He was running and looking back toward the trellis where she usually waited, when he tripped over her, sliding across the grass on his stomach. His knee had punched into her shoulder, knocking her flat to her back.

"Jeezus, Val! You almost broke my friggin' neck!" He was up on his knees rubbing it.

"Oh yeah? What about my back, you stupid idiot!" She rolled up on her knees and brushed off the seat of her pants, irritated as hell. Dark again, the moon's light swallowed up by clouds, she crawled on all fours looking for the cigarettes.

"Here dummy. Here they are—" He'd already lit one up and was waving the snuffed match in the air in front of his face, leaving a trail of sweet-smelling smoke. Leaning back on his hands, he watched her pick fresh-cut grass out of her hair. With his bare foot stretched forward he used his long toes to brush loose grass off her knees, thinking her skin felt unusually smooth, opposite of his.

"Enid know you're out past midnight?" His voice was low, grown husky over the summer and strange sounding, especially in the dark.

"Oh sure. She just told me to behave myself and tossed me the keys when I walked out the door—"

"Climbed out the window again, did you?" He shook his head, laughing, and put another cigarette in his mouth, lit it up and handed it to her.

"Thanks—"

"Welcome—"

The moon reappeared and she saw that his jeans had a hole in the knee, an old hole with fray around its edges. Blond knee hair stuck through like tiny white springs and she thought of Reilly and Enid and the noise of the bed and looked away. A night breeze barely stirred, rustling the wide green leaves of the magnolia tree in the front yard. Sitting next to him she smelled outdoors, a leftover smell of heat and grass and skin that reminded her of swimming the creek and the way they'd always lounge naked on the sand afterward while they let the sun dry their skin in its own good time. She bent down and sniffed her arm and smelled only Lux. She had a reason for being there and the sooner she served it up, the sooner she could get home to her hot-water bottle.

"About last Sunday—"

"Forget it."

"Can't—"

"Try." He inhaled, pinched his nose closed with his fingers and blew smoke out his left eye. It was some perverse sinus anomaly he'd been born with. Some flawed tear duct. Clown work. It was his only trick and she grinned even though she didn't want to.

She listened to the wooden sound of leaves blowing, sad all of a sudden because this was the way it had always been between them. Huge, library-sized arguments full of hard-edged words and accusations, and then a hurried apology as dusty and brittle as an empty cabinet in an abandoned house. It was one more thing she hated. One more thing she considered a curse. Why growing up meant that words could be slung and then tamped down like fresh dirt on a grave, she'd never know. But it had always been their way. More his than hers in all truth, and like it or not she felt relief their fight from Sunday was over. That he was sitting on the grass beside her blowing smoke out his eye. That her only friend liked her again.

"I'm still going to the creek—I'm still going to see her, but I don't expect you to go. I don't even want you to go anymore," she said.

"How come?"

"How come I'm going? Or how come I don't want you to go with me?" She looked at him and caught him grinning.

"How come you don't want me to go?"

"Because you don't want to."

"I never said that." Jackson snuffed out his cigarette and split a blade of St. Augustine to make a whistle.

She looked at him then, amazed by his amnesia, shocked her mother had been more than halfway right about something for a change. "Act like you don't want a guy to do a thing, and they'll break their neck doin' it every time," had been her comment concerning the motivation of men.

A light came on in the back room of the house across the street and she heard a lid being lifted and then replaced to a garbage can. His elbow nudged her, bumped her for attention, and looking his way she saw a trio of rings linked together drifting above his pale, blond eyebrows. He had grass stuck to his back from rolling over her, and careful not to break his concentration, she reached around and picked it off while she counted new rings puffing from the corner of his eye. Six.

"That can't be good for you. Every time you do it, your eye's red for a week. You need a new trick," she said.

"Yeah? You think so?" He rubbed his eye where it hurt.

"Yeah."

"Well, why don't you ask Enid to show me one of hers—"

She fished for something she'd heard the boys say once. Finally remembering she said, "You're too young. Enid eats boys like you for breakfast."

"Yep—that's what I heard." He studied her wide-open face and found it clean as the sky. Valuable didn't have a clue about anything. He reached over and thumped her knee.

"Hey—I'm joking, okay? Bad joke."

She nodded, rubbing a hand across her stomach. Yawning wide and deep, she wondered if her lips disappeared into hard thin slashes like her mother's when she did it, or if they kept their shape. The moon disappeared again, erasing the rhododendron and the hydrangea from the side of Jackson's yard, erasing the trellis and the magnolia tree, erasing everything, even Valuable tracing her fingers along the lines of her mouth, testing its shape while she tracked a yawn.

3

THE REALITY
OF THE NEGRO

"I THINK IKE WORE OUT his balls those forty years in the army."
Even heard this and the rustle of a newspaper when he opened his
front door and stepped out into the hot. Canaan had made a seat for himself out of a crate turned on end and was perched there, his Ben Franklins
on his nose, his legs crossed like a professor's. Patient as sunrise, the old man
would sit outside waiting, and soon as Even stepped out the door, he'd speak.
Whatever words came tumbling out his mouth were meant to be that day's
discussion. Today, apparently, it would be the president's privates. Turning
around, Even went back inside and poured up a second cup of coffee.

Handing Canaan his cup he saw the man's paper was folded into one
long quarter, so he could read two columns at once without the thing being
spread open and victim of the wind. Canaan said without looking up, "Ike
used up his rocks fighting. Got no balls now for dealing with the reality of
the Negro."

Even Grade knew he was not speaking of his thesis. He was speaking
of the theory behind it. His thesis—"The Reality of the Negro"—was
something else entirely.

Spread out on Canaan's kitchen table, the actual thesis was a broad sheaf of work. Five inches thick at least. Set next to a Mason jar holding pens and pencils and a brand-new screwdriver still in its package and large stacks of books concerning philosophy and the study of triangles, the work was tagged in sections by various things. A turkey feather. A broken-off pen. A spoon. The day Even had stumbled across it, Canaan had been outdoors chasing away the goat. Thumbing through half of one stack, he was amazed by the heft to it, noticing the man's penmanship was flawless and unnaturally straight with his cursive loops to letters *b* and *d* and *g* absolute and nonvarying. He knew the man was somewhat different from the rest. That he thought highly of people long dead and Greek. That he could spend hours chewing on a matchstick and pondering. "But I didn't know this. I sure as hell didn't know this." He placed the stack labeled "The Reality of the Negro" back where it had been, straightened the edges and stood watching the goat run down the street to the pink-trimmed house on the corner. Canaan had come back inside and walked straight to the sink, where he stood washing goat from his hands. Even, still curious, tapped a finger down on the first stack covered with red strikeovers and scribbling inside its margins. At first glance it seemed to be a sea of red on white, like some teacher had weighed the work and found it wanting.

"You in college or something, Canaan?"

Canaan wiped his hands on a dish towel and said, "We're all in college, Even Grade. Most just don't know it."

Even had never read "The Reality of the Negro," but he admired the size of it.

Now a year later hearing Canaan's comment on the balls of the president, Even stood considering the man's wide berth of study while he looked out over what was supposed to be a yard. Lush green grew thick to the road outside his fence without benefit of fertilizer or care, but grass shied away from his yard and this was a puzzle. All he could figure was that a pack of roaming dogs picked his place to park during the day. There were sizably bare, dog-sized spots all over and he'd come up on old crumbly shit along the side of the house.

"I think Willie Mays gonna burn out before the season's through—"

Even said, not interested in the president's balls. He could still smell the toast he'd burned that morning.

"Ain't no way." Canaan rattled his paper and leaned forward. The reality of Ike erased by the reality that Canaan loved Willie.

"I'd bet my left nut, he does." Even sat down in his green chair and leaned on his elbows, pleased to be off politics. "A man can't keep climbin', without slidin' down a time or two. I think he's 'bout due."

"Maybe. Maybe not." Canaan appeared to think on it. "But you gotta go back to that first time at bat. There he was. The whole world waiting. That scout up in the stands like a big shot lookin' down at his prize colored boy. And what happened?"

"Struck out."

"Yessir, he did. Didn't get a hit until twenty-four at bats. Every writer in the world was sayin' his bark was worse than his bite. What's that tellin' you?"

"He still had what it took—"

"That's right. Still had his balls. Not like Ike, who lost his scrawny pair to the army. Him sitting on that bony ass of his sayin' to everbody who'll listen, 'Ole Ike don't fix what ain't broke, nosirree.' Sittin' up there in Washington, D.C., while we pull dead fourteen-year-old niggers out the river." He turned to a new page and then requartered his newspaper. "Problem is, ain't nothin' broke for nobody but the colored man, and there ain't too many breakin' their neck trying to fix anything there, anytime soon." He shook out his paper, like it was dirty.

Even studied him, small and owl-like, his neck puffed like an angry bird's. "They trying over in Arkansas and Birmingham—" remembering how the man took comfort in the slow move of things. How he'd said in hot disagreement with Even that an uprising, no matter the merit, would burn up what he called the "wheat" along with the "chaff." In his opinion Canaan's slow and easy policy was like a sour fart in a tailwind. Nothing but stink was ever gonna come of it.

"Like I said—not but a few tryin' to fix a thing. Just a few."

"Yessir, but what you said concerning 'those few' was—"

"I remember what I said—" Canaan bent over his coffee.

"What you said was, 'These high-minded *Nee*groes gonna get us niggers kilt.' That's what you said. Tell me if that ain't what you said—" Even sat back, amazed by the man's turnaround.

"I remember—"

"You had a change of heart concerning the activity of *Nee*groes, Canaan?" He was delighted.

"Nope."

"Well, what then?"

"Caught a bottle upside the head is all—" He looked up at Even from his perch on the crate and Even saw the puckered questioning scar above his eye.

Glancing up the street, Even saw a group of kids had found the renegade goat and tied it to a rope and were leading it around in circles. It usually roamed free, up and down Bellrose, and until he'd found the dog shit at the side of his house, Even thought the goat was the cause of his missing grass.

"You got plans for the day?" Canaan watched him, put out and irritated as a dipped rooster.

"Well, first off, I'm gonna cut what grass I got left. There's weeds around back that need pulling up. Then I'm gonna go to the hardware store—you need something done over at your place?"

"No, just thought you might be heading to the creek draggin' a woody."

Even kept his gaze steady-fixed on the man until Canaan looked away and down at his newspaper. "She ain't what you think," he said.

"How do you know what I think? You're about as talkative on that front as a thief to a judge."

"I know enough not to open it up with you. She's nobody's business." Even crossed his arms and looked at his grassless yard.

"She's trouble. I got nothing but your best inter—"

Even held up one large hand. "Canaan, you know why we've stayed good friends?"

"I got me a reasonable guess," He swatted at a fly with his folded-up newspaper.

"You may have a guess, but here's the truth of it—we don't try fixing what ain't broke. Now, leave this alone—" That's all he said, and then he got up from his chair and went inside to make a fresh pot of coffee before he started on the hot work of cutting grass and pulling weeds. When he came back out he saw the crate had been placed back in its original spot underneath the window. The only sign Canaan had ever been on the porch was his empty coffee cup, upside down on the rail of the porch.

The weeds piled up by his fence for the goat to eat, Even left Bellrose and walked toward town, meaning to buy some paint. Once that was done, he intended to head to the woods that bordered Little Black Creek.

With his sleeves rolled up against the heat he walked the two-lane toward the center of town. Petal was farm country. A place of fences and cattle and farmhouses set way back off the road. The Quarter squatted between the bigger farms that ran north and town, and a person driving through, with no knowledge of those inlaid farmers, might think Bellrose and Shasta and Morning Glory, three streets crowded with colored, were all there was to Petal.

Close enough to town to see the blinking caution light, he approached Hillcrest Loop, with its long winder that ran almost vertical to a cemetery on top of the hill. The Korner house, built by a man who'd thought he was a farmer once upon a time, sat narrow and white and trimmed in blue near the ribbon of the road. He saw the old man's tractor embedded in tall grass now, rusting steady out under a back shed. Enid, the only one left to home-stead besides a teenaged girl, stood on the porch decked out in a dressing gown the color of blood. On her feet were flat, slappy-type house shoes with big red powder-puff-looking things across her toes. It was nearly noon but she looked dressed for bed.

"Morning, Even Grade!" She waved as one parade bound.

He threw up a hand and called out, "Morning," while he walked straight and away. If she'd been inside where she belonged and not out on her porch in a stalk, he would have hiked his way up to the cemetery. Old stones dating to the Civil War leaned weighted and neglected in one over-grown corner. A morning of study had been his intention but the woman on the porch had soured it. He'd seen her all over town and he'd heard the talk, and the last thing he needed at this point in his life was a gin fan tied around his twenty-seven-year-old neck.

"Hey, Even—wait up!" Her shoes slapped across the yard like applause and he found himself within four feet of her. Nothing between but a thick hedge of prickly green. It was a strange sight, too, the red of her dressing gown rising up out of the boxwood, and for some reason he pictured a nervous Adam and how he must have sought out barriers—trees, animals, maybe water—as a way of putting space between sinning with his woman and staying clean.

"You know where I can find somebody to fix my lawnmower?" She was slightly out of breath, standing with her arms crossing her chest, like she was trying to cover herself, and he felt momentarily better about things. Her dark brown hair fell heavy to her shoulder like a heavy, shiny curtain, too long and needful of hemming.

He scratched his head, "No ma'am. Not right off, I don't."

"Hell, I can't get it cranked, and Reilly's gone until Monday evening." She pushed one heavy fold of hair behind her ear and he saw a tiny gold hoop in her narrow lobe.

He swallowed hard because at the business about Reilly being gone, she'd looked him straight in the eye. Just one quick, hard look and then her eyes shot back up to the hedge between them. Red feather boas bordered the front of her gown. Plumes of some sort, irregular and jarring against the backdrop of the too-tall grass and the dirt road that led up the hill to the dead. He saw old man Korner's tractor back a ways in the shed, an Allis-Chalmers, one of only two in Petal, its body eaten by rust, the core of itself reduced to dusty piles around its long-flat tires. And it seemed sad to see the wasted dyed feathers of some exotic bird in the foreground, and the blood rust of something so hardworking stuck out in a shed. The woman looked down at her feet. Her only change in behavior the nervous running of one hand across the top of the freshly trimmed hedge.

"Yazoo?" he asked, clearing his throat.

"I think so. It's red and Lord, it's big."

At the word "big," she looked at him again and he took one step backward and to the side. He noticed she matched his movement, and he thought, Have mercy, she is not Eve, but serpent. Out loud he said, "I'll sure ask around in town, Miss Korner. See if maybe somebody there knows somebody who does—" He put up his hand and took another step away from her, meaning to wave good-bye, meaning to head back toward town.

"You know anything about lawnmowers? You look like you might."

"No ma'am, I sure don't." He had rebuilt more than two dozen from scratch.

"I thought all Negroes knew machinery like they know the backs of their hands." She had put both hands across the top of the hedge like she meant to attempt a leap.

"No, ma'am. Not the ones I know." He didn't know but one who couldn't fix just about anything that was broken—Canaan, who was more interested in the study of philosophy than the business of screwdrivers. He took one more step to the side closest to town.

She matched his move, saying, "Like I said, Reilly's gone 'til Monday—"

"Yes ma'am, I heard what you said—" He was pouring salt.

"I need my grass cut and I got money to pay." Even watched the prickly point of a leaf catch on the front of her red gown and pull a pucker across where her breast must be, like a badly healed scar. Her eyes traveled from the hedge to his eyes and back again, as if she were sizing it up for a place to lie, testing it as a place of support.

Stepping sideways, his thoughts away from him and scattered, he said, "Grass don't look too high to me—it probably wouldn't hurt to wait 'til Monday, and your man is back." Sweat had beaded itself along his upper lip and the air felt bitter hot when he pulled it inside his lungs. August has dug its claws into my back, he thought. And that's what she's aiming to do, too, if I don't git from here. He wiped his upper lip with the back of his hand and then wiped his hand on the seat of his pants.

"Lord, you're burning up—you want some water?"

"No ma'am. I've got business to tend to. I'll sure spread the word in town, though." He had just lied to the woman for the third time inside of five minutes, and trying to put his mind in church, he drew as comparison Simon Peter and his three lies before the crow of a cock, but his brain hung up on the words "peter" and "cock," which led back to the woman behind the hedge with dark hair falling like a curtain. This is a maze with no out, he thought. Every step goes back to her feathers, but I have never coursed a white woman and I don't plan on starting with this one here.

"Won't be back 'til Monday evening—" She looked straight at him, crimping up one corner of her painted mouth as if out of control. As if making a standing slut of herself against the hedge was something she didn't want to do. "A woman can't have things around that don't work— know what I mean, Mr. Grade?"

Clearing the salt off his face, feeling it pool in his palm, he turned his back to her. Walking away he thought on weird things with no obvious bearing. Canaan's thesis. A dead whale tied down on a rail car. Curly dock growing tall by the side of the road. He sensed her trailing him along her side of the hedge, calling out things about grass and the mower, and how she had more than enough money to pay someone to fix what was broken and not running. Midways down her row, the talk became more pointed and she asked him if he were a *big* man, if he'd had a woman in a while, if he'd *ever* had a white woman, and he walked faster. The hedge ran thick and unbroken, straight into the broadside of a fence that was as old and tired as Petal itself. Split gray rails, crossed and set, ran away from the road, back toward the cemetery, but first, to old man Korner's once industrious tractor.

Even kept his gaze steady on that boundary line, that fence coming forward that would mark an end to it all. In between all those other thoughts that had no bearing, he gauged the distance left to go and spoke aloud to himself, saying, "Just ten more steps now. Easy does it. Have mercy and breathe. Just under five now and we'll be done with her."

Once he passed the corner of the Korners', leaving her just a swatch of snagged red net behind him, he wondered at the phase of the moon, and if some tidal pull were under way, because August had not seemed this strange for as long as he could remember.

Walking hard and fast and away, he saw the caution light blinking steady above the empty intersection and the hardware store right up the street and felt calmed, finally.

Canaan, on more than one occasion, had theorized that the buying power of the Negro dollar is not, and never will be, equal. Even thought of all the man's examples as he walked past the Sinclair service station, two stores down from the hardware store. Even had spent long dregs of time across from Canaan, sipping coffee, thinking on other things such as work and pleasure and long-ago Memphis, always nodding at the older man's

one-sided dialogues but gone elsewhere in his mind. Canaan would be saying, "A plot of land's for sale. Two men show up willing to buy, holding
good cash money in their hands. One's a Negro, the other White. Who's
goin' home the landed gentry?" or "Two men show up at the counter of
Feed and Seed at the same time, both holding money, only one's colored.
Who's gonna get waited on first?" As he approached the hardware store he
dismissed Canaan's examples and went on in the store confident. Colored
or White, paint was paint, and Even had not judged paint a hard thing to
buy.

Clemens made him stand in line and wait for the Walkers and the Mitchells
and the Hensleys and the short, sweaty, fat kid who didn't want a damn
thing other than a conversation and a piece of bubble gum. The juggle of
paint cans against his stomach pinched in more than one place and there
was a smell to the store of pesticide and dried corn that burned his nose
and fired up a headache. He had wanted a longer time to search the shelves
for a lilac or sage, but the weighted stink hanging in the air settled dust-
like to his skin and dug into his clothes. He put his nose to his shoulder
and wiped his face.

"What you want this paint for, boy?" Clemens, near skeletal with a
vague goose-like look to him, asked this. Even concluded with one quick
glance that the only things nongoose-like to him were his thick, bushy eyebrows that grew straight across before heading for his ears. There were arti-
ficial workings in his mouth, false teeth, or a plate of some type, that
knocked around like wayward gears. When he talked, his gums—black at
their base—smelled like something three days dead by the side of the road.
Even remembered the short fat kid who'd leaned up hard on the counter
waiting for bubble gum and he thought to himself, There is a Reality here
that these people will tolerate anything while using their buying power.

"You deaf, boy? How come you need this Benjamin Moore?" Even
backed away from the odor and stood staring, considering the man's question.

"I mean to paint with it," he said.

Clemens snorted out his nose and looked down at his hands, firm and
flat on the counter, saying, "We got us a strange one here, buddy boy," as
if his fingers had ears. "What I mean is—" he spoke slowly, as if to a half-

wit or retard, "you ain't gonna paint up the water tower or the underpass, are you?"

"No, sir," Even said, puzzled paint should seem a criminal purchase for a black man.

"Last paint I sold ended up on the side of Little Black Creek Bridge. The *artist*—" Clemens accented the word, "—left the cans sitting right there by the water. Green paint. Sage, I think. Or Kelly, maybe. Smeared *Michael McGee is a needle-dick bug fucker* up and down the Runnelstown side. Big green letters for everybody to see. How you think that made Michael McGee feel? You think he wants all of Petal calling him *Needle-dick the Bug Fucker?*"

"No sir, I don't think he would."

Canaan, who loved to gossip as much as he loved to read, had told him a while back that Clemens's lanky daughter, a loose-limbed girl as freckled as a pup, had dated McGee for a short span of time. According to Canaan, who got it straight from the manicure girl at the beauty shop, McGee had broken it off because a cheerleader had winked at him from the balcony of the Saenger. Even had a pretty good idea who had painted up the Black Creek Bridge.

"We got enough meanness here. We ain't needin' more. You get what I'm saying to you, boy?"

Even felt himself growing angry and wishing he'd read Canaan's thesis and studied those theories. He spoke as carefully as Clemens. "Yes, sir, I do. There's enough meanness here, for sure." He leaned back at the waist and held his breath because Clemens's odor was hot as the sun. The *cha-ching* of the cash register finished their business but the proprietor made slow work of putting the cans inside a brown bag. While his tongue dredged along his gums he picked up the can of Harvest Gold and read its label, finding an interest in its properties. He finally put the last can to the bag and sat down on the high stool by the register, folding his arms across his chest. Even walked out the door thinking, I've got a chapter for Canaan here. He didn't look back, but if he had, he knew he'd see the man staring after him, his eyes made suspicious and narrow, believing a nigger wanting color was a nigger up to no good.

Leaving the store, Even walked across the street and headed up Highway 11 and within a short span of time found himself in open country. No houses in sight. Just long drives that led back to where he knew houses sat next to barns and silos. The only proof of occupation an occasional mailbox with a name printed on the side, leaning up near the highway.

The river Leaf ran parallel to the highway sending out streams and creeks that ran free before winding back to their source. One was the Baby Black. The Bogue Homa was another. For the most part these waterways roamed unmolested, hemmed in as they were by trees thick as cane along their banks. He thought on how the Indians, long gone now, must have floated speechless in their canoes and paddle boats, the single call note of gnatcatcher or mockingbird the only sounds other than that of their oars dipping and breaking open tea-stained water.

To the right of the road underneath towering broadleafs, he saw a downed grove of ironwood trees. Blown there by storm or tornado, their steel-like limbs scattered like tossed bones, bleached now by weather and time. A nuthatch made pulp near the base of a rotting trunk, enlarging an opening for nesting. Even thought it a boast of the region that within four feet of the road his feet were trodding down, the bird had not broken and flown. Just kept lowering and raising its white-striped head, pecking and pitching at splinters as regular as a metronome, scattering the ground with flesh-colored dust from a long-dead tree. I am the stranger here, Even thought, and it was a thought that made him glad.

As he approached the half-moon-shaped bend to the road, he began to think on her—the small polished sticks she wore in her hair, the way her lips moved around her words when she spoke, her stabbing cheekbones, the way he seemed to smell Africa in the dark crease of her neck. He thought of her hands, the way she held them still in her lap, her fingers steepled, and the way she seemed to soak up their differences until they were moderate, but waived. From a distance north, he saw a dark cloud approach, its outside edges stretching and warping, chasing at its center. Closer now, he saw the cloud was actually a sky full of blackbirds, and as they settled and filled the upper limbs of two sweetgums to the right of the road, black was the king color stirred into the leaves—leaves already made early purplish red by the approach of autumn. Hearing the clamor he thought on his current situation and why he had put off this thing—why he let it grow so large it lumbered like a beast, lost and home-

less and starving. He would have picked at this thread until fully considered had he not heard singing coming at him from the final loop of the
curve. Stopping, Even saw a wheel crest first and finally a grown-up-sized
trike of some sort showed itself. A man was seated on it wearing a red-
and-white-striped shirt and a green hat pulling a busted lawnmower
behind him by a rope.

Even stood watching while the blackbirds in the sweetgum pitched
their fuss to one high key and ruffled their feathers, showing an undercoat
of blue. On approach, he noticed the wheels to the trike were mismatched
and thin-spoked, like those off a series of wheelchairs of different models.
The mower at the end of the rope swayed back and forth onto the highway like a wagon loaded too far back of its axle. When the lawnmower man
was within twenty feet, Even Grade held up a hand.

The man piloted the trike one more turn, and with his left foot still
on a pedal he lifted his right leg and crossed his knees, sticking both hands
in his pockets while he sat back on his seat and waited. Dignified, Even
thought. That's as dignified a move as I'm ever likely to see a man on a trike
pulling a lawnmower make.

"You got a need of me, or you just like stoppin' folks for no reason?"
the man asked.

"You know how to fix those things, or you just pull 'em around from
place to place?" The smell of witch hazel and honeysuckle drifted up from
the woods.

"You got one that's broke?"

"Not me. Somebody back there." Even nodding with his head toward
town. "She stopped me this mornin' on my way out. Said hers was broke
and needed fixin' and I said I'd ask around."

"Where in town?" The man lit up a cigarette with hand movements
straight from Hollywood.

"Hillcrest Loop. Not the loop end. The end closest to town," Even
said.

"White house with blue trim? Old man Korner's place?"

"That's the one."

The man blew gray smoke out his nose and stood up tall on the pedals of the trike, reminding Even of a bone-thin dragon. "Get thee behind

me, Satan!" he shouted, pointing his finger at Even. "That's a garden of sin if ever I seen one, and I ain't going! I been spending *years* tryin' to cut down my own garden of sin! Been scrapin' together mowers from here to East Jesus tryin' to find one able to mow *down* my garden of sin! Been searchin' all over the country tryin' to find a blade sharp enough to cut *down* my garden of sin! And I ain't *about* to take on nobody *else's* garden of sin. You hear what I'm *saying*, nigger! Do you?"

Even backed away and to the side and stood on the grassy shoulder thinking, If worse come of this and it surely might, I'll take the first can of paint my hand touches and bash in his skull. "Whoa now, you just hold now—" was what he said, holding up one hand.

"Whoa now! Whoa now! You ain't hearing word one of what I'm sayin'. Do you *hear* what I'm sayin', brother, about the garden of sin?" He was shouting and flushing birds. They broke from the sweetgum like a noisy plague—a blustering, screaming sea of black.

"I hear you. I hear you," Even said. Me and all of Petal and most of Ellisville and Runnelstown, too. He reached in and lifted out the Harvest Gold.

"I *been* in a garden of sin and I *knows* how it feels!" The man threw off his green hat and it sailed up to a splayed-off branch of a sycamore.

"I been so low-down *deep* in the garden of sin I lost all hope! You know what took me there, brother?" He was still standing on both pedals shouting, pulling off his shirt now and wadding it up into a tight little ball. His hat already gone aloft to a tree, his shirt followed. They both hung from branches too high up for retrieval by anything other than a fire truck. All that was left in the order of clothing on the man were his pants and shoes. His black chest heaved, naked and ribbed.

"You know how I got so low-down!?" he shouted.

"No sir, I ain't got a damn clue!" Even shouted right back, looking back behind him for the approach of a car or a mule or anything supportive.

"Guess! I want you to guess what sent me to my garden of sin!" The shirtless man panted like a chased-down fox and his legs, from standing upright on the pedals of his trike, twitched and jerked at the knees. "I'll give you three good guesses!"

Even set the brown bag on the ground. "You calm down and I'll do your guesswork. You keep screaming like a runover cat and all you gonna get from me is this can upside your head."

Wild-eyed as a show dog the man clamped his hands over his mouth and nodded.

Even tested the weight of the can. "My guess would be a woman. A woman led you there?"

The man shook his head from side to side and made a "naaa" sound from behind his hands.

"Liquor?"

Same sound.

"Numbers?"

Same sound.

"I give, then. You sit your ass down on that seat and breathe easy. You want to tell me what led you there, okay. If not, I'm goin' on down the road."

The man shook his head and said, "Naaa."

"Suit yourself. I'm leavin' now and the road you're wantin' is that-away—" Even pointed in a direction back to town, away from the bend in the road and the creek beyond.

Leaving. Walking backward for a while to make sure the man didn't leap off and chase him down and kill him, he watched him sit himself down on the seat of the trike.

"Don't you want to know what led me to the garden of sin?" he called out as Even approached the middle of the curve.

"Not no more I don't!" He could see the man a hundred feet away from him and how he had turned himself on his trike so that he could watch Even's departure.

"It was me! Me who led me there!" he shouted one last time, and then Even heard the sound of mismatched wheels moving forward again, making a league of their efforts in order to pull.

Well, that's as true a thing as I ever heard come out the mouth of a crazy man, Even thought as he hurried on down the road. A crow sitting in the top of a pine on the side nearest water sent out a nasal call that seemed in agreement.

4

CREEKSIDE

TWO MILES DOWN HE FOUND the bramble bush growing out of a rusted tin can and ducked in on a trail. It was marked by several things. A rock with a shape to it of anvil. A broken-off stump wide as a car. A pine tree forming up split, like the spraddled legs of a man standing upside down, his head buried in the sand. Once there, Even turned back once to make sure the man hadn't followed, not because he was scared, but because he didn't want to be disturbed or interrupted. This done, he stopped and did something he had found himself doing since his very first time by the creek: he pulled off his shoes and socks, tucked the socks inside, laced the shoes together and draped them around his neck.

A winding trail led down at an easy grade. For the largest part there were no mosquitoes. Just a buzz now and again around his ear, and he tallied their absence to the cool inside, where underneath trees so tall light fell through in pale ribboned green. Soft underfoot and padded by leaves, it seemed a place of sweeping angles—forty-fives and nineties, mostly. The tallest of the trees, a pine that had been ignored by odds and hurricanes and God, grew nine feet in circumference with two of its oldest roots raised and exposed and lined with lime green moss that gave it a look of a low velvet chair. He stepped over the roots and headed on down the slope.

A rock too large to be called a rock but too small to be called anything else rose out of the ground at an angle akin to thirty degrees. Rounded and humped, on approach it had the appearance of a big-shouldered giant squatted on his haunches, sleeping, his head ducked and hidden, his back to the world. Studied from the opposite side, it showed itself to be a hollow area, cave-like with insides frosted the color of milk by some type of dust or mold. Even named it Paradox Rock because what it was was different from what it looked to be. He patted it as he climbed down, thinking what a strange thing that a rock could be such a fitting look at the reality of man in his varying extremes.

As he stepped out into the clearing the cans of paint swung together and caught the skin of his leg, pinching hard, startling him to the point he let a loud fart. Frozen by embarrassment and blinded by the sun after being under such a heavy umbrella of shade, he stood poleaxed at the edge of the woods, a soiled blind man not knowing what to do, wondering if she had heard.

"Well, at least I know you a human man and not some angelic being sent down from heaven," she said.

His eyes adjusted and he saw her. Paint cans clanking, Even was too embarrassed to move. Too shamed to stay. This is a reality not even Canaan could imagine.

"How *is* Canaan?" she asked as if she had read him, which she hadn't, because she couldn't. "And come on over here and quit being foolish. I can tell you ain't ever lived with a woman—you standing there thinking farts are a man's pleasure. You think I don't break wind?" She laughed low, her arms crossed over her overalls with nothing under in the way of a shirt. Just blue bib and straps and metal grabs against dark. Between visits he forgot she was a tall woman, almost as tall as him, which made her close to the top end of five feet. Five ten was his guess, since he stood at six one.

"I asked you how Canaan is," she said.

"Suspicious." He moved finally.

"About life in general, or just me?" There were onions in a wooden bowl under her arm.

"Mainly you."

"Good. That's good then." She picked up a heavy stick of wood and put it on the fire.

"Good?"

"Suspicious means he's still considering. Mean'll show up once he's made up his mind fully. Suspicious is better than mean any day of the week, I'd say." She sat down and picked up a knife and began paring the onions. Nodding with her head, she asked, "What you got in the bag?"

He set the package on the flat rock she'd named Mama Girl. "Paint," he said while he ran a large hand over her head, feeling the polished sticks, fingering his favorite. Year Eleven. A tiny blue one with silver dots.

"Paint?"

"That's what I said."

"Real paint?"

"Yes ma'am. You gotta promise not to paint up the underpass or the bridge, though. There's enough meanness in this world."

She handed him her bowl of onions and stretched a hand to the bag and lifted them out. Barn Red. Plymouth Blue. Harvest Gold. Running a long finger over the lid of the last can, the yellow one, she looked at him and said, "Nobody ever give me paint before. This is a good gift, Even. Thank you."

"Harvest Gold almost ended up out on the road." Still holding her onions, he sat down and pulled up his pants legs to midcalf so he could cross his legs like an Indian. Rubbing his thigh where he'd been pinched by the cans he thought of those hard Lutheran fingers that had marked him more than once back in Memphis. "I just about decided most of Petal is crazy—"

"Crazy's not all bad."

"Mostly it is."

"No. Crazy you can work with. Those crazy stay open to gifts: Liquid. Air. God. Food."

"Satan. Don't forget how they leave that door open, too," thinking on Clemens and the man with the mower and the Korner woman who wanted his sex. He dug his heels into sand.

"Him too."

She took the onions from him and dumped them into a pot of something bubbling over the fire. He thought he smelled chicken and rutabagas and winced. She knew just about everything there was to know about root and herb and animal, but not a thing in the world about cooking. It was a weakness she shared with Canaan.

"You hungry?"

"Not yet."

She sat down cross-legged with her hands folded in her lap, her fingers steepled, and he thought that for the most part she was just like the woods, a woman of severe angles. Her forehead sloped easy over hairless brows that ran to the small polished sticks she wore braided in her hair. One stick for each year of her life done up in different colors and decorated with various designs. Her neck dropped sharp to her wide shoulders, which appeared almost tray-like on top of corded arms that were muscular but not overly so. Through her overalls he could see hip and knee bones, these as sharp and striking as her high cheekbones.

"They ain't nothin' even or halfway straight in this old world—who give you such a name as Even Grade?" She asked this regularly. Seeming to like the question for some odd reason.

"It's a long story."

"I ain't goin' nowhere." She looked at him, her eyes so black they appeared pupil-less.

Not in a frame of mind to discuss his lack of history, he switched. "Canaan's got an attitude going on over something. Thinks the president's balls are shrunk up like grapes, for a start."

"He seen them recent, has he?"

He grinned, feeling good over being out of his box and able to talk freely. Sometimes he imagined that the only time he was truly plumbed was when he was creekside. The rest of his time was spent canted, off-center. "Can't say on that. Seems like that bottle upside the head changed his way of thinkin', though. Started him readin' about Arkansas and all that meanness. Set him off on Emmit Till again. Lord knows there ain't enough words on that one, though. Made me feel foolish and stunted for repeatin' back to him what he preached hard against just last year—"

"Canaan ain't the Eternal Voice. I spoke to you in a dream and you were smart enough to find your way here, weren't you? Or maybe you beginning to think bein' here with me is a sign you're near witless."

He grinned at her again and dug his toes into cool sand.

"You keep grinnin' like that, I'll start believing Canaan's right—you foolish and stunted."

"You think I'm stunted?" He winked at her.

"Had crossed my mind. I ain't checked you in a week. You hungry yet?" she asked.

"You sure didn't act like you thought I was too stunted last time. Acted scared of it, if I remember right."

"For a orphan, you mighty full of yourself. I asked you if you was hungry—" She was stirring her pot of strong-smelling food.

"For chicken and a sour turnip?"

"That's what's in the pot."

"I may be foolish but I know what sounds God-awful and what sounds good and I ain't thinkin' chicken and rutabaga." He grinned and leaned back on his hands and while he watched she unfolded herself like a lean trap, the food forgotten.

"Merciful Jesus . . . Sweet, *merciful* Jesus—" he whispered soft against her ear.

Her heat left him weak as a newborn, barely able to breathe or control his bladder. The full measure of this feeling was as much a forgotten thing between visits as her tallness.

"You the only one I can't read. You know that, Even Grade?" She said this in a low puzzled voice.

"I know," he answered, realizing that whatever happened between them would have to be traveled tenderly as one learning Braille.

He felt her growing hungry for her clothes while the sun disappeared behind the trees along the creek bank. It still burned red at some low, buried point, sending spindled fingers of light up through the crowded trunks.

"How's Canaan's head?"

"Healing. Looks to be a scar of a question mark where the bottle hit."

"That's as right a thing as I ever heard," she said against his arm, kissing the bend of his elbow before standing. His way of pondering issues had traveled over to her somehow and he wondered over it.

"Who they say I am this week? Not Canaan. I know he thinks I'm 'bout as evil as Satan. I mean everbody else." She worked her way back into her faded, clean overalls while the frogs chorused across the creek. Flexing her long fingers she bent and scratched at her ankle.

"They sayin' about the same thing as always—you the crazy nigger woman, and Canaan don't think you're Satan. He just thinks you're pain on the way." He leaned on his elbow and spit in the fire, his water making a hiss as if part of a potion. He could see the tattooed markings on her legs above her ankles—dots and slashes and inked lines that resembled extracted molars—and he looked away. The way they threaded around and up seemed similar to beginning cracks in black temple marble. "They say you throw a mean-ass spell and stop the rain," he continued, considering her feet. Large for a woman's, and her toes appeared agile enough to do a proper job of snapping beans. "Not much agreement on the price of beef or Eisenhower, but you say 'crazy nigger woman' and just about everybody south of Ellisville knows right off how they feel about you. And they ain't feelin' charitable, either."

"They feel like payin' me good money just to tell them things. Sounds like *they* the crazy ones."

"You keep telling folks things, there's gonna be trouble. Baptists don't like that shit."

"Then how come it's Baptist women puttin' food in my mouth—bringin' me fresh corn and rump roast just to open up my mouth and speak?"

"'Cause their Baptist men don't know they're doin' it." And this was the truth.

Stretched out on his side, he watched her stir around the fire rearranging the cans of paint on the squat Mama Girl rock. Blue first, then yellow and red. When she bent, her age sticks caught the light and lit her up like a just-struck match. All those lacquered coats pulling color from the yellow of the fire, the full gleam of the moon. Reflective spears slid down her face like multicolored war paint. Watching her, he felt swallowed up. Back in the womb again with no breath of his own.

He looked toward her lean-to, domed and mounded, its layered plaits of woven oiled grass. For such a shanty, it wore a remarkable beauty. Much more than his place with his yellow Formica kitchen table and his tin canisters and his floor that always needed cleaning. Tribal and round, hers seemed pregnant with something without benefit of male seed and this made him jealous.

"Tell me now—what they say about me?" She leaned back on her hands, curious.

The little finger of her right hand was missing and he looked away.

"They think you're trouble, that's for sure. They think you foul the creek. That you scare the bulls and make 'em hate the cows. They think you the *craziest* somebody they ever heard of." He saw his pants crumpled up on top of his laced-together shoes.

"Do *you* know who I am?" She quieted him. Her hands folded in her lap now. Those cans of paint lined up behind her like tin gods, listening.

He forced his eyes to watch her. "I know you're Judy Tucson to me and it don't matter about Canaan, or anybody else. I only care 'bout one thing—what I know to be true. Nothing else, nobody else matters."

She looked away from him and he wondered why.

Stretched to his side, he noticed the settle of night. More tired than he thought, he felt himself falling asleep, lulled there by the always of the woods. There was always her fire and there was always the sound of the creek and there was always a benedictional mist coming from the meeting of the two. Soft fog lifted off the moving water and crept up and away in wilting swirls. He watched it float over palmetto and prickle pine until it covered his feet first and then his legs, but never hers.

"I saw a queer thing. Guess what it was." She was more talkative than usual. Even shook his head, yawning.

"Come on, Even—guess."

"You tell me." He yawned again. This queer thing could be anything from an albino snake eating itself into a knot to a dark horseman aiming for the town librarian.

"I had visitors. Two naked white kids floated face-up in the creek, right out there in front of my house." She pointed to the dark water. "Boy and girl. Thought they was two boys 'til I saw her teat break the water. They drifted by, like I weren't even here. 'Bout the same age. Fifteen or sixteen years old, give or take a month. Don't that seem funny? That they'd float by naked as sea turtles?" She was snapping up pole beans with her strong fingers and throwing them into a cast-iron pot for tomorrow's meal. It sounded like a song, those different *bing, bong* sounds the vegetables made when they hit the pot's bottom.

"Hmmm. Maybe they was tryin' to cool off, 'cause it's been so hot. Everbody and their uncle tryin' to find someplace cool." He turned his head and watched her. Tonight she looked more like thirty-five, and if the moon would flash for longer than twenty seconds, he could count her sticks.

"I got a readin' when they went by, too. The boy'll be here next week to ask about the split pig. The girl's got questions too. Ain't about no pig, though." A deep chuckle and more music in the pot. She began a subtle rocking motion in rhythm with the creek.

"What pig?" He had counted his way to number twenty-seven. The blue stick with tiny white circles and diagonal slashes.

"The boy dreamed it. Dreamed it was wintertime and he was in a big car with scratchy seats, in the middle of freezin' cold rain, and a pig was floatin' belly-up out of the ditch to his right." She stirred the fire with a metal poke. "A big-ass pig, too. All white and pink around its teats and snout."

He raised on his elbow. "Judy, folks got electricity back in town. You don't need to camp out here."

"Sow was split all the way down to its privates and the window of the car was steamed up because it was winter and the girl floating down the creek was in there with him, making him breathe hard, making other things hard too, but he don't know it yet because he ain't learned the 'hard' lesson yet, except what he does on his own." She frowned.

"You got all this while they floated by?"

"Maybe 'cause they were naked. Maybe not. Anyhow, in this dream he rubbed himself a little peephole in the window of the car and saw that pig rollin' up on its side and startin' to pull its way out the ditch." She made swimming motions in the air. Acted it out and he found it disturbing.

"Like it still had life. Muddy ditch water kept catching inside the cavity and washing out through its teats, like chocolate milk. The dream scared the boy. Hell—scared me just reading it while he floated by, and I ain't one to scare easy." She stopped rocking, tucked her hands under her armpits and bowed her head as if praying. There was quiet on all fronts, no frogs, even the sound of water seemed quieter until she raised her head and the frogs started singing again. She turned to him, smiling. "That's all I saw before they floated by. Just a pig dream and me knowing the two of them will be by next week, give or take a day."

"They say a talkin' pig dream means a storm is comin', or a change is on the way." He was wide awake again.

She brushed her hands down her overalls, swept away his comment. "You think you could get me some pork? I got the money. Some good bacon maybe, or some ribs?"

"That ain't too hard a thing. But why don't you come on home with me? I got a place. Got lights and a fan that blows cool all the time. Got a refrigerator. Got all kinds of things." Sitting up he wrapped his big arms around his knees. He could still smell Africa on the tips of his brown fingers but it was fading. He watched her eyes, wanted them. "They ain't gonna leave you alone, Judy. Sometimes I feel such a big thing comin', I can't breathe. You know that, don't you? You know how bad I worry."

"I know." But she looked at him solid, straight on and fearless, like he hoped his mother might do if ever he were to meet her. Proper and proud on some busy street where the instant they saw the other they would know. Judy looked at Even that way and something in her look pulled at him from points all over. Made him crave the breast he'd never had. Watching his eyes, she reached over and undid the left clasp of her overall bib, folded it down, took her own sweet time. "I've said this before—you the only one I can't read fully. You remember me sayin' that?"

"I remember." His mouth pulled again and he wanted to suckle.

"You the only one that don't send out nothin' but a thin little stream. You know that, too?"

"I'm sorry about that." And he was. He wanted her to know things about him. Tell him something more than Lutheran memories out of Memphis. But she didn't and he knew she never would. He looked at the train trestle over his head, tried to ignore her breast for as long as he could because it made him feel near starvation and small. It was close to ten. Southern Ohio be by soon. The slope was steep and there were vacated bird nests high up, locked into wooden corners.

"One good rain and they gonna fish your dead body out of the river," he said, and his voice sounded old to his ears.

She laughed then and it cut him like her paring knife. "I be long gone before the rain, but I ain't gone yet and Joody Two Sun think big ole Lutheran orphans never do get over leavin' the tit." She hummed a lullaby in some lost minor key and with slow hands undid the other clasp. While beans boiled in a pot and the frogs shouted encouragement across the creek, he shut his eyes against her. Kept them clamped down tight against her warning. Her leaving too large a thing, too horrible a thing, to imagine.

5

A SIX-SIDED WOMAN

JOLEB GREEN HAD FLAT-OUT LIED. The black woman didn't smell any more strange than his mother's white slip and didn't even come close to measuring seven feet tall. And as soon as I see him again, I'm kicking the shit out of his skinny hebe ass, was what Jackson McLain thought in those first few minutes.

"Only thing we know for sure is whether we got it, or whether we don't. Either way we know."

He stood out by the creek listening to their low voices, as much of his back to them as he dared. Let Val move on closer to the half-crazy nigger. He wasn't about to and he wasn't parting with any money, either. Not for words concerning whether a person has love or not, coming from a woman not that tall and not that strange-smelling.

"Now you—you think you different. That it ain't ever gonna come. You think they's some mark covering you, makin' you lost to it. But that ain't a worthy fear. How old are you anyhow?"

"Fourteen, almost fifteen."

"You caught the Blessing of Blood yet?"

"Excuse me?" Valuable asked, puzzled.

"Your moon cycle. Bleeding," Joody explained, her legs splayed open like a man's while she chewed on a twig of something.

Valuable looked toward the spot where Jackson was standing. Jackson, who hadn't heard anything of the question but the word "blood," was looking in all directions for a sharp stick in case this thing got ugly. He watched the dark woman lean in to Valuable and say something but he wasn't close enough to make it out.

"Bleeding is a gift. It ain't nothing to be ashamed of. And don't you mind the boy. Most men envy a woman's emissions," was what she had said. "Now we cleared that up, answer my question: you caught the Blessing yet?"

"Yes ma'am—four times since January. Only my grandmother called it a curse, not a blessing."

Valuable spoke low, and over the thick noise of water and cicada, her words were partial at best. Jackson took one step closer to her fire.

"Lord have mercy on the three-sided woman!" He did hear this.

Valuable glanced his way. "We had a fight because of it last Sunday. Only he doesn't know that's why we were fighting. I didn't even know that's why we were fighting, I just—"

Now why in the world was she bringing up *that* old news again, he wondered. Jesus! I might as well strip down and expose myself, bend over and let them count the hairs on my ass!

"So you're younger than that one by more than a year?" Her black head with all those sticks had bobbed in his direction.

"Yes ma'am—"

"I remember fourteen. Just barely, but I do remember. Fourteen's hard, ain't it?"

"Yes ma'am, it's turning out to be."

"Well, Miss Valuable Korner, who give you such a beautiful gift of a name?"

"Let *her* tell you, Val, that's why we're here, ain't it!" Jackson moved two steps closer to the fire, but no more. "Ask her about your name. See if she knows."

"Young boy!" The woman jumped to her feet and the hair on the back of his neck stood up right along with her. "You come over here by my fire if you want to address me. Don't you stand there yelling at me like I'm some nigger field hand out picking a row somewhere. I ain't screamin' over the noise of frogs and I ain't goin' back and forth all night between two worlds!"

He had heard that same tone right before his eighth grade geography teacher beat him with an augured-out paddle. In a slightly more respectful tone he said, "No ma'am. I'm fine where I'm at." He glared at Val then, who was refusing to look at him. All dressed up in her Sunday best she was kneeling shoeless in the sand like she was visiting Jesus. Her flowered dress was pulled down over her knees and she kept tucking it behind her legs like there was something there to hide besides drawers and a slip. Like there was something to her he hadn't seen at least a thousand times already. Her shy behavior made him furious. This was the same creek they swam in, for Christ's sake! Same sand, wind and sky! The same everything. What a priss she'd turned into, was his thought.

Calmer, easier, the woman said, "You come over here, white boy, and I'll tell you 'bout that pig that nearly scared the life out of you." Her voice rode on a peculiar pitch, enticing and melodic, not unlike that of a tent preacher's.

"It wasn't that bad. Just a dumb pig."

Valuable was looking at him puzzled. He had kept the pig dream to himself. Good for you, priss. Teach you I got secrets, too. "I'm fine where I'm at. I don't care that much about the pig."

He stood with folded arms and studied the creek. At night it was queer. Its edges gone. Everything was black-brown with no in between, and the lack of effort required to see, or rather, not see everything around him, made his eyes feel rested and cool with unexpected energy set aside for roaming. The frogs were used to him again. Invisible to sight but an assault on the ears. Their noise had stopped when he first put his feet in the shallow brown water but had returned full throttle.

The strange beauty of the place hit once and then rolled off his back like water off a duck. Disappeared like last year's dream. He scratched at his nose, worried over Val's adoration. Where this thing might lead was as clear as a map drawn by a blind man. But where it had its beginning was plain as day. I will surely beat the ever-living shit out of Joleb Green over this one, Jackson promised himself, while a bobwhite gave its call from somewhere hidden in the grove.

It had been hot that first week of June as the dead center of August, and where he stood leaning against the wall of the barbershop was burning his back, baking his shoulder through his white T-shirt. Joleb Green had been there, mumbling around his cigarette. Some type of total boring bullshit about the woman by the creek.

"I swear, Jackson, there's a smell coming off her jawline like the inside of my brother's clarinet case. I swear it was revigorating."

"*In*vigorating. The word's invigorating," Jackson had answered. "And what's so great about smelling like a band instrument?" He looked over at Joleb and weighed their differences. Joleb was almost four inches shorter and opposite in every physical way. Dark and skinny. Nearsighted and neglected. With a great pointed beak that made him look like a hebe.

"She's magic. I swear. I walked up to her and she held my hand and I fainted dead away, and when I woke up, I felt immediately smarter."

"Oh yeah? Well since you're so newly smart maybe you can answer this. What's the difference between the Seven Dwarfs and a Brownie Troop?"

Joleb pushed his glasses up on his sweaty nose and ran a hand over wiry hair. "What?"

"Well, the Seven Dwarfs are a cunning little band of runts—" Jackson held his hands out, palms up, waiting for the obvious.

"Yeah? So, what does that make the Brownies?"

"Jeezus, Joleb!" Jackson whooped and hollered and beat his knees. "Jeezus! I think you better go back for seconds!"

Val came out her mother's beauty shop then, drinks cradled in her arms. Jackson waved at her, still laughing.

Joleb, clueless, continued. "I swear, Jackson, I woke up outside Owl Drug," he pointed down the street, "my dick straight up like a spear, grown out a whole inch with hair sprouted on my balls—"

"And you were smarter, too. Don't forget that." Jackson doubled over laughing again.

"Yeah, that, too. I swear, man. You need to go see her."

"Fuck *me*. I already got a big dick, Joleb." He elbowed him in the side while he snuffed out his cigarette on the side of the building. Joleb watched Val approach the curb, "Here she comes. Beware a Korner bearing gifts. Next stop might be for penicillin."

"Stop being an ass, Joleb." Jackson slapped him in the chest.

Valuable passed around three Nehis. Including one to Joleb who snatched it away without saying thanks.

"What's so funny?" she smiled easy.

"Go on, Joleb, tell Val what's up. I'm sure she wants to know."

Her dark hair was behind her ear, and when she squatted on the ground Jackson noticed how tiny her ears were. "Come on, tell me—"

And Joleb did, leaving out the dick part, highlighting the nonessential stuff instead. "There's a nigger woman down by the creek who knows stuff . . . ," he said, and that was all it took. Val was hooked and started working on Jackson the very next minute.

All that week and into the next, they bickered way outside their normal boundaries. Every single word that had come out her mouth had been about the woman by the creek. What she could do. What she might say. Things she might know about the both of them.

"I ain't listening, Val. Now shut up, will you?" This was Sunday past when they had headed to the creek to swim.

She'd clammed up. Just walked fast with her arms folded across her chest, disrupting her balance. He laughed out loud when she tripped on a stump and almost went facedown in the saw grass that tangled around their knees. At the next fence line, she let the barbed wire fall down early and his skin was snagged, jerking a bleeding scratch about four inches long. She swore it was accidental but that didn't stop him from punching her hard in the arm and cussing her up one side and down the other. Once by the water she sat her ass down on the sand and pouted. Said her stomach hurt or some lame lie and that she didn't want to swim after all.

"Well, shitfire and fuck *me*." He picked up a rock and sent it skimming across water.

She snorted through her nose, "You know, every time you say that it sounds like an invitation. 'Fuck *me*' this, 'Fuck *me*' that—I hate it. It's crude and vulgar and I think you're disgusting. I think you should be ashamed of yourself for having such a filthy mouth *and* I think it's a blessing to the entire Western world that you're an only child." She burrowed into the sand. Made graves for her small bare feet.

"Oh, yeah?" he'd said, flabbergasted. "Well, I think you've got me mixed up with somebody who gives a flyin' fuck about your opinion." He was furious. "Furthermore, I think leaving you dead center of a quilt was the smartest thing Enid Korner ever did. Why she bothered to come back, I'll never know!" He threw another rock across the water that fell short and plopped. He turned and pointed. "You know, Val—Joleb's turning into better company than you, and you know what a bore he is."

She'd jumped up then, holding her stomach, and headed to the palmettos at the fringe of the woods. To pee he figured. Or cry. Or some stupid girl thing. When she had finally stepped back out, she headed to the water and said, "I think I'll swim."

"Well, don't do me any huge favors."

They both got spanked when they were kids for wandering home wet after swimming in their clothes. They swam naked after that, folding everything up into small neat squares far enough up on the sand to keep them dry. Their skin never seemed naked out in the sun, at least to Jackson, who'd seen everything about her for so long it felt like nothing, but when she turned her back on him to undress he felt like he'd been slapped; like a curtain had been pulled.

"What the fuck're you doin'?" He couldn't believe it. Standing on the sand all she gave him was her shoulder, slender and tan, her hair braided and falling midways down while she'd slipped out of her jeans. Going deeper in, she put her hands over her tits and, standing waist-deep in water, glared at him. Lifted those eyebrows like "So?" and he was furious. It hadn't been that he wanted so badly to see her. He had seen her a week earlier and nothing in the world could have changed in that amount of time.

"Christ, Val! They're markers, you know. Not even tits yet. Not by a long shot." He was standing on the bank, naked as a jaybird, a lit cigarette dangling from his mouth. "Fuck *me*. You should've warned me you were gonna turn into a girl, that way I could've brought my camera—"

"Go to hell." She said it so quietly he knew she meant it.

"You *cunt!*"

"Cunt!" she screamed. "Cunt!" and her voice rose even higher. "What in the world is a 'cunt'? Never mind! Don't tell me! I don't want to know that any more than I want to know the difference between the Seven Dwarfs and Brownies!" She cupped her hand and threw water at him with strong arms and good aim and his cigarette broke at its center, soaked. "Sometimes I hate you so damn much, it makes me sick to my stomach!" She went under then and came back up wiping water from her eyes, and those two things she'd taken such pains to hide in the first place showed themselves. "You think you're so special! But you're nothing! Nothing! I hate your stinking guts!" She disappeared then, cutting through the water with hard strokes, brittle and clean.

Jackson, angrier than he had ever been in his life, angrier than the situation deserved, dove in after her meaning to drown her, or at least make her think she was drowning. He had forgotten what a good swimmer she was, though, and by the time he caught up with her, he was exhausted and close to drowning himself. Rolling over on his back, he floated speechless through the water, watching clouds overhead, hearing familiar sounds that didn't sound familiar anymore. Felt immersed in water that seemed a stranger. Everything is different now, he thought to himself while he watched the sky. Everything in this world is different because of the stupid woman by the creek.

And here I am. Cold. The loser of the group. The boy who got himself told off by a nigger woman.

"Shitfire." He watched them chum up around the fire like long lost buddies. Glancing away he wondered again over the queer look to the creek. The differences between night and day at the place made it almost worth seeing, he supposed, wishing he had a cigarette so he could sit and think on all the wide contrasts.

"There's a pack of Lucky Strikes over there on that rock," the woman said, pointing to a shape near the creek that looked like the head of a horse coming up out of sand. Then she turned back to Valuable and said, "My daddy was a Injin. You know that?"

"Choctaw?"

"No. Drunk—" Leaning over she patted Valuable's hand and Jackson felt his head go hot at the touch. It hadn't registered yet that he had only "thought" about a smoke, not mentioned it out loud.

He sniffed the air—just creek. Just wet moss and rotting leaves. Like the house gutters in fall after a week of drizzly rain. Nothing more. Against the fire, he thought Val looked like a hunchback in a party dress trying to keep the wind out of her drawers. He snorted, noticing that she was still up on her knees, staring like a hypnotized chicken at the woman's black mouth, hanging on her every word, and the adoration there made him want to slap her hard across the face. Like his daddy slapped his mother. No, harder than that. He wanted to watch Val's head snap back like a loose rag doll. He wanted to do other things, too. Muddy, unkempt things that made him short-winded and stiff just thinking about.

Trying to calm himself, Jackson walked over to the horse-head rock and took a cigarette out of a brand-new pack of Lucky Strikes. Lighting it up with the one lone match set by the pack, he walked back to where he could hear their words, but sat with his back to them so everyone concerned would know exactly how he felt about things.

Smoking, thinking the forming mist on top of the water looked like a failure at meringue, he thought about how his father had slapped his mother while she cooked in the kitchen. He had hated him for it. Still hated him for it in a way. And because it had been about Enid Korner, he blamed Val for it in a way that seemed perfectly reasonable. All his mother had done was call Enid a whore. Everybody in Petal knew it was true. The last thing Jackson had ever expected was old John Henry to stomp over and knock her silly.

It had to be more than that, he reasoned. Something worse than telling the truth. Maybe his mother had done something. Maybe held her arms over her tits while John Henry stared. Maybe whispered between her teeth, Go to hell, same as Val did. He thumped his cigarette into the water and watched it sink, thinking that whatever it was his mother had done, she must have deserved it because men don't want to hit a woman unless they're pushed. Even though he'd never hit a real girl and hoped he never would, he had punched Val in the arm once or twice, the walk to the creek this Sunday past was proof enough of that.

He heard them laughing at him behind his back and refused to turn around. Chatty as cousins. He might have joined them around the fire if she asked again and he sat still, waiting for an invitation. Finally fed up with it all he jerked his shirt over his head and threw it to the sand. He undid his jeans and put his hand there and squeezed, the voices behind him making him furious again, making it harder to do what was usually so easy. After a minute he stood.

"Valuable?—" He unzipped his jeans. "You make *her* tell you the story. You hear me?" She looked at him, her eyes large and liquid and dark as he stepped out of his pants and turned to the fire.

I'll show them. Show them I got something holier than a head full of twigs. Val's eyes shot away immediately but the black woman's gaze never faltered. She stared, smiling easy, her steepled forefingers unimpressed with his semi-erection.

"Joody Two Sun thinks little is much when God is in it," she said, pointing.

It didn't make a bit of sense but he was thrilled to see Valuable's fingers twisting nervously in her lap.

"Looks to me like you need to spend a little more time prayin'." She laughed a great booming laugh. "And you don't know what to do with what you got anyhow. Do you, boy?" She hooted like an owl, his dick as hilarious as he found Joleb's nose. "Lord have mercy!" she said between howling while she beat her bony hands down on her bony knees. Splashing like a plopped rock, he was two hundred feet downstream before the frogs stopped screaming and the woman stopped her laughing.

Underneath the water at night the sand looked like ground-up bits of silver. Bluish-brown pieces of silver shining like sunken music. He made shallow dives, scooped sand up in his fingers and watched it sink slow to the bottom again. He rolled over on his back and with his face still six inches underwater, opened his eyes. Through clear night water the moon looked crazy, like a warped moon pie, not round at all, just weird and untrue to any known geometry. It shifted and changed, first oblong, then back to almost round again while it glowed pale and bluish brown like everything else around him. The tall pines. The banks. Sand. All just shapes of bluish brown that rested cool behind his eyes. Objects his eyes swallowed without thinking. Pulling his hands over his head he cut through the water and sent himself floating backward in the direction of the train trestle. I bet I look like a silver snake, he thought to himself. A silver snake in all this blue-brown. I bet the moon sees me and wishes it weren't a moon. He cut through water like a knife, felt its velvet, felt its coolness, and sent himself drifting away from two crazies huddled around the fire.

"I believe in you," Valuable said.

That simple.

That horrible.

She stretched out a hand then, as if to shake the woman's, and when their fingers touched it was as if a deal had been meted out between them. She met those black eyes and was glad that Jackson with his luggage of noise and disbelief was down the creek and away from her. This is it, Valuable judged. This is my course. At the woolly apex of Joody's head was a faded blue stick with twin dots along its ends. Valuable reached out carefully and touched it. Rolled it between her fingers to the limit of its give. While she did this the woman sat still as stone, closed her eyes and sighed once as if she had been here before, knew what she was being asked to do and was made terribly tired because of it.

"I know your story but I don't know his, yet," Joody said, nodding toward the loud whoops under the bridge while she picked up a stick midways along its process of polishing. The ground was full of them—colored, shiny markers stuck in the sand around her feet like a buried but highly decorated porcupine. "Your mama's a whore—" she said, finally, sadly, placing the stick in the palm of Valuable's hand.

Valuable waved this news away as if shooing flies. It was nothing to her. "Ma'am, everybody in town knows that. What Enid does with herself doesn't matter to me—"

"It's good it don't matter, 'cause it ain't gonna change with time." Joody stopped, confused by something. Something she caught off the girl when she waved her hand in front of her face.

Off her knees and cross-legged Indian style, Valuable dug up sand and put it in the valley of her dress. "All I ever wanted to know from Enid was who my daddy was, and all she ever said that first year was, 'take your pick,' and that was that. I realize she's not all bad. But like I said, I just want one thing from her. I asked her the same thing again when I was eight and she told me he drove a truck down in Brownsville."

"She lied."

"She did? You know who he is?" She sat up straight.

"I know he don't drive no truck. And I know you been playing the quiet game at home with your mama ever since. And I'm gonna say a true thing here—" Her head was beginning to hurt in the spot underneath her eleventh year. "Valuable—mean is mean. It ain't no more right for you to clam up and make a mute of yourself than for her to not tell you about your daddy."

"But—"

"No buts about it, girl. Mean is mean. And a woman mean is weak, not strong. Most women get so caught up in meanness, they forget what they goin' after in the first place. Besides, who in the world said whores don't need kindness? Who you think God's gonna look down on—the whore or the one who hates the whore?"

"The whore," Valuable said, but she wasn't so sure anymore.

"You lyin' now, girl. You still ain't convinced." Dear Lord, but her head hurt. Her dark hand waved over the fire. "Don't do that to me. It's like all that splashin'—" She pointed down the creek. "Lyin' don't do nothin' but throw out noise that kills the grass and disturbs the living, and meanness don't do nothin' but make you small."

She stood then, stretching her arms to the sky, popping joints that cracked like gunshots and as a test of what was true and what wasn't, threw off a smell like that of folded-up velvet. Blue velvet lining inside a diamond watch case. Like a jeweler would use. It was easy to do because she had seen it clear as a bell. It hadn't come from the girl, though, but traveled up and cradled alongside her neck from the direction of the creek, where the boy was swimming.

"Now—I'm gonna tell you 'bout your name 'cause white boy out there needs proof, and whether or not he settles in and hears it right this minute ain't important. You'll know. And you'll tell him in your own good time and he'll listen, because like it or not, you're a lot more important to him than he realizes. I'm gonna tell you some other things, too. I ain't sayin' word one 'bout your daddy, though. Not because I don't know. I do. And Lord! what a sorry man that one is. Not worth the spit God gave a goose. Knowin' him won't stop what's already moving any more than a feather'll stop a moving train. So you just sweep that hope out of your heart right this minute, 'cause I ain't sayin' word one."

Joody jumped her fire in one broad leap and landed square in front of Mama Girl rock. There she bent and lifted the can of red paint. Disappointment was large as a bull behind her. A terrible, injured bull. She stood still, waited for it to snuff itself out and pass. Holding the can pressed to her stomach, thinking on Even, she looked up at the blanket of stars and found her pattern. Pleiades—the Seven Daughters—resting securely inside bull Taurus. She said over her shoulder to the disappointment, "You ever sing a song and paint a nighttime rock?" Movement, slight and shy, drifted up from behind her. A rustle of cloth. The sound a foot makes digging into sand. That's a right, good girl, Joody said to herself. Ain't gonna know your daddy, but you gonna know other things that'll suit you better. Just you wait and see. To the movements behind her she said, "You mean, you lived here in Mississippi for fourteen years and ain't never painted a rock out under a lunatic moon? Girl, you ain't lived at all 'til you done that."

A cloud passed over three of the seven daughters while in the lower corner of the spread of black, twin stars flung themselves out, leaving trails the size of spilt salt that looked like diamonds. Her signal. With the fire behind her she smiled, put a hand to the shortest and oldest of her sticks—her Number One with two gold dots. The stick placed in her nappy head after a hard birth on a hot day that wore out the insides of her mama. Jolene's tired, wet fingers had twined polished wood into Joody's barely fuzz on Arizona's day of two suns, and once she kissed her and wiped her clean, she named her daughter accordingly. Lifting her thin arms to Pleiades, Joody turned and saw that the girl breathing hard by the fire had stripped down to her white cotton slip, pulled the undergarment's excess up through her legs and somehow made bloomers of it. Her lean legs were exposed to midthigh like a young warrior's, and light from the fire found her ivory skin and blazed her up with red shadows that danced like tattoos. Valuable had done something else, too, and seeing it Joody felt strange along her spine.

"Lord have mercy," Joody said, wishing she were Roman and knew their rites of crossing hand over chest. "Lord have mercy," she cried, not knowing anything else of equal value to say.

Standing there blazed and marked, Valuable had taken up the paring knife and shorn her hair. Pruned herself neatly at the base of her neck. The braid—gleaming like a headless black snake—dangled from her hand. Its weave still intact, but dead now to scalp and skull and soul.

"I've killed hope, Joody. I've killed hope and here it is—" She shook it out, breathing so hard her nostrils flared. Out under that lunatic moon she looked gloriously ready, and Joody's one prayerful wish was that the boy in love with water could see his sister now.

Everything in place, the woman who knew everything and nothing at all, answered her, "Yes ma'am, you sure have killed hope. Joody Two Sun thinks you killed hope so dead, it ain't ever gonna show itself again. And that's good, 'cause hope deferred makes the heart sick—"

With that Valuable threw her hair in the fire and they both sat twin-like, watching it burn.

"Enid's your mama's name," Joody said after the proper amount of time had been allowed for the burning of the hair. "Disappeared the night you was born. Up and hitched a ride outta town with a trucker, to a place I can't see right now. Maybe because leaving was bigger to her than where she was headed. Just wanted to leave. Anyhow," she sighed heavy, "she showed back up seven years later on a June day full of rain and flash floods that killed fourteen people up in Port Gibson. Showed up exactly three weeks before your granny died—" Joody stopped then, seeing a broader scope of edgework. "Your granny Luvenia named you. You know that?"

"That's what she told me. When Enid came back, she tried to get me to change my name to Louise and her and Granny had a big fight over it. Granny finally chased at her with a broom and she stayed gone somewhere overnight." Valuable was speaking slower than before. "Granny never had anything bad to say about anybody but Enid, and she hated her so bad just talking about her would give her a headache. All she ever said bad about me was that I ruined her quilt."

"'Ol' Prizewinner.' That's what she called it, ain't it? Called it 'Prizewinner.' Give it a proper name 'cause she won a blue ribbon at the

Neshoba State Fair over that Amish. She found you screamin' your lungs out smack-dab in the middle of it."

"How do you know these things?" Valuable felt worry feather up and down her neck because only God and Satan knew things and this woman was not God.

"That ain't important. I just know. I know you was named after a 'For Sale' sign off Main Street. 'Property for Sale. Valuable Corner,' it said. Luvenia named you Valuable so you'd know you was, 'cause your mama sure weren't. Your last name begins with a K, though." She shook the can of paint. Underneath the moon, the red inside the can looked dark as blood. Joody bent to it and sniffed its queer oily smell.

"Like I said before, love's the biggest something there is in this world. You know this thing? Know 'bout love? I think you do—"

The girl was staring into the fire. "I don't know anything, anything at all."

"Yes, you do, you just don't *know* you do—"

"No. I don't know the ass-end of anything!"

Joody held for a minute, disturbed. Knowing was like coursing. If you went too fast, it ruined it. "You just feelin' sorry for yourself 'cause your granny died and your mama's a whore and you ain't gonna find out who your daddy is." She spread a long red slash on a large rock between her knees with a combed-out piece of cane. Valuable had a smaller piece in her hand and was playing its edges against her palm, still staring at the fire, beginning to worry now over her dead, scorched braid and what she was going to say to folks. Especially Neva and Bea.

Joody continued, "You know the creek feels good. Know it feels like it stretches forever. You know you got you a good friend in that boy splashin' like a fish. Rude or not, you know he'd chew off his arm to save you. Looks to me like you know lots of things."

"I don't want to know lots of things, then. I don't want to be a woman." She reached across the fire and picked up a rock while she spoke in a monotone, like one spirit-vexed. "When I was seven, Granny picked me up and set me on a stool and the last thing I saw as a girl were the redbirds. Once she set me down I was somewhere in between. Not girl. Not woman. Just lost somewhere in between and afraid."

"What in the world did she tell you bad enough to make you not be a girl no more?" Joody asked, genuinely interested.

"You don't know?"

"I see broad pictures, girl. Not details. I got your name and its reason because it's such a big thing to who you are. Now what'd Luvenia tell you while you watched those redbirds?"

Valuable whispered low, "She told me about bleeding—"

"That you'd be cursed? We already covered that—"

"Yes ma'am. And how a woman should take a towel to the marriage bed with her to clean up after a man howls at the moon and empties his chuck wagon—"

"Lord God in Heaven have mercy!" Joody jumped to her feet and then spit in the fire. Wiping her mouth she said, "I heard it called rod, log, dick, cock and peter. But I ain't ever in all my life heard it called chuck wagon. Lord God have mercy on the three-sided woman!"

"I was set to ask her about some things, but she took Prizewinner to the cleaners to be cleaned and fell down dead in front of the Coca-Cola machine."

"Luvenia didn't have no respect for fluids. That's what kilt her. Lord have mercy, if I had doubts before, they all cleared up now. Yessiree, they all cleared up." Joody reached over and guided Valuable's hand, helped her make a queer design her mother showed her once. "You birthed on that quilt—you marked it. Your first essence soaked through that quilt and if your granny'd had the sense God gave a goose, had listened to what that quilt was sayin', she'd have stayed clear of the cleaners."

Valuable cocked her head and listened.

"Birth fluid is just as important as breeding fluid. A woman should know these things. Lord have mercy. A towel?"

"Yes ma'am. For the chuck wagon."

"A woman gotta get back to Deep Mother to understand these things; to understand the proper way to be a woman. Deep Mother is six-sided. Like this—" A near perfect hexagonal got painted on a rock with a red-dipped cane. "Feeling, Seeing, Knowing, Smelling, Tasting. Hearing. Anything less, ain't Woman. Luvenia was three-sided at most: Seeing, Smelling, Tasting. She took good care of you. Fed you, taught you how to

keep yourself clean and smelling sweet. Taught you how to behave in front
of the world. Taught you how to make a proper biscuit and sew a straight
seam, but one thing she didn't teach you, 'cause she didn't know it herself,
was to walk soft around fluids."

"How come she didn't know this thing?"

"'Cause her mama didn't teach her. A woman who thinks to herself, I'll
just take this dirty thing down to the dry cleaners and get this great, ugly
spot outta Prizewinner, or I'll just bring me an old ratty towel to bed to
sop up my man's nasty spill, or I'll just call that life-stem hanging between
his legs a chuck wagon. A woman like that ain't capable of no more than
shadow work—"

Out in the dark where she supposed he viewed himself safe, the boy
was sitting naked on wet sand, shivering, his legs pulled up and wrapped
by his arms. He'd lacked proper foresight when he tossed his clothes over
by their fire. Joody looked over and squinted. Good. That's a right good
boy, she thought. You just sit your ass down there and listen hard. Maybe
you learn a thing or two about how to be a man.

Inside a deep casket of a dream, Even saw her painting rocks around a
smoldering fire burning low blue and dying.

"Do you see her?" a Big Somebody asked.

"Yes."

"Watch close, 'cause this will be the thing that finishes her. This will
be the last thing she will do."

"She's just painting rocks!"

"No, Even, you're wrong. She has filled the barrel 'til it split the seasoned oak. She has burned the last of the hometown fodder. She has done
this thing again and again. This will be the last thing she ever does."

"Ain't no harm in what she's doing—she's just paintin' rocks, Mister
Big Somebody. Ain't no harm there. Can't nobody be hurt there!"

"She has set her hand to stir the pot one time too many. This will be
the last thing she ever does."

"I'll tell her to stop, then! I'll find her, and tell her to stop!"

"Too late."

"No!"

"Sharp with her shuttle she struck, and bloodied her hands."

"No! She's Judy Tucson is all! From out in Arizona—"

"She was a princess once, of an ancient house, reared in the cave of the wild north wind, her father. Half a goddess but child, she suffered like you. You remember this. You talk to Canaan of this—"

"No!—"

Even woke screaming and the sound of his own voice, high in a beggar's cant, bounced back over him from the hard walls of his bedroom. He had thought he heard gunfire or some deep shattering. But there was nothing but a moon shining full and brilliant. He saw by its illumination that the hands of the wall clock were set at 1 A.M. Naked and hot, he kicked off his sheet and climbed out of bed.

The window had slid down at some point during sleep and he'd lost the benefit of breeze. Sniffing, he smelled sealed-up dust and kitchen grease and old, worn-out shoes. This is a male house, he thought. Nothing but stains, odored-up shirts and smelly socks. And it'll always be male, he realized with a sudden heaviness that threatened his throat.

He pulled on jeans and walked through to the front door and stepped onto the porch where there was still a partial breeze, but just barely. Listening for thunder, expecting to see some evidence of rain or distant lightning, he sniffed hard again, but came up empty. Bellrose was quiet. No rain in weeks. The dirt streets were dry as old scabs, their wheel-worn ruts dusty and deep and hard-ridged. Canaan's place seemed dead and vacated. No light at all. The only movement from his yard was a bucket on its side rolling in a lazy arc. Even sniffed again, to the east this time. Knowing wind and weather was as natural a thing to him as breathing, and there under a moon more like a sun, he felt a change in the pressure of things, a subtle slippage so slight it almost went unnoticed, but still a change.

"People call it lots of things, it don't change what it is." She was speaking of the moon. Addressing its state of being, regardless of name.

"Colored, White, Chinese, Coon Ass, don't matter what they *say* it is, it don't change the *what* of it. You look at it now—tell me what you see."

Joody's fire was lower and she had grown so far beyond the word "tired," that it wasn't a word anymore, just the memory of a memory of a word. Feeling close to being gone, her ages weighted beyond the range of light-weight polished wood, all she wanted for the moment was to be done with this thing, park her body on her hemp pallet inside her hut and sleep the sleep of the righteous. "Go on now. Tell me—"

Valuable looked up at a light so loud she squinted. The low sounds of frogs mingled with cicadas, off-key and jarring, but slower, their tune shallow of melody. "I see a pearl," she said and yawned. "The moon looks like a great, giant pearl."

"Talk to the moon, then, tell him what you think of him. Stand up and address him properly. Down here, we're nothing. The moon looks down on us and sees how small we are and has pity and opens up his ears. Talk to him. He's so bright, he gotta be hungry." Joody laid her head on her knees, glanced over studying the lumped shape of the boy and yawned herself to sleep.

Valuable crossed over. One minute one place. The next, somewhere else. A litered pine knot exploded inside the center of the fire, throwing off a storm of sparks that rained all around but landed harmless. The woman next to her seemed deaf to it all and gave off a small, snuffling snore like that of a small dog or baby bear. Once Valuable judged the sleep real and the snore genuine she knew the decision of speaking or not speaking to the moon was to be a private thing. Her instructor, who had been so insistent she feed the hungry pearl, was out like a candle.

Private or public, the deal was done, because for what felt like a very long time she had stumbled along. Cascaded into chance empty-handed. Carried with her fingernails bitten to the quick and bloody. Enveloped as she was in the coating of night, it was easy enough to believe someone had decided she was to be a six-sided woman. A completion not based on heritage, but something else. Something set in motion involving more than dust and weariness and helpless wondering. And so she opened her mouth, not knowing what would come in or go out of it, just doing it because it seemed a part of a bigger design, and the words when they came were not the type of words she would have put together at all. Resembling those of the tongue talkers who bark like dogs and roll themselves around underneath smelly tents, her words were about as clear as a muddy pond after hard rain:

> *Moon of pearl, see me small and have pity on my nothingness.*
> *Love me. See me as I am. You and God and Wind and Sky see me*
> *and take me up to you.*
> *Love me. Love my three sides looking for three more.*
> *Love my heart searching for Deep Mother.*
> *Judge me worthy and send me my Pearl.*

Okay, said the moon, *here it comes,* and what came seemed to echo from the inside of a metal tube. *Fate has terrible power. You cannot escape it by wealth or war. No fort will keep it out, no ships outrun it—*

"No—God, no."

The moon hushed then and seemed to blink one slow blink like the lone drunken eye of a great-headed man. She felt her arms—cold and stiff. Ran her hands across the back of her hair—short with one blunt, flipped-out curl. She saw her braid, severed and burned, wiry and frizzed, like hair off a doll. Swallowing hard she pulled in a breath that came in syncopated. Like the drag of a hand across a sticky counter. Next to her dying wood was shifting. Orange to blue to gray to nothing. She heard plopping sounds of fat acorns hitting creek water and the unhurried settle of night. Valuable heard all these things, and all she wanted of any of them was Jackson.

He was frightened at first. Scared almost senseless and close to the point of shitting himself, and then he gave up. Just gave up and let it wash over him in tall waves. Beat him up with heavy fists. Whittle him down to a sliver and be done. Cold. He sure was cold, though. The crazy nigger had seen him, he was almost sure, but Val was under some conjure spell and until it fizzled, he'd just as soon stay put, even though he was freezing to death and sand was caking up in his ass.

Crawling up the bank slow as a snail, the first thing he'd noticed once he'd found his spot in the dark was that the two of them were involved in some kind of girl talk that was so God-awful it made him want to puke.

But as soon as the colored woman put her head down on her knees and nodded off, Val began jabbering like a crazy-ass mute with a fresh-grown tongue. Spewing mumbo-jumbo and philosophy like a harelip Plato. He listened for just about half a second, beaten up enough by fear to ignore her babblings, finally able to enjoy the ordinary sounds of water at night. With that, he stretched out on his side and shut his eyes.

Thirteen. Inside his dream they were thirteen and fifteen again. Swimming together. Diving together. Just like when they were little and doing it for the first time. He saw his cigarettes up on the bank beside his clothes while Valuable went under in a splashless dive. She came up saying, Look at the silver, Jackson. There's silver down low, just waiting, and like magic, he was suddenly down under and low, where the loose, shuffling grains felt rough to his cheek. Needing air he rolled over too soon and touched velvet. Her velvet. Her velvet breast had landed inside his palm and made him come up choking. When he broke the surface, she was nowhere in sight. Gone. Vanished as cleanly as one wipes a chalkboard. Going under again, he stirred up mud that clogged his nose and eyes, settled down his throat to rest on the back of his tongue. He tasted it and the taste of it was huge and bitter. But then he felt the velvet again and squeezed and felt his dick turn hard as a rock. Felt the thrill of it rush clean up to his throat. When the water cleared, her face was floating next to his, pink and white, floating eyeball to eyeball, and when he winked, she winked right back but her eyes were different. Pale blue and blind, not dark gray as a dove, like before. Pushing away he saw her legs and they were not hers at all, but those of a pig. A gutted sow with tits catching in the current. Before he could move, she pulled him in. Sucked at his neck and then went lower, tearing at his heart.

"Ahhaaa!" He woke up coiled and cold and wondering why he was outside naked with sand up his ass. He looked over his shoulder and saw them around the fire, and remembered. Saw the colored woman sleeping. Saw Val curled up and covered by her dress. Saw his clothes, placed closer to him than he remembered and folded neatly, like when they used to swim in the creek. Val did that, and he knew it was true. Crawling over, careful as an old turtle, he pulled them on. Warmed by the fire, they felt good as a hot towel after a shower. He yawned long and hard and then he stood, feeling drugged and sleepy. Zipping up, he walked back to where he had been sleeping and listened to Val's snore. A snore more like a hummingbird's wings than snore. A cute sound. A sound that made him smile.

Looking at the trestle to his right, he heard a groan along the suspended tracks and knew a train was on its way. The Southern Ohio probably. Miles away still. While he sat and waited he heard the sounds expand underneath the old trestle. Heard the straining whine of metal. A cluster of nests in the trestle's corners gave way and began to drop straw down onto the water like dried-up rain. He saw it all. I'll wait and see the train, too, was what he thought to himself, yawning terribly. But he was fast asleep before the locomotive pulling twenty-six cars of coal ever broke through the mist and roared over the Baby Black Creek. He had fallen asleep sniffing the air like a happy hound. Dreaming instantly of cigarette smoke and the smell of sand and sun on skin, and the smell of Valuable who, curled up and sleeping around the fire, was throwing off a scent like that of velvet.

Joody Two Sun knew she would have to wake them—wake the boy over by the water, curled on his side and snoring softly, wake the girl next to the fire, sleeping underneath her crumpled, flowered dress. Joody knew she'd have to send them back to wherever they were supposed to be, to whatever they were supposed to be doing. She knew she would have to help them rearrange their clothes. Help them recover from their dream-sleep. But for the moment, she just sat and waited and did nothing at all because a powerful something had happened inside the orbit of her creek world and waiting was appropriate. So she sat—long after the train passed over headed south—her forearms resting easy on her knees, her hands dangling, while she studied the blues of her fire. She didn't mind the wait, either. To a six-sided woman, jostling awake too soon after such a powerful something has happened was shadow-living and beneath her. To a six-sided woman, jostling awake too soon and shortchangin' the dreamworld was as ill-mannered and deadly as ignoring life's precious fluids.

6
DREAMS

NEVA AND BEA BOTH WOKE at the stroke of midnight, needing to pee. Light from their bedroom window smuggled through tapestry stitching, and its illumination across the foot of their bed took on the appearance of twin scabbards, complete with swords. The weaponry continued up into the wall, finding its final mark in twelve-inch dental molding imported from England sometime shortly after the Civil War. Bea's first thought on waking was that the house was being split in two by light and would shortly fall apart into two halves—the bed's remains on one end, and the dresser and antique chaise on the other. Neva's first thought upon waking was that they needed better drapes.

Lesbian and polite, unlike those foolish men they had married so long ago, each waited for the other to finish their business and the toilet to flush before broaching the subject they'd both agreed to discuss in the morning.

"Somebody needs to talk to Enid," Neva said.

"She's lost, that's all. Everybody gets lost now and then."

"She's got the clap, Bea. That's a little more serious than being 'lost,' don't you think?"

There was silence followed by one loud exhalation from the bathroom. A habit Neva hated. All loud breath and booming silence that forced a response. She continued, "And she's got that particular calamity because she whores around like there's no tomorrow. Not to mention that business about Valuable." She walked across the oak floor, climbed up on her grand-mother's stuffed chair by the window and tucked an army blanket over the scrolled iron curtain rod. The gabled house was a headache. Deep porches in the front that were totally useless because the street was ugly and there was no reason in the world a sane person would want to sit in a rocker and study ugliness. No decent porch at all in the back, where the plum trees bloomed and the butterfly plants waved purple cones all summer long and the couple's painted birdhouses were always occupied. No porch at all where one should be. No grace at all, either, for the bedrooms. Sun fading everything of value. Every shantung stripe, every hand-embroidered flower, every damask rose—while the moon, even quartered and pared down to a sliver, multiplied itself against the bed and the polished wood floors. Neva hopped down and threw herself across the bed, bumping the bedside table, making the china figurines from Bea's marriage knock and ching.

"I'll tell you something else, too—" she reached over and steadied the china pig blowing the trumpet, "—somebody's gonna get hurt over this and I'm not talking about Enid."

"You really believe that?" Bea said this around her toothbrush. Foam slathered down to her chin in a white goatee. That was another habit Neva hated. The way Bea brushed her teeth every time she got up to pee.

"For God's sake, quit being stupid. They're half brother and sister and running around all over town and not knowing it. Jackson's sixteen now. I know sixteen. Hell, I remember sixteen."

"Enid's never said it was true."

"Enid's never said the truth about a single thing in her life, either. Somebody better talk to her, that's all I'm saying." Not that she would lis-ten. Neva had seen her at work and it was almost a sickness, an ignorant sickness as well as an embarrassment. Fine if she were living alone, with nothing better to do than run the beauty shop and fuck everybody in pants in between shampoos, but there was the issue of Valuable and the boy. Lord! Family is a curse as bad as the clap, she thought to herself, realizing

Val was stealing their sleep more effectively than their topped-off bladders and the white-hot moon. Neva looked at her watch. Twelve-fifteen. Throwing an arm over her eyes she called out, irritably, "We need rest, Sweet. You can do your partial in the morning—" No answer from the bathroom. She didn't really expect one, just halfway hoped she might hear the water shut off and then the click of the light switch shortly after. "Can't you finish that later?" Still nothing. Just the sound of wet cascading over china, and energetic hands brushing against dentures, along with the low sound of old plumbing straining itself at midnight.

Underneath a thrown light from a green desk lamp Canaan's head nodded down and hit a stack of books level with his chin. Once his mind was let go of the dream, he raised his head and sat back stunned.

There was not much new to see at night inside Hattiesburg's library and he found that a peculiar relief, having the visions inside his head to calm and wet down and catalogue. Relieved then by the familiar, he turned his eyes to the corridor nearest—578–698, birds, plants, geographical mapworks, gardens of the world—and called to mind a book in the center of the highest shelf. *The Wonderful Birds of the Northern World*. A full-color slick covered the book and it was thick with a promising heft but as full of nothing as the dust-filled work of a taxidermist, for it was page after page of garish, unbecoming photographs taken by a man who obviously hated birds. There were pictures of birds shitting. Birds regurgitating. Birds mating. Birds eating the eggs of other birds. Birds eating the shit of dogs. Birds dying in time-lapsed segments that filled ten pages. Canaan called it *The Abominable Book of Birds* and found out through lazy investigation it was a conglomerate piece put together by a group of ornithologists as part of a thesis. In truth he thought they missed their true vocation and should have settled on a hobby closer to their happy nature. Like mortuary. He thought on this particular book because it was the only volume in the library that he hated, and thinking on something he hated always cleared his head.

The library at night had always looked like nothing else he'd ever seen. Tall corridors hurled black shadows all the way across the black and white squared tiles. Leather chairs snug to round tables seemed to hold shrouded shapes placed there in detention. There were ten tables in the lower level. Four chairs per table producing forty fixed phantoms who sat locked in place until light of morning. Unsettling at first, he'd grown accustomed to these long shadows, these interruptions of light, and had come to think of them more as pools of marooned wisdom looking for a boat than as evil.

He had finished earlier than the night before. Broom and mop and bucket of scrub brushes were back in storage. Sinks scrubbed and cans emptied. The four toilets and two urinals more fitting for punch than offal, and when he polished up the sink, he saw his face sent back to him, smiling. He had spent the rest of the night a man of leisure, a scholar alone but for stacks and stacks of books piled up on the table by the dark east window, the window facing the alley. He paused only to make coffee and smoke an occasional cigarette on the small grated landing out the second-story fire escape.

He especially loved the old philosophers—their keen awareness of human worth and their belief in what a human could accomplish, both good and bad. And he loved the tragic poets—Aeschylus, Sophocles and Euripides. Canaan had no clue as to the proper saying of their names. The way they twisted coming out his mouth was as unimportant to him as the true color of his colon. Colon was colon. It had a duty to pull regardless of handle, and so did the poets. He knew their words, their songs, the cold truth behind the poetry, but he settled on calling them Ache, Soph and Europee, accordingly.

Tragedies came closest to the meat and marrow of the southern Negro was his belief, and of the three great tragedians, Soph was his favorite. *Oedipus the King, Antigone.* Plays proving a hard truth that unwittingly man is both innocent and guilty simultaneously, and more often than not, winds up dead as a knob because of it.

Minutes before the sow visited, he had been reading *The Libation Bearers*. Part two of a trilogy by Canaan's least favorite of the three, Ache (Aeschylus):

> *But as for me: gods have forced on my city*
> *resisted fate. From our fathers' houses*
> *they led us here, to take the lot of slaves.*

And mine it is to wrench my will, and consent
to their commands, right or wrong,
to beat down my edged hate.
And yet under veils I weep
the vanities that have killed
my lord; and freeze with sorrow in the secret heart.

Canaan had yawned and scratched his head and gone to the back cubicle for coffee. Fresh, hot, black, he made it up the way he liked it at home, planning on clearing the evidence an hour or two before his shift ended. Once it perked, Canaan used the assistant librarian's favorite cup. A Woman's Work Is Never Done was printed on its side. Ain't that the God's truth, he thought, and the thought was not charitable.

On his way back into the main room, the glare of the moon was shining so full he could read tomorrow's sermon topic on the outdoor glass sign of the Methodist Church across the street. "The Chastisement of the Lord." Canaan shook his head. I think if I were preaching a hard word, I wouldn't broadcast it. But then those Methodists are about as hard on sin as the Episcopalians. Meaning they weren't very hard at all. Sometimes it seemed to him the pagan Romans with their penance and deeds had the only truth of it—make a person pay today for what he done yesterday in order to avoid punishment come tomorrow.

At that point he had sat himself down and headed back into his reading, but the words clotted on the page and made his eyes tired and itchy. Stretching out his legs, he thought, I'm just gonna sit here and think for a while. Think on all the business in Montgomery and Birmingham and Arkansas. Think on how long it might take that business to cause a wrinkle in the fabric of Petal. Yessiree, I'll just sit here awhile and think. Canaan never knew when he drifted over from thinking to sleeping. He just came to some level of knowing that his ass was in a leather chair and his arms were folded across his chest and he was watching a pale and gutted-out sow make slow work of walking toward him.

"Good evening, Canaan," the sow finally said, pulling out a chair and sitting herself down. "Don't bother getting up—it seems a heavy world tonight, don't it? Heavier than most?"

Alarmed at her gape—the way her ribs were pried open and her teats disaligned—he watched her lift a front leg and wipe her brow and then she smiled. But the smile carried a slight edge of embarrassment to it like a highly dressed lady who's fallen flat on her ass in front of a crowd. Aware of his eyes, she reached and pulled her sides together and then folded her arms across her split middle.

"Who in the world did this ass-awful thing to you?" Canaan had managed to ask, pointing to the incision that ran from puckered anus to base of snout.

"Why, the whole world did this to me, Canaan. You of all people should know that. Whole world been after me for a long time now—" She wiped her forehead again and her left side opened up and he saw a cavity as dark as the inside of a snake.

"Thy God, you've got rocks in your mouth—"

She raised her pig's foot and pointed it. "Why, I think you're mighty bright for one so colored."

Likewise, Canaan thought, for one so lacking in internal organs. He continued, "Just like that man. That Greek man down on the shore—" Canaan snapped his fingers, trying to remember.

"Demosthenes," the sow said flawlessly around the pebbles in her mouth.

"That's the one."

"You know, Canaan," she crossed her legs and her incision took on the shape of an *S*. "One thing that puzzles me, almost to the point of breaking my heart, is man's futile search for the core of things."

"Thy God, do tell," he nodded in agreement.

"Why, I mean, mankind in general, black and white, Coon-ass and Chinese, all bank on the worthless seam of things—the fragile seam of the universe. Expecting that old tuck to hold up through eons of time, but in the end it splits wide open. Just like this—" She jerked open her incision and Canaan jumped back in his chair, horrified. "Everything spills. Like a bladder in a bucket." She sat looking at him, her eyes filling, her snout crimped up on one corner. "You've really disappointed me in your efforts, Canaan." She gave him such a look of profound sadness he felt like weeping.

"How in the world?"

"You shore up breaches that ain't even opened up, ain't never gonna open, and you ignore the canyon in your soul."

"Lord have mercy, have I done this thing?" He put a hand over his heart, alarmed.

"Yes. You build a case where none is warranted and ignore the true reality."

"You sound more prophet than pig."

"Thy God, yes, I 'spect I do." The sow nodded and wiped at her cloudy blue eyes.

"Why this concern over true reality? Why this reconsideration of the activity of *Nee*groes? Why visit me now?"

"Why, a smart colored man like you should know this thing." She grinned and three books flew off his table. Pages fanning. Blown by some wayward wind.

"I don't. I don't know."

"Why, you catchin' a bottle with your head brought me here, Canaan. A man can't bleed all over town and not draw attention. You remember this you hear. Even Grade needs you to remember this thing. He'll need it now and he'll need it later down along the bay." She pushed back her chair then and stood up, a great wallowing heap of flapping skin and unbound seams. A rock she'd held in her mouth fell straight through her slit-open frame and hit the tiles on the floor.

"Are you Demosthenes come back from hell?"

"Hell? You think that jewel went straight to hell?"

"He killed himself, didn't he? Preachers say—"

"You think man is big enough to say to God who goes down and who don't?"

"No, no I guess not, I guess most might—"

"You're right there so shut your mouth. You ain't big enough for that." She put her entire foot in her mouth and took it back out again. "Can you do that?"

"Thy God!"

"Not quite—"

"Who the hell are you?"

"My name's a riddle and not important," was what she said as she turned and walked away, strowing rocks behind her like tiny turds. He watched her shuffle between the shelves holding books on religion. Canaan's head had touched down then and he sat up straight in his chair. Not a man to give hold to a dream he simply directed his eyes to the shelf holding the abominable book on birds and tried to still his heart.

The profaned birds didn't do it, so he rose, lifted two books off the table and climbed the stairs that led to the balcony, and once there, just minutes after his dream of the gutted sow, he stood and leaned on the walnut balcony at a point where a weak light cast a beam the width of the book held up in his hand. And there, from that point, sent down to the captive ears of the forty frozen phantoms, Canaan read out loud passages from *Antigone*.

> —*If I die before my time, I say it is a gain.*
> *Who lives in sorrows many as are mine*
> *how shall he not be glad to gain his death?*
> *And so, for me to meet this fate, no grief.*
> *But if I left that corpse, my mother's son,*
> *dead and unburied I'd have cause to grieve*
> *as now I grieve not.*
> *And if you think my acts are foolishness*
> *the foolishness may be in a fool's eye—*

"Here's the chorus now, boys. You listen up, maybe ole Canaan let you out of school early tonight." He sent this down to ghost number three sitting at the table by the broad front door. "You an unruly spirit. Always itching to get out early. Just like Even Grade." He shook his head, still thinking on sow but not so much as before. He continued, his clear, deep voice filling the hall.

> . . .*These rigid spirits are the first to fall.*
> *The strongest iron, hardened in the fire,*
> *most often ends in scraps and shatterings.*
> *Small curbs bring raging horses back to terms.*
> *Slave to his neighbor, who can think of pride?*

"Small curbs—I know about small curbs. You just ask any colored man about small curbs diggin' in his backside and neck, he'll tell you good and true 'bout those small curbs." Every word came back twice, such were the acoustics

of the building. He cleared his throat and picked up another volume, a bigger
one that once spread open lost its outside edges to opaque shadow. He directed his eyes and read the lines from *Oedipus at Colonus:*

> *. . . Though he has watched a decent age pass by,*
> *A man will sometimes still desire the world.*
> *I swear I see no wisdom in that man.*
> *The endless hours pile up a drift of pain*
> *More unrelieved each day; and as for pleasure,*
> *When he is sunken in excessive age,*
> *You will not see his pleasure anywhere.*
> *The last attendant is the same for all,*
> *Old men and young alike, as in its season*
> *Man's heritage of underworld appears:*
> *There being then no epithalamion,*
> *No music and no dance. Death is the finish.*

There was a long silence, then he spoke softly, not to the phantoms but
to his heart: "No music and no dance. Death is the finish." He paused, arms
crossed over chest, the book underneath next to his heart. *And though he has
watched a decent age pass by, a man will sometimes still desire the world,* was what he
opened his mouth to say, but couldn't. All he could do was stand confused
inside a meager light and clutch to his chest a book that didn't belong to him.

7

THICK AS GRITS

WATER AGAIN. The sound of it in the back bathroom of 42 Stockwell Street reached through three walls—bathroom, bedroom, long portion of hall—and even over its long reach, Joleb Green could hear Grace singing:

We goin' down to River Jordan
No worries there, the price done paid
That train done come and we a boardin'
La la la laaa, de laa la laaa . . .

She'd been singing the same song over running water for years and he was yet to hear word one of the last line. He brushed his teeth and thought on it and what words might rhyme with "paid" because he didn't want to think about what else Grace was doing in the back bathroom with his mother slung naked and soapy wet in her harness.

Dropping his toothbrush in the glass, he had a little talk with Jesus. It was one-sided as usual but he did it one more time even though he was fast approaching the point where he would give up entirely on that slippery eel of a Savior, having come to the conclusion that the once dead but forever risen vice president of the Trinity was damn shy about living in a heart dark as Joleb's.

He pissed long and hard, washed his hands and went into the dining room, a smallish room too cramped for the short sofa against the lemon-colored wall. Through the broad picture window he saw more of the street than he cared to, but there was a bird feeder out there in the middle of it all and week before last a pair of indigo buntings showed up and sat squat by the camellia bush—all cobalt blue against deep fruity green—and seeing such a thing as that had been a pleasure.

Water shut down in the back room and he could hear Grace talking to his mother. "We gonna get you fresh as a daisy, Miss Mary, gonna get you fresh as a newborn baby. You just sit back and let Grace do her business now. Don't you fret and squirm. You just rest now—"

Joleb thought of the sling and the diaper and wondered which parts were still naked before he could stop himself. He smelled fruitcake set to season in the dark china cabinet across the room and the sweet smell of it made him want to puke.

("Where'd you get this heavy notion of sin?" the black-robed man asked.

Stunned by lit candles and gold and carvings, Joleb sat there stupid as a retard for about three whole minutes.

"How'd you come to believe you're bound for hell?" The man didn't seem impatient, but he did seem concerned.

If he had known then that his name was Russ as he found out a few minutes later, Joleb could have said, Well, you see Russ, I went to Vacation Bible School when I was ten years old expecting to build a birdhouse out of matchsticks—you know, the kind the prisoners up in Parchman were famous for making and sending out by their relatives to sell at the craft shows so they can have cigarette and gambling money and a way to buy candy. All I wanted was a birdhouse. Maybe my handprint in some plaster of Paris that I could paint blue for Christmas. But a tall man had something else in mind. We finally got the Kool-Aid and the cookies, those who still had the stomach for it, that is, after hearing of hell and damnation.

Me and sixteen others, Russ. I ain't the only one running all over town looking for Jesus . . .

Joleb could've said those things. Put the blame back a few years, but it was stupid and weak sounding so he kept his mouth shut and watched the wax slide down the cylindrical sides of a whole sea of candles. Over the candles was a statue of Mary wearing a crown and the Christ child at her tit.

"Sin," Joleb said finally. Not as answer or explanation. Just as topic. "Hard to imagine a word with three little letters could be such a ballbreaker, sir. Seems to me a word that carries such a God-awful weight should have lots of letters and be difficult to spell, at least to my way of thinking."

"I'm concerned by your disproportionate anxiety over this," he said. Joleb noticed his robe went nearly to his feet. Like a garment a judge would wear.

Anxiety? Anxiety? I could preach you a sermon, my man, Joleb thought while he watched the candles melt, wondering the whole while if Mary had nursed Jesus with her own personal tit or hired out a wet nurse to do it like all those royal folks did.)

Joleb sat back on the sofa with his hands behind his head and looked up at the ceiling. There were rust-colored water stains from where the roof had leaked and he saw a piece of silver tinsel still attached on top of the doorframe. They had been the last family on the block to get rid of the Christmas tree. Waiting for a tardy Santa who got lost somewhere in transit. Waited 'til most of February was gone and then they quit waiting and hauled the thing out. Joleb remembered what a helluva good time he had watching the sonofabitch burn, too.

("What's that gold box for?" Joleb pointed past the long table with a carved-out Last Supper scene at its base. One of the disciples was leaning on marble Christ, crying like a titty-baby and Joleb hated him for such a show of weakness.

"You mean the altar?"

"No, I mean that gold box behind that carved-out table?"

"The table's called the altar and the gold box is the tabernacle that holds the consecrated host."

"What's a host?"

Joleb got the abbreviated version, which boiled down to Jesus Christ being reduced to the size of a vanilla wafer that is then consumed by the congregation with the leftovers being put aside in the gold box until later when folks got hungry again.

"You're shitting me—" Joleb blurted out and the man gave a hoot of a laugh.

"No, I'm not. It's the consecrated host—used to celebrate Mass with the shut-ins and the sick. We can't just toss it out like so much bathwater. The priest drinks all the leftover wine. The host goes in there." He pointed to the gold box. "Some people come for adoration," a time of contemplation he explained, "they kneel and pray before the Blessed Sacrament."

"So you folks believe Jesus turns himself to the size of a vanilla wafer and people eat this wafer like they would a daily vitamin." Joleb stood leaning against a pew watching a flickering red light inside a tiny hanging globe.

"Well, somewhat—"

"And people actually believe this? Believe they're eating the body of Jesus? Because, mister, it sounds like something most people wouldn't dare admit to, pardon my rudeness."

Grinning, the man sat down and stretched way back. "Who in the world *are* you?" he asked.

"Joleb Green, from over in Petal. I'm not Catholic and don't intend to be one, either. This is just my last stop in a whole string of churches. Mostly Baptist and Holy Rollers—"

"I see. How old are you Joleb and what brought you to Sacred Heart Church, you not being a Catholic or ever intending to be one, for that matter?"

"Fifteen, and I can't get shed of my sin, sir."

"You can't get shed of your sin—"

"No sir, I can't."

"Tell me about your sin, Joleb. What's got you running to every house of worship in the region?")

"Joleb! You out there?" Grace yelled this from the back bedroom. "You Joleb!"

"I'm here—"

"You come get your mama now while I change out the bed."

He stood and stretched and then went down the hall popping his knuckles.

From the side she looked asleep but he knew she wasn't. She was nodding her head all right, but she wasn't asleep. Taking the handles in both hands he wheeled her down the hall and into the dining room.

"You get her a fresh bib, too! Don't forget that—I think the green one's in the kitchen somewhere!"

Moving the wheelchair until he got her maneuvered just right, Joleb set the brake and went into the kitchen looking for the bib. Morning light was just coming through the back window over the sink. Cutting over floor and wall and door. Running a sharp angle straight into the stainless steel of his mother's wheelchair behind him. Caught there, it went up and over the frozen feet resting in fuzzy white slippers parked on the metal footrest.

Thick as a rock. Thick as grits left overnight in a bowl. Thick as grits—

After plundering in a drawer he found the plaid green one with long ties and went back into the dining room where he sat on the small sofa and watched her.

"You got her bib, Joleb?"

"I got it, Grace—"

"You tie it on yet?"

"No ma'am, not yet—"

"You tie it on now, you hear? I got her bathed and sweet smellin'. That's a new housedress she's got on."

"I'm about to."

"That's my good boy—"

"Yeah, right," Joleb said low, more to himself than his mother. The tinsel stuck over the front door was bothering him.

"I sure hate Saturdays, Ma. Lazy-ass Burris is still sleepin' and here it is close to noon. I think that's a damn shame." He brushed a fly away from her hair. Her pale blue eyes looked like glass deer eyes, only glass deer eyes looked more real. Frozen in a startled stare like her last glance at the world of the living had been some horrible vision, he knew she would sit unblinking for an amazing stretch of time. Forty-five seconds according to his Timex. He'd tried to hold his eyes open for the same amount of time but couldn't.

"He went out last night and looked for the face of God again. I think up along the trestle at Baby Black. I'm not sure, though. His shoes are muddy, so maybe it was a different place this time." He smoothed out a wrinkle in the lap of her dress.

Grace hurried through carrying an armload of laundry. "Get these nasty things in the wash and out on a line. I do say, ain't enough hours in the day for what Just Plain Grace got to do. I tell you—"

"You need me to help, Grace?"

"No, but you can tell Burris if he wants clean sheets he can get his sorry self up next time. I ain't waitin' on him while he sleeps 'til noon."

Joleb stood and went to the tinsel and jerked it down. Wadding it up to a tiny ball, he swallowed it. He could hear Grace slopping clothes around in a sink full of starch.

"I don't think Daddy knows it, either—about Burris slipping out. He climbed back in his window about two A.M.—"

"You talkin' to me, Joleb? You got to speak up if you're talkin' to me!"

"No, Grace, I'm talking to Ma." He leaned low to his mother, "Anyhow, Daddy kept right on snoring, like he never heard a thing. He told him last time if he caught him on a trestle again, there'd be hell to pay but I don't think so. I don't think Daddy's got the balls to do much of anything anymore." He rested his forearms on his legs and glanced outside. The twin girls across the street were trying to hopscotch.

"You want me to read to you, Ma?" He leaned forward, his arms straight down between his legs—

("I murdered my mother is the what of it," Joleb blurted out. Then, "What's your name, sir? Seeing how I'm sitting here spilling my guts all over this damn marble floor."

"Russell. Father Russell to most, but since you're sitting here spilling your guts and you have no intention of ever being Catholic, feel free to call me Russ."

"I've been baptized fourteen times, Russ. Five times Methodist. Nine times in combination Baptist, Methodist and Pentecostal and I still can't get shed of it."

"The sin of murder?"

"Yes sir, that's the one."

"Well, murder *is* a mortal sin, Joleb. But I think one baptism is all a person needs, even a murderer. Anything over the first one—that is if it's done in accordance to Scripture—is null and void. Much like gassing up an already full car or trying to put water in a glass that won't hold any more."

"I don't follow, Russ—"

"You can be baptized until the cows come home, but it's a waste of good water, is what I'm saying." Russ cracked his fingers and then undid the white collar around his neck.

"So all this running around I'm doing—"

"Is a waste of time," Russ said.

"Are you tryin' to tell me it has nothing to do with being saved? All those times I've gone under the water? Well, the Methodists sprinkled, but I was dunked everwhere else. Held under 'til I nearly drowned by the Pentecostals, and you're saying it don't mean a thing?"

"If by the term 'saved' you mean 'a ticket to heaven'—" Here Russ had shrugged. "I don't know. Whether or not we end up in heaven is up to God. We believe. We hope. We struggle to be as good as we can possibly be. All those things. Your baptism places you inside a community of people who believe in Christ. Where were you baptized the first time?"

"Mars Hill Baptist. Actually in the Bogue Homa Creek, but through that particular church."

"Well, the Protestant faith is different, but the basic precepts of belief are similar as far as baptism goes. They baptize in the name of the Father, Son and Holy Ghost. So the baptism was valid. But as a Catholic, I believe that to embrace Christ solely as a 'personal' savior, or someone to guarantee you make heaven and bypass hell, is missing the mark. There are no guarantees. It's a perilous journey at best."

"You talk like a man who's pretty sure, in spite of things, he's goin' up and not down. Like a man who sleeps nights and ain't afraid his balls are gonna roast in hell—"

"You don't sleep?" Russ asked.

"You know anybody who's killed their mama who does?"

"Murder's a mortal sin, Joleb, but forgivable," Russ said.

Joleb saw a candle go out. Snuffed itself cleanly, as if to prove the man a liar. "Well, you can't prove it by me. I still feel like a sinner. And it's gettin' worse, too."

"Have you confessed your sins?" Russ said.

"You mean have I told the police?"

"No, actually what I meant was have you confessed your sin to a priest?"

"I ain't Catholic and my daddy's a Mason. Thirty-second degree and they hate papists."

Russ looked at him. Grinned so wide his face split. "Papists. Strange."

"Most preachers want to know right off how I did it. Don't you wonder?"

"That's something for the confessional." He nodded toward the back and Joleb turned and studied the three wooden phone booths with red and green lights on top. The door to the left one opened and the light turned green. A woman wearing a shawl on her head walked out and stuck her finger in a bowl of water fixed to the wall before she left the church.

"You mean those phone booths back there?"

Russ laughed so hard he had to stand up and walk over and lean his head on the sill of a stained glass window. When he came back he put a hand on Joleb's shoulder, "Excuse me, Joleb——" He was wiping his eyes with his handkerchief, "but you take the cake, son. I'd love to set you down in a room full of Jesuits."

"You mean because I'm stupid?"

"Good Lord, no! That's not it at all." Russ started laughing again and a woman polishing the wooden pews looked up and frowned.)

The Mystery of the Haunted Mill was on the dining room table.

"I'll read the Hardy Boys to you, Ma, if you want." He could stomach that, but not the other. Grace had walked back through, her arms loaded down with fresh sheets, and had tapped her finger on the big family Bible. "I think the Book of Job would do you some good, Joleb." She mentioned this again on her way back into the kitchen, where she stood wringing out the dress shirts. The laundry would go into a pillowcase up in the freezer until she got around to ironing it.

She tapped the book again when she came in to check the towel between his mother's legs. Nodding with her netted head while she slid a hand up under his mother's housedress, she said, "When was the last time you walked with Jesus, Joleb? I think walkin' with Jesus would do you a world of good. Make you feel better 'bout things."

"Jesus ain't in the Book of Job, Grace," Joleb said patiently, his head resting sideways on his hand, seeing his mother's feet and Grace's face can-terwalled.

"Don't you be tryin' to tell me where Jesus is or ain't like I ain't got no idea what goes on inside a church. Jesus all in that good book, cover to cover!" She swelled up like a bullfrog and huffed her way into the kitchen, leaving Joleb to baby-sit a woman as empty as a locust shell stuck on a pine tree. Sighing, he stood up and followed Grace, not so much because he was sorry, but because in his heart, he felt he'd offended his true mother.

("I thought Grace was my mother for years. Called her mama in my head and everything. I never even noticed she was colored. Even when someone pointed it out to me, I still didn't notice."

"How so? Who pointed it out?"

"Oh, some moron on the street. Yelled out in front of Hal's Music Store, 'You Green boys are nigger lovers!' and I looked up at Grace and said, 'What's a nigger, Grace?' and she squeezed my hand and said, 'I ain't got a clue, baby, but I know I ain't one.'" Joleb turned and watched people filing in by twos like they were hoping for a window seat in the Ark. "You got something goin' on here tonight, Russ?"

"Mass in half an hour, but I'm off-duty. This woman Grace sounds like a special person."

"She is. My aunt said she just showed up one day when I was about a week old and got hired on. Daddy was lost. Stuck with a newborn, a three-year-old and a brain-dead wife, and Aunt Louise said on a good day Beryn, that's my dad, might be able to fight his way out of a wet paper bag, but that was about the limit of it. I used to think she was being mean. But it's true. The man is simple. Is thinking your father's stupid a mortal sin?"

"No. Maybe venial if you demean him in some way. I think maybe you should try to see your father in a new light. Appreciate him in some way." He sat up. Leaned his elbow on his knee. "So you were a baby when your mother had a stroke?"

"No, I'm the *reason* she had the stroke, Russ. You ain't been listenin'. You got a Coke box in this place?"

"How about a sandwich?" He looked at his watch. "I missed lunch—you want one?"

"Sure." Joleb stood, wiped the palms of his hands on his pants and followed Russ toward a dark hall. When the man crossed the front of the large carved-out table in front of the gold box holding the Christ wafers, he kneeled down on one leg and made the sign of the cross.)

Grace was holding up the grocery list to the light coming in from the kitchen window as if the sunlight filtering through might uncover its meaning. She was forty-two years old with a world-class memory, but she couldn't read a lick. She must think we're brainless, Joleb thought.

"You want me to read that to you?"

"My eyes is tired is all—"

"I know. They sprayed for mosquitoes last night. Everybody's eyes are burnin'." He took the note his father had scratched out before breakfast and read off: "Cereal. Half gallon of milk. Four pounds of sausage. Round steak, two pounds. Bag of onions. Shortening. Paper products. Barq's root beer." She nodded her head at each item, assigning them each a finger, then she went to the cabinet and lifted down a coffee tin and fished out a ten-dollar bill.

"I'll be back in about an hour. I got to go clean across to Hattiesburg to buy her some support hose. Her legs are knotting up around her ankles. You watch her, you hear? Don't let her straggle—if she starts to straggle, call your brother."

She always said "straggle" for "strangle." Joleb knew this and usually made a joke about it. He didn't this time because he had lied to her about the root beer.

"And if you have to go somewhere in an all-fired hurry, you wake up lazy-ass Burris and tell him to sit his mom. You understand what I'm sayin'?"

"I'm not stupid, Grace."

"I know that, but sometimes I come back from town and she looks mussed up or something. Like somebody," and she put her hand on her hip and glared at Joleb, "ain't been watchin' her. And if she straggles and dies, I ain't gonna be the one blamed."

Joleb held his hands palms upward like what else in the world do you want from me?

Grace looked him up and down a time or two then walked into the dining room and checked out Mary. Once she was sure she was fixed in her chair and wasn't sliding this way or that she tapped one more tap on the Holy Bible and walked out the front door, headed to the bus stop at the corner.

("Burris claims the only reason Grace was hired on was because nobody but a colored would wipe a grown-up's ass and agree to cook and clean for five dollars a day." He took another bite of turkey and cheese sandwich and watched the man across from him. Russ had already finished his and sat there smoking a cigar.

"Burris is your older brother?" He tapped the ashes into a thick amber ashtray.

"Yes, sir. He's weird, though. Claims he can see God in the face of a train. It's some sort of habit he's got—like smoking or something. If it's a foggy night he picks a trestle and stands on it and when the train breaks through the mist he jumps off to the side. Weird, huh?"

"Dangerous and foolish is more like it. What does your father have to say about this behavior?"

"Dad's quiet on most things." Joleb burped. "Excuse me."

"You're excused. Now Grace—she tends you? Cooks and cleans and takes care of your mother?"

"Yeah. Even after all these years, Dad still can't stand having a colored around. Wears his glasses at the table and lifts up each forkful for inspection against hair and toenails, which he says colouds like to drop in white folks' food." Joleb stood and went to the fridge and poured himself another glass of milk.

Russ was swearing long and loud behind him. Joleb sat back down and stared, never having heard a man who claimed to be holy let out such a string of four-letter words.

"Grace stands her own, though, Russ. Don't you worry there."

"I find that hard to believe—"

"No, it's true. Aunt Louise said that when Grace came on with us, Dad sat her down in the chair in the kitchen and listed out the rules of the house. He said, 'Grace, I ain't got no problem with how you come or go as long as you come and go using that there back door.' Then he says, 'And I ain't got no problem with you pickin' up and answering the telephone just as long as you rein in those thick lips and say Green Residence in a plain, precise voice.' Then he says, 'But one thing I will not tolerate is other niggers over here in this house lollygaggin' around when I'm away to work.'"

"Lord, God," Russ said.

"Exactly—but then Grace, as big as you please, says, 'Well, now you've listed out your rules, Mr. Beryn Green, I guess I better pull out mine and see if they meet up halfway or else you gonna be out there on the street lookin' for somebody else.'"

"Did she really, now?" Russ leaned forward, smiling.

"That's what Aunt Louise says. And there was more. Grace looked at Dad and says, 'Well, since I'll be changing your wife's shitty diaper and bathin' her on a daily basis and keepin' her in fresh drawers and powdered and clean as a baby, and cookin' every bit of food that goes in your mouth, not to mention washing and ironin' and sweepin' and moppin', I don't figure you have a say in which door I come in and out of, or how many of my friends I want to see once you're to work!'"

"Well I'll be damned!"

"You know what Dad said?"

"I can't imagine," Russ said.

"Why, nothing. Nothing at all. He just sat back and blinked a few times and then Aunt Louise said he looked at Grace and said, 'Well, I ain't never worked for a colored before and I'm sure glad we got things straight round here.' And then he put his hat on and walked straight out the back door!" Joleb grinned, loving the story as much as Russ, who was laughing so hard he was about to choke.

"Joleb, you may think you're bound for hell, but it sounds to me like you got a guardian angel working her ass off trying to look out for you!"

"You think so?"

"You bet I do.")

Joleb walked down the hall to where Burris was sleeping and listened at the door for his snores, then he walked back into the dining room and sat by his mother.

Her bright red hair was yellowy gray now and pale white fuzz was growing across her cheeks and upper lip. Fuzz climbed to her ears where each fold seemed coated in white moss.

"You want me to read to you, Ma?" he said, leaning close to her ear. Seeing the soak, he decided to change the bib. Carefully, as if handling a newborn puppy, he untied the ties and pulled it from around her neck, rolling it up while he held his nose because slobber stinks, no matter whose. Taking one hand and tilting back her head, he placed the fresh, plaid green bib under her chin, then let her head fall forward easy until it rested on her chest again. He tied it behind her like an expert. Not too loose, because drool would run down her shirt and get smelly as hell. Not too tight, because she might choke up phlegm out her mouth and nose and possibly die. Again. He stuck a finger behind her head to make sure it was just right.

"You want your monkey? You want me to get it for you?" She liked the stuffed gray-striped one made from a sock with the orange triangle for a mouth. "I think it's back in your room. I'll be right back." She blinked twice, which surprised him and made him sit back on his ass and think, Well, Good Lord.

He walked through to the back bedroom and jerked up his mother's gray sock monkey from the clothes basket in the corner. He hated their beds, the way they faced off foot to foot like gunfighters, his dad's with a *National Geographic* spread open on his pillow, his mother's cranked up with a pee-pad across the center.

Back in the dining room he saw Mary was staring out the window at nothing. Outside on a feeder set near the center of the yard two redbirds were eating, throwing a storm of black sunflower seeds down to the ground like dark snow. He looked back at his mother to see if there was a glimmer of anything there, anything at all, but all he saw settled in her eyes was something similar to a reflected cloud. He stuck the monkey to her side and patted her leg again. "There you go, Ma."

Joleb sat back on the sofa and crossed his arms. "Aunt Louise said you stopped traffic in your yellow coat. Do you remember that? Stopping traffic out in the middle of Front and Mobile Streets? Almost stopped a locomotive, even. She said you were the most beautiful woman in Hattiesburg." He thought how cold he must sound and tried to apologize, "You're still pretty for one so afflicted."

He studied her light freckled skin and pale blue eyes, stretched out his hands and set them side by side to hers and noticed the differences. Night and day. That's how loud it was.

"I used to climb in your lap when nobody was around and pull your arms around me. Do you remember that? Grace caught me once and whipped my tail. Said I'd mess up your kidneys sitting on your stomach."

He adjusted her buttons thinking that her breasts seemed worthless as graded-off hills. Grace didn't even bother putting her in a brassiere anymore. He reached across and patted her shoulder to make sure and all he felt was bone and a fleshy pod along the backside of her arm.

Releasing the brake, he backed her away from the window and deeper into the narrow shadows of the room. Pulling a chair out of the dining room he set it in front of her and bent to her mossy ear, putting his arms around her neck. His view of the world changed. Turned canterwalled again. "You should see these birds, Ma. Sideways they're strange. Off. Not like birds at all. Like something else." He tried to pull himself closer but the chair bumped metal. "Next week's my birthday. Sixteen. Did you remember? No? Well, that's okay. I guess it was a bad day all the way around. As sideways as those birds out there." He slid his arms down—one behind and one in front—and linked them together around her waist while he shut his eyes. She smelled like baby powder and menthol. After a few minutes of smelling her neck he lifted his hand and put it on her tit.

("We've got a good parish softball team here. We always need recruits—"

"I'm not much good to anybody where sports are concerned, Russ. But thanks. Thanks for the sandwich, too. That was nice." Joleb stuck out his hand and shook the man's. "I like your church. It smells nice and old, and that cut-out railing up there reminds me of *Heidi.* You ever read that?"

"I've read it—Joleb listen, you've got a lot of good in you. You've got a good heart and I'm sorry you're carrying such a load. I don't think that's something God intended."

"Well, whether or not God intended it don't mean squat, does it, sir? Pardon my rudeness."

Russ didn't seem to know what to say so he put his hand on Joleb's shoulder. "I want you to think about laying this thing down. You may have to work at it, but I know it can be done."

The church service was over but there were still a few people kneeling holding beaded necklaces while they prayed. "Anyhow, I'm through chasing water, Russ. I had pretty much decided that before I came to see you."

"You don't need to chase anything, Joleb. You don't need to run all over the country looking for answers—")

"I went to see that colored woman by the creek, Ma. The one Grace said ought to be run out of town—" He heard Burris stirring in the bedroom. Coughing. Snorting. Hawking up his night snot like an eighty-year-old smoker. "I climbed out my window just like Burris. You know what she told me, Ma? You know what that colored woman said?" Burris was opening and shutting drawers in his bedroom while Joleb kissed his mother's fuzzy cheek, "She said I'm 'thick as grits left overnight in a bowl.' Does that make sense to you? Because it don't to me. I don't get it. Do you get it?"

"Joleb!" Burris yelled up from the hall.

"I've got a secret, Ma—something I'm gonna do for all of you on my birthday. It's the right thing to do, too. The only thing I can do to set things right again." He leaned in to her ear and whispered it in great detail. Told her everything. His hand was against her hair first, then her shoulder.

"Joe!"

"What!?" Joleb sat up and straightened out his mother. Smoothed her dress. Ran a hand over her hair. Looked for a blink.

"Where's Grace," Burris yelled.

"Why!"

"'Cause I wanna know, you little shit! Now why can't you give me a straight answer! Tell me where she is!"

"She's gone to town—" Joleb stood up while he rested his hand on his mother's shoulder and patted it easy.

"What for?"

"Support hose—Ma's got knots in her ankles." He moved to the front door and stood there with his hand on the knob, not looking back.

"What's for breakfast?"

"Whatever's left, Burris—it's noon for God's sake." Joleb heard a great sleepy yawn coming from his brother followed by a loud burp.

"You mind your own business—who's tending Ma?"

Nobody, Joleb said to himself as he opened the front door and walked down the steps, startling the birds. Nobody. Nobody at all.

Her wheelchair in the half light, half shade of the dining room, Mary Green blinked nonstop for ten minutes straight while the redbirds outside on the lawn dug at their seed.

On a cloudy night absent of moon the colored woman had said to him: "Joleb Green, you thick—thick as grits left overnight in a bowl. You got a core to you that's dirty. One you brought on yourself. Now get on outta here—" He'd run away from her, up across the sand, out through the woods, bringing back to Petal an ugly scratch and a mild case of poison ivy, but that was all. He had lied to Jackson about fainting dead away and his dick growing out an inch and his balls sprouting hair. He had lied to Jackson about waking up outside the drugstore and how he felt so much smarter about things in general. Joleb had lied to Jackson about every single thing except her smell. He was true on that one.

Grace took the Number Two bus to South Nineteenth, disembarked and walked to a house done up in the style called Spanish—all red tiles and out-of-place arches that in her opinion looked just plain silly. "Mornin', Miss Ivy," she said to the old woman in a clean white dress sweeping the walk. "Ain't got no rain yet. But we can keep on prayin', can't we?"

"Folks is getting worried. Farmer's Market full of shriveled-up squash and that's 'bout it, too."

"Well, we got to keep prayin', is all."

"Too late for prayers is how I see it," the woman said. She nodded with her head. "He's in there—go on in." She kept on sweeping, her corded arms lying about her age, which she kept to herself but most knew was approaching seventy.

Grace pushed open the door and walked through sniffing the air. She could smell dirt a mile away and she was pleased Ivy was living up to things, keeping the place clean. The hallway stretched out to a sunlit kitchen with green and white tiles on the floor but she turned left and went into a dark library lit by a desk lamp. He was sitting in a leather chair on wheels, his back to the door, and the world for that matter. At first glance, it seemed he was making out bills.

"There ain't been no change that I can see—"

He sat up straighter. "No change at all? Nothing?"

"No sir, not a thing."

"The doctors said as much, didn't they?"

"The doctors said as much sixteen years ago, Mr. Lieberstein, that's how long it's been. Now Mr. Beryn's wantin' to put her in a home is what Miss Louise says, and Lord God from what I hear, that'd be a hellish way to live and if she ends up goin' there, there ain't no way I can get in and out and make sure she's bein' taken care of."

The man turned in his leather chair and took off his glasses. His hair was mostly gone now and what was there was gray-white, but he was still handsome in his strange Jewish way. "You leave Beryn to me, Grace. He'll not interfere." He rubbed his eyes. "Mary stays put where she is or she comes here once and for all." He crossed his legs. "Sit, please. I'm sorry— I should have offered sooner." He pointed to a leather chair beside the desk and she sat herself down and looked around the room. Books everywhere.

"How's the boy?"

"Too quiet for me. Now Burris talks a blue streak around the moon, foolish as ever, still chasing trains—"

He waved it away. "Joleb—" he said. "Tell me about Joleb."

"Like I said, too quiet. Mopes around, especially these past two weeks.

He's quit all that church business and maybe that's good and maybe it ain't. I don't know. His birthday's next week. But I guess you of all people already know that." She fingered the clasp to her purse, embarrassed she'd brought up such a heavy thing.

Opening the center drawer to his desk he pulled out a white envelope. "I put something extra in this time, Grace. Something for you and Joleb. Buy him something and address it from Mary. And do something for yourself, too." He turned back around and faced his desk as soon as she took the envelope from his hand. "There's always the store account, in case of emergency."

Standing to her feet she said, "Mr. Lieberstein—I know this ain't none of my business, but I loved your mama and daddy. They were good to me when I was in a real hard place and I was good to them in return because of it, too. And you're a good man in a hard place, too. And I know you might think I'm too big for my britches to be saying this here and now, but I think the boy needs you. Needs something. You're right, Burris is a fool and so is Mr. Beryn, but Joleb's lost. Lost."

"Thank you, Grace," he said, without bothering to turn around. Then while his pen scratched across paper he said, "I'll take that into consideration."

She looked around at the three walls of books in the room. Floor to ceiling packed down with dried-out seasoned words. "You got years of reading to hide behind, don't you, sir?" Knowing she'd stepped over the line she left him and walked back down the hall to the front door. Waving to Miss Ivy who had swept the walk clean, Grace walked to the corner and stood waiting for the Number Three bus clutching her purse.

"Lord God spare me from foolish-hearted people!" she said, wishing for rain.

8

MAN IS BORN OF WOMAN

MAN IS BORN OF WOMAN, but I carry no proof with me, Even thought. Then, For such a sorry orphan, I've found myself sotted with expectations.

Truth told, he'd found himself so missing of the basic rustle of newspaper every morning that he'd taken to leaving out the back door and walking through an overgrown alley to the main road, just to avoid the memory of companionship. It had been almost two weeks since he'd heard word one from Canaan, and man born of woman that he was but had no proof of, Even had found himself thinking weak womanish thoughts: How to make things right? How to call back words? And what words? Which had been the most offensive? And so on and so forth. Finally, on the morning after the dream of Judy doing that thing that would be the end of her, Even walked outside and stood on his front porch, sick to death of shying away from the truth of a thing. Get thee behind me, Canaan, he said to his heart, and felt better immediately.

Stretching his arms over his head, he heard the rustle of the heavy starch in the sleeves of his white shirt, startled it could sound almost twin-like to the rustle of newspaper. The iron had burned his finger when he went to touch it. Blistering it up easily to the size of a peanut. But he knew the shirt looked good and didn't repent of the hour he'd spent pressing in a crease hard enough to slice medium cheese. That rustle again. He hadn't moved his arms, though.

"I had me a dream last night hard enough to stop my bowels for a year—"

He turned and saw Canaan. Sitting back closer to the wall than he used to sit. The distance a larger span from Even's front door, as if it would be a while before things were as they had been. But he was there—his skinny butt sitting on his upturned crate.

"Mornin', Mister Mosley," Even said.

"Mornin', Even Grade." Canaan opened his newspaper to the center and folded it back. "I spent most of last week lookin' all over town for a pair of attentive ears. Had a woman at the meat market tell me she'd rather swallow the cud of a dying cow than listen to one more word out my sorry mouth—" He looked up at Even and Even grinned at him, pleased as punch, in spite of the distance between them. Canaan shook out his newspaper like it was an unruly child. "I sure could use me a good cup of coffee."

On his way back into the kitchen, Even's face felt strange, like he'd ground down on his teeth all night and woke with a sore jaw. Putting up a hand to his mouth, he felt a smile was all, and he told himself, Watch it. You gettin' your heart up like a queerboy. Watch yourself and quit being foolish. This is just old sharp-tongue Canaan. On his way out, he picked up off the table the scrap of paper he'd hovered over for most of an early dawn hour. After crossovers and substitutions he'd finally come up with: *She was a princess too, reared in the cave—*

Back out again, Canaan took the cup from his hand. "I've always prided myself on knowing the reality of myself. Spent the past ten years theorizing and projecting my thoughts to paper concerning the reality of others. And after last night, I feel I've wasted at least fifty-seven of sixty-three years."

"Must be the weather. I woke myself up screaming. Can't remember but a part of it, though. This—" Even handed over the yellow scrap of paper to Canaan who read it through about fourteen times.

"Thy God—" Canaan said.

"What—it mean somethin'?"

"*Antigone.* What you doin' dreamin' on that one?"

"I wasn't really just dreamin' on that. There was other stuff, but that was in there. And the person sayin' it said I should ask you about it," Even said.

"Did a large pig deliver this?"

"Nope. Just a Big Somebody. All voice. Big spookish voice."

"Thy God," Canaan said again.

"Canaan—"

"Save it, I ain't needin' no apology—"

Even snorted, amused. "No, it ain't that. I don't know what it is exactly. All I know is I ain't saying this to make you change your mind one way or the other. But in the middle of all those words, I dreamed Judy was doin' something last night by the creek that was the death of her." Even sat down in his green chair and rested his forearms on his legs.

Silence then until a door slammed down the street and someone yelled, "'Cause I said so, and if you ain't ready to do it just 'cause your mama say so, I think you better be findin' you somewhere else to park your sorry ass!" They both leaned out and saw Clorena with a raised broom over her head beating her sixteen-year-old son Otil about the head and shoulders.

"'Bout time on that one," Canaan said.

"You say that true."

Canaan sat back, looking thoughtful. "A gutted sow visited me at the library. Dropped rocks out her beehind as she walked away." He slurped his coffee. "And I tell you one thing for sure—you won't catch me eating pig for a while. Call me foolish, or call me hebe, don't matter one way or the other. I ain't eatin' pork."

Even laughed, finding it funny for some reason.

"Where you goin' all dressed up? Courthouse?"

Even shot him a glare and Canaan held up his hands, "Courthouse wouldn't be bad. Courthouse wouldn't be bad at all. You old enough to get married without anybody's say-so."

"I aim to go into town, is all," Even said and stood up.

"Where in town?"

"Lieberstein's."

"Well, that's a good thing too. Lieberstein's is good, not bad at—"

"Canaan—"Even looked at him grinning, "if we gonna do this thing, I want it like it was—you disagreeing with every word that comes out my mouth and me bracing up for an argument each and every time. You keep being so agreeable, you gonna bust."

Canaan shrugged and held up the yellow paper. "I'm gonna think on that dream of yours. And I'm gonna say something here, too, since you're so concerned I might bust open. Dark is hard. I ain't talkin' about the color of our skin. I'm talkin' about the not knowing of things. It's hard to live in that place. We all do it and we hate it. Everbody in Petal been running down to the creek to find out things they don't have no business knowin'. Everthing we need to know about ourselves comes from here—" he looked at Even solid and tapped a dark finger on his own chest. "And if we can't find it here, it ain't worth knowin'. I ain't got nothing against your woman other than her not using the proper wisdom in what she's saying. Now, maybe I'm suspicious and uneasy because I don't know her, haven't met her. And if that's the case, I'm willing to try. Much as I hate a bog, I'm willing to meet her fresh and sweep all this dark stuff under the rug. That's all. That's all I got to say on matters." He wet a finger and turned a page in the newspaper. "Lieberstein's a big-ass store that don't like niggers, Even Grade," he said, peering over his glasses. "Now they tolerate *Nee*groes, but not niggers."

"I thought you'd said all there was to say on matters—"

"I'm talking shoppin' now. I never said my mouth was sealed on matters concerning shoppin', and I know you gonna be about as welcome in that fancy store as the Bellrose goat."

"Well, I guess as life goes there's a first time for everything—including goats." Even stepped down and walked across to Canaan's yard and fetched his bucket that had rolled clean up to the old man's mailbox.

"Yeah? Well, that's what they told that Till kid, too—'Go whistle at the white woman inside that gas station, Emmit. It's a first time for everything!' He ended up dead as a knob, that one did."

Even threw up a hand in a wave. "There's more coffee inside. Feel free," he said, and then he walked on down the road, headed for Hattiesburg.

I belong here as readily as the Bellrose goat, Even said to himself thirty minutes later, sick at heart.

Lieberstein's on Pine sent out two wide curved window displays to midsidewalk that broke the flow of pedestrians as politely as bales of hay on a flight of stairs. Inside the bump-out, a trio of mannequins did things contrary to the stifling August heat of southern Mississippi. One pulled on a leather boot while the other's fur-trimmed coat was caught midfling on a third mannequin's arm. There was a dark bottle of what looked to be champagne next to a trunk that looked to be going somewhere. Stickers marked Brazil, Puerto Rico and Jamaica were plastered up and down its side. They're geared too hot for those places, was what Even thought while he studied the store and wiped the sweat off his face. Taking in a good breath in case it was his last, he moved to dual doors that were heavier than they looked. Once in and blasted by air colder than winter he found himself standing on a black marble entrance pad that ran square to a field of maroon carpet. A white-gloved doorman, all blue wool and gold buttons and shined-out shoes, stood dead center and tipped his pillbox hat in Even's direction. Even's first thought was, Well, he ain't from around here. Not dressed like that.

He stepped forward finally and found himself picking up his feet like an old, arthritic chicken who's suddenly unsure of the standard run of his ground. Moving stiff he passed amber glass at waist level that cased in watches, scarves, perfumes and wallets, catching a glimpse of his face looking back at him from small brass viewing mirrors set at the level of his head. A dark pumpkin in a picture frame was what he thought, for everything in the store was amber lit and the color of bad beer. I'd be as surely lost in New York City, Atlanta and probably even Vicksburg was what he was thinking while he wandered along like scared poultry. Finally, by sheer luck, he found a printed sign next to a set of automated stairs. Following the directions, he rode stiff-legged up to the second floor where, thankfully, there were long stretches of aisleways without the blood-colored carpet. Once he was there his stride finally lost its chicken appearance and took on that of man's again. He ended up in front of Women's Wear trying to discern sizes from a distance of three feet.

He barely understood the scope of a woman, much less her dimensional size, and the numbers on the small tags held as much comfort as Latin. Ten. Twelve. Eight. Six. Four. Numbers divided up dresses on round stand-alones. How could he come close to knowing the circumference of a chest or waist when he knew the actual measured distance would exceed the highest of numbers presented, which if he were seeing correctly, stood at sixteen. I never seen a sixteen-inch-waisted woman and pray to God I never do. He made a circle of his dark hands and peered down through them to the floor, opening them up until they seemed true enough to Judy's waist.

"I guess you thought we was all one size?" she said.

Turning, he saw a tall Negro woman with more girth to her than Judy, more flesh around the face, but tall enough to fit into the right range of height. "Pretty much," he said, noticing how striking she was.

"Don't pay for a man to think, then, I always say."

He kept quiet on that one and guessed her age to be somewhere in the early range of forty.

"I'm here for support hose. Not for me." She stuck out a nice leg as if he needed proof she had all the support necessary. "For the woman I sit. Invalid woman. You stand still long enough, salesmadam will help." She nodded toward a woman of such slight movements, he had thought her to be a mannequin. "You have to open your mouth, though, white folks can't mind-read." She elbowed him in the side.

"No ma'am, I guess not."

Leaning back her head she frowned, like she was trying to recall where or when or if she had seen him. "Grace Johnson, to most everybody this side of the river. Just Plain Grace to folks from Petal." She extended her hand.

He shook it. "Even Grade—just plain Even, no matter which side you find your feet on."

She laughed hard then, like a man. "I ain't never met you, 'cause I would've remembered you for sure. How long you lived here?"

"Four years." He thought her hands were absolutely beautiful. Large, clean, capable.

"Uh huh—" She circled him as if admiring a mule.

"Four years, six months—I work at Hercules Powder. The 'Bull Gang.' As a pipe fitter." He shifted on his feet and gripped his elbows.

"I do say—four years and Just Plain Grace ain't never run across you."

Her voice was low alto and he thought what a strange girl she must have been, all high breasts and bass voice.

"And here you stand in your starched shirt lookin' at dresses for somebody. I guess somebody done run across you, for sure. Either that or you got a mama you love more than Jesus." And she gave out a hoot of a laugh.

"You said you sit for someone?" He licked at the salt on his upper lip.

"And by that trapped look I see in your eyes right now I guess it ain't your mama you shopping for, or else you'd be braggin' about her birthday and how you love her so—"

He just stood staring at her rich lips. Struck dumber than a dishrag by her teasing.

Grace reached out and patted his arm. Ran a finger down the hard crease of his sleeve, "I ain't forgot your question, Mr. Grade. I just turn fresh at the sight of a starched shirt." She adjusted the belt to her dress then grew serious. "Yes, I do. I sit the invalid woman over on Stockwell Street. Lord God, you think you seen sad, 'til you see what sad is. I sit her and cook and clean for the menfolks."

"Men?" he said.

"Men? You worried about me cookin' for a houseful of men? You don't think I could handle just about anything that needs handling? Or is it you might be wonderin' if I got me a man on the side to care for as well? No? No, I sure don't and I ain't lookin' for one, neither. Stopped that years ago 'cause there ain't nothin' worse than dealing with a man without a brain in his head. So you think I can't handle a houseful of white folks, or you think maybe I just can't handle men in general?" She stuck out a strong leg and crossed her arms and smiled.

"No ma'am, that ain't what I'm sayin'." Even thought to himself, I said but one word and was handed back a thesis. The Reality of this Negro is that she can talk to rival Canaan.

"Grace. Call me Grace."

"I was just curious about your occupation is all."

"White folks. The Greens. Two boys and the father. Good money, too." She cocked her head and seemed to rethink herself. "How broad's your woman? And don't you be shy, 'cause I know you got a woman. Now come on. Is she this or this?" She measured with her hands against her own hips and extended the width the second time. He could see she had thighs like a well-fed pony and he felt drunk, as if he'd had a fifth of something cheap.

"More like the first," Even said while he cleared his throat, feeling salt run from his temple to the neck of his shirt where it soaked, turned chilly in air-conditioned air.

"Her waist bigger 'n mine? Or smaller, like that woman's—" She pointed to the petite salesmadam who was standing behind a counter writing something in a small notebook.

"Hmm. I guess somewhere in between the two—"

"Well, there you go—" She punched him in the arm. "Best guess I got is size ten. An eight might bind, and skin needs air to itself. You stand here and wait, and tell that woman a ten's what you want." She crossed her arms, pleased with herself. "She can take it up if it don't fit. I ain't found a store-bought dress yet that don't bind at the arms." And then sticking out her hand again she said, "Pleased to meet you, Mr. Even Grade. You just about made my day for sure. Grace Johnson is mighty pleased to meet you." She winked at him. "And I tell you what—if you ever find yourself in need of shopping advice, I live down on Shasta. Two-ten Shasta. I'm there most nights after seven. I got a goat for a pet and he gets mean if I don't break him out and let him roam. So I always try to get home by eight at the latest."

Her dark eyes gleamed like polished rocks and he grew hot at her string of words. Then before he could express his thanks, she turned and walked away on the best-looking legs he'd ever seen in his life. That one would breathe life into Canaan's dead wood for sure, was what he was thinking. Then, It's a crying shame she belongs to that goat.

"What'd she say?" Joleb asked. "She had to say something to make Val go and chop off her hair like that—"

"I told you. I swam the creek and Val and her did all the talkin'. You want to know something, you go ask her." Jackson was sitting on a round stool in Kress drinking a chocolate soda through a red-and-white straw.

Joleb was there. His hair coated by Butch Wax that made him look like a scared bear with a crush on Elvis.

"I *did* ask and she said for me to ask you—"

"Well, there you go. You asked and I answered. Drop it." Jackson saw by his reflection in the mirror across the counter he needed a haircut.

"The way everything's been scrambled in my brain, I'd have to say it's some type of voodoo spell on me that ain't worn off yet." Joleb began pushing himself around in slow circles on his stool.

"Uh huh." Jackson slurped the last of the chocolate through his straw.

Joleb grabbed the counter and stopped his motion. "She say something different?"

"Nope,"

"She call me a liar?"

"Nope," Jackson said again.

"Well, what then, 'cause I can tell you think I lied or something—"

"Shit! I'm not thinking anything of the sort, Joleb. All I was thinking is that school starts in three weeks and it's hot as hell and this is the worst August ever." Truthfully, he was thinking that the sky outside was too steadfast blue for August, too deep in color, almost cold-looking early in the morning. That it had a feel of autumn to it, without benefit of cool weather, and how he wished Val was sitting here beside him instead of Joleb.

"God's truth, I didn't lie about one single thing."

"Okay Joleb, I believe you."

"I came out of the woods and found her crouched over her fire like a witch." He began spinning himself around again on his stool. "Then she stood up—too tall to be a woman was what I was thinking—took off those overalls, I guess because either she read my mind about me doubting her being a woman or she wanted me to see what a naked colored woman looked like. I was standing by the edge of the woods and she called me over and put a little spit on the end of her finger and touched my head and before I knew it some kind of spell was cast and I was flyin' backwards."

"I thought you said she blew hot air on you and sent you flyin' backwards? And this is the first time you've ever said anything at all about her being naked—" Across the counter, in a mirror behind colored bottles, he saw the two of them had grown taller over the summer. When they both sat straight up, their chins rose higher than a green bottle of tutti-frutti flavoring.

"Well, I did. I did say that. But I'm remembering other things now because the initial shock of the spell was so big." *Thick as grits left overnight in a bowl.* "She was scared of me, too, I could tell that right off."

"Now you're lyin'," Jackson said.

"I swear it Jackson, I swear it!"

"I know better."

"You don't know shit!"

"I know there ain't a thing in the world that one's afraid of."

"How do you know?" Joleb asked and really seemed to want an answer.

"I just do. Now drop it, Joleb. I've said all I'm gonna. It was a strange night. I wish I had never gone. I guess Val got in deep shit over her hair because she looks ugly as hell but I don't know that either, because I haven't spent more than ten minutes with her since then. Now shut up about it."

"I'm tellin' you, she was scared—" *Thick as grits left overnight in a bowl.*

"Burris still chasing trains?" Jackson asked, looking for a diversion, wondering where Val was and what she was doing and if he might be able to talk her into swimming.

"Yep." Joleb slumped his shoulders; his arms dangled between his legs. "She sure smelled strange, though. I'll give you that much—" His voice was quiet, church-like.

"She lives in the woods. What'd you expect?"

"No, I mean she smelled *good*, like good medicine. Like a clarinet case. Or Butch Wax. Something spicy and sweet and strange. Kinda like Sacred Heart Church." Joleb looked at Jackson. "And you're absolutely positive she didn't tell you something about me?"

"Like what? What in the world do you think the woman would say?"

"I don't know. Anything. Maybe that I'm sick or something and you shouldn't hang around me—"

Jackson looked at him and had to look away from what was there. "Joleb, you're not as bad as you'd like everybody to think you are. What happened wasn't your fault. You were just being born is all. Nobody could've known it'd mess up your mother." He didn't know why he said it.

The words just up and popped out before he realized it, and as soon as they were out, he was as embarrassed by them as if he'd shit himself on a city bus. Elbowing him again, Jackson said, "I'm outta here," and hopped off his stool and headed for the door, afraid to look back.

Jackson whistled his way to Main Street, angling toward the Saenger Theater so he could read the playbills. He was window-shopping for nothing, aimless in direction, just enjoying being on the Hattiesburg side of the river when a strong arm connected to his elbow, hoisted him up and maneuvered him into an alley. He was led the distance on his toes. Lifted up like a two-year-old being dragged off to a doctor.

"You breathe easy, you little shit, and this won't hurt a bit. Not one little bit—"

He spun and saw Neva Moore, who still had his elbow clasped between both her hands. She flung him away finally and he fell into the back wall, bumping into a hanging drainpipe covered in rust.

"You want to explain to me what happened to Valuable out in those goddamn woods?"

Looking around he saw a stray yellow cat missing part of its tail perched on a garbage can six feet away. The two small windows high up that faced the alley were painted white, made blind should a body be left to bloat in the alley. He licked his lips and plastered himself against the wall, so startled it took him a solid minute to get that I-don't-give-a-shit look back on his face. But by then, it was too late. He was lost.

"Seems Valuable went out in the woods with you and came back missing something. And I'm not talking about her virginity, either." Neva poked a rock-hard finger in his chest that hurt like hell. "Did you think it would be funny for her to come back clipped like a mongrel? To have the whole town laughing at her? Calling her ugly?"

A black-and-white pirate, that's how she looks, Jackson thought while he tried to find enough spit to speak. Her shirt was so white it glowed, and she was wearing black pants, cinched by a broad shiny black belt. God help me if she's got a pistol or sword stuck in there, he thought. God help me, anyhow. Helpless, he held up his hands. "Now wait a minute, Miss Moore, I didn't have anything— "

"Oh, so it's *Miss* Moore now." She poked him again in the same exact spot and he looked down at his chest expecting to see a large hole gushing blood. She stood back away from him and he was amazed at how small and vicious she was. Like a terrier whacked out and crazy.

Afraid of her dark eyes, he looked to the side nearest the street.

"I'm only going to say this thing once—" She poked his chest again. "If you *ever* lead that girl anywhere in town or out, anywhere at all, and she happens to come back missing anything on her body—hair, fingernail, eyelash, anything, anything at all—if she *ever* comes crawling back after one of your nightly raids minus something she had before she went, you, young man, are gonna lose your balls. Are we *clear* on that?"

He swallowed hard and it made a clicking sound in his throat like one of those desert beetles that spend their whole lives banging their head on hard sand looking for something. Up close she looked younger and less strange than she did from across the street, where she always appeared slumped and lumpy. He held up his hands, intending to press her off of him, and she suddenly gave and brushed her hands together, as if she'd gotten them dirty poking at his chest.

As she walked away, her shoes catching every crunch there was to catch in the alley, her shadow out in front eating up the garbage can and the yellow cat missing part of its tail, he thought that with that cropped-off dark hair of hers, she looked more real than any pirate he'd ever seen in the movies. Right before she left the alley and hit the street again, she looked back once, clicked her heels together and saluted him with her middle finger.

"Well, fuck *me*! Well, fuck me! Shit! *Shit!*" He threw his fist up in the air while he kicked the alley wall with his foot. The cat sat still and stared and gave one flip of his half-there tail. This is fuckin' great! Jackson thought, breathing hard while he pressed a hand to his chest, massaging where she'd been poking him, sure he was bleeding.

9

THINGS PARTIAL

E VEN'S FIRST THOUGHT WHEN HE broke through the last border of trees was that she'd gone. Colored in a shade that felt more end than beginning, the place seemed to have an emptiness about it like that of a campsite recently abandoned. Red-faced rocks still circled in the center of the clearing, but there was no fire. Just a hump of cold, dead ashes, spotted here and there with burnt-down kernels of wood that had overnight turned into near weightless coal. The area was clean-swept, void of footprints. All proof of humanness vanquished. Even slapped his neck, killing a yellow fly, and stood considering, holding the cardboard box to his side. Looking down, he saw blood in the center of his palm.

Across the way, toward the creek but vaguely to the left, wild redfern that he'd never noticed before grew in clusters around palmettos. Fanning their ruffles against the spiky green, they made it look as though small flames were springing up out of the sand. It was there, laid carefully to the side of the ferns, that Even saw her twine-tied saw grass, and he understood. Using her homemade broom she had walked backward to the spot, sweeping to hide her footprints. He had read of Oriental gardeners whose dirt knew them—knew they'd be swept clean and decorated beyond their limits—and this is what came to mind when he thought of her: a woman tender of dirt and fire and water and sky. And thinking of her in this manner made him clutch the cardboard box at his side, crimping it and dampening up its edges.

Walking through, Even found the beginning of a path. It was thick with moss and once on it he wished he had taken off his shoes. All along the way curious pinkish fern fronds uncurled like fuzzed snakes standing upright, concerned by his approach. The path wound down to a place he'd never seen, an area that opened up on a small beach where all that remained of a fire was another heap of cold gray. He felt as though he had come on some private something that was meant to stay underneath the sheets. More proof that as deep as her aloneness was, it wasn't deep enough. Unable to help himself, he walked down onto her sand closer to water and saw twin rocks jutting out into the widest neck of the creek, and while he wondered what the name of those rocks might be, he saw their purpose. Creek water funneled through, creating a cove with its own small waterfall. This is as pretty a thing as I'm ever likely to see, he thought to himself. Bending, he pulled off his shoes, tucked in his socks.

The water rippled when he leaned in; he studied what he saw. Against a background of blue sky, there was his face, broad of forehead and overly long, and he was surprised at the new look of age on him. To everybody else, I must look ten years beyond twenty-seven, he thought, and it made him glad. Even had begun to fear gaps and what they might mean. Wide-spanning spaces between age and its weight of language and ability had begun to feel like easy reasons for saying good-bye. He saw inside the calm reflection a gull flying high over his head, braced by clouds drifting east toward Runnelstown.

Turning back, he walked north around moss-based trees and finally found her digging wild onions growing thick next to fern. With her back to him she said, "Tired does one of two things—either builds the soul or breaks the heart. Can't decide which it is right now. All I know is I'm tired." At her voice a cloud of yellow sulphurs lifted off the scrub behind her and flew scattered, as was their nature.

"Take a break, then."

She turned, seeing him for the first time, and smiled wide. "I do say, Even Grade, where you goin'? To a birthday party?"

"Sorta." He walked over and kicked aside a dead limb and sat, leaning back against what looked to him to be a pretty good dogwood. He unbuttoned the top two buttons of his starched shirt and smiled.

"What you got in there?" She pointed to the box.

He placed it on the ground in front of her bare feet and pushed it toward her dark toes. "I don't know my birthday—" he said. "Sometime in August of '29 is the best they could figure from all their combined memories. Which may or may not be a good guess." He rolled up his sleeves. "It was a bad year, the cook up in Memphis said. Told me '29 was full of mean storms and war talk and doin' without. And that's how I carried it in my mind—" he tapped the stiff pocket over his heart, "that Even Grade, whoever he is, was born in a year rich with pain. Thinkin' this way's been a weight." He looked at her. "When or not I was born of body, or who I was born of, ain't important anymore, at least not to me. From here on out, my birthday's gonna be the day I found you picking pine nuts underneath that great big tree." He hushed, embarrassed and scared. Inside the pause, he rolled up his crisp sleeves to his elbows.

"Hold still, Even—" She held up a hand, like she was trying to stop traffic or stop the rain or stop anything bearing down on her that needed stopping.

"No ma'am. I ain't gonna stop. You can shut your ears if you want to. But I ain't gonna hush. I held still too long. I ain't holding still no more." Leaning forward for want of something to do, he knocked the dirt off a wild onion and played it against his hand.

"You can't read me," he said. "I can live with that. But because you can't read me, you gotta know these things out of my mouth, 'cause there ain't no other way you'll ever know them—"

She raised a hand again.

"Nah, I ain't—you just sit and listen." He looked at her steady. "The first clean memory I can call up was being set down hard at a long table with six or seven other boys. All white and bigger than me. Set down hard in front of bowls filled with something hot that smelled good—some type of vegetable soup, I think. But I was so short the edge of the table fell higher than mouth level and all I can remember seeing from where I sat was scratching along the edge. Like a cat or dog had reached up, clawing and digging, looking for food. And I remember a big, dark woman, broad as the table, wearing an apron around her waist, taking my hand then, and putting a spoon in it and sayin', 'You eat, now, or I'm throwin' it to the pigs.' Then she walked away and tended the other boys and I was left reading scratchings on a table and holding a spoon—"

A lost malachite lit on the lowest branch of the dogwood. Its pale turquoise wings opened and shut like a Japanese fan shot through. He watched it for a second and then he spoke again, "She told me about my name. How they found a note stuck next to me with words from my true mama. The part she could remember went like this: 'I'm headed back to Mississippi. Tired of the ups and downs of Tennessee. I'm ready now for a more even grade.' And that's how they named me. Even Grade. Named after some colored woman's good-bye note. The reason I'm explainin' this is because when I met you, I had dark motives—I heard talk in town." He smiled to himself, looked up into the sky and away from her eyes. "About what you knew and saw. Anyhow, I set out to find you for my own reasons. I didn't really want to know you any more than anybody else in town did— I just wanted you to find me some other memories. Something other than a cold spoon and a large room with a scratched-up table."

"Even—"

"No, wait. I gotta say this. By the time I realized I wasn't ever goin' to have more than what I'd been given, I didn't care. I didn't care. And that's why I brought you this." He tapped the box. "It's not near enough. Not close to as much as I feel. But I wanted you to know you're more than just a divining rod or a four-leaf clover. You ain't those things to me, and I wanted you to know."

She looked at him long and hard and then she picked up the box and opened it. Inside crisp layers of gold tissue paper was a flowered dress of soft cloth. Small Chinese marks ran a pattern against a yellow the color of good butter. There were tiny round black buttons that ran to the black patent-leather belt, textured to resemble the skin of alligator.

She picked up the corner of a collar and rubbed it between her long brown fingers. Stroked it with her hand. "Sometimes partial things can break the heart." She bent her head and to his surprise he saw the soft, yellow cloth turn orange in spots and knew she was tearing up, dropping salt.

She talked so low he had to lean forward to hear, "My ma'am was so black she was blue. Sometimes she'd stand outside in the sun and from wherever I happened to be it'd look to me like she'd stepped into a big hole that swallowed her up. There'd be light all around her, but no matter the squint, I couldn't see her eyes or the turn of her mouth." She ran the back of her hand across the bottom of her nose and wiped it on her overalls. "I was her first to make it. There'd been three others all born dead and she told me once she'd just about given up when I came along. But I tore up her insides getting out. That didn't stop Injin from comin' at her, especially when he was drunk." She lifted out the dress and placed it across her lap where it lay like a limp yellow body.

Watching her, Even thought, That yellow dress looks of dead Christ draped across Mary. Like that stone carving done up for a church somewhere overseas. He had seen the picture once in *Life* magazine and tacked it to his wall. Never having been one to appreciate the coldness of statuary, he still thought the carving the most beautiful thing he'd ever seen. Only one thing bothered him about it: for someone so precious and freshly dead, it seemed to him Virgin Mary would have held dead Christ higher up and closer to her face. Close enough to breathe in his smell. Most mothers would. Most mothers wouldn't allow such a distance, not even in death. The Virgin's peaceful distance bothered him to such a point that after a month of consideration, he'd taken the picture down, folded it up and stuck it in a manila envelope. But he never stopped believing it to be beautiful.

Judy said, "Like I said, Injin wouldn't leave her be and she lost two more babies after me, and each time, when she'd stand in the sun, she'd look darker. Darker and smaller. Like the sun was eatin' her. After a while I give up trying to see her eyes when she was outside. I'd just sit and wait wherever I was and hope Ma'am would be comin' back outta that hole soon. She wore sticks in her hair, just like me. And people used to come from miles around because she knew healin' ways and she knew when there weren't no healin' possible, and on those times, she'd try to give them a ground-down sweet herb to brew up, or a carvin' she'd done from a bone. Something. Ma'am always tried to give them something—"

Judy was undoing the black belt, running a finger across its bumps, playing with its silver buckle. Even sat still as stone and thought, This is her first telling of this.

"One of the last times I saw my daddy he was wandering up drunk across the yard and singing like a fool. He was a medium-size man with hard planes to him—cheekbones, nose, chin and the meanest eyes I ever seen in my life. I never could understand why Ma'am was with him. I never could understand that part of her, how they met, how they took up together and made me and five other dead babies. That part was always a puzzle. He beat her bad that time, too, that time he walked across the yard singin' like a fool. I was in the corner, squatted down, watchin' chairs break over her head. I got hit with a splinter in my cheek that dug in and festered and later had to be spliced out, but that day it was just a splinter sent into the side of my cheek by something that was dying across the top of Ma'am's head. So many dead chairs that day. Lord God, I thought they'd never end. Injin busted over her head every chair we had but one—a cane-back rocker he'd brought with him from wherever he was from. I sat in the corner holding my cheek, thinkin' nothing in the world could be worse than this, and then he fell on her and pulled off her clothes, turning her over this way and that like a dead bloody sheep. I fell asleep watchin' her eyes watchin' me. I only saw part of her face. The rest was pressed into the bed and the part that I saw didn't look like Ma'am no more. She winked then. One single wink that spoke up clear as can be, 'don't mind this baby girl, I too big to be kilt by a chair.' That was my first time of reading something that come off of somebody else, and I rolled over right then and slept, 'cause I knew there'd be at least one more mornin' on its way where she could walk out in the yard and stand in full sun and step into that hole."

A quartet of Indian pipes sprouting out a long-dead log bobbed and nodded their sad droopy heads.

"Next morning Injin was up, straightening things, movin' quiet, tip-toeing around broken-up wood, picking up a piece here and there and lookin' at it like it was the queerest thing in the whole wide world. I woke seein' him studyin' the room as a fresh puzzle, then Ma'am made a groaning sound from the bed and he went and asked, 'Can you walk, Jolene? Can you walk, sweet baby?' She tried to answer back, but her mouth was swole up to the size of a pear. She just rolled her head from side to side and Injin scooped her up and carried her over to the one chair that weren't lyin' in pieces—his cane-back rocker. He knelt there, straightened her clothes while he made little clucking sounds and kissed her knees. He finally left to go find his bottle and I ran across the room and tried to find her face inside all that swelling. She looked down at me and said through those cracked-up lips, 'Partial kindness breaks the heart, Joody—don't you never forget that.' And that's all I remember 'bout that day. Injin kilt her with his carved-up jawbone in the winter of that year and I ain't seen or heard from him since."

The Indian pipes stood upright and trembled.

"Sometimes partial kindness kills a person as bad as partial knowin'." Judy said this while she hugged the dress. "But then sometimes partial kindness and partial knowin' is the two best things in the world."

She lifted out the card he'd put inside—just a simple to Judy Tucson from Even Grade—and laughed.

"Here you sit knowing the inside of me like nobody else has ever knowed and you missed the spelling of my name. It's J-o-o-d-y T-w-o S-u-n," she said. "My given name is Lorene Walker, but my ma'am called me Joody Two Sun 'cause I was born on a day Arizona looked to carry two suns in its sky."

A parhelion, Even thought to himself, knowing weather and sky, and still the news of her being born under one of the rarest things of atmosphere made gooseflesh. A mock sun seemed a powerful something, and what with Canaan's foolishness over messages old and Greek, some sixth sense said, Keep this one to yourself, Even Grade. This is one broad thing that needs to stay creekside.

10

ELIZABETH TAYLOR

SO MUCH PINK HERE, I feel a puke coming on. The woman clutched her purse to her ample lap. Pink plastic butterflies dangled from wires. Spun in slow circles courtesy of the mounted wall fan.

"I don't know, Miss Korner, my niece got a wild hair once. Thought she wanted to change her major and study drama or art. Finally ended up in Birmingham doodling for the newspaper. Never went back to college, either. Last news we heard, she was expecting her third and still not married to the beatnik poet she's living with—" The woman stopped, remembering the circumstances of the woman who was holding her head within drowning distance of running water. "I mean, I don't think I'd let this thing go on . . . this silence, I mean. If what everyone is saying is the God's truth, that is. I mean, do you think she'd sheared her hair if there'd been an open door of communication? I just don't know—"

"Frankly, ma'am, I don't know much more than you about that one." Enid squirted a coil of shampoo into the palm of her hand and lathered the woman's head, whipping up a cap of suds from nape to eyebrows like there was no tomorrow. She was good at this—this scrubbing thing. Sometimes she pretended she was working for the Royal Family or someone in Hollywood like Kim Novak. Looking out her storefront window, in between suspended butterflies, Enid saw her daughter sitting on the curb in front of the barber-shop fanning herself with a paper fan from Braswell's Funeral Parlor.

"Did she say why she did it? Cut her hair?" the woman asked.

"No ma'am, she sure didn't." Enid rubbed hard at the knobby base of the woman's skull, working her hands upward the way the woman up in Jackson had taught her.

"So it's true then, the two of you do not speak?"

"Yes ma'am, it's quite true." And it's quite true you're a rude, fat-ass nosy bitch, Enid thought to herself.

"If you don't mind me asking—how long has this been going on, this silence, I mean? I trust this is the first time the girl's cut her own hair with a butcher knife."

Reaching over the top of the woman's head, Enid opened a cabinet and got the cream rinse down and ready to mix. "I guess seven years."

"And she talks to other people?"

"Yes ma'am. Talks a blue streak."

"But not to you."

"No ma'am, not to me."

"Hmm." The woman tightened her grip on the handbag in her lap and this did not go unnoticed.

Leaning over her, Enid sighed and adjusted the water, testing it against her wrist before she switched the nozzle and rinsed. Leaving her head leaning back over the porcelain bowl, Enid mixed four parts water to one part cream rinse and stirred it with a spoon 'til the water turned blue and then she poured it through Mrs. Overstreet's already gray hair.

"Now you hold tight for two minutes and I'll get you rolled and under the dryer with a good magazine." Enid set the egg timer on the shelf and then went into the back and brought back two Coca-Colas and opened both with her bottle opener. She set one for her customer on a small square paper napkin and smiled. There you go, you nosy old bat.

The woman was not a regular. Nobody was a regular anymore and it was just as well with Enid. Too little, too late for this sorry-ass town. This one—and even money said she was a Sunday school teacher of some make or model—was another referral from somebody over in Hattiesburg. Actually, from a dead somebody, or rather the relative of the dead somebody over in Hattiesburg. Thanks to a do done up to resemble Marilyn Monroe for a corpse over in Braswell's, Enid's business had tripled inside of two months. All she needed now to head to the West Coast was three hundred bucks. And don't think I won't do it. She took a long drink of her soda and looked at Valuable fanning herself across the street. Lighting up a cigarette, she sat down in the chair next to the window and pulled apart the blinds to watch her daughter.

The egg timer went off and she rinsed out Mrs. Overstreet for the last time and then sat her up while she patted her hair dry, making sure she wiped out the lady's ears. Checking the towel and smirking when she did it. Turning her to face the mirror, she made a part down the middle.

"How old are you, dear?" the woman asked.

Well, here it comes. "Thirty this past March."

"I think I knew your mother, Luvenia."

"Most did." Enid had three rows down, nine rollers total. Only two more all the way around and Miss Nosy here will come out from under the toaster looking like Shirley Booth. Enid dipped her comb in setting gel and worked it through.

"A remarkable woman."

"How, exactly, did you know her?" Even money says the woman never heard word one more than scattered bits of misshaped gossip.

"I can't remember right at the moment—maybe the Ladies Guild or the Missionary Circle."

"No ma'am, I don't think she was a member of either of those. You might've met her at bingo. She had an itch for that, for sure." Gotcha, Enid thought to herself.

The bells jingled and Valuable walked in and for the first time in a great while, Enid was glad to see her daughter.

Mrs. Overstreet sat herself upright, crossed her fat legs at the ankles and folded both hands over her purse.

I guess she thinks we're a pack of gypsy thieves, ready to run off down the alley with her fake alligator purse. Holding a total of what? Ten dollars? A tube of ugly lipstick?

Valuable, slouched around the shoulders, sat down in the dryer chair.

She really is a beautiful young girl, Sally Overstreet thought to herself. Looks like a pair of giant pinking shears got her hair, though. But those eyes! Not blue. More gray. An almost lavender gray as different from her mother's coal black ones as night is from day. Must be a gift from the father, whoever he is. She noticed that the girl's small mouth was bow-shaped, and while she could see the resemblance between mother and daughter, there was something else that spoke of the father. The set of the shoulders and the girl's large hands and feet maybe, and something about the set of the chin.

Enid looked across the room where Valuable was sitting with her feet looped around the legs of the chair. "We've got dinner tonight at the River House. I'll have time after this appointment to shape your hair. I thought maybe a shingle down the back where it's ragged out. I didn't figure you'd want Neva and Bea seeing you with it messed up the way it is and going off about it—"

Silence.

"And the knife jagged it for sure over your left ear, but I can feather it out and maybe feather your bangs a little. That is, if you can wait for me to finish up here," she pointed the comb at her, "and don't you think about running off with Jackson again. Those days are over, young lady. I should've stopped that a long time ago and this just proves it."

Silence.

Enid chewed on her lip. I've let this thing slide. I should've stopped it years ago. No matter what folks said.

Valuable sat back and crossed her arms over her chest and kept her mouth shut through the woman's entire drying cycle and comb-out. She picked up a movie magazine once, thumbed through it and folded it back to a certain page before laying it facedown on the chair next to her.

There was a disproportionate amount of fuss over the hair spray. Sally Overstreet maintained that since it was Friday, she wanted her hair sprayed down to a near state of permanence. Lacquered hard as a helmet for Sunday. And since she had the Farmer's Market to visit in the morning where wind whipped through the stalls, the stiffer the hair the better. "I think it's poor business practices, dear, to charge someone eight dollars for a do and have it disappear in a rush of wind because you're stingy with the spray. Something like that could get around and hurt you in the long run." She sniffed once, glancing at the girl in the chair who was crimping up her mouth trying not to smile. Gosh, she's a beautiful child, the woman thought.

"Well, if you feel that way about it, I'll oblige, of course." Enid sprayed a near full can on Sally Overstreet's beehive.

Sally, who didn't see the ridicule in all her spraying or the way Enid had winked once at the silent daughter sitting in the chair opposite, simply thought she'd won her argument. And she did like the do. So Hollywood. Like nothing any of her friends had had the courage to attempt. She paid for the coiffure, tipped quite nicely, too, and then walked out the door, turning back only once at the border of the window, checking one more time to make sure it hadn't been a quiet game, and she the dupe. All she saw were two females set at odds, staring each other down from across the room.

Enid lit a cigarette with her pink Zippo, the one Steve, or was it Brent? had given her when he took her dancing up in Jackson. Fed up and embarrassed besides, she turned to Valuable, "Look—do you want me to do your hair or not? Because dammit, if you don't, you can just head on out of here and go home."

"Can you do it like this?" Valuable had folded a page back to a picture of Elizabeth Taylor with her new husband, Michael Wilding.

"I don't know, but I can try."

"Well, okay then."

Valuable climbed in the padded chair and her mother put her foot to the bar and pumped three times, raising her to eye level. She spun her around then so that she faced the mirror and could watch every cut of the scissors.

"Enid—Jackson didn't have a thing to do with me cutting my hair. And even if he did, it's none of your business. I'll see him whenever I please and there's nothing you can do about it. In fact, you can tell Neva and Bea for me that he's coming to supper tonight down at the River House."

"Oh, really? Is that what you think?" Enid held the scissors by Valuable's left ear.

"No ma'am—that's what I know." Valuable, not intimidated in the least by a pair of scissors, crossed her legs and sat back in her chair. Her days of silence over.

II
BOGUE HOMA

———————⟋⟍———————

THE *HATTIESBURG AMERICAN* and the *Clarion Herald* were in a pissing contest involving adjectives. Lou Walters, usually quiet about things, sent down a memo from the third floor of the *HA* stating, among other things, that if he happened to open up his paper one more goddamn morning and see the words "scorched," and "parched" he would personally soak the offender's car with gasoline and set it on fire. Go get me some news, boys! the memo said. Something other than weather. The memo circulated its way around the press floor until it wound up back on Walters's desk covered with notations. A dehydrated threat at best, one read. Excuse me, but is your brain parched or is it just my thirsty imagination? was another. Sounds as if your charred creativity is as shriveled as your penis! was the one he hated the most. He penned another: Report without embellishing or your ass is out on the street—that's what we're here for. He got only one response to that one. Pardon me, but you ended your sentence with a preposition—how'd you ever manage to land on the third floor? He tracked it to a part-time mail clerk hired on from William Carey College. An elementary education student at that. He fired her on the spot without blinking an eye.

Adjectives aside, the summer of 1956 had turned into the driest summer in close to a hundred years, what with August ready to close itself
down and still no hint of rain anywhere south of Jackson. There continued to be hope—a deceptive hope, but still hope—due to a low pressure
front that swirled across the east coast of Louisiana up from the Gulf of
Mexico. But it did little more than whip up clouds that trapped the heat
and give the red dust the means of traveling across the lower southern
states. Most farmers, after a week or two of hope, decided hope was a cruel
thing to believe in and turned to the National Guard instead. Olive-drab
tankers rolled in from Camp Shelby and dumped water into tanks so the
cows could drink. Too bad about the cotton, though, those army boys said,
yawning deep, glad they played with guns and live grenades and not trac-
tors. Most cotton was burnt, having never stood a chance, all those early
blossoms falling to the ground like so much hand-tossed confetti. The
farmers stood scratching their heads or their balls, wondering if it were too
late a thing for Jesus and a fast or two, or what about those planes their
federal taxes support that go up and seed the clouds? Having nothing to
do other than stand around and study their dried-up fields, some took to
going to town and leaning against the light posts or sitting back on the
loading dock of the Feed and Seed, feeling weak and diseased with this rare
thing called time on their hands.

Valuable walked past a blue-jeaned group out on the loading dock and
listened.

"... medicine man up in Collins—I say we get him on down here for
a dance. I ain't beyond begging, either."

"Sally's buried dishrags under the front porch for weeks now. Says her
grannie swore by it for dryin' up the running squats—"

"That bein' the case, seems it'd do more to stop a thing than start—"

"By God, it does, don't it?"

"Hold on Sam, those Catholics bury Saint Whatchamacallit upside
down in the yard to bring on a sale of something. I say we send somebody
over the river to see what they got that we can bury so's it'll rain."

"Hold now—it ain't that bad."

"You say. There was a black chicken that stayed in the middle of
Highway 11 for seven hours straight—"

"Lord, I heard about that—"

"Me too—"

"That ain't good, Jack. A chicken undecided about things is a heavy omen. I say if we got to go to the Catholics we best go."

Someone else, and Valuable couldn't see who it was, said, "Endtimes, that what this is—endtimes!" There were nods and sounds of agreement while streams of tobacco juice shot out to the street.

"I say we repent. Go to prayer and fast from food and sex with our women—"

"Ain't no way!"

"I agree—ain't no way! I say we go with the Injin up in Collins and if that don't do it boys, we might as well bend over and kiss our ass good-bye for this year, I tell you."

"I agree with Tom here. Man up in Collins might know something—some old cure. I say we make the call, give it a try," he said.

"Amen. I lean to a course of hiring out a rain dance rather than a called fast from fuckin' or a statue burying."

"Amen—"

"Me too—"

"Me three—"

Valuable walked past, thinking to herself, So this is where we are. Calling on Indians and burying rags under steps. She coughed, tasted trapped dust in the back of her throat and wondered if the medicine man would be allowed his dance out in the middle of Central and Main, or if it would turn into some secret thing like what the Masons do, or the women of the Eastern Star.

Turning on Hillcrest Loop, passing her own house as she headed up the hill, she ran a hand along the back of her neck and liked what she felt. Whether or not anyone else liked it, she did. She wished to herself she had whacked off that childish braid years earlier.

Jackson lived closer to the cemetery than Valuable, and once she could see his house and him outside cutting grass, stirring up a storm that blew in all directions, she headed away and through the gate of Hillcrest Cemetery. In late summer she thought most on her. It had nothing to do with the date of her death. That had been winter when every day was wet and cold as a frozen root cellar. Winter held its own code. One that required all energy to be used in the business of keeping warm. Summer was for grieving, and that's what she had done and that's why she found herself thinking on Luvenia while she wiped the sweat off her face.

She found them near the back edge of the field—Katie Luvenia and William Dixon Korner. A line of maple trees squared off behind them, headed north away from death, and Valuable sat herself down and waited. She didn't have a lot to say in the way of information. Everything current already had the feel to it of old news. Most of what she wanted to say couldn't be spilled in the middle of tombstones. Most of what she need-ed to say she was saving for Jackson. Over the sound the hot wind made in the tops of the dried-out trees she could hear his mower whining and coughing. Looking over she saw his dust cloud had spread until it covered three houses. So much dirt, so much dust on life here in dried-up Petal. Valuable bent and swept Luvenia's footstone clean.

William Dixon's footstone had a locomotive carved under his name because that's how he'd spent his early days before retiring to become an unlucky farmer. Katie Luvenia was carved into her grandmother's. That and "She Who Loved Much in Spite of Things." Valuable was almost positive Bea had been responsible for that because that's what she had wandered around saying all during the graveside service. The daughter and the father were laid out side by side. There was no hint of the wife of William Dixon or the husband of Luvenia, and for the very first time, Valuable wondered where those two were and why there'd been no mention of them as far back as her memory allowed. Just the two of them. One an old man, the other a tall, lanky woman with big hands and feet. All she could remember was Luvenia's claim to being a widow. Her tale that her husband had been killed when his tractor rolled over on top of him on a downward slope. As for the missing great-grandmother—the mate of William Dixon—Luvenia had never in all her days said word one about her mother.

"I'm talking to Enid now," Valuable said finally to the right side of the headstone marked Korner. "I guess you're happy about that. Or maybe not, but I'm doing it anyway. And I don't know how it's gonna go, but I'm tired of being quiet about things. She's still with Reilly, but she's been going dancing a lot and you and I both know what that means."

She fanned her shirt away from her and watched dust fly. Her shoes were red, their white canvas having kicked up tiny dust tornadoes on her walk up the hill. "Tonight's the River House for supper. I cut my hair, too. It looks sorta like Liz Taylor's. At least I think it does."

She usually talked for an hour and felt better afterward but this time it was as if Luvenia had finally gone somewhere else, somewhere permanent. A neighborhood dog yelped and howled and Valuable looked around, chilled inside the heat. The sound carried from Jackson's house across the field of the dead and back again. You're gone from here, aren't you? Gone for good just like the rain. Thinking this didn't make her sad. Instead it made her feel like there was more room inside to think on Jackson, a thing she'd found herself doing more and more. That damn dog again. Yelping in a wave that crashed then built back up again. She pulled up a handful of dead grass that was curling over the wheels of William Dixon's locomotive. "Maybe you didn't want me to cut my hair. Maybe me staying a little girl standing up on a stool was your idea all along—"

"Yaaaa!" Hands grabbed hard at her waist and Valuable screamed loud enough to wake half the field. Turning, she saw his blue-jeaned legs moving away from her in a run and she made a grab, bringing him down hard across the Korner's dead neighbors named Runnells. Jackson rolled up laughing.

"Wow!" he said, sitting back on his hands, looking at her hair. "Wow." Softer this time.

"Enid cut it." She reached across and pulled him up off his butt. His face was dusty red and where he'd sweated, channels of true skin color showed through, running lines up and down his face like bars.

"You look like a boy in prison." She pointed to his face. She still had his hand. He hadn't pulled away; instead he held it, wrapped his fingers around hers in a way that made her stomach feel funny.

"I am in prison." He looked at her long and hard and Valuable felt the whole meat of their conversation had moved away from dust and cutting grass and dead relatives. Moved seasons away from where it had been only yesterday. Jackson pulled her backward and they scooted until they sat on Luvenia and William's heads, still holding hands and looking at each other.

"We're sitting on their heads." He pointed down. A brown cloud of birds—sparrows or field thrush—lit in the dogwood and in the upper stretch of tall pines along the break in the woods, but neither one noticed.

"I don't think they'd mind."

"You think they feel us through the dirt?"

"They're dead and gone, Jackson." It made her feel good to say it. The dog quit its howling. Everything was still.

"It's nearly three. I need to get cleaned up."

"No, don't leave yet." She squeezed his hand, amazed at the way her stomach was behaving. It felt full of butterflies or bees and where they were moving around was sending a charge all the way down to the spot between her legs.

"I stink," Jackson said, but he said it soft and he squeezed her hand when he said it.

"No, you don't. You don't stink—you just smell like somebody working hard on the last day of summer."

"I've never kissed a girl," he said then in way of an apology, as if she had been asking him for a kiss, and she looked at him.

"Yes, you have. You kissed me when I was eight and tripped on your steps and knocked out my front tooth. Remember?" Valuable said. "You kissed me six times on the mouth."

"I don't think that counts."

"Why not?"

"'Cause I didn't know what kissing meant then."

"And you do now?" she said.

"Maybe. Maybe not. But you're sitting here with all your teeth in your head and all I can think about is wanting to kiss you." He reached up with his other hand and brushed at her short hair. "You're really a pretty person."

There was a moment then when a kiss could have happened but he seemed to reconsider and stood to his feet, embarrassed, pulling her up with him. "I want to be clean, is all," he said finally in explanation.

"I've got to go to the River House tonight for supper and I want you to go. Enid's driving. We could pick you up around seven." She didn't want him to let go of her hand and she pulled him back until their rears were leaning on the headstone.

He laughed a snorty laugh. "I don't think Neva's gonna be too glad to have me there. Threatened to kill me if I ever led you anywhere and you came back minus anything again."

What he'd just said about her coming back minus something made her weak and flushed. "I know and I'm sorry she did that to you. Joleb told me all about it."

"I'm not scared of Neva. She just startled me there for a minute."

"I don't care if Neva wants you there or not. I want you there. Besides, she owes you an apology." She had breath at the beginning of the sentence but by its end she was near fainting.

"You okay?"

"Yeah, just hot."

"Me too." He grinned. "Are you sure of this?" He squeezed her hand one more time while he looked down on his house, clipped and neat but dry as a bone.

He wasn't speaking of supper at the River House or the August heat and she knew it.

"I'm sure, and after we eat, maybe we could go to the creek—"

He shook his head. "Not the Baby Black," or even the Tallahalla, he thought, which ran into it. "I don't think I'll ever go there again—"

"No, not that one," Valuable said. "We'll go to the Bogue Homa this time. Up on 42." She could smell sweat and dust and something else coming off of him that made her want to kiss him hard on the mouth. She felt thick and heavy between her legs and her eyes felt swollen and puffy. Putting up her free hand she felt alongside her face but all seemed normal.

"Well, okay, as long as you're sure."

"Are you sure?"

He looked at her thinking, if she touches me with those tiny fingers, I'll faint dead away, and then he felt like a stupid, farm-dirty fool for thinking such a sappy, sissy thought. He picked up the tail of his shirt and wiped at his face, freeing it from prison. "I'm sure," he said.

"And you'll kiss me then?"

"Yes," he said in his new deep voice. And I'll do other things, too, if you let me, he thought.

Stepping off William and Luvenia's dead bodies, they walked back out through the gate and headed in separate directions with nothing more than a wave between them. She studied her hand as she walked down the hill to her house, and while it was covered with fresh dirt and sweat, she thought it the most wonderful thing in the world.

Even dragged the Bellrose goat by a frayed rope and thought, If this is a small measure of what it's like to take the bull by the horns, I'll pass to something less ambitious.

Up Shasta he went, headed to the house on the end that stood empty all day long. He had passed it before and wondered how it kept that lived-in look, what with fresh flowers and swept porch and neat curtains in all the windows. He understood now, having met the woman Grace in the middle of a swank department store in downtown Hattiesburg.

"This best not be wasted effort," he said to the goat, which darted up and nipped him on his ass. Even turned and swatted him hard in the face with a rolled-up newspaper.

"She ain't gonna like it one little bit you hit her goat in the face." An oldish woman was leaning on a ratty fence, her hair done up in rollers. He looked to her feet and saw mismatched shoes and wondered if any Negro woman in all of Forrest County owned a matching pair. And then he remembered Grace. Her house stood quiet on the other side of the woman's fence.

"Well, you can help me on this matter," Even said. "I got her goat here," he shook the rope as proof. "And what I'm needin' you to do is tell the owner of the goat that her pet is tied up over at 14 Bellrose. And if you'll do that for me, I'd be obliged."

"You would, would you? Sounds to me like you ain't never met the owner of the goat." She picked at teeth remnants with the plucked bristle of a broom.

"I met the owner and I still want you to do this thing for me."

"Oh, I'll do it all right. I wouldn't miss doin' that *thing* for you for all the money in the world." She laughed a croaking laugh. "Don't know what you got in mind, but I'll sure as hell do it for you. Buy a ticket to what Grace is gonna do once she sees her goat tied up like a dog, too. Yes, sir, I sure would buy a ticket to that one," and then she turned and walked up her rickety steps to her front porch, still laughing.

With no other dialogue between them, Even headed around the corner to his place dragging the goat, bleating and stubborn the whole way. He had come on it eating grass up by the main road and pulled out the rope he'd carried to work for the past four days, hooking it neatly with one toss. Gotcha, he thought to himself, feeling briefly like a cross between cowboy and Cupid. While he shortened the lead he said to himself, "Canaan, the rest is up to you and that old dead wood of yours."

12

SUPPERTIME

"I DON'T LIKE ROAST AND I got work to do besides."
"'The Reality of the Negro' can wait. Ain't no new changes I seen
in the wind since yesterday or the day before that, and it ain't gonna dry up
and blow away by waitin' one more day. Besides, you got company comin'
and I think a clean shirt and pressed pants might be good. If you'll bring
'em out here, I'll press 'em for you."

"Who's comin'? I ain't invited nobody nowhere. And since when'd you
become my mama?"

"If you was half as smart as you think yourself to be you'd put on a
fresh shirt." Even pointed a fork in his face. "You want to spend all your
days chasin' a goat out the yard? If that's the case, you just sit there wearin'
something I can smell clean over here. You want a little peace and quiet,
you go clean up a little and maybe your problem'll go away." And if luck
has anything to do with the scope of life maybe somebody's tube snake will
rear its one-eyed head and show itself. Even Grade smiled to himself. "You
want me to iron your pants or not?"

"I got ironed pants hangin' in my closet."

"Starched?"

"Nope. I hate starch. Don't do nothin' but chafe and make my eyes run."

Even was standing in the other man's kitchen searing a rump roast in a black iron skillet. He poked it through with a fork and shoved in bits of fresh garlic and turned it on all sides until it was brown and crisp. This done he lifted it out and put it in a bigger pot with cut-up potatoes and carrots and wedges of crisp cabbage. Into the leftover drippings he sprinkled flour and chopped onion and made up a roux.

"Sure smells good to me," he said turning, but Canaan was out of the room. He could hear him in the back opening up drawers, slamming them shut. Complaining the whole while. The goat was behind the house, the cord around his neck tied to a clothesline where he had plenty of play, Even having rigged it so the goat could graze and shit in peace.

"Why you so contrary, Canaan? I thought you'd jump at the chance to spout your theories all night long to a pair of virgin ears—" Even yelled this out over the sound of sear and pop.

"I ain't contrary. I just hate surprises." He had moved back into the kitchen and Even jumped at the close sound of his voice. Turning, he saw him buttoning up a fresh shirt. He was still in the same pants though, wrinkled around the knees and pockets.

"I've known you four years now and you ain't ever had a woman over once. If I hadn't caught you eyein' Clorena a time or two, I might be tempted to think you were a queerboy," Even said.

"You think what you want, all you want 'cause it don't matter a fart's worth to me. I was married once and it was one time too many, and if bein' a queerboy's what it takes to rid women of their ways, then I say all men best bend over and get on with it."

Even frowned down into his gravy. "You're making about as much sense as that goat out there. You got anything good to say 'bout anything at all?"

"Nope, I sure don't."

"Well, that's a real shame now, 'cause company's comin' and she might expect something on a little higher plain."

"Don't matter to me what she expects. What she sees is what she gets—"

"What she's gonna see is Canaan—tough and mean and thinking tits are a waste as well as what a woman's got between her legs. You're a sad man. A sad little angry man."

"I ain't had nothing good to say about a woman in thirty years and I ain't seen anything around here to change my opinion yet. Women is women. They're slow-witted and fast talkers and they don't mean a word they say 'bout love or carin' or anything in the world 'cept leaving. They mean that. You better believe they mean that."

"Maybe you just ain't met the right one yet." Even had been confident but was worried now.

"The hell you talkin' about? I'm sixty-three years old! I ain't got enough time left on this world to be meetin' anybody. You think I'm gonna change my ways at this point of things? Maybe take up golf or fishin'?"

"Relax, Canaan. This ain't a bad thing. Nobody's asking you to change. She's just a nice woman, is all."

"You relax. You ain't the one sitting here wonderin' why I suddenly need starch in my pants and what big thing's coming round the bend."

"Not too big. 'Bout five six. Hundred and thirty-five, forty pounds and the best set of legs you ever seen in all your livelong days."

"Thy God, what've you done to me, Even." Canaan pulled out a hand-kerchief and wiped his face. His scar glowed like a traffic light.

"God ain't got nothing to do with this one, Mr. Mosley. More like the goat you've been complainin' about for months and the stiff starch in a shirt I wore a while back."

"Well, you can cook and you can hope, but I got me an opinion on things and it'd take more than a good set of legs to change it." He moved to the sink and made false motions toward perking coffee. Picked up the tubed pieces. Put them back in the sink. Opened a cabinet door. Studied his coffee cups. What he was really doing was looking out the kitchen window in the direction of road, curious as a cat. "I ain't changin' my mind bout nothin'." he said.

We'll see 'bout that once you see those legs, Even thought while he cut the hard ends off broccoli and tossed them in the pot. They made sad, familiar *bing bong* sounds hitting against metal and he thought on Joody and wondered what she might be doing down by the creek in the middle of all this final hellish August heat.

The River House was seven-gabled. Built by a Northern man so in love with Hawthorne he knew whole passages by heart. But that was all he knew. For the architect he had hired, a one-eyed Boston man short of vision in both ways literal and figurative, had built the seven-gabled house with its ass to the river, setting the front door to face a dead field of saw grass and scrub with the only trees in sight forming a hard brittle line that ran north into nothing. The Northern man, who traveled down from Springfield, Massachusetts, expecting to be able to see his river from the wide bow windows set center of his bedroom or from a chair set on his deep porch, imagining a bluff and a steep flight of stairs that could eventually lead to a dock to which a boat could moor up bearing visitors, had found nothing of the sort. There was a river—brown and sluggish—somewhere on the other side of a thick arm of trees that did little more than provide cover for mosquitoes and biting flies and brown water moccasins. The Northern man lived there a total of six months and then he sold the River House and bought a small piece of land on a New England bluff where his vision stood a better chance—somewhere close to Boston, so the story went. The River House wound its way through a series of owners before being purchased by Luvenia Korner's uncle Benjamin in 1920, who in turn left it to his only granddaughter, Bea Korner Gondst, who instead of being thankful for the gift, thought it the ugliest house she had ever seen in her life.

"I want you to behave," Bea said quietly while she scooped out the melon balls.

"My reputation is exaggerated—I always behave."

"I guess that good behavior made you attack that boy on the street." Bea looked over her glasses. "Enid told me about that, and frankly, I'm embarrassed at such a show."

Neva was silent—just reclined crossways in a Queen Anne wingback swinging her leg.

"I've baked a goose with orange sauce and wild rice. I thought you could be nice and make dessert."

"I doubt they'll be here long enough for dessert, dear." Neva undraped herself from the chair and walked over to the liquor cabinet and poured herself a Scotch.

"See? This is the element. This is what I mean—you stand there so threatening and honest to God I think you must see yourself as Rhett Butler or some similar sort of bully."

Turning and lifting her glass to Bea she said, "Frankly, my dear, I don't give a damn—" Bea just glared back, her hands on her hips. "Hey, I'm joking. Lighten up for Christ's sake." Bowing formally Neva said, "I promise to behave, Sweetheart. I'll be so courteous you won't recognize me and my scalawag heart." She sipped from her drink and winked.

"And what about dessert?" The cut crystal bowl of melon balls went center of the table.

"There's pound cake from Koshes' Bakery out in the kitchen and I picked up a gallon of strawberry ice cream from Seale Lily. Now see? You still think I don't care?" Neva said.

"I'm withholding my opinion until after supper."

"Dinner, dear. It's dinner."

"We say supper here, Neva, now get off your high horse."

The doorbell gonged its eight-level gong and Neva held up a hand, stopping Bea. "I'll get it. You get the ice in the tumblers and pour up the tea." She turned once before she reached the door and said, "and I'll behave. Just you wait and see."

The wide door swung open and Valuable bounced in, Jackson right behind. "Aunt Neva—gosh, it's good to see you." She gave the woman a bear hug that was surprising in its intensity.

"Hey! Wait a minute here, you're choking me." Holding her by the shoulders and making her stand back, Neva studied the girl while Jackson hid himself inside a shadow. "Lord, you're a picture. Bea come here and see this—I never would have thought it, either. Who did this?"

"I did. Copied a picture of Elizabeth Taylor in a movie magazine." Enid pushed her way into the large hall, dropped her pink plastic purse on a table and walked straight to the bar where she poured herself a drink.

"And I guess we have you to thank in the long run of things," Neva addressed Jackson.

"Aunt Neva—" Valuable warned.

"No, I'm serious. Forgiven?" It was the closest she would allow herself to an apology because the closest she ever came to feeling maternal tenderness was what she felt for Valuable. Neva stuck out her hand to the boy. Well, hardly a boy. Undo the scared shitless look to him and he was really something to look at. Shit. I wonder if Enid knows what's going on here? Shit. Don't tell me I'm the only person in the world worried about this thing—

Jackson stepped forward and took her hand. "Yes ma'am, you're forgiven and thanks for having me for dinner."

"You hear that, Bea?" Bea was standing in the doorway in a flowered dress that made her look like Miss Kitty from Gunsmoke. "Dinner. Jackson said 'dinner.'" Neva linked arms with the two of them and herded them into the long dark dining room.

The roast smelled like a big, juicy piece of heaven and this was a fortunate thing because Canaan was in a dark hell of a mood. Contrary and mean, he sat reading the same page of his thesis over and over; pulling out his pen; carving at the words with red.

Wiping his hands on a dish towel, Even set two plates down on the end of the table without stirring Canaan's thick stack of papers.

"You suddenly forget how to count? I only see two. Don't you dare tell me you ain't stayin'!" Canaan said in disbelief.

"I ain't stayin'. I got things to do."

"Uh huh. Well, ain't that a great big pretty picture! Trap me here with a total stranger—"

"You won't want me around anyhow once you meet her." Maybe not you. But she sure might after she spends five seconds with Mr. Demon here, was what he thought.

"She must be one ass-ugly woman, you wantin' to run out so fast and all."

Even heard the slung supposition as he walked out the living room on fast legs. Not much living been done here, he thought. Sad too. 'Cause life is short as a dream, once you stop and ponder it. He had looked out the kitchen window while he whipped up the potatoes and seen her walking up Bellrose. There were words to be said, a few warnings and advance apologies to make before he officially introduced the two. If it ever got that far. He walked down the steps to the porch and met her with outstretched hand as she turned in the gate. He smelled of roast and wore Canaan's ratty green dish towel over his shoulder. She smelled of rose water and was wearing a royal blue dress that made her look like a dark, gleaming queen. Her legs were bare and she must have thought something was up other than goat, because she was wearing a pair of low black heels. Lord, she's a vision, Even thought.

"Now before you go and shoot me over the goat," he said holding up his hands, "I got an apology to make. I made a mess of things here—"

"What'd you do, kill my pet and cook it for supper?" Grace was squared up with him. Steady and calm in the eyes.

"Lord no."

"Well, what then? What's so wrong you need to build an apology before you offer me a glass of tea?"

"I ain't been honest here. I had somebody I wanted you to meet. That's why I did this thing. Stole your goat, I mean." Why in the name of Almighty Jesus had he ever thought of doing this thing? Strike me dead, Lord, if ever some thought crops up like this again. "Your goat's fine. Out grazing behind the house. And I got supper cooked and he," here he point-ed to the owl-like face looking out the kitchen window, "don't know a thing about this. This was all my doin' and I realize now it was a foolish thing, too. So if you gonna get mad, go ahead. He's mad as a wet hen right about now, so you ain't gonna be by yourself on that one." He stopped, flustered and foolish, having talked more in that one minute than a month.

Grace had one hand on her hip. "You mean you stole my goat just to get me over to this man's house for a date?"

He saw Canaan was still peering out the window, craning his neck try-ing to see. "Yes ma'am, and I'm sorry. I got foolish is all."

"You ain't got to tell me you got foolish! What's the matter with this man anyhow? He a cripple? How come he can't get his own woman?"

"'Cause he hates women and I just found this out. Got married once to a mean hell-bitch who drove him to it, is what he says."

"You don't say." She didn't believe word one of his lies.

"This is a fool thing I've done and I'm sorry."

"Sounds to me like you think Just Plain Grace too ugly to get her own man—"

"Oh, Lord no! That ain't it. That ain't it at all, ma'am. I just thought the two of you might get along, but I didn't know he hated women. I wish he didn't 'cause Lord God, you're a sight. I just got to thinkin' ever since I met you how good a match it might be, is all."

"That's why a man ain't got no business thinkin'," Grace said.

"I know that and if you'll strike this one up as forgiven, I promise I ain't ever gonna think on thinkin' again." He grinned at her, unable to help himself because she was just so damn good-lookin'. Her arms looked polished as well as her cheeks. He'd never seen such white teeth and large healthy hands. "I'll fetch your goat now and walk it home, and again, I'm sorry." He put a hand to his chest and felt the dishrag and thought, I am a blazing fool. A pure-d blazing fool. Embarrassed, he ducked his head and made to go round to the side of the house.

"No, you just hold up a minute, young man. I'm here now," she patted his arm, "and I'm all dressed up 'cause Rosa said who it was who slapped my goat in the face and I meant to look good while I tore up your ass— but that's another somethin' I'll deal with later."

"You tearin' my ass up sounds more pleasin' than painful." He was shocked at himself and his face grew hot, but there was something so sexual to the woman he found himself blurty as a teenager.

"Now you're flirtin'." She smiled and pointed a finger.

"Maybe. Maybe I am." He was grinning so wide his face hurt.

"Well, Even Grade, if your roast is half as good as the smell in your shirt, at least I'll get a good meal out of this. Lead the way to this man. What's his name, by the way?"

"Canaan. His name's Canaan Mosley."

"You say a woman made him mean?"

"That's what he says."

"Is he a smart man or dumb as a stump?"

"Smart as they come."

"We'll see. Just Plain Grace will sure see about that, 'cause I ain't met a man yet smart enough to be let loose for longer than two minutes."

Even led her up the steps and opened the front door to the house, and after she walked into Canaan's living room, he removed the dishrag and stood outside on the porch for a long minute wiping down his face. He was hard as a rock and all he could think on was coursing.

Jackson had never had goose before and he found it greasy, good-tasting but greasy. He'd never eaten off such good dishes, either, or had wine with a meal, or had to wonder about which fork to use while he sat at a table so long it could have easily fed twenty. Valuable was across from him, set down there by Neva who still had a mean look to her underneath all her show at politeness. Once or twice he caught her watching him instead of eating and he forced himself to chew slowly while he lowered his hand down in his lap instead of propping it up on the table beside his yet to be used coffee cup.

There were paintings on the dining room wall framed up in gold with lights above them. The paintings themselves had such a look of amateur to them Jackson knew they had to be expensive, shipped in from some place other than Mississippi. A mirror seven feet tall stood on heavy claw feet and multiplied the soft light of the chandelier suspended four feet above the dining room table. Light seemed to shoot out from every point. The gold frames. The crystal. Valuable's dark shiny hair. Jackson picked up a fork and moved it sideways and watched light fly off and hit the ceiling and the wide molding over the door that led to the kitchen. He winked at Valuable and she winked right back.

"Jackson, how is your family? Your father and mother?" Bea asked this while she passed him a boat of gravy.

"Mom's fine. Dad's over in Vicksburg 'til Sunday at a trade show." She looks too old and tubby to want a woman, he thought to himself, not sure what that meant but thinking it probably meant he thought her too old and tubby to want sex of any kind, man's or woman's.

"And Enid, how's business? Still reaping the results of that Marilyn Monroe do over at Braswell's?" Neva asked.

"Contrary to popular opinion, there's not too many out there willing to service the dead," Enid replied, chain-smoking Camels.

"Oh, I quite agree. I was married once to a very dull man. Servicing the dead can be a real challenge."

"You making fun of me, Neva? Because if you are, it's a waste of effort."

"No. I'm simply agreeing that service to the dead is something not everyone is willing to do and I think it's remarkable you found yourself able to it." Neva put a bite of goose in her mouth and smiled. "Of course, service is your specialty, isn't it? You aren't eating, dear. Something wrong?"

"I think you know exactly what's wrong. And I think you're baiting me. And I think goose is a terrible thing to cook in the middle of all this heat. Goose is for winter, or at least the fall."

"I think you're mistaken," Neva said. "Goose is good any time of the year, if you can find it. And you're a guest. It's rude to be so picky about food when you're the guest."

"Not in my book—"

"And which book might that be?" Neva said.

"Why'd you invite us here, Bea?" Enid looked at her older cousin who was nervously refolding her napkin. "D'you invite us here so your bulldog could insult us?" She lifted her third Scotch toward Neva in some sort of a toast. Her words were slurred.

"You're drunk, Enid," Valuable said, putting down her fork.

"So?"

"And we have a guest here. Shame on you for such a poor show of manners." Neva reached over and tapped Bea's arm and mouthed "coffee." Bea nodded and rose.

"Who, Jackson? S'that who you're talking about being our special guest?"

"Enid—" Valuable said.

"And you, Miss Priss, can just go right back to keeping that mouth of yours shut. You think I don't know how you feel about me? You think I'm stupid as well as being . . . as well as . . ." She struggled for a thought that had been there a second earlier.

"A whore?" Neva spoke up.

"Neva!" Valuable and Bea yelled this out.

"Hey—I say we put everything on the table once and for all," Neva said, wiping her mouth and grinning. "How about it, Enid? You want to do that? You want to put all our cards on the table? You owe us back rent on your shop, for one thing. The whole town's talking about you, for another." Neva fondled her knife, throwing light across the room.

"Neva, you promised——" Bea said, quietly.

"Bea, I promised to behave and that's exactly what I'm doing. I'm behaving exactly the way someone should have behaved years ago when this behavior started."

"Well, excuse me! I'm just the *whore* here, but it sounded to me like you were just being rude as hell!" Enid shouted.

"Bea, darlin', why don't you make yourself useful and go make coffee?" Neva said.

"What's going on here?" Valuable said in a small voice that sounded seven again, and Jackson stuck his foot under the table, feeling for her leg.

"We're just being adults is all. You'll learn it fast enough." Neva picked up as spoon and breathed on it, looking bored.

"Well, it sounds rude to me. And mean and something I hope I never learn." Valuable was near a point of crying.

Jackson thought that there was a feel to things then like there had been out in the cemetery earlier. Like things could head off in a million different directions and while he held his breath and waited to see which way this thing would go, Neva pulled her parts together and clamped shut her mouth like a premature trap. She slouched down in her chair and didn't look happy about it, though. What a fruit, Jackson thought. What a total fruit. She'd dressed the part, too. Purple pants, shirt, tie. Like a prune with a royal vendetta. All she'd managed to do was make herself look foolish for picking on a drunk. Apology or no, he knew she was one mean bitch hiding undercover.

"Anyone want dessert?" Bea asked in a quiet voice. "We have pound cake and ice cream. Jackson, would you care for dessert?"

Most of his food was still on his plate and he was as near throwing up as a person could be because of goose grease, but thinking a break in the activity, that one person exiting might break up whatever was going on there, he said, "I'd like some coffee, ma'am."

"Me, too," Valuable said in a small voice.

He looked across at her then. Heard the small sound to her voice. Slipping off his penny loafer he ran his socked foot up and down the soft side of her calf, not thinking on what might or might not come later if they ever made it to the creek. Just thinking she might need comfort right then and there, was all. And there in a roomful of females siding up like wet cats ready to pounce, Valuable and Jackson sat still and waited for coffee speaking a secret conversation through identical gray eyes.

Even stood out on his porch with his hands deep in his pockets and tried to pick apart the words he heard every now and again. But all he could hear with any regularity at all was the hoot of a lost owl somewhere barely north and the hot wind blowing against the metal billboard at the break of the road. What the sign used to read was a too-old puzzle now for anybody to remember, seeing how all that was left was part of a man's leg down in one corner and something that looked to be a jar with a red lid on it in the upper right. The letters were gone as well as the memory of what those missing letters advertised. A buffer was all that sign was now—a catch for wind that once it was caught threw out a sound like that of false thunder. He saw the light in Canaan's kitchen was still burning yellow, and once or twice he saw vague movements as if one had been sitting at the table and then stood to do something—maybe make coffee for real this time. Earlier, about thirty or forty minutes after an introduction as pleasant and relaxed as one might find the cleaning of a polar bear's teeth to be, Even had walked out leaving them both standing in the middle of the kitchen, their arms crossed, each with one foot stuck out in some sort of declaration. Worried and more than a little curious, he had wandered over once the sun was down and he wouldn't be seen and stood under the open kitchen window, smelling roast and soap, like dishes had been scraped and left to loosen in the sink. "How long you been working on this?" he heard Grace ask. "All my life," Canaan answered. "Well, I think it's a cryin' shame you spendin' all your waking days and wasting your big old brain writin' 'bout something just so you don't have to live it." Well there you go, Even thought as he hurried away, salt beading across the top of his lip. She's put her sharp teeth to the heart of the man and I bet there'll be a dead goat before morning. But that was three hours ago. There'd been no bleat of dying goat or female scream or outburst of any sort. There'd been a cloud of laughter once—Canaan's. And once or twice he heard Grace's voice over the sound of the wind. Canaan's light still burned yellow and the nag of a goat was still tied up in the backyard underneath a clothesline, hunched down on top of its legs sleeping. While he listened to the sound of false thunder, Even Grade wondered over it.

13

SIMILAR TO AN OYSTER

WHERE THE FLOOR OF THE BABY BLACK seemed made of cool ground silver, the bed of the Bogue Homa was more inclined toward gold. Sun caught and held its face to the water, still enough of late summer left to it so that every place it touched glowed ochre and brass and a peculiar green-gold that seemed fire-lit and precious. Jackson and Valuable stood on the lip of the metal truss bridge—no cars as company, just a bird or two up nesting inside a rusted angle—and watched this thing, this movement on top the water from bright gold to a red closer to purple than red. There'd been no rain and the water ran narrow, leaving wide banks dyed and thirsty and scattered with hopeless logs.

"I think we need to go down the other side. Looks like someone thought of maybe buildin' a boat ramp at one time. See?" He pointed to a trail of tire tracks that cut through the tall grass.

"You think someone's down there now?"

"I don't think so. We'll check though. *I'll* check." Jackson held out a hand to her and saw the questioning look on her face. It seemed to take her an hour just to touch his hand. "You still want to swim? Are you scared?" he asked, not thinking on swimming but something else.

"I still want to and yeah, I'm a little scared." She was an excellent swimmer and he knew she was speaking of something else, too.

"What are you afraid of?" He moved closer to her until their shoulders touched—his inside a shirt but still able to feel her warm skin. He spoke low and soft. His voice sounding unsure and strange to his ears. He cleared his throat thinking, I'm the older one here, I should know these things.

"Of everything. Of not knowing what to do first. When to do what and how and where—" She brushed her hand across her eyes while she crimped up one corner of her mouth.

"Hey—it's okay. I'm scared too." And he was but he looked steady at her when he admitted it, instead of to the side, this new thing of looking into her eyes so fresh it felt like some sort of a gift. He opened his palm skyward and looked down at her hand and traced her fingers against his palm, amazed by the margins. Looking away and back into her eyes he said simply, "I love you—let's head on home and forget this thing. There's time enough for this later."

"No. It's hot and I want to swim."

"Okay, we'll swim then. But that's all."

"No. You promised you'd kiss me. You have to at least do that much." She linked her fingers through his.

He looked at her grinning, relieved he wouldn't have to figure out the mechanics of anything more complicated than a kiss. Pulling her forward he walked with her across the Bogue Homa bridge. Valuable looking down the whole while, careful not to step on any cracks.

"Does it bother you about Enid?" Jackson asked.

"What do you think?"

"I think it does."

She didn't answer. Just squeezed his hand while she stepped over a crack.

By the close of the meal, Enid had been too drunk to drive but not too drunk to remember the telephone number of some guy up in Richton who knew a good blues band down in Hancock County. She rang him up and when he showed up thirty minutes later in a grinning Mercury convertible she had sobered enough to tease her hair and put on lipstick, but that was about it. Stumbling to the car, leaving her daughter and her daughter's dinner guest, she had tossed her pink plastic purse into the front seat and then collapsed against his side. He hadn't seemed to mind, though, because he propped up her head with one hand, waved good-bye with the other and then tore out the driveway, throwing up a spray of gravel clear to the wide front porch.

"If there's anything you'd like to say, now would be the appropriate time," Bea said, glaring at Neva.

"I'll drive her car in with the kids—"

"Taxi service is not what I had in mind and I think you damn well know it!"

"We're all responsible for our own outcomes, Bea, even Enid. I had no idea she would take one little thing I said and twist it the way she did. Hell, I was just trying to be cordial was all."

"I think you had your heart set on a cock fight is what I think—"

"Well, you're mistaken, dear. Now where's the key to her Ford?" Neva had walked back to the hallway table. Opened up a drawer. Rummaged for the keys.

Valuable spoke up. "You might as well forget about the car. Enid took the keys with her in her purse. I want to walk anyway." She went down the broad brick steps to the walkway and turned back once. "Aunt Neva, I don't want to seem rude, but you embarrassed me tonight."

Neva had come back out and stood leaning on a post, her hands in her pockets. "We're not a normal family, Val. It's foolish to expect us to behave as one."

"I'm not expecting normal. I'm expecting decent. There's a difference."

Neva looked from Valuable to Jackson. "You can't walk back to Petal after dark. You really shouldn't, it's at least two miles. Bea, tell them it's not safe to prowl home after dark and for God's sake quit stalling and go back the car out the garage."

"It's barely dark and we won't be prowling," Valuable argued, standing near the boxwood hedge, halfway to the road at that point. "It's not even eight and besides, we've done it before—you know that. Enid can figure out how to get her car home tomorrow. But I'm walking." She had turned her back to them then. Just waved good-bye with one flip of her hand, leaving Jackson silent as a stump on the porch between the two women.

He had been standing there watching the flickering light from the gas lamp light up the back of Neva's dark head, thinking how the unstable illumination made her look like she belonged in an illustration in *Tom Sawyer* or *Treasure Island*. One that included a dark-mouthed cave and handheld lantern. "Thanks for having me for dinner, ma'am, and I'll watch out for her," he said finally, going down the steps after her. These were his first words since the fiasco in the dining room.

"Really? Well that's just charming. And who, may I ask, is gonna look out for you?" Neva, an ugly little smile on her face, had stared down at him from her spot on the porch, her hands deep inside her purple pockets, the gas lamp throwing light across her face accentuating and lengthening the lines along her nose. Jackson shook his head and looked away thinking, Whatever this cold queer is feeling—it's no kin to concern.

"They don't seem related to you. Are they?" Jackson asked quietly.

"Somehow, way back. Bea's father was Luvenia's uncle or something like that. I just call them 'aunt' because it's easier." Valuable picked up a rock and sent it skimming across a pool of gold-colored water. Her shoes were off and she stood midcalf in the swirl.

"Do you think they're mean as they seem?" He was sitting cross-legged back a ways on the sand.

"Sometimes I think Neva might be, but not Bea. Bea just seems scattered. Dim-witted. Sorta like Enid only Bea likes women and not men."

"Why you think they're queer?"

"I guess for the same reason we're not. They just are." She sat down at the edge of the water, her dress getting wet and changing colors underneath her ass.

He scooted down by her and rolled up his pants legs. "Do you think they kiss and stuff?"

She thought about it. "I know they used to. I saw them stretched out on their bed once when I was about ten years old and Luvenia was in the hospital that first time for her heart. They were kissing then, up in that big bed of theirs. They didn't even jump apart or anything, not even when I climbed up and asked them to read a story to me. *Peter and the Wolf.* I think that's the one Neva read. But that was years back. They're kinda old now. But yeah, I'd guess they still kiss. They share the same bed and I can't imagine them not kissing a time or two, at least good night. You think they kiss?" She looked at him.

"Sounds sickening now that I know them." He leaned back and kicked at the water. "A couple of years ago, when I first found out what 'queer' meant, I used to like to think about it. You know—two women kissing and maybe taking off their clothes and rolling around bare-ass naked and stuff. But after meeting them up close, I can't imagine those two doing anything other than being mean to one another. Kissing seems too soft a thing for them, somehow." He put his hand on the back of Valuable's neck and felt her brush of hair, ran his fingers up to the back of her skull. She was sitting still as a rock. Her arms wrapped around her knees.

"I used to swim with you and feel your braid brush my arm and think it was a snake."

"That seems ages ago."

"Just two weeks back. Not so long a time as you might think." He lit up a cigarette. "When we'd float on our backs, our arms would bump together, or our legs and I'd wish you'd move over and get away from me. Now all I can think about is getting close."

His voice sounded so soothing and deep, it made her sleepy. Overhead was a sliver moon, curved and hooked, low in the sky but steady-climbing. Like something in a fairy tale that would hold an elf or a cow would jump. A fool's moon, Luvenia used to call it, for it drove foolish farmers to plant earlier than they should, thinking they'd get a jump on the full-faced moon with their collards and greens. She felt Jackson's warm hand up at her neck undecided about the buttons of her dress and smiled. He would touch one or two as if calculating its position and the number of maneuvers required and then his fingers would go back to her hair again. She smelled cigarette smoke and wet leaves and rot—those dank smells that live a narrow life at the edge of moving water. The crickets and frogs were loud here, but not as loud as at the Baby Black. Here their chorus seemed unrehearsed and untethered to anything resembling order. Everything at that other place seemed preordained and connected to some antique notch in time that rolled around once or twice a millennium. Here at the Bogue Homa, moving along the creek and in the trees and inside the sounds falling back on top of other sounds, was the feeling of choice. As if she still had a say in the way things might go.

Still watching the moon she reached behind and unbuttoned her dress. Aware that he was watching, she pushed the flowered material down around her waist. There were similar sounds beside her. Fingers to buttons and zipper. But she still watched the moon. When there was nothing but the crickets, she said, "You're mighty quiet."

Jackson swallowed and it felt like a cob had gone down whole. "Shit, Val, I don't know what to say. Or do. I don't know shit about anything at all——" He saw the bra she'd pulled off lying in the sand and it seemed too similar to what he saw of his mother's hanging on the back of the bathroom door. He pushed it behind him.

Valuable turned around and faced him—bare-chested, her dress loose around her waist like a draped sheet. They sat there squared off. Stalled. His eyes trying to be well mannered but failing. Valuable just leaning back on her hands watching his face.

"I want to see you," he said, swallowing hard.

"Where?"

"Down there." He pointed to what was still hidden under the drape. "If it's okay."

The moon went behind the clouds and for a second or two he lost her—as if she'd dropped off the face of the earth, disappeared down through a hole in the sand. When light came round again, she was on her back, her knees spread. Her head resting on her arms.

With hands that shook, he pushed her legs apart and studied her by moonlight. "I can't see good—you're so inside."

"I'm all inside. Opposite of you. Everything you've got is out in the open." She heard the sound of the Zippo opening—the one with the green four-leaf cover on its case, and knew he was using it for light. He held it far enough away not to burn, but close enough for her to feel the heat of it changing location. She listened to his breathing, wondering why it sounded raspy and ragged.

"Does this hurt?"

She bowed at the back at the foreign placement of his finger. "No." And it didn't.

Her voice was different, muffled and thick and he looked at her, trying for her eyes but they were shut and her head was thrown back. He snapped his Zippo shut. Didn't want to see her anymore. Studying her and her differences made her seem far away from him, like an alien form that had sprung from a pod or something. It was all too strange and cold. Moving his hand, he pulled her legs together and lay down beside her looking up at the stars. "Looks similar to an oyster," he said. "All pink and gray with ruffled edges. That inside part, I mean."

She put one arm around his neck and reached down with her other hand and held him. Felt it jump inside her hand. "Luvenia told me men like to empty their chuck wagon better than anything in the world. For a long time I wondered over it, what it meant." She squeezed and felt the changes. "She meant the male organ, I know that now, but I still don't know why she called it a chuck wagon."

"Jesus, Val. Stop for a minute. Please." He covered his face with his arm. "You scare me. *This* whole thing scares me. I don't know how to do this." Blond from summer sun, he turned silver in the quarter moon, a prelude to how he'd look years from now when this thing he didn't know how to do was as ordinary and common as night breathing.

"Just kiss me, that's not too scary is it?"

And he did, kissing for what felt like a very long time. Testing different ways. Playing it out to the limit of what kissing offered. Then, breathing hard, while the moon disappeared, they began the rest of it in stops and starts similar to a rushed-up song. Like music that wouldn't be music until time broke it apart and made it better. But still like music. "You want me to stop?" he asked at one point, his breath lost and ragged. Dear God, please let her say no, he prayed while he held himself halfway inside her with his hand.

"No. Don't you dare stop—" she said. And he didn't.

It seemed like a slow season, but it was barely more than an hour. She bled on her dress, though, in a spot high up on its bodice, bunched as it had been underneath her bottom. While they walked home—their hands linked easy—they talked about the night sky and the unnatural brightness to the stars and the lay of the trees along the banks of Bogue Homa Creek. The stain caught the light of the moon a time or two and in Jackson's frame of mind made Valuable look marked. As if she'd been shot through the heart and left to bleed out slow with nobody around skilled enough to stop it.

"Where in the world have you been?" Bea asked. She was wringing her hands over by the telephone. So terrified of being alone, she'd vomited twice, losing her goose as well as her coffee.

"Out walking."

"Out walking for more than an hour? I think you're lying. Where'd you find to go around here?" She wiped her eyes on the tail of her dress.

"The creek," Neva said, and then she walked to the cabinet and poured herself a Scotch.

14

GOOD BAIT

———————

GILBERT MORRIS set out his trot line at about nine o'clock that Friday night hoping to catch something big. There was a steady stream of constant rumors around his region that catfish, one hundred pounds and up, slugged along the muddy bottom of the river Leaf. He had no personal proof, but a man up Wiggins way caught one that filled his bathtub and ended up with his picture in the newspaper and a new boat parked beside his house. And if a man from Wiggins, a place with no claim to the river and only partial knowledge concerning the art of the fish, could catch one that size and find prosperity hand delivered, it seemed only proper a man from Petal, where the Bouie birthed, ought to be able to do the same. Trot-line fishing was poor fishing at best. A lazy man's way. But Gilbert Morris was a weak man who never saw clear proof there was a need to be any other type, and so he never pursued thought on his weak-styled ways—simply accepted them with a shrug. He was pretty sure though that rolled dough would prove the best bait for the trot line. Rolled dough with raw bacon stuck inside. Worms were good, too, and he reasoned if he could find a way to set a worm inside dough and make it stay put long enough, it would be a feat indeed. One that might lead to the naming of a certain type of hook or brand of bagged flour after him, but that was for another day and another hour. Because he hadn't bought groceries inside of two months other than liquor and cigarettes and day-old cinnamon buns, tonight he would be limited to just dough. After he'd made up enough to fill a bucket, he drove the eight miles to the river and left his truck running, its lights shining down on him so he could see what he was doing. Sliding down the hill on his ass, he remembered the bad brakes his truck was wearing and he prayed the damn thing wouldn't roll and kill him while he was trying to catch a fish and win a boat. His thoughts took a turn then on the hilarity and perversion of being killed by one's own rusted-out Ford wearing a set of worn-out brakes and he got so tickled he nearly pissed his pants. Then, at the thought of what had almost happened—him almost pissing himself while laughing at the thought of his own death by his own truck—he laughed so hard he dropped his bucket. Sitting down hard while he held his stomach, he watched half his bait roll down the hill like white turds and plop into the water. "Well, there you go, boys, I done laughed so hard I lost my balls!" He whooped and hollered then, rolling on the ground, kicking his legs up in the air. Done in to the point he finally did piss himself while he was flat on his back laughing his ass off, he knew he'd have to air himself out or go home and change his pants before he headed to Riverman's to get drunk. The thought of detour sobered him to the point he managed to sit himself down, his crotch wet and clingy, and get what was left of his bait set to hooks. Once the line was tossed, those orange floats working away from him, he stationed one end to a stob on the west bank of the Leaf River and climbed back up the hill to his waiting truck. A trestle ran over-head and he reasoned the rumble would stir up the catfish and make them hungry, disturb them from their slugging ways long enough to herd them toward his hooks, that way his picture could end up in the *Hattiesburg American* and he could win himself a boat.

The man who seemed at first look out of place with the rest couldn't take his eyes off the woman dancing—the way she rocked forward from the hips, her arms bent and doing a strange pulling motion against her sides with each offbeat, her fists clenched like she was low angry and trying hard to hide it but couldn't. Whichever or whatever, the woman was gorgeous. All dark hair and pale, pale skin. A tiny woman, perfectly shaped. She stood, her feet planted firm on the wood floor, her head raised as if in some sort of worship, while men and women of all ranks and colors flanked her front and sides. Most in the club were regulars—a strange thing for such a place as lower Mississippi in such an upside-down time as 1956. The sign outside the door explained a measure of it: "Music lives here. Everbody else don't count." And music did live there—inside this place named Belos by a man so long dead, no one could remember why it was named such anymore. Colored, White, Coon-ass, true Cajun, Swear-to-Gods, Creole, each and all seemed accepting of their role as stranger as they ducked through the low, off-angle door. The man on the outer edge of the circle who at first glance seemed out of place with the rest was no exception.

He could see a flash, now and again, of thin arms and thrown-back head as it ducked then rose again from inside the ring where she danced. All the men in the club, most with women leaning on their arms, had moved their chairs until they formed a ring around her, leaving an opening at center where she did something too basic to be called a dance but too rhythmic to be called anything else.

The KeyTones out of Picayune played the Robert "Snake" Sims song, "West Coast Lover," with a beat so loud the tune seemed breathable as gas and nearly as toxic. The woman kicked off her shoes—both flying over the heads of the circle and landing by the piano—and rocked so far back with each beat it seemed a hard miracle she maintained her balance in the center of the floor. "Holy God—" the man who seemed out of place with the rest said.

"Ain't that the truth," said Cleve the bartender, who'd seen a lot but never anything like this.

The Negro on saxophone blew out a language older than English and the glasses on the tables trembled.

Her eyes still closed, she worked her hands up through shoulder-length hair and the room broke to a cheer. She shook her head against it, her long hair swinging side to side, as if the cheer broke some train of thought too holy to lose.

The Negro on the trumpet, a rubber plunger on its end, moved center and stood in front of the woman dancing while a glass bowl on top the piano walked clean to the edge and crashed to the floor. Nobody even noticed.

The man smoked while he watched, his crisp sleeves rolled to the elbow, one elbow leaning on the bar. The dancing woman's pink purse had been set down on the counter next to a huge jar of pickled eggs and Cleve stood guard as if it were the Holy Grail and held some secret to her. Something other than what she was showing to the world in the middle of Belos.

"Where she come from, dat one?" the man asked, trying to hide his Arcadian tongue and failing.

"Lord, I don't know. Man who brought her got his head broke and crawled away—"

"He da one got throwed out?"

"Yep. Needed manners, I say. Ain't polite to yell out 'You gonna dance for the niggers all night or you comin' with me?' in the middle of a Negro bar. Ain't polite 't'all. A man could get himself kilt doin something as rude as that."

Three of Belos's biggest had jumped him. Quick-jabbed him in the ribs and kidneys and dragged his ass out the door. Tossed out onto the gravel, the man spewed once and then lay facedown in his self-made mud and whimpered. He eventually raised up and crawled away on all fours in the direction of the cornfield parking lot. "You show up back in Hancock County again, us Picayune coloreds gonna kill your white ass!" the tallest of the blacks had yelled. The woman stayed in the center of the room and danced. Not drunk on anything but KeyTone blues.

A run on the piano and the KeyTones went into "All Alone I Sit and Cry" and the room settled round the woman who was pulling up her dress to midthigh. "Oh Baby! Oh Baby!" they all yelled while they clapped and stomped and cheered.

The man checked his watch and ordered another Pabst.

"You ever seen such a sight?" Cleve wiped a glass clean and set it to his side.

"Nah—and I don't think once is gonna do it."

"You say!" Cleve ran his rag across her purse. "Handed me her bag and then she took to the floor. That she did."

"Dey know the Johnny Otis song 'Baby, Baby Blues'?"

"You must be wet out the womb not to know they know everthing they is to know—you know that?"

"Ask him to play it once and then wind down for the night. It's close to three." He handed Cleve a twenty.

"You know, I'm feelin' a mite tired myself." The bartender grinned and walked over to the drummer and stuck the money in his shirt pocket.

Thirty minutes later, on two opposite sides of Mississippi, things were set: Gilbert Morris had hooked the catch of the year underneath the river Leaf, and Enid Korner was on her way to California with a man said to specialize in repossessions, a Cajun man, dark and good-looking, who carried a snub-nose .38 in the back of his pants.

15

THE FACE OF GOD

―――――――――――

VALUABLE WAS DEEP IN A DREAM concerning butterflies. They covered her head while she bent to the creek and all she could see were spots of yellow, blue, green and gold that stole the color of her hair and made her head look topped by a hat of flapping wings. Inside her reflection in the water her image moved, as if someone were shaking her. Making the butterflies take off from on top of her head—

"Wake up!" It was a whisper.

"Whaa . . ."

"Wake up, Val—" A hand ran along her cheek and she felt a kiss there like that of a baby, soft and bumbly and wet.

Valuable opened her eyes and saw Jackson kneeling by the side of her bed. Judging from the night breeze, his way in had been through the open window. She had locked her bedroom door against Reilly in case he came off his run earlier than expected and wandered through looking for Enid and found her instead. The house had been empty when Valuable finally made it home. No trace of Enid anywhere.

"Jackson, come'ere." She put her arms around him and tried to pull him into bed with her.

"No. Listen to me—Joleb's missing. So's Burris." Her gown smells warm and good, he thought. Like some type of Thanksgiving spice. Maybe pumpkin.

"Missing? What're you talking about? How do you know?"

"Old man Green just left my house about ten minutes ago scared shit-less. Says Burris and Joleb haven't been home all night." Jackson was still whispering.

"What time is it?"

"Three in the morning."

"Do your parents know you're here?" Valuable asked.

"They think I'm out looking for him and I am in a way, I just thought you'd want to come along." Even sleepy-eyed she's so pretty it hurts, he thought.

"When did you see him last?"

Jackson thought on it. "I guess three days ago at Kress." He sat back on the floor by her bed, Indian-style. "The day Neva came after me and threatened me in the alley."

"Was he okay then?"

"Sorta. As okay as Joleb can be. I think I know where he is, though, and I ain't goin' there by myself." He sat back and watched her rub her eyes.

"Turn around then, and I'll get dressed." She threw back the covers and swung her feet over the side.

"No, I'm watching."

"It won't be the same as the creek, you know? It'll be different here inside the room." She ran her hands through her short hair.

"I don't care, Val—I'm still watching."

She stood up and moved to the chair holding her clothes and pulled her nightgown up over her head and threw it back to the bed.

She was right. It wasn't the same. But it was still good.

Even Grade was sleeping, curled on his side, his back to the window. Sound asleep for once, too, inside a calm place without a dream. A dark cool place of no color or noise other than an occasional knock that floated up like a bucket set bobbing against a wharf post in low tide. He heard it again and woke, realizing it wasn't a bucket inside a dream but a steady urgent knock at his front door.

"Hold now!" he yelled while he climbed out his bed and pulled on his pants. Walking through the kitchen he was alarmed to see the lights were on over at Canaan's. The man is dead, he thought, stricken. Probably of heart attack in the middle of coursing after such a long season of dead wood. Dear Lord, what have I done here—

He opened the door to the dead man, frumped and close to wringing his hands, but with a new smooth look around his eyes in spite of obvious agitation.

"We got us a situation over there—" He nodded to his lit-up house.

"What kind of situation?"

"Those Green boys Grace sits are up and missing. Beryn Green, the boys' father, came round about an hour ago thinkin' maybe the youngest— Joleb—had wandered off to her place." Here Canaan chuckled. "Didn't know her house number but knew she owned a goat. Rode around slow, searching every house in the Quarter 'til he found the one with a goat."

"Yours—"

"Mine. And I don't even own the damn goat—"

"But the man sees it tied up out back—sees it's the only house with a goat and he gets out his car, knocks on the door and asks for Grace?" Even said.

"That he does," Canaan said.

Even raised his eyebrows. "Was she there at three in the mornin'?"

"She was."

"Readin' 'The Reality of the Negro,' I reckon." Even grinned.

Canaan looked at him and lifted his chin. "Maybe. Maybe not. But that ain't the issue here at the moment. There's more and you need to hear this, too. She didn't want me to tell it because she's embarrassed over the look of things, her being over there and all, but I think I might need to and I think you better be a gentleman about it, too. It's a mess, Even, and it ain't started good yet."

"I'd say supper went pretty good for a man so against it," Even said.

Canaan was silent but he smiled.

"I'd say for somebody dead set against roast, you made a regular pig of yourself." Even felt a peculiar mix. Pleased it went as planned. Pissed it went as planned. I'm unstable and loose, he thought, shaking his head, realizing he needed Joody. Needed to course long and hard 'til he lost his breath and his face shed salt.

"You ain't gonna make this easy, are you?"

"You say that true." Even saw the lights go on in the house across the street and remembered how voices carry. Lower he said, "Hold tight. Let me get in a clean shirt and I'll walk on over." He stepped out to the end of his porch and put out a hand to the night, spreading his fingers wide and waving it side to side then holding it still while he felt for a sure directional on the wind.

"Good. That's good then. You dress and walk on over." With that Canaan headed back to his house, jumping a bucket that loved the center of his yard.

Even stood still and slowed his breathing. He sensed a true change to things. A pickup in the wind. Northeast, an unusually strong northeast, too, as if it held a reluctant front by the hand and was leading it south.

"'You keep doing this thing—your daddy gonna send you away to a mental home or hospital. It ain't normal.' That's what I've always told him. Told Burris," Grace said, her beautiful face contorted with worry.

There was something about her dress that was wrong. It rode higher up on one tit than the other and seemed bunched and catching under one arm. Even remembered how she'd never been able to find a store-bought that fit her proper and sized it up as such. He stood watching the two of them, his ass leaning on the kitchen counter, his arms crossed. Canaan and Grace at the table, their hands at the center touching on occasion. The old man's books and Mason jar full of pens and pencils and still-packaged screwdriver, as well as the thick sheaf of his personal life's work, stacked on the floor beside the pie safe. Candles on Mason lids everywhere. We are at a new point of reality here—one that doesn't need recording, Even thought to himself, and it felt like a sad thought, a turning place, as true a signal as the drop in barometric pressure. Looking at the now empty table where the papers had lived for as long as he'd known Canaan, Even saw a spot on its back edge, a black scorch mark shaped like that of an iron, solid black, loud as thunder concerning the man's habits of bachelorhood.

"You say this boy chases trains? I don't understand," Even said.

Grace explained, "The why of it's lost on me. Just somethin' he picked up from God knows where. Once when he was 'bout twelve I sat him down and we talked our way around it again. He claimed it was a game, nothing more'n that."

"He thinks he sees the face of God in the train." Canaan said this as if it were a reasonable thing to expect to see coming down the track and threatening death. "Right before it breaks through the fog, he says a prayer and throws himself off to the side, jumping clean."

"Sounds crazy and foolish to me—" Even said.

"Oh it is. It sure is crazy all right." Grace rose and went to the sink to make coffee. "Those boys ain't normal. Never had a chance to be, what with everything that happened—"

Even moved away from her and strolled over to the table and sat. Her back was to them and he saw her misbuttoned blue dress had left a large portion of her dark back naked to viewing. He looked away and kicked Canaan under the table. When he looked up Even nodded with his head in her direction.

Standing, he went to her. "Hold a minute, honey," and while she did he rebuttoned and smoothed her over, running a dark hand down the back-side of royal blue.

Honey, Even thought. Lord have mercy, the man said Honey.

"Thank you, Canaan—" and she patted his hand while she still looked out the window.

Even cleared his throat. "So what's this younger one got to do with all this? Maybe it's just two boys off to no good."

"Mr. Beryn Green found a note from Joleb saying he was going to find the face of God," Canaan said. "He's been troubled lately on things. Not himself."

"And you two think he's off somewhere standing on a trestle with Burris?"

"No," Grace said, looking at Canaan.

"What then, and what does this have to do with me?" Even asked.

"We think he's gone to the creek," they both said in unison while they looked at him.

⚶

Louise Green knocked over a water glass when she answered the phone by her bed.

"Lord have mercy, Louise, I've made a mess of things——" the voice on the other end said.

"Beryn? Christ! What time is it?" Louise fumbled for the lamp toggle, hearing a snap somewhere south of her she hoped wasn't her glasses.

"Close to two, I guess," her brother said.

"Is it Mary?"

"No. It's the boys. They're gone." There was a long pause and she heard the sound of a nose being blown and she imagined what he must be doing—how he was probably sitting at the phone table in the dark winding the black phone cord around his finger.

"What in the world are you talking about, Beryn? Speak clearly here."

"They're gone. Both of them—Burris and Joleb. Gone and I'm all alone."

Oh Lord, she thought. "Where's Mary?"

"Oh, she's here. Back in the bedroom, I mean. She's here sleeping."

"Then technically speaking, you're not really alone, are you?" She sat up in bed and felt around for the glasses she never remembered taking off. He had never answered her question, not that she expected it. He had a water glass with him and she heard him slurping.

"I've got to go out looking and I can't leave Mary alone. Can you come over?"

"Where's Grace?"

"She don't live here, Louise—Lord! You think I'd have a nigger sleeping under my roof!"

"If you were a smart man you'd have cleaned out that back room and offered her a place years ago," Louise said. "Been more convenient for everybody, all the way around."

"I'd never in a million years——"

"I agree. It'd take a smart man to think such a thing beneficial."

"You better believe it." All she heard in his voice was relief that she had been in agreement.

"Give me twenty minutes and I'll be there. And Beryn?"

"Huh?"

"You go to Grace's first. Joleb's always been partial to her," Louise said.

"Joleb?" Beryn said it as if he didn't know who in the world she was talking about.

"You said he was missing, didn't you? Isn't that what you said—that both the boys were missing?"

"Yeah, but I was thinkin' on checking on Burris first, what with his taste for train trestles and such—"

I just bet you were, she thought. She reached under her rear and pulled out her broken glasses, thankful she'd seen the prudence in purchasing a spare. "Has Joleb ever in his life done anything like this?"

"No, not that I know of." He blew his nose again and she heard him sipping water.

"Then Joleb's your biggest worry. Burris has been stepping out for years. You find Grace first and I'll bet you find Joleb, and if he's not there, call for the police because my first thought is that something foul has happened."

"You really think—" was all she heard before she replaced the receiver.

Once Jackson and Valuable ducked in on the trail marked by a spraddled pine tree, it seemed as if they entered another place—a place more like a mist-filled cathedral than forest. One built by a man who knew how to set a post to the greatest effect in order to reap the greatest reward. Tall pillars of trees stood quiet inside the thick of it all, their tops so high and covered by night they were erased from sight, from memory even, and all that was left appeared as rough posts forming up a worship place of sorts. Jackson shone his flashlight down the path which was steady downhill, not afraid anymore. He played the light first to one side and then the other, watching the blue of the night break open and expose straggly limbs that looked like arms. They seemed soothing, though, like helpful hands. Not spookish or graspy at all.

"I don't remember this path," she said.

"It just looks different at night. It's the same, though. I recognize it."

He breathed in deep, smelling pine and honeysuckle, thinking, This place seems sanctified at night. All cool mist and blended shapes. Like something that would cure anything. "Hello! Hello!" he yelled out. It echoed back three times from unknown points and he heard the sound of wings flapping overhead—like an owl or large hawk irritated at being disturbed.

"What in the world are you doing?" She grabbed at his arm.

"Just listening to the echo. Hello!" He yelled it out again. "They say if it comes back three times, it's good luck. And if it don't come back at all—you're about to die."

"Thank you very much," she hissed.

"Hey, what's wrong, Val?" When he stopped she bumped into his back and he lost the flashlight.

"This isn't a game, Jackson. Enid's likely to be back before me, and what then? What am I goin' to say then?"

"Since when do you care what Enid has to say about anything?" He tried to find her in the dark, but she had moved. "Maybe she's not the problem. Maybe it's something else." He picked up the light and put it under his chin so he could see her eyes but she was looking away, toward the dark. "Are you sorry we did it?" God, he hoped not because he wanted to do it again. Real soon.

"You look like a ghost," she said, irritated, thinking of the way he blew smoke rings out his eye and how he seemed a regular trunk of tricks at times, without even trying.

"Maybe I am a ghost."

"Maybe you're an idiot, you mean." She felt swollen and sore between her legs and was tired of walking.

"Idiot? Me?" He covered his heart and grinned again. "You're killing me here—"

"Can I hold the light, please?" She looked around and leaned into him, spooked. There was a huge rock that looked slumped and animal-like, like a great beast hunched down and sleeping.

"If you'll give me a kiss. A French one, like before."

"Haven't you had enough for one night?"

He tapped his watch. "It's a new day now—time to start over." He was taller than she was even with her standing on the incline.

"You don't sound very worried about Joleb—shouldn't you be?" Valuable reached out and felt his earlobe. It was perfectly shaped. Not too big. Not too small. She felt around behind his head at the way his hair was cut close to the scalp, but still silky.

"Maybe. Well, yeah, I guess." He wrapped his arms around her and his flashlight played through the trees behind her. What a heavenly place, he thought. What a wonderful blue-black place. "Here, you can hold the light. Just hold it low to the ground so we won't trip on roots."

Something lighter than night was coming through the trees from the east. Not true daylight, but something working its way up to it. The tops of the trees that had been hidden before were showing their lower limbs now and the place was losing its look of cathedral. The path finally stopped its downward cant and they knew they were there. When they stepped out of the woods onto the wide clearing of sand and saw her fire, they stopped short, bumping into each other again because there was some- one else standing by her fire. A tall man with his arm around her. But there was no sign of Joleb.

16

MERIDIAN OF TRUTH

THEY SAT SILENT AROUND THE FIRE for a series of minutes that didn't seem that long or that strange. Just seemed protective somehow. Like a cloak waiting to be shrugged off once it was time and everybody was warmed up enough.

Still cold, Even looked the trio over. He had been kissing Joody when the two broke from the woods and drifted up out of the dark and Joody had pushed him away, held him off her with her hand. Which did seem a strange thing and not at all warm like a coat.

This Joleb must be a boy of some consequence, he decided after the girl spoke up and told them who they were after. Either that or he's a bothersome nuisance. A boy whose only chore in life is to interfere with good sleep or coursing on the way.

"He ain't here," she had told them, same as she'd told him a half hour earlier and the feeling was back. That wallowing, sinking feeling that part of the truth was still back a ways in her throat, waiting to be said.

He and the boy—a tallish one with blond hair and what looked to be gray eyes, their color hidden at that point, the night being dark and still having its hold on everything around—watched the two others as individuals might watch a carnival exhibit. Suspiciously. Even had seen a prehistoric giant on display once in Batesville and walked home sure his foolishness had registered on his body. That every pedestrian he encountered knew he'd just paid a dollar to see a plaster of Paris manshape as old as yesterday's milk. This boy knows there's more, too. And Even Grade found the thought disturbing.

Even watched him while Joody prattled. The way he kept himself close to the girl. Always touching somewhere. Hands. Side of the leg. Arm. He added up the sum of it, wondering at their timing and how two so tuned into the same need had managed to interrupt his primary intent. Even had initially wanted to check out the woods for Grace, who was still back at Canaan's worried sick. But as he walked down the path, passing the paradox rock, his thoughts had strayed to coursing and Joleb Green became just an afterthought. He watched the girl, who seemed awestruck, as if Joody's talk of roasting pecans was more than recipe. She leaned on her hand listening like she had all the time in the world while Even looked at Jackson McLain, whose face said he'd come to the same conclusion. All things considered, I'm as randy as a goat, he thought, and not likely to feel a remedy anytime soon by the look of it. Even Grade dropped it then, and took to wondering over Joody's lie instead. Why she'd cut them off and said she didn't know the boy when it was plain as that missing finger of hers that she knew a lot more than she was saying.

Joody, tired of the pecan talk, said, "The young man here's the one who dreamed of the gutted sow, and he's yet to work through it all. But he's tryin'. Grown himself two new sides in less than two weeks, I'd say." She grew quiet then and wrapped her long arms around one knee.

At Joody's spilling of his dream, Jackson crimped up his mouth, embarrassed, and Even thought, This crimping of the mouth seems a trait of Petal somehow. He'd seen the young girl's slut of a mother do it on the other side of a hedge, as well as Canaan and Grace while they stood by the sink. But never Joody.

"My friend Canaan dreamed of a sow," Even said. "The thing walked on hind legs and visited him in the library where he works. Came up out of shadows."

"Was it dead and slitted?" the boy asked.

"Don't know about the dead part, but he said it was cut from snout to ass—all its bacon gone. Told me the thing had rocks rollin' round in her mouth and spouted philosophy." In recall it sounded ridiculous and if anybody other than Canaan had done the telling he would have counted him fool or drunk, or possibly both. "How come you two down here looking for the boy?"

"I was about to ask you the same." It was the first time the girl had spoken.

"Somebody who knows him thought he would be here is all," Even said.

The boy looked across the fire. "All Joleb's talked about for two months solid is this place and meeting you." He studied Joody suspiciously, as if he'd just realized he'd been taken by a hoax.

"He ain't here and he ain't been here." She threw more pecans on the grate and Even knew she was hedging. As far as he knew only one other woman had ever lied to him, and that one lie had cost him a week's wages. Set him up, was what that one had done. Pretended she was interested just long enough for the one she was already interested in to beat him senseless beside the train tracks and take his money. He woke up the next day with a broke arm and noplace to go, determined to head south, as was his original plan. Now Joody, whom he'd judged to be beyond falsehood, was lying as brightly as the stars, the reality of it sending out sour waves as smelly as farts.

Joody stirred a metal poke at the pecans and avoided his eyes.

"I heard in town they're hiring an Indian to do a rain dance to bring it on. The rain, I mean. Some folks are burying dishrags under the steps, too," Valuable said, trying to draw her out, wondering why the woman had grown a prickly edge. "I hope if they do we get to see it. I mean, there's not a lot to do there and I . . ." She hushed and looked up at Jackson.

"So—you ain't seen Joleb?" The boy's eyes had narrowed. "Small. Dark hair. Big nose. He wears glasses and he's missing. Him and his brother, Burris. Burris is older and chases trains—"

"I only remember him once and that was early summer, or maybe late spring." Joody kept her eyes on Valuable. "Why do you think this Joleb would come find me?"

"'Cause he thought highly of you—of what happened here at the creek when he came to see you." Jackson said this and it had a sound to it of accusation.

She sighed heavily and unlaced her fingers until they dangled like bones. "Well, he ain't here. Joleb ain't his name, by the way."

"Yes it is, Miss Joody. Joleb. Joleb Green. He's sixteen years old." Valuable was smiling. The boy patted at his shirt pocket, like he was looking for a smoke, and Even shook one of his out for him. They both lit up, Even with a match, the boy with a good-looking lighter decorated with a four-leaf clover.

"Joleb's his tag, but it ain't the name he was meant to wear. Not the one picked out for him. Sometimes folks hit it but most times they don't. All I know is Joleb ain't what he was supposed to be called." She reached into a burlap bag at her feet and got another handful of nuts and spread them clean to the edge of the grate.

"—the hell you talking about?" The boy leaned forward.

Even was thinking the very same thing.

The girl spoke and stopped both of them. "Do you remember when he came to see you? Joleb, I mean?"

Joody rubbed her hand over her eyes. "I seen so many, I lose track . . . I just remember knowing the name Joleb weren't meant to be his name, is all."

"If Joleb's not his real name, what is it? What's it supposed to be then?" Jackson blew smoke hard through his nose.

"I ain't sure."

She's lying, Even thought. She knows this thing and ain't sayin'. He leaned around and looked at her. "What's goin' on with this boy, Joody? You may be telling the truth, but you ain't saying all of it." She waved him away and kept her mouth sealed all the way across in a new and different way. A stubborn way.

"Something strange is going on here," the boy said after a long pause.

"I think you're just about right on that one—" Even was irritated. Tired of puzzles.

"Lord God! A body gets set-to just by trying for some peace and quiet! I went contrary with him, all right? You happy now? There, now eat some of these pecans," Joody said. "First time I went contrary since year eleven, and if you ask me that ain't such a bad record." She waggled her right hand, drew attention to her missing little finger.

"How'd you do this, go contrary?" Even asked.

"He came on me here in the woods one night after everything that day had been crossways. My beans had burned early on. A woman from Purvis wouldn't leave 'til I spread her whole life out in the sand. Another woman, a Holy Roller from Sumrall, came at me with a blessed prayer cloth and tried to cast Satan out of me and grew mad as a hornet 'cause I wouldn't agree that my soul was home for six hundred devils. Anyhow—he, this Joleb, came on me after a day like that and I said he was 'thick as grits left overnight in a bowl,' quick as I saw him. When I read hard like that I usually try to soften it first, maybe clamp down my mouth on part of it. But not that time. I tried to find him after, to give him something to ease it, but he run off. Straight through the woods."

"Why in the world would you say such a hard thing?" Even asked.

"I think I just told you the why of it—"

There was silence all around and this time it hurt.

"Like I said, I repented of it—" Joody picked up a handful of nuts and put them in her mouth.

That ain't enough, Even thought. That ain't nearly enough. He thought on Canaan's reality words. On how everything a person needs to know is carried in the heart. Just waitin' there for us to listen. He watched Joody chew her pecans and suddenly felt as if he'd walked on bloody hands and knees all the way across the earth and found himself landed in the wrong place.

"Problem with all of you—including you, Even Grade—is that you think I'm perfect. That my voice is the only one. Ain't nobody perfect. Ain't nobody's voice truly wise. Nobody's. Only perfect things in this world and beyond is the things we can't see and most don't want to be still long enough to listen for them. I'm mere human and it still ain't enough for folks. They always want more. Always want me to do their hard work—" She raised her hand and waggled her missing finger again and they all saw it.

Joody handed her a pecan and Valuable felt faint. It had started near the outside range of her sight where everything broke into dots that spun while moving to center. The rich smell of pecans made her head hurt, and immediately after she put it in her mouth, she felt sick to her stomach.

"Valuable, look at me," Joody was saying in a voice that sounded double. Outside the ring, the man Even Grade, as well as Jackson, seemed to be dozing. They weren't actually asleep because a part of her was still listening to their conversation and watching them share cigarettes. But she seemed outside of things. Locked in tight quarters with Joody. A closet-sized room with a limited amount of air where every time the woman moved her black head, age sticks knocked together like chimes.

"Hold still and listen. This is just me and you—hold still." Valuable felt water in her mouth, as if her glands had revolted.

"Valuable, hear me. I can brew a drink and stop this thing. Give you an herb and stop it right this second." Joody's mouth was shut, but she was talking. Valuable heard her clear as a bell.

"No," Valuable said, glancing up at the pearl named moon.

"Look at me. Not the moon—"

Valuable looked at her steady and said, "No," in a clear voice.

"You know what you're saying?" Joody said this quietly within the normal range of her voice. It was sadder though, and full of sighs.

Even Grade looked over, wondering if he'd missed something. Jackson had heard about the accident at Hercules and wanted to know more of it, if those two really had been decapitated and so badly burned they had to be shoveled up. The two of them had been talking on it while the females ate their pecans. The moon cleared for a moment, broke through the clouds, and Even saw by fresh light the boy's eyes were gray after all, as gray as the girl's.

"Jackson—Joleb's not here. It's time to go," Valuable said, standing up, reaching for his hand.

Even watched them disappear back into the woods. Except for losing his desire to course, it was as if they had never visited. I'm glad I'm wearing my pants, he thought, missing his smelly house for the first time that he could remember. I'm glad I ain't stayin'. That my pants ain't crumpled up on top of Mama Girl. That I'm not squatted on the sand, my privates dangling.

"I know you disappointed in me," Joody said.

"More surprised than disappointed."

"Now who ain't telling all of it?" She spread out her hands and studied her nine fingers. "Seems like maybe we don't know each other good as we thought." She sighed. "Truth lives inside a meridian, Even Grade. Goes from one broad border to the other. There's spaces inside that feel like lies, but they ain't. Quit judgin' me so hard."

Hurt, he sat still as a rock thinking truth was truth. Deep and cold. Straight and narrow. She put a hand on his knee and watched her fire.

"She's new with child," Joody sighed, sounded exhausted.

"Who? The girl just here?"

"Yep. Valuable."

There didn't seem to be a full menu of things to say, so he settled on, "She seems too young, though."

"I lost my finger 'cause I wouldn't repent in year eleven," she said, her story piecemeal as was her custom. She had stretched out her legs and he saw the tattoos and the way they disappeared into her overalls and he knew what a sacrifice it would be for her to wear that yellow dress in the middle of town. Still hurt, but not so much as before, he put his hand over hers and waited.

"Black man came to me outside Yuma in Arizona 'cause I was rumored to have the same healin' ways as my ma'am. He wanted his daughter cured of a cancer and I couldn't do it. 'She'll be dead inside a year,' I said, 'cause it was true. I was only eleven. Only had eleven sticks in my hair at the time and it was back when I was livin' off can goods down by the rail yard with a bunch of hobos. I was foolish and young. Didn't have nobody tellin' me when or not to open my black mouth. Hadn't learned to hear Deep Mother purely, either. Anyhow—I thought he'd want to know this thing 'bout his girl so's he could spend what time was left makin' it special. He didn't. 'Cure her—Cure her now!' he yelled. And hard as I tried, I couldn't do it. Couldn't repent of what I'd read. You ever do something like that?" She looked at him, waiting.

Even thought on Canaan and how the man had leaned in on all those large things he felt for Joody, and said, "Yes."

"Three of his friends held me down out in the yard by a chicken pen while he whacked off my little finger with a fishin' knife—"

"Lord God——"

"I didn't repent, though. The girl's mama showed up then and made 'em quit. Took a shotgun and made those men walk away from me or I'd have lost the rest. I didn't repent, though. I sure didn't repent——" She paused and looked at Even. "I knew those two that just left here were related. Knew from twin readings they had the same whore-chasin' daddy. Saw they didn't know heads or tails of it, either, and I kept my peace, thinking on how I blurted out one time too many and lost too many things in the past. I value what's left of my fingers, Even——"

"Of course, you do. We all do, Joody. Hold on now——" He clucked easy, broken clean away from his anger. There is no back to her cave of sorrow, it just runs on and on forever, he thought.

"——And now she's carryin' her brother's child and she don't want to stop it, either, 'cause I said I had a drink that would and she said 'no,' big as you please. Big as any full-grown six-sided woman would say. You got to swear an oath you'll help me see this thing through, Even. Help me help 'em if need be——"

"How can I make a swear like that? How could any man?"

"'Cause you ain't just any man. You're Even Grade. Truly named by Deep Mother before you was ever born."

"Lord, have mercy——" Even didn't have a clue about this Deep Mother and his suspicions concerning Joody's sanity loomed as large as the giant pine with velvet along its roots. In spite of it, he put an arm around her and felt the casing bones alongside her chest, his fingers finding that center rib that always made him want to reach in and hold her heart while it beat inside her chest.

"Christ, have mercy," Joody said and laid her head in his lap, a high cheekbone stabbing him hard in the groin.

Her years fell across him and rattled and he felt their weight and what he felt burned him, made him want to cry because of consequences on the way. "Lord, have mercy," he finally said, completing things, while he rocked her underneath a cloudy moon and let her cry.

17

THE HATTIESBURG AMERICAN

G ILBERT MORRIS GOT SO SHIT-FACED down at Riverman's Friday
night, he spent all of Saturday inside his cluttered house trying on
various remedies for his king-sized headache. He slept through but for
spells of spewing tomato juice and vinegar into a bucket on the floor, and
by the time Sunday morning's sun climbed midway over his yard of
rusted-out cars, settling temporarily on the '37 Buick with the missing
doors and hood, he was recovered enough to remember the rolled dough
he'd set on the hooks of his trot line out under the Leaf River trestle.
Moving slow because his head felt heavy as an anvil and fast movement
seemed to impede his memory of where he'd put the croaker sack, he
walked as a man on low battery through rows of salvaged relics. Relics
that held as much hope of future service as tits on a chicken. He found
the sack finally underneath a trio of cardboard boxes holding parts to car-
buretors and mufflers and gears. By the time Gilbert jerked it free and set
out for the river, the sun was done with the '37 Buick and halfway up his
tower of balding tires. He steered down his dirt road toward the river,
squinting the whole while against the sun and reasoned that the trot line,

set now uninterrupted for over twenty-four hours, was sure to be heavy. Was sure to win him a boat.

Parking in the shade of a mimosa tree he was relieved he'd come on his spot absent of niggers and their poles. Church, he summed it, glad he'd never bothered to cultivate a belief in the Maker beyond the limit of swear words. Out in the brown water he saw his floats still bobbed in the easy current, at least two of them did. The fourth and fifth were missing and the line seemed to drop away at a point near the middle of the river.

"Holy Jesus!" he said while he slid down the bank on his bottom. "Holy Sweet Jumpin' Jesus!" he said again, his hands so shaky he could barely undo the line tied to his stob, so shaky he jigged it up until it was knotted and tangled. "Well, shit fire while I piss rocks," he swore low, smelling his own rank breath as he cut through the line with his knife. This done he tossed the knife up the incline of the bank where it landed buried to the hilt. Studying the knife in the hot sun he giggled at the thought of it, thinking the thing's brown handle looked like the stuck-out tongue of a fresh-buried man.

He wound the line four times around his wrist to keep it from drifting and then he walked to the edge of the water. Even with Petal's lack of rain, the edge was still bogged out and mushy and Gilbert sank to midcalf at the first pull of his line. "I need me a boat. A boat sure would be the proper thing to have in such a time as this. I could drift out and sit in the sun while I pull up my catch." His breath was so foul, he advised himself not to speak aloud again, to think his thoughts instead. Once the *Hattiesburg American* popped his picture, a boat might be his future, he thought. Who else deserved such a thing other than a drunk who managed to hook a hundred-pound catfish on rolled dough and bacon? He tried to lift his feet out of the mud so he could back up a ways to dry land for better balance, but they were sucked in as snug as if buried in cement. Testing his weight by bouncing a little on his legs, he felt his feet on some type of firm foundation and reasoned he'd not be eaten by mud before he pulled in his fish.

He tugged at the line and felt it clear of snags but weighted heavy, putting a deep crease across his palm. Holy Jesus! And what a day for it, too! He imagined how the fish would look—its size and the length of whiskers and width of jaw—and once his sober brain cultivated these imaginings, he began to wish he were free of the water and back on the dry bank. He didn't relish the thought of something so large flopping around his ankles and possibly gigging him in his prides with one of those nasty spines.

His stomach rolled at the thought and he grew sweaty in the stiff wind. With one hand on the line he leveraged his arms, tried to free his feet again and couldn't. The mud sucked steady with solid smacking sounds that reminded him of the process the mouth makes during food consumption. Quicksand is a real possibility here, he reasoned, remembering a woman who disappeared six years earlier from up Ellisville way. He'd seen one or two Tarzan movies, as well. Proof positive quicksand could eat a man or woman whole but for the hats on the heads. Gilbert tried again and Lord God if he didn't find himself lower, closer to his knees with brown water lapping up, making him wet, hiding all evidence of his brown work boots.

"Help! You up there! Help!" he yelled, but all he heard was a quartet of crows up on the beam of the trestle, calling out screams that sounded brass-plated.

"Help! You niggers on the road—help! I'm down here and sinking!" He gave up on the trot line, forgetting the fish and the *Hattiesburg American* and the thought of ever owning a boat. The line fell straight down back into the muddy water at an angle that was away from him. "Good—you go away now and wait 'til I get free. You go away fish—" Caught off balance, he fell back on his ass and brown water soaked him to waist-level, splashed up to his pocket, drowned his cigarettes. Trying to push against the mud he felt his left hand going down and becoming locked around his wrist as if trapped in a vise. "Holy Jesus help me!" he screamed long and wailing-like, suddenly sorry now he'd never bothered to cultivate a belief in the Maker, who had been sent to earth for such a time of emergency as this, too, he reasoned.

Caught and held fast by two legs and an arm, he kept his one free arm up out of the water so he could wave down traffic. Think, Gilbert Morris. You're not an unthinking man. Think on this and get yourself free of the jam. He worked his feet again and Lord God if he didn't feel mud over his knees now and still hungry. Be still then, he thought. Don't think anymore.

That last thought of yours fed the river two more inches. Don't think. Just be still. "Help me!" he yelled to the empty road and the laughing crows. He felt something brushing his wrist above his trapped hand, and looking down he saw slack in the line, drifting forward, traveling slow and steady to the surface.

"You fish! Stay away now!" He slapped at the water, hoping to scare it back down, but all the hand slap did was send a choppy wave that played itself out to the middle of the river.

"Yaaaa! Go away now!" He reached behind him hoping for the stob, thinking he could jam it into the ground and pull his way free or at least use it to poke the catfish in the eye, but all he caught in his one free hand was cracked dirt and dried-up marsh grass.

The slack was loopy now, so loose the first and second orange float bumped between his legs, knocked into his soaked thighs. A medium-sized catfish had hung up and died on the second hook and Gilbert could see one sightless eye peering up in a way that seemed accusing. The gray tube of its body barely broke the surface. Its whiskers limp as sogged noodles. "Holy God—if one that size still let the float break the surface, I've caught me a monster for sure! Holy God! I'm a goner with no favorable place to land once gone, either!" He thought on hell and all its attributes, and as bad a possibility as that place seemed to be it still had larger appeal than what he imagined would take him there.

Swallowing a sudden abundance of spit, he sat still as a turtle in the sun for what felt like a great while and called up prayers. Salvation mostly. The blessing of food. A Saint Paddy's Day prayer he remembered hearing at a bar down in New Orleans. A Christmas prayer that was partial at best because he was usually drunk as Cooter Brown two days before Christmas Eve. He prayed them all out loud with a fervency and frequency that hurt his head. God was deaf to it, though, for His only answer was a sudden hot wind that pushed at the line, bringing it and whatever it held steady forward.

Two Negroes found him, spied his truck first, parked beside the tree at the edge of the trestle, and when they peered down over the side toward water their first thought was that the stranded man had drowned in a squatting position while having a seizure. Scrambling down they stopped dead when they saw the rest of it—what was facedown in the water between the squatting man's legs. The squatting man's face was active in a silent scream, his voice having played out an hour earlier when a bleached body had found its way to shore and settled its head at the crotch.

"He needs help, James," the taller of the two said.

"You go pull 'em out, then, 'cause I sure ain't. I ain't gettin' closer than where I'm at right this very minute."

"We can't just leave him—"

"You go flag a car and get help then. I'll watch here, but I ain't goin' closer than this very spot." James yelled between his hands, "You hold on, Cap'n, Raymond's goin' for help! You hold on now—won't be long now." Lord God, two seconds with that thing between my legs would do me in, he thought.

The man turned a pleading, desperate face to them, the past jaw workings of his mouth so brutal it had cracked at its edges and bled down his chin. While the taller of the two scrambled back up to the road, the man pushed steady at the bleached head of Burris Green that kept creeping forward to his crotch. The teenager had been hooked in the ear by the last hook of the trot line set out two days earlier. Gilbert Morris's pale face made the front page of the *Hattiesburg American* after all. But there never was any mention of a boat.

18

SOMETHING LESS STRINGENT

LOUISE GREEN POURED FRESH COFFEE into her brother's cup with mechanical precision. She then pushed a plate of crisp bacon and eggs forward to the man humped and crying at her kitchen table. A severe woman of considerable bearing, tall and solid as a steel tube with hips, she was dressed in gray, an appropriate noncolor for all occasions in her book of style. The flash to her other than her brilliant blue eyes was a bright yellow scarf looped around her neck. Her glasses, when they weren't on her nose, were kept attached to her neck by a no-nonsense silver chain.

"The body needs food regardless of the situation. Eat, Beryn. It'll make you feel better." She patted his hand. Because it came air-conditioned and equipped with a Steinway upright, her front parlor would be used for the wake, which meant she'd need help in cleaning and waxing.

Glancing at her watch, "You never saw the need for a church, have you managed to contact anyone willing to handle the service?"

Grace stood by the stove dishing out a bowl of oatmeal for Mary. Setting it down on the table to cool, she went to the fridge and looked for the cream.

"It's in the door, Grace," Louise said without turning her head. "Come sit with us while it cools. Please."

Beryn Green looked up at his sister and frowned. "I'm bereft of reason, Louise. Bereft of reason. How can I think at a time like this? Especially about trying to find a man of the cloth." He unfurled a white handkerchief the size of a small flag and blew his nose. He swabbed at eyes in what seemed to Louise to be an overly dramatic fashion.

"That's nonsense, Beryn. You've suffered a blow, is all. I'm sure you can manage to think if you try hard enough."

"I'm bereft of comfort, Louise—"

"It's a hard place, but not the end of the world." He must have stumbled across the word "bereft" recently in *Reader's Digest* and been tagged by it, was her thought.

"I'm bereft I tell you, bereft of comfort—"

"You're bereft of a brain, Beryn, is the truth of the matter." Irritated, Louise sat up straight in the chair and sipped her coffee and nodded at Grace, who had just taken a seat.

Grace stirred in two spoonfuls of sugar, thinking, Lord have mercy.

"Ain't that the God's sorry truth—" Beryn paused, thought a minute, then blurted out in a stammering way, "Did I hear you right, Louise? Did I hear you call me brainless out your very mouth?"

"Yes, I'm sure you did and if you insist on blaming our Heavenly Father for this unholy mess, claiming His holy truth as 'sorry,' I'll have to ask you to leave my house."

"I'm not blaming God—"

"Well, that's good, because the only one I see to blame is sitting right here at the table. And I'm not speaking of Grace, here." She leaned over and patted Grace's brown hand.

Beryn looked the two women up and down. His wife was in the doorway in her wheelchair making wheezy breathing sounds but she didn't count as part of the audience. Pointing a finger he said, "You know, Louise, this whole town's been saying you're cold as a witch's tit for years. That you couldn't get a man if you strolled naked down Hardy Street, and I've been *brainless* enough to defend—"

"Only true word I heard, Beryn, was 'brainless,' and that you surely are."

Grace pushed back her chair meaning to leave this fight to play its own course without her having to listen. Grief had a bad enough smell without this loud horseshit.

Louise held up her hand, "You don't have to leave, Grace. You're as much a part of family as anyone."

"S'cuse me, but I don't think I want that honor," Grace said.

Beryn pointed his finger at his sister. "My only son is waterlogged dead and you sit here cold as ice, judging me stupid—in front of hired colored help, at that!"

"I think what you meant to say, Beryn, is that your *first*born son is waterlogged dead." Her eyes went from Grace to Mary and back to her brother again.

"That's exactly what I said! My firstborn son hooked like a fish, and you dare tread on my grief by calling me brainless?" His voice ended high, incredulous and screeching.

"That's because you are, dear. And I'm treading nowhere fresh. There's a regular path worn wide as a truck, made by people who have said as much."

Grace stirred the oatmeal and watched out the window for signs of rain and thought on Canaan and the way he had read to her from a book of large words.

Louise said, "There's still Joleb to consider. And frankly, I wonder why you aren't out there on the streets. Do the police have any fresh news?"

"They're still looking. They got the flotilla out dredging the Leaf with their hooks—"

Grace squeezed her eyes tight at the words and stood. Her brown hand gripped the oak ladder back. White folks sure know how to use that knife of theirs. "S'cuse me. I've got Mary to see to." She pulled the chair alongside the wheezy woman and spooned up mush with a shaky hand.

Louise sighed. "You need to eat, Beryn. You have a long sad day ahead of you."

Beryn Green stabbed at his egg with the edge of his toast and glared at his sister. "I may not have a church, by God! But I'll find a preacher. I'll do it for my boy. I owe him that. Just you wait and see—" He seemed to want to say more but couldn't quite spit it out, managing only a series of mouth openings and closings in a landed fish fashion.

Louise said tiredly while she rubbed the front of her head, "Leave the arrangements to someone with a brain, Beryn," meaning herself, and this seemed to be his limit for tolerating insults. He pushed his chair back, knocking it to the floor, and stood trembling with her green linen napkin stuck in his shirt. Louise saw he needed to use it, too. That he had a dab of egg showing on his face. "Let someone capable handle this thing," she repeated.

"That's exactly what I intend to do!" He shoved his hat down on his head and left through the back door still wearing the napkin.

"Sounds to me like you were a mite hard on him," Grace said. Mary opened her mouth in a mechanical fashion. She would blink between swallows and when it was time, she sucked orange juice through a straw. Age had worn a crease at the corners of her mouth and oatmeal spittle ran down her chin to Grace's waiting bib.

Louise picked up the knocked-over chair. "I guarantee you he's forgotten every word I said even now. My brother's immune to insults."

Grace looked at the woman and kept her mouth shut.

"Mary was a sweet woman who deserved much better than a ground slug for a husband." She looked over at Grace. "She came to me when she met Joe and asked my advice on the matter. I told her then and there to leave my brother and God knows she tried. Beryn said she could go but Burris was staying. My brother said she could have her Jew, but not the boy, too."

"He's tried to be a good man, considering things." Grace held the straw to Mary's mouth.

"That's not enough in my book," Louise said. "You know why I fault him?"

"No ma'am, and I'm not sure it's somethin' I got a right to know—"

Louise waved her comment away. "Joe brought you in on this from the beginning. You've got to be curious about some of it."

"Mr. Lieberstein brought me in because I'd just lost my baby girl and I still had milk. He needed a wet nurse and that's what he got, and for a season of time, I had me a baby at the breast again." Grace stopped and wiped Mary's mouth. "I've been up most of two days worried sick over

Joleb, but I've got to sit here and tend the mother when I'd rather be out turning over ever rock there is to turn over lookin'—"

"I'm sorry, Grace. I've been foolish and insensitive." Louise stood and went to Mary, brushing back a clump of her sister-in-law's heavy gray hair with one hand while she put the other on Grace's shoulder. "I guess I need to call Joe and tell him what's up. I'd hate for him to read the Sunday paper and see it there."

"Do what you got to—"

Mary was between them, her mouth opening at the prompting of the spoon. Her wet-sounding breath the loudest sound in the room.

Back in the room, Louise picked up the conversation as if it were suspended in the air.

"—used to come to me and we'd talk for hours on what she should do about the situation. Have you ever noticed how women think spinsters know things? As if we've stayed away from men from some acquired knowledge of their shortcomings. Have you noticed that?" Louise began cleaning her glasses on a green napkin.

No, I've been too busy wiping the ass of your sister-in-law to spend dawdle time on thoughts concerning white women. Grace was silent. Leaning forward while the woman babbled, she put her wide hand to Mary's chest. What she felt there was sea-like and alarming.

"—seemed to me early on, all she wanted was conversation. That's what most women want in my opinion. Somebody to talk to. Share common interests with. A little recognition. I don't think sex was the biggest of it, either. When Joe came along she was ripe for it." Louise wiped at the clean table. "I know you think I'm hard. But Beryn is missing some ability to engage fully in life. I've seen but one expression on his face for most of his life—bewilderment."

Grace squatted herself in front of Mary and tilted her head until it was even and straight, feeling along the cords of her neck. For an instant it seemed Mary looked at her. Really looked at her. The glaze dropped from off her eyes and what came shining through was similar to the startled look a deep dreamer gives off once waking.

"Mary? Mary, you listenin' to me? You know where you're at?" Mary blinked twice and Grace noticed how near to red the whites of her eyes were. She put her ear to the woman's chest and took her wrist to count off a pulse. "She's sick, Louise." Grace turned around to the woman. "She's feverish and her chest sounds rolly as an ocean. You better call us an ambulance quick. And call Mr. Lieberstein back and tell him, too. Tell him I think we got to get her somewhere."

"Dear me, Grace, I've got the funeral man coming in half an hour, I can't possibly—"

"Well, if you don't get yourself up and on that phone right this minute we gonna have two funerals is what I'm saying! She's sittin' here drowning while you sit and dawdle on why or why not Mr. Beryn's bewildered about the puzzle of life—" Grace sat again and held Mary's cold hand in her warm one and rubbed it. "There, there . . . be a sweet baby. You be still and sweet now . . . Grace is here—" Turning, still seeing Louise in a sitting position around the table, she hissed, "Go on now—call. Get up and call!"

The ambulance showed up first, followed immediately by the hearse, and to the neighbors who had lined the street, made curious by the carnival of formal-looking cars, it must have seemed like a failure in diagnosis. As if someone who was initially thought sick was actually dead or was expected to be dead in a short amount of time. Joe Lieberstein pulled up right after in his large black Imperial and jumped out and ran inside. With the help of two attendants he got Mary settled into the back of the ambulance station wagon and it pulled off silent, but with flashing lights.

"I'm following in my car, Grace. Would you like to come?" he turned to ask, but she had already climbed in the front seat of the Imperial. With one foot in the door he yelled at Louise. "Any word from Joleb I want to know right away! You can reach me down at Methodist Hospital—"

"I will, Joe. They're dragging the river right now, but there's still no sign."

Grace was glad to see him flinch at Louise's words. So glad she wanted to grovel at his feet and kiss his strange Jewish hand.

"Just unlucky Burris, so far." Louise nodded her head at the waiting hearse. Inside the back she could see the gray hulk of the coffin holding her nephew.

Front door opened wide, Louise stood waiting inside its entrance, ready to guide the men into her parlor. She studied her long camelback sofa in a raised rose brocade and the Steinway upright that still needed dusting and mentally adjusted her schedule to accommodate.

Three Negroes maneuvered the casket, which was riding on a metal cart, up onto the porch and into the hall. Once there, they stepped aside to make room for the mortician, a small, stocky man, fresh from Jackson. He rubbed a finger across the tiny mustache he imagined gave him a bearing similar to a Parisian and surveyed the situation. Looked the parlor inside out. Ran his eyes to the crown molding and tiger oak piano. Silent beside his temporary transport cart bearing Burris but for fingers shaped like cigar minnows drumming on the casket.

"I don't think the piano bench will hold," he said in a dry voice, looking round the room.

"Excuse me?"

"I said, I don't think the piano bench will hold." He nodded in the direction of the padded mahogany bench in front of her piano and then looked down at a small notepad for confirmation. "Mr. Green voted 'nay' and I don't see anything else in here that'll do the trick."

"What did my brother vote 'nay' to, exactly?" Louise put on her glasses as if to steady herself for the answer. What a tiny obnoxious man. And that mustache! He must have some perverse, misplaced admiration for Europeans.

"Renting a stand. For twenty-five bucks you get a portable viewing stand and he—Mr. Beryn Green—said no he didn't want it. That he had something else in mind. Something more personal and sentimental that he was planning to construct himself."

She rolled her eyes and shook her head. "You're absolutely right. I don't think the piano bench will hold."

"Not likely—this boy's waterlogged and heavy." He patted the gray steel casket affectionately. "You're talking five hundred pounds, including casket."

"Okay. I quite understand. There's no need to be graphic."

"Yes ma'am, I think there is. I am skilled at seeing ahead of a problem.

That's why I suggested renting the portable stand to Mr. Green." He looked at his notebook again.

"You may be skilled at seeing ahead of a problem, but in this case, you stopped a yard short and extended your suggestion to the wrong person."

"Whom would the right person be?"

"The person with the brain." Simple as that. "Would you like coffee while we discuss our options?" She walked on steady legs toward the kitchen.

"No ma'am. I don't drink coffee."

"Well, you're the first—what type of man refuses coffee? What is your name, by the way?" She looked back at him.

"George Willard out of Jackson, and to answer your question concerning what type of man refuses coffee my answer would be—the type I am." He licked his lips and thought, You are a stately challenge, Ma'am. Followed by, I would eventually like to extend more than a suggestion in your direction, too. But what he said was, "I apologize then. But for twenty-five dollars you would've gotten full steel support on wheels that lock in place and a slide-around pleated screen to hide those wheels while viewers pay their final respects. And a hydraulic lift." He watched the kitchen door swing shut behind her. Looking at his men, he rolled his eyes and mouthed, "women." They stood silent and expressionless wishing for water or tea or something wet to kill the hot.

"My brother had something else in mind?" This as she came out of the kitchen with a cup in her hand.

"That's what he said—"

"Something sentimental? That he intended to construct himself?"

"Yes ma'am. Those were his words—"

"And where is it?"

"That is the crux of it isn't it, ah . . . Mrs., Miss?"

"Miss. Miss Green as I'm sure you can read on the invoice hiding in that little notebook you favor." She sipped her coffee. "Apparently my brother was struck by grief and unable to see this 'sentimental' project through."

"Well, that's a damnable shame, pardon my French, 'cause short of setting the deceased on the floor, I don't see a ready solution." It was already three in the afternoon; the wake was to begin at five. The body was to be picked up by eight. He checked his notebook again, irritated she held back her given name. When he glanced down he noticed her strong ankles and her shoes. Large and expensive. Shiny brown leather. Underneath her skirt he could see the tabs of her garters. He licked his lips again.

"We set the Parden child on the sofa," she said.

"As I recall the Parden child was a newborn," he said, still looking down at his notebook and her shoes. I bet she's easily a ten and a half. Possibly eleven. Wide width, too.

"Yes, that's correct."

"Thirty pounds, tops. I'm no genius, but I don't think a waterlogged eighteen-year-old is going to weigh the same as a newborn." He looked at her and smiled and put his notebook in his pocket.

She shot him a glare that was usually sufficient in making bigger men or harder women back down, a look he served right back in equal measure, which instantly made him seem interesting in her eyes even though he was unusually short for a man. Five seven up on his toes. His memory is a sharp one, though. The Parden baby *had* been a newborn, living only four hours, born as he was minus the major portion of his brain. In Louise Green's book, George Willard out of Jackson immediately moved up three more notches.

Blushing, she brushed her hands together as if knocking off flour dust from a recent, disappointing bout of baking. "Sir, I'm afraid we have no choice here but to try the sofa."

"You're sure of this, are you?" This is a fine woman—high firm breasts, a strong neck and plump upper arms—and he regretted having set her at odds with him earlier. Coupled with regret were his dual specula-tions on how a woman of such strong features had remained single for the majority of her childbearing years (she'd never met the proper man, was his conviction), and how such a woman would look laid out as a brochure model in the top of the line premium casket, the Heavenly Supreme (heav-enly, was his estimation). "You're absolutely positive?" he asked.

"Yes sir, I am. Burris will fill the sofa, I'm sure. But I'll place chairs at his head and feet, to secure the coffin. I have overweight relatives with bad feet who will consider it a privilege to do nothing but sit and perch and

weep the occasional tear." She looked around him to the hallway, dismissing him until later. "I believe your hired help is waiting on the porch. Call
them in, please, and let's be done with this." She clapped her hands together three times.

Admiring the woman more and more by the minute, determined not
to wait on mercurial death to initiate their next encounter, he called out,
You Boys! to his waiting Negroes, and together the four of them placed
the gray coffin on the camelback sofa. It was such a tight squeeze it bowed
out the ends. A flaw he considered more blessing than curse, for it served
up a reminder of the possibility of other tight squeezes.

Louise Green stood in back of the room and studied the placement,
realized it would be a lower than usual viewing and more likely than not,
the boy would spill at some point during the evening. I'll let Beryn scoop
up the spilled beans, she thought, not concerned in the least that her sen-
timents were less than charitable or Christian or even familial. "I may be
blood kin but I'll not carry his weight and smell into my dreams. Not in
this lifetime, I won't," she said to no one in particular. The mortician standing by the door simply smiled and judged her statement admirable.

Mary Amelia Green drowned at four-fifteen that afternoon. Roughly forty-
eight hours after her son met the face of God head on and found himself
thrown into the river Leaf, his ear jerked by a hook. "It's a wonder she made
it to this point," the doctor said while he scribbled notes on his pad and
slapped it shut, done with her. Mary had died at about the same point in time
that her sister-in-law was saying good-bye to the mustached mortician who
had placed her deceased firstborn son on a camelback sofa.

The man who loved her was by her side when she passed on, as well as
the woman who may have felt something less stringent than love but had
the hands that had proved reliable at the true business behind the word for
close to sixteen years. The two of them stood outside in the sterile hall of
the emergency room after all was said and done. Joseph Lieberstein buried
his head in an antiseptic corner and cried. The Negro woman stood tall
and tearless while she clutched the bag holding Mary's belongings to her
stomach, wondering over Joleb.

19
THINGS VERTICAL

There was a mediocre skirmish between the brother and sister when Beryn arrived and found his son's coffin wedged onto her couch. Actually the skirmish was little more than a pull at her arm delivered in an almost loud tone of voice. Mediocre because the man lacked the energy and wit to fight or grieve or love effectively.

"You cheap old maid—I can't believe you held back twenty-five bucks! My son is resting on your sofa for God's sake!" He yelled this (halfheartedly) while standing by the hall tree within clear earshot of the first mourners to arrive. All men. They stood out on the porch, turning their hats in their hands like steering wheels.

"That's because a man bereft of brain made the arrangements," Louise said, irritated. "The mortician made it clear to me that you said you were planning something sentimental, and since nothing sentimental showed up before Burris, I made do the best I could. Now get hold of yourself. There's news I need to share. Please wait for me in the back hall—" And with that she breezed by him and extended her hand in welcome to the mourners waiting on the porch. Ushering them in, she saw cars beginning to line up on her side of the street, bumper to bumper, casserole laden.

Turning to Beryn, seeing him waiting with spindly arms just like she'd ordered in that darkish hall, she softened. "Come with me, please," and she led him gently into her bedroom. She could tell by the feel of his suit that it was stiff-new and she studied him front and back looking for tags.

Her room had a smell to it of old. Wrinkling his nose he glanced over her bed and studied her racks. Display shelves with scrolled wrought-iron brackets had been mounted above her brass bed by different crews of handymen, each working no more than a day before throwing up their hands and quitting. The shelves cost her more in installation than Beryn made in a month of hard work at the power plant and held the frivolous duty of showcasing old instruments mounted on brass holders. Silver cornets. Gold-plated trumpets. Black oboes. One of only four playable Civil War–era flutes known to exist was on the second one up, its fat black body and ivory mouthpiece lit up by an overhead display lamp inset into the crown molding.

"I tell you what, you wasted a truckload of money there." He nodded to the wall. "I could've built you something twice as good at one-tenth the cost, should you have called me to do it."

"I know, Beryn. Something sentimental, I'm sure." She rubbed at her eyes. Where to begin?

He sniffed and nodded, his head bobbing on top his long neck, comical.

He really can't help who he is, she realized while fingering her necklace. "Beryn, maybe you should sit down for this—"

"Where?" All she had was a high bed and a dresser and he couldn't see himself perched on either. "You need a recliner in here, Louise, or something usable. The room's big enough for it." He sniffed. "I don't see how you sleep with the smell of old wax. Ma and Dad never had anything stinky over their bed."

"It smells wonderful to me. I drift off at night imagining what music was played last out of each one. What that last note might have been. I have a whole list, you know."

"You're weird as a two-headed turtle, Louise," he snorted. "It's no wonder to me you were never a bride and wound up all old and cranky."

"And you're stupid, Beryn—your wife is dead."

His wails, overly loud she thought, but who was she to say at that tired point, filled the hallway and spilled out onto the front yard, drifted clear down the street. She felt like kicking herself for losing her temper and blurting out the news. "Nooo! God nooo!" Up and out like the wail of a train nearing a crossing. The mourners, most of whom seemed to appreciate Louise's ingenuity on stuffing her nephew into the sofa, ran back and filled the bedroom. Crowded through the doorway. Elbowed their way up the hall for a look.

"Is it true, Louise?" he cried.

"Yes, Beryn, it's true. We tried to find you, but couldn't."

"Was Grace with her?"

"Yes. She was there. Mary wasn't alone."

"Where is she? I want to see her—"

"She's down at Braswell's. That's day after tomorrow, Beryn. Tonight it's Burris. Come on now. Sit up and compose yourself."

"Noooo! Nooo—" It began again and then stopped abruptly, as if he'd run headfirst into a wall. "Hard luck comes in bushel baskets, Louise!" He looked around the room at the spectators. "Thousands of bushel baskets! God's hard luck orchard is full of bitter, bitter fruit!" Several watching nodded their heads and appeared ready to cry.

"There, there Beryn," she said. Dear God, he's gone to poet now. A bad one, too.

He had climbed center of her bed and pulled the covers over his head and was rocking side to side, causing the brass head frame to bump the wall. Louise turned to the first two she saw standing in her room. "Tom? You and Marge herd up the crowd please and spread the news. Explain the situation here. We'll be out after Beryn pulls his parts together." She patted what was either back or bony ass. Covered as he was she couldn't be sure.

"No! NOOOO!" he screamed from under the covers in a high screech like that of a shot-down owl, and the room cleared in three seconds flat.

"Now, now Beryn—"

"You got your teaching, Louise. You got your work at school. You got something! I got nothing! No family. No son. Nothing at all!"

"Why, you have the power company, Beryn—you have your work. Just imagine where we'd all be without electricity . . ." She patted the hump that was her brother and watched her wall, especially the heritage piece at center that had served its time in the Civil War. She'd paid close to a thousand dollars for it at an auction up in Memphis.

Jackson watched the crowd in the parlor and thought, Best thing that could happen here would be for Burris to spill and roll across the rug and clear this room so folks could breathe.

"You think he'll spill?" He reached for Valuable's hand.

"Lord, I hope not. Have you seen him?"

"Just from here and that's bad enough. Shit, I'm glad Joleb's not here. This would send him over the edge for good." He squeezed her hand.

"You've got to promise me something—"

"What's that?"

"Promise me that if something happens, you won't let people gawk at me."

Jackson looked at her, saw how serious she was. "I promise."

"I'd do the same for you, you know. I wouldn't let people stare if you were messed up like that."

"I know you wouldn't." He saw his mother watching him from across the room and let go of Valuable's hand.

"Enid show up yet?"

"Not yet. Reilly's given up I think. He packed a bag this morning and left a note on the table for me to call if she comes back around."

"What'd Neva and Bea say about it?"

"They don't know—"

"You can't stay there alone, Val. It ain't proper."

"Well, I don't have a big choice in things now, do I?" Sally Wills, who had grown large boobs over the summer, stood across the room watching Jackson, a smarmy little smile on her face. Valuable glanced down at her own meager chest and folded up her arms for cover.

Viewers walked by in a squat to get a closer look at his pierced ear, which was swollen and jerked to twice its size. Valuable watched the procession for an hour, thinking the viewers looked funny, like they were looking for a pee spot in tall grass. Jackson's mother was there, dressed in a dark blue dress with pearl buttons up the front. His father was absent, traveling again at a trade show. Lucy McLain looked lost and uncomfortable and Valuable smiled at her, but the woman looked away.

Valuable felt his arm around her again. "You know, there's something intimidating about the shape and design of a coffin," she said.

"Hmmm." Sally Wills had winked at him big as you please. He moved closer to Val; leaned forward and smelled her good-smelling hair.

"Seems to me, if this wake thing is for the comfort of the family, coffin makers would come up with a way to make it better. Build one shaped like a bed or an easy chair. Maybe place the dead on their side with a book over their stomach, like they got caught dozing while reading something dull."

"You think?" His mother was frowning in his direction and he stared back, leaving his arm where it felt best this time.

"Yeah, if they couldn't build one shaped like a bed, then a platform like a pallet or something. Drape the person while they're on their side, maybe put the dead's hand up under their head like they're napping—it's the flat on the back look that makes them look so dead."

"They *are* dead, Val."

"I know that, but when they're flat on their back it seems so uncomfortable and final."

"Come on, let's get out of here—we've seen enough." Jackson pressed his hand in the small of her back.

Careful not to hold hands around so many spectators, Valuable left first, walking through the room while people stared. Sally Wills and her circle of friends snickered and put their heads together when she approached. "Hey Jackson—" she heard three voices behind her say. She couldn't hear if he said "hey" back or not and she was afraid to turn around to see. Clutching her elbows, careful to keep her arms folded across her slow-growing breasts, she headed to the porch and finally out to the sidewalk where there was clean air to breathe.

"Hey—you goin' to a fire, or what?" Jackson caught up to her.

She smelled aftershave and looked at him. Those crinkle smile lines around his eyes like his mother's. That nick on his chin from a fresh shave.

"No, I just thought you might want to stick around and talk to those girls. Thought you might need some time to yourself, away from me and everything."

"Why in the world would I want to do that? What's going on here? You act like I've done something to make you think that, and I haven't."

"I just feel strange, is all." Valuable shrugged her shoulders.

"Hey—are you jealous?" He bent down. Tried to find her face.

"No. Just giving you room to roam. In case you wanted to."

"Well, I don't, so stop acting this way."

"People were staring, Jackson—"

"So? You're beautiful. That's why they're staring. You're the prettiest person here, that's why they were looking—"

"No it's not and you know it." Looking round at the trees blowing in the hot wind and the neat street with its sidewalks and clean gutters and all the cars lined up in perfect order, she felt ages beyond the place. As if she'd been transplanted to a place where order was as over-the-hill as make-out games and seating arrangements in homeroom.

"Val? What's with you?"

"I don't really know. It's just—" She ducked her head and looked at her shoes.

"Jackson! Jackson, come here a moment, please!" He saw his mother standing on the porch, hands on her blue serge hips.

He put a hand on her arm. "Hang on. Don't you disappear, I'll be right back."

Piano music was coming from out of the Green house. A poorly executed version of "There Is a Fountain Filled with Blood," played by someone unfamiliar with sharps and necessary flats. Even with the discord, people inside were attempting to sing. Valuable watched Lucy McLain put her hand on Jackson's arm, the same way he'd just done with her—hooking four fingers near the bend of the elbow—while she stood up on her toes to place her mouth to his ear. Valuable could see Jackson's face from where she was standing, those smile lines around his eyes highlighted by the yellow light of the porch, and she realized he had learned a new trick after all—how to keep anybody from seeing what was really going on there. His expression stayed the same. His mouth opening once or twice while he looked across the yard at her and winked. Valuable read the muscle running from jaw to ear and knew that for some strange reason he was clenching down his teeth.

"It's not good to get so exclusive with one person. You have friends back inside that you're neglecting—you've known the Greens for years. It's rude to run out so early after everything they've been through." She was practically up on her toes. He'd grown a foot over the summer and by sight and smell and the nick in his chin, she knew he'd begun to shave on a regular basis.

"So?" He could see she had tiny lines coming out from her eyes. Her hair steady-going gray at the temple like most of her friends. He breathed in Oil of Olay mixed with Jergens for those wrinkled hands she was wearing and thought, She's turned old on me. Just like Gran.

"I think you're old enough to develop some new friendships. To be friends all the way around. You and Val have been almost snobbish when it comes to others—"

"So?" Valuable was standing under the light waiting, looking small and like a child. Jackson looked at his mother and weighed their differences. Wondered if she'd ever looked so helpless while swatting July flies underneath a vapor light.

"Things happen when a boy and girl your age spend too much time together. Too much close physical contact without the benefit of others can lead places. Lead a boy to do things that he wouldn't do otherwise—"

"Like what? What're you talking about?" She's yet to look me in the eyes, he realized. All she's done is study my mouth and face and shoulders and feet.

"I'm not stupid, Jackson. I was young once. I know what's going on here—"

"What's going on here?"

Lucy McLain looked across the yard at Valuable standing in the beam of a streetlight. "You're headed into the eleventh grade. You've got your whole life ahead of you—the last thing in the world you need right now is to get that girl pregnant—"

"You're crazy!" He snorted and stuck his hands deep in his pockets, not sure over the bigger insult: the speculation of the act, or the way she'd called her "that girl."

"Don't you dare talk to me this way. I'm your mother—"

"I know that, but that don't mean you're not losin' your mind—"

"You watch it. You're not as big as you think you are."

"You know what I think, Ma? I think you don't want me to have anything to do with her because her mother's a whore and you think it's catchin'. That she's gonna turn out to be like Enid or something."

The whole while they'd been talking, they had never raised their voices. People milled around like tourists. Moved in and out to blow smoke rings. Return empty dessert bowls to their cars. Talk about the weather. Set down in the middle of them, Jackson and his mother stood like statues, barely breathing, their faces drawn and hard, as readable as granite.

"We'll discuss this later at home," she said in a low voice. "I don't want to involve your father in it, but I will if I have to."

He couldn't believe it! Here she was using the same man who'd slapped her hard in the face a month back, as a threat. "You're the one who brought this up. Who's already got me getting her pregnant. Jesus, it seems you'd trust me more than that!" His father loved Valuable. He'd be on his side if it came to it. Behind her head Jackson saw an unbelievable sight—lightning jagged in the western sky over Hattiesburg.

She leaned back and looked at him. Searched for some sign that he was lying, but all she saw were the same blue-gray eyes she'd been watching for sixteen years. She'd never been able to tell when John Henry lied, either. One more way they were similar other than the size of their feet and the same smelly brand of aftershave.

"Like I said, we'll talk later," she said.

"No, I don't think we will. Not about this. Not about her." Jackson turned around, putting his back to Valuable for the first time, and spoke low. "You never have liked her. Never. Not once in all these years can I remember you saying one good thing about her. In your book, she's been second-class since you met her and it's not fair. Not fair at all."

"There are elements here you don't understand—"

"What elements?"

"Just elements." She paused and took a different tack. "Jackson, I feel sorry for her. She's been on her own for so long, I don't think she's had a chance to make other friends like most girls her age. Do other things girls should be out doing."

"Like what?"

"Like going to parties and such. Or shopping. Or church. Does she have one female friend? Even one?"

He thought about Judy and then Neva and Bea and finally Enid and realized the truth of it. He stared back, silent. "I'm her friend, Ma. It'll have to be enough. I'm going now. I'll be home late, so don't wait up."

"Jackson——" She pulled at his arm, hissed through a clenched jaw, "You've already done it, haven't you? You wouldn't be this defensive of her if you hadn't. I remember just last month when you said you never wanted to see her again as long as you lived. But something's changed now. That's it, isn't it?"

His mother's question put a new hateful light to it. Tried to shame it. End it. Destroy any proof of it, and he felt his hands come out of his pockets and turn to fists by his side.

"No, I haven't done a thing. She's my best friend, is all. You're the one who's turning this into something dirty." That much was true.

"I think you're lying to me."

"Well, I'm sorry you feel that way, because I'm not lying about a thing." He walked off the porch, thankful lying to his mother had been such an easy thing to do. When he got to the center of yard, it was empty. Looking around in all directions he finally saw her four houses down, headed to the highway. Alone. Running to catch up, feeling like he was in a constant state of chasing a shadow, he felt a drop of rain hit him square on the back of the neck. The weight of it so heavy it felt like a rock.

Louise stood between kitchen and parlor and watched the crowd. Thinning finally, thank the good Lord. Thank the good Lord Beryn's grief was down to a bare idle, too. Better than before, when it roared and ranged the living room, loud as a loose muffler. The door to the kitchen swung open and she saw him holding court around the kitchen table. The room was full of crow-like women she barely knew (thank God). Their hair done up high and Pentecostal. They hovered in a half circle around his back and clucked regular as fast-egging chickens. Her brother had dropped the poetry, stopped picking fruit out of God's bitter orchard, and was traveling a new path. One powered by less imagination since it involved the simple pronouncement of all his many failures. He was negligent in changing the oil in his automobile on a regular basis. He was an inconsistent husband and an absentminded father. He threw out the salt pork Grace was saving to season dry limas three times in a row. He made these declarations all the while running a hand through his too-long hair, one bony elbow placed dramatically on the table. A plump, large-haired woman Louise thought might be related to the Seventh-Day Adventist across the street kept disagreeing with his accusations and tried to encourage him with a cup of coffee and a tuna fish sandwich shaped like a star.

The air conditioner had done its work Louise could see. The curtains flanking it were damp along their edges and would need dry cleaning come tomorrow or soon after. Once all the dead were buried. Once her brother was shuttled off to his own place four blocks over. Once they had some clue about poor Joleb. Louise watched Beryn pump a departing woman's hand like there was no tomorrow. His hand clutched her elbow like a coupling to a pipe. This is it, she thought. This is my life. Where I've found myself, finally. Guard of the dead and protector of a moron. For the first time since all the news of death, Louise felt tight of throat and heavy behind the eyes and tired enough to drop. She looked over at her nephew, the bleached tip of his nose showing above the gray metal sides like a corner piece of molded cheese.

Hours back when Burris had first been delivered, short minutes before the mortician had rolled his empty cart to the hearse and prepared to leave, Louise had studied her nephew's dead body, waiting for something to break loose inside and let out the grief she knew was an obligation. But all she'd managed to sense was that she was looking down on an incomplete exam. An essay in the impractical. An assignment poorly researched and absent of theory. Walking to the air conditioner in the window, she had set it to high, then headed toward her polishing rags, dry eyed and tired. She had checked the hall tree for dust. Opened drawers and counted silver. Realized by her best estimation that she'd swing way short in servings. She had pulled out the linen, cleaned up the coffee pot. Gone on, finally, to all those other things that needed tending. On her way through the hall to freshen up, she noticed the traffic areas of the oak floors needed refinishing. Worn down to raw wood in places, it made her sad to look at it. But that had been all she'd felt while her nephew chilled in the parlor. Distressed over floors and insufficient silver.

I am as dry a lake as Beryn, she thought, still studying her nephew's nose. Thunder sounded then. The boom of it so long a stranger, it seemed like something out of Hollywood. Outside the window she saw the flash of lightning and counting down to five, she heard the thunder again. Closer this time. So near it rattled the glass in all the windows and stirred up excited talk in the kitchen.

At least the sky will cry, Louise thought, still dry-eyed and tall. A fitting tribute to all the dead. Burris. Mary. Joleb in all probability. Even Beryn, a man more dead than alive. At least in spirit and all those other essential corners that make one human and deserving of human love. And she did love him. Had always loved him. But her love was tall and vertical. Stretching high without much reaching out to it, so it came off her cold and like something other than love. But it was love. Louise was almost sure of it.

Shutting the door to the parlor and heading to the phone to call the mortician, she saw the deer heads mounted high up and dismissed them. Their glass eyes just marble, now. No threat at all. She remembered Beryn waiting underneath them, his hands helpless by his side. Someone coming in had shut the door behind her and killed the light. Lost in the shadows, for an instant he had seemed the person from the softer time. The time when they were young and used to run squealing under the stuffed heads that always seemed to watch them from the wall. Beryn would hold her hand while they ran, pulling her along to the kitchen, shouting, "Don't you look up now! Don't you look up!" The memory was a sharp one and for that instant in the hall, he had seemed young again. Seven or maybe eight. No more than nine. Then the door opened and let in more light and she'd seen him as a man, his limbs too long for his cuffs, not afraid anymore, either. Just pitiful, now. His growing up a bitter disappointing fruit, after all. Her love too high and vertical to overlook it.

20
PROPER PUNISHMENT

JOLEB WAS KING OF A DEAD WORLD and it suited him. He sat cross-legged on the ledge and squinted his eyes trying to see. He noticed two things: the light through the trees left tiny spots the size of hands all over the floor of the woods, and the greens came in two colors—a bright shade of lime and a darker, mossy color similar to broccoli. That was it. That was all he saw and he only saw this within twenty feet of his ledge. He squinted again, trying for an in-between green, something similar to lettuce, but couldn't find it. The handprints were nice, though. The way they turned the ground all freckled, like the coating on a new deer or maybe a baby leopard. That was the extent of his vision—handprints on the ground and two shades of green. His glasses had fallen off when Burris shoved him off the trestle and at best, his immediate world seemed foggy and detached and harmless. As if he'd been caught up and wrapped in a gauzy curtain and then set down someplace still wholly wrapped. Brown tree shapes waved in the breeze at his sides. The pale sun was overhead and seen only occasionally through the thick top of a tree. Just a noncolor winking light that blinked through the day, in and out from above waving branches.

Everything else was brown or brownish related. Brown night. Brown dirt. Brown leaves. Brown everything. Even the sounds had a feel of brown to them. Coming as they did mostly at night when every call and hoot and chirp blended into one muddy noise he couldn't pick apart. It was the same during the day because like it or not, his vision was related to his hearing somehow and everything he heard sounded more chorus than solo. Joleb grew tired of wishing for an aria and settled for brown noise that helped him nap. He nodded once, twice, his chin touching down on his beat-up chest.

Joleb! You crazy little shit! What the hell are you doin' here?

He flinched like he'd been shot in the back and shook his head hard. Made it go away.

The sun sure felt good, though. Good and hot. He leaned back his head and took a deep breath. Breathed in the smell of mold and dried-up leaves and dust. All those late summer smells that signal the end of something and the beginning of something else. His hearing was back fully and he heard the call of what he thought must be a mockingbird. Its wide range of songs executed and thrown out like one boastful and drunk on talent and not ashamed to show it.

He held the pocketknife clutched in his hand. A good one, too. His brother's. Somehow it had flown out of Burris's pocket and struck the back of Joleb's head while he rolled down the hill like a bowling ball. Put a king-sized knot there, too. The knife had edgework cut from ivory and he could feel that Burris had his name carved into it. Burris Nathanial Green. Joleb traced one jagged fingernail along the G and then he opened the knife up and shut it, again. Opened it. Shut it. Opened it. Shut it. The point cutting into his palm until blood ran down and soaked his one remaining sleeve.

I can't believe you followed me! You little sneak—what're you doing?

Leave me alone, Burris. This is my business, not yours.

The hell it is! Get up off the tracks! Get up from there this fuckin minute or I'm gonna kill your scrawny ass!

Joleb shook it away again and crawled back inside his cave on his knees. The rock scraped him, dug at his skin, and it felt satisfactory, like good and proper punishment. Leaning against the back wall he took a finger and dipped it into his running blood and drew a shape like that of a cow on the side wall where it curved. No, a bull. He drew horns and made it into a bull and sat back, looking at his work. A white frost of some sort lined the cave, made the bull look like it was aging and gray and too old to give a full-steam fuck to a cow, but it was still a bull. He picked up more blood and put in an eye and one nostril and the slash of mouth. The smell of his blood was metal-like and stinky and he stuck his hand between his bare legs and pressed in, feeling sweat sting his palm. This, too, felt like proper punishment. The white frost or mold made his nose itch and pour snot like a faucet. But it was warm inside the cave and this would help when winter came and true frost covered the ground and squirrels dropped frozen from the trees, dead of hunger. Tired. He sure was tired, though.

He'd lost his pants when he'd rolled down the hill. In such a hurry to catch up with Burris he'd taken off that night without his belt. Already thin from summer heat and lack of appetite, he'd felt his jeans snag on something—tree limb, root, finger of God—and turn inside out down his legs, stealing his sneakers, leaving him barelegged and barefooted in his shorts.

*Give me your hand! Give me your hand, goddammit! Give it to me now or we're both dead*GIVEITTOME—

He blinked hard and it went away again.

A crunching sound was to the right and he pulled his legs up from where they dangled. It usually meant a squirrel or armadillo. Either one was okay because one ate nuts, the other slugs. Raccoons were mean though and liked to steal. With claws that scratched and tiny teeth that felt like razors, they had a way about them that was bad-ass mean. Joleb put his hand on his pile of dark blue berries. It was all he'd managed to find to eat besides pine nuts that tasted bitter and one or two fat slugs that were pale green, shot through with a blue he figured for intestines. Where summer heat had stolen his appetite to the point all food made him want to puke, the business of being a murderer twice had made him hungry enough to eat the ass end out of a horse.

His ankle felt somewhat better. It was still swollen and blue in places but was moving steady to a green that was closer to yellow. He'd torn one sleeve off his shirt and wrapped it around his heel and back up a bit, and by putting his weight down carefully, he could take a few steps now. Three of his toenails had been torn off and for the life of him he couldn't remember it happening. *I should, too,* he thought. *I should remember that because it's one more form of proper punishment. But damn if it ain't gone from me as surely as my pants and shoes.*

He'd run miles that night in bare feet on rough pavement. First he'd climbed the incline and pulled his pants loose. Not thinking worth a shit he'd tossed them down into the Leaf River instead of putting them on. Standing there in his underwear he watched them float for a few minutes before they soaked and disappeared from view.

I want to see God, too, Burris! Leave me alone!

This ain't a game, Joleb! Feel it? Feel what's headed over? Now move! Give me your hands!

What's the matter with you? What's the matter with you? Are you fuckin crazy!

Yes! Yes, I'm crazy, now leave me alone!

Come on—come on down from here!

No! I ain't leavin!

Joleb! JOLEB!

The lights then. Huge, hard lights as big as the world and a horn that blew out his ears until all was quiet as a grave. His back was to it and he felt Burris dig in, breaking his finger while prying him loose. Kicking him in the back of the knees to free up his legs. Then he felt his brother's arms under him and that sudden feeling of the bottom dropping clean away. Joleb's mouth opened wide in a scream he couldn't hear. Everything around him was light and vibration that rattled his teeth and tongue and the insides of his lungs.

He hit hard earth then and rolled. Legs folded up under him like a wooden puppet's. Knees busting into his chin. Night sky and dirt turning, tumbling all around him, changing places. The moon up one minute. Gone the next. Up one minute. Gone the next. The taste of dirt and blood and grass in his mouth. The smell up his nose. But no sound. Landing on his back, he felt down his legs surprised they were still attached to his body while overhead a bird soared through the brilliant light. No. Not a bird. Burris! Burris doing a perfect jackknife off the center of the trestle! Beautiful! Joleb raised up on an elbow and watched, amazed. *He'll put his fingers to his toes and then he'll fold out again, just like Johnny*

Weissmuller! And he's lit up like he's performing in a spotlight, too. A spotlight as bright as the sun. Hands moving to toes. He was falling now and Joleb could see. No, wait—he was backwards. Backwards! The backs of his hands were touching his heels. By God, the back of his head was touching his ass! Backwards! That ain't right, Burris. You'll lose points that way. You gotta go to the front just like they taught us at Jaycee pool. Can't go backwards at the waist like that. Can't touch your hands to your heels, you fool! How'd you do that anyhow? How'd you do that, Burris?

Still on an elbow he watched him hit the water, soundlessly. Good points there, Burris, on entry. Good and quiet. Ripples circled and ran at him like tired rings while he crawled to the edge of the river Leaf.

Burris? He still couldn't hear a thing. Not even the beat of his heart. Not even the sound of his voice, *Burris? You're done now—let's go home, okay?*

Working his way to his feet, he watched the water. The train was a long one, the shape of its cars barely visible in the thick fog. Coal dust rained down on his head and Joleb held up a hand and watched it turn dark and gray. The surface of the water was still as a pond. Silvery and flat. Solid looking. Like all it would take to walk on it was faith and a good pair of shoes.

Houdini stayed under a while—but he almost died. You know that. Now stop this. Come on up— A glimmer of something then by his feet and he bent and picked up Burris's pocketknife and he knew that somehow Burris had made it out of the water and was right that minute racing home to tell on him. Tell how foolish he'd been out on the trestle. How he'd almost gotten them both killed. Seeing his pants as proof up on the hill, once the train went over, he climbed up and tossed them down. *Now let's see you try to prove it, Burris. Let's just see you try to prove I was ever up here!*

He ran then. Up the road and away from the lights. Ran harder than he'd ever run in his life. Running from the lights that were breathing down his neck, running from every single thing he'd ever known. He turned in on a path that felt right somehow and lost his balance and rolled down a hill, turning his foot. Landing finally at the base of a giant pine tree that stretched so tall it had to reach to God, Joleb glanced over and saw what looked to be a bear hunched down and sleeping, its slumped head resting on its paws. I'm done with things, Russ. Done with things, he said or thought he said, he wasn't exactly sure. Either way, it didn't really matter, seeing how he'd decided to crawl over and offer himself for supper. I'm done with this business of sin. Russ was there, too. Standing to the left of the tree named God, wearing a long black cloak and a Brooklyn Dodgers cap on top his head.

"I'm concerned with this preoccupation concerning sin, Joleb," he had said while he patted the tree and looked up, as if checking God's nose for trash.

"Well, that's just too fucking bad, 'cause I'm done with it, Russ. I'm this bear's supper and there ain't no way you're gonna pry my hands loose from this one."

Joleb had crawled over then and into the mouth of the sleeping bear and fallen sound asleep. He woke up the next morning stiff and bloody and with an ankle the size of a cantaloupe. He wasn't in the bear's stomach though. But inside a cave. A cave covered with frost beside a tree that stretched to heaven.

Two nights had passed and things were getting worse instead of better. At best he could figure, he'd gone one and a half to two days without water but it felt like a year. His breath was foul and dead smelling and he felt his brain had shriveled down steadily inside his skull while his tongue had swelled up to three times its normal size. He'd bitten through it when his knees shot up into his chin, and even without the burden of speech, it felt worrisome and heavy, as though all it would take to break off its end was a hard and hurried breath. He had come deep enough into his senses to realize where he was. Who it was who lived down from him by barely a hundred yards. What it was that flowed wet right past her place.

Water will help me heal, he reasoned. Lots and lots of water. The berries had given him the running shits and his stomach was so sore and knotted up he had spent a whole span of daylight trying to straighten out to a reclining position. I'll wait 'til night. Wait 'til she's sleeping, then I'll slip down and drink at the creek. Maybe soak my foot, too. He had it stretched out in the sun, hoping the heat would take down the swelling that had grown worse, not better, even though the color was closer to normal, except around his toes.

It took him most of the night to make it to the clearing. Once or twice he caught a glimpse of her fire out his side vision but kept pulling forward on his belly. Water first. I want water first. He smelled the rot and wet all wrapped up to a smell like that of spice. Her spice. That clarinet case, again. There's the water, Joleb. Go get it. Three more pulls and you're there—he felt hands then. Hands grappling along his back like harpoons, rolling him over like a dead seal. Hands that were going to keep him from the water that he needed to live. No! Nooooo! he tried to say, and then he saw her face, those sledgehammer cheekbones protruding like knives, those eyes, deep-set, inky black.

"Shhhh—be still, boy. Hush up now and don't you move—"

He rested then and gave himself up to die. The moon clear and large and harvest looking. Like the one that liked to shine around Halloween when the pumpkins are lit and set on porches to shrivel up just like his brain. Harvest Moon. Shine On. Joleb thought he felt rain then, or tears from the moon. Wet fell on his face and he tasted the creek. The way it would taste when water would get up his nose and wash down his throat.

"Here—drink this. Drink it down." She held a cup to his mouth. "There, there. You be still now and don't move. Lord God Almighty, what a mess!"

He heard her running through the sand. Watched her scoop down into her pot and stir it with her finger, dip something in that shined. And then she was heading back, sprinting forward, a runner. Lord, all she needs is a torch. Joleb looked up at the moon thinking if he were about to die, about to be brained in the head with one of her painted-up glowing rocks, he wanted something nice to look at while it happened.

"You got folks scared half out their minds, and some of these folks ain't got much to work with neither, from what I hear!" She spread a blanket by his side and lifted him over and wrapped him up like a mummy. "Running off like you a convick or some type of criminal! You ain't got nothin' to run from—here, drink some more. That's a good boy. Don't gulp now, you'll throw it back up. Don't you talk, neither." Joleb tasted mushrooms and some kind of sweet nut taste, like that of wild exotic honey. Something in the wet made his raw throat numb and cool. When he was done, she put the empty cup center of his wrapped-up stomach and lifted him, carried him over to her fire, grunting the whole while under his weight. When she stood up, she stretched her arms over her head and popped out her back.

"Mama Girl gonna watch over you while I mix up some medicine. Don't you move now 'cause she's watchin'. She's a good rock, too. Won't hurt you a bit. Just lay back and listen to her talk a while and rest."

Busy as a bee, that's how she looks with all this running around. She sang, too, some off-key stupid song about healing ways. Joleb listened past the rush of the water:

> Ain't gonna repent of healin' ways—
> No Lord. No Lord.
> Ain't turning back from this feelin' day—
> La da da da

Just like Grace, he thought. Only this one sings to the tune of "Camptown Races." But she sings it the same way. Sings three lines and blurs the fourth with nonsense. While he leaned up and watched the rock that did have a somewhat maternal look, Joleb thought on words that rhymed with "Lord" and came up empty. The closest to it being "hoard" and "sword," but neither seemed appropriate for a woman who had lifted him up and set him down easy by her fire and seemed determined to save his dark and crusty soul.

21

STICK IN THE MUD

HAVING STALLED FOR AS LONG AS HE DARED, Even ran through the
mud, knocked on Canaan's door and stood waiting. Soaked through
from sprinting across a yard he'd spat across with little or no effort, he stood
shivering underneath a porch roof that leaked a river at nearly every seam.

Even had seen rain like this but once. Up in Memphis during the
spring of his tenth year while he was learning the business of pipes and fit-
tings from a crippled man hired on by the Lutherans as janitor. Squatted
down on a leg six inches shorter than its mate, the man had said, "God ain't
never gonna let it rain such as this ever again." Sixteen people had died the
week previous. Including his six-month-old twin nephews who got swept
out their mother's arms while she hitched a ride in back of a truck to higher ground. "Not ever again," he swore while he worked a wrench and sticky
black grease around a series of bolts that wouldn't give. "God done
promised me by answering a fleece I set before him night before last. Said,
'No, Jacob. You ain't gonna cry no more over a thing like this. This rain's
the last of its type ever to fall south of New York City. I give you my word
on it.' That's what God told me, boy. I'm square on with that one."

"You say," Even had said, glad God had promised such a bold swear, because cold gray rain that fell for days on end made him feel the low ceiling of orphanhood as nothing else he'd ever encountered.

"That's what He said in my fleece. Said no more bad rain. Maybe up north, but not for us folks—"

Seventeen years later, it seemed God had forgotten his word concerning rain. Steady-falling in Petal for three hours now, it cut off visibility as soundly as a tarp draped over a lamp. Objects and their identifying colors—shrub-green, clay-red and goat-shit brown—were washed away along with their defining clues. Everything losing its edges and switching to an anonymous gray that made one feel blind and cut clean off from the world of the living.

As soon as he made it home from work Even had stood out on his own front porch and watched the runoff, realizing the bone-dry land was acting more as slick glass than sponge, knowing Joody would be swept away inside of an hour. Two at the most. Man is no match for a forgetful God, Even thought. Fleece or no. Thankful his nose had seen what was coming when he walked into work that morning and made arrangements for a truck. He had known then, just by watching the turning of the clouds, that by night Petal would feel the breath of something seen only once or twice this century. The clouds warned him, as well as the smell of the morning and the feel of air to his skin: that drop of pressure the tips of his fingers noticed when he went to drink coffee or scratch his nose. Trapped inside the guts of Hercules Powder, Even worried past the point of normal, having yet to see the sky. Just feeling the evidence of things pull at him from points all over his body. Preoccupied, he let a pressure reading go to red while two were under digging in sludge looking for a leak. Cutting it back to a normal range, he thought, Hold now, Even. Hold on now. You'll be no good to her dead as a knob.

But once he'd climbed up the metal rail and seen the sky, he wished he'd gagged himself to the point of vomit, spewed in front of the foreman maybe, and left early on sick leave. The sky was too deep to be called purple, belonging more to the hateful family of black. When he hurried over the bridge that spanned two places, not stopping long enough for one single consideration, the sky was the color of old oil, stretching forever in all directions. Ground held the last of the day's light, took on the color of a ripe squash. Trees fell to the color of the insides of a caterpillar. Made greener by the black of the sky. This is a backward palette here, he thought. All light at bottom and dark at top. Stiff-mouthed and panicked, Even barely noticed the blinking caution light, blown so hard it was horizontal in the wind. All he saw was Bellrose, straight ahead up Highway 42.

"Canaan—you Canaan! You in there?" He pounded on the door again with his fist.

"Coming—hold your horses." The door swung open and Canaan pulled him in. "Get on in here, Even—thy God! Since when we on knock-ing terms?"

"Since you got a goat tied up out back." Even shook water off his arms and out his hair.

"There ain't no goat out there that I can see," Canaan said.

"No?"

"Nope." He was wearing a fresh shirt, newly starched, and Even thought, Well, there may not be a goat, but there's proof in the sleeve crease the starch-loving owner's been over.

"Grace gone?"

Canaan nodded his head but looked calm about it. "For now. Not for long, though. No sir, not for long. I tell you what, you think you at the end of it all and Lord, if it don't start all over again. Just like new. No— better'n new. Like a gift—"

Even prayed he'd go no farther.

Canaan sobered. "She's got grief to deal with. The woman she sits died this afternoon, as well as the son. She prefers to do it alone. Took her goat and went home to pray over things." Canaan scratched his gray head and squinted up his eyes. "Wouldn't even let me see her to the door. Seems she thinks 'cause we fornicated—that's her word, not mine—we broke some heavenly rule concerning man and woman and God pulled out his club and beat her across the head for punishment."

Canaan seemed glib. I think this one overestimates the power of his wood, was what Even thought, impatient with the old man's tale of tail.

"—I said we got hit by a thunderbolt sent from God himself, but she's AME and got some strange—"

"I ain't thick, Canaan—I get the point." Even slapped his legs and watched water splatter to the floor.

The light blinked off and then on again out in the kitchen. "We gonna be losin' our power come the next hour or so."

"That's why I'm here. I got to get Joody away from that creek. Water's risin' and I ain't got long." He stripped off his shirt and walked to the sink, twisting chambray into a knotted tube. He could see "The Reality of the Negro" was still on the floor by the pie safe. There was a fresh starched tablecloth hiding his iron print and the place smelled new, fresh. Fresh as a woman with a goat.

"I figured she'd be over there right now dryin' herself out—" Canaan said.

"Nope. But she's gonna be. Like it or not—"

"Whose truck you got parked out in the yard?" Canaan was looking out his kitchen window.

"Shebbie Sterns. He dropped it by an hour back." Even didn't offer up how the rental had cost him a week's pay and the promise to fix a busted-up mower that hadn't run inside of ten years.

"I didn't know you could drive," Canaan said, surprised.

"I can't. That's why I'm here."

"Thy God, Even, I can't drive that thing! Can't see well enough to, especially at night. Not with these old eyes. If I could see, I still wouldn't know how to." He sat down at the table and leaned on his hand.

"Well, shit!"

"Amen to that." Canaan picked a fresh toothpick out of a glass holder Even had never seen before in his life and picked at his straight teeth.

"I been running it around in my head trying to come up with how to do this thing and I thought for sure you'd learned how to drive at some point in your life."

"You mean, 'cause old Canaan so decrepit and gray, he oughta know how to drive an automobile?"

"Something like that."

Even spread his shirt out over the stove, not hoping for dry, just hoping the pilot light would give off a little bit of warm. Leaning against the kitchen counter, he rubbed his head while rain fell so hard it sounded like nails being driven into tin by a thousand heavy hammers.

"Shebbie know you ain't got a clue on drivin?" Canaan asked.

"Nope. I told him I been drivin' for years. Told him I used to chauffeur up in Memphis—"

"Well, all I got to say is he's one stupid Negro. Can't believe the Bull Gang ain't blown themselves to smithereens with that one on board." Done with his toothpick, he broke it into three tiny pieces and set them on ends like a miniature teepee. "And I guess you too proud to ask him to drive you."

Even turned his shirt to the other side and heard the steam. Watched it rise to waist level like halfhearted incense. The lights blinked off and on again twice and on the third time stayed down, sending the room to black.

"Well, there you go. We in the dark now." Canaan felt his way to the pie safe and got out the candles, cradling the lot of them against his stomach.

Even saw five or six white candles set on Mason jar lids, used recently, too, by the look of the fresh drip along their bottoms. Canaan lit them all. Lined them up from the tallest to the least, like a close-knit family of wax. Even saw an imagined picture then of what they'd been used for, what act had called for the soft light a candle throws, and the picture of those two coursing—on the floor, the table, against a doorframe—filled his head as surely as the smell of his own wet shirt warming filled up the kitchen. Lord God, my woman's drowning and I stand here thinking on this!

"Well, shitfire, I'm goin'. I'll figure it out on my own, I guess. Hell, drivin' can't be too hard a thing if Shebbie can do it." He pulled the keys from his pocket and studied them. Concluding the biggest key turned the damn thing on.

Canaan, still at the table inside his ring of light, casually brushed busted toothpicks into his hand. "Grace knows how to drive," he said. "Drives the Green car all over creation. Had to learn how 'cause the woman's prone to need doctorin' every hour of the day. Said Mr. Green—"

"You think she'd agree to?" Even heard an upsweep in rain noise and swallowed hard against what he was feeling.

"Can't say, with her being so into grief and repentance and such—"

"Well, give me your umbrella 'cause it ain't gonna hurt to ask. You can put some space to your coursing and she can repent later." Even finished buttoning up his shirt, still wet but steamy warm, and headed to the door at a trot. He heard Canaan right on his heels behind him, but it didn't matter. Canaan or no, he was intent on getting to the creek within the hour.

Grace seemed pleased to have been asked. Seeing it as a chance to do something other than stay down on her knees in prayer, was what Even guessed. Either that or she viewed it as a last heroic act she could die doing in order to win back God's favor for what she'd done earlier while candles melted down on Mason lids.

She went to a trunk and pulled out a pair of dungarees and a man's yellow long-sleeved shirt and disappeared into the dark. Once dressed she took on the air of fire truck operator, calling out orders like, "Even—get you a flashlight from under my kitchen cabinet. They's three of them there and be sure and check the battries," and, "You, Canaan, grab that quilt off the top of my bed and fold it up tight and stuff it here." Taking bags that had been used to cover dry cleaning she stuffed in the quilt and a couple of men's shirts and another pair of pants she had jerked from the trunk. Watching her step into boots that looked suspiciously like a small man's and reach for a hat—again, a man's—Even glanced at Canaan, caught him studying the clothing and the trunk, the question mark on his forehead crinkling. There is a reality here that this woman had a life previous, Even thought while they all ran up the street and crossed over to his flooded yard where the truck sat.

Climbing in, Grace studied it. Pushed in on the clutch and fiddled with the gearshift. "Straight shift," she said, sounding knowledgeable, but Even was worried. The way she bounced up and down while putting her hands to the steering wheel seemed too childlike, too pretend-like. Like driving a truck was something she'd always wanted to do but had never actually done. "Get in now, we goin'!" she said, revving up the motor, fooling with knobs, finding the lights and turning them on and off and back on again. Backing out the drive, Even saw the wind had blown his green chair clean to the side porch rail. It sat leaning back in a reclining position. Like a ghost who loved rain sat there, cooling his head underneath the angry runoff of the roof.

As she pulled out onto the road, she honked once for no reason and

Even grabbed at the arm handle, convinced she had never driven anything other than a man crazy. All lies, he thought. Drummed up to impress an old man who'd been just as easy without the need of bragging. I am a dead man, Even said to himself. Dead as a knob, just too dumb to know it.

They were met by a caravan that under any other circumstance would have brought a variety of comments. Cars. Trucks. Trailers. A tractor pulling a cart loaded down with a couch. A man riding a mule holding a dog by a leash. Every means of loading goods one could imagine had been done by more than a few eager to get out of the way of the river. It ran parallel to Highway 11, separated at places by little more than two hundred yards. Forgotten during the dry spell of August, it carried a hot dead smell of the urgent now. A thing to be feared and gotten away from. Quick. The caravan played out once they left the skirt of town, leaving just one or two cars coming their way every couple of minutes or so. Faces in the windows of those cars looked out at them like they were crazy and misdirected and foolish. "The flood's thataway! You're headed straight into it!" one woman yelled out the window of her car while she pointed in the direction they were going. Another one, a man in a red truck, did much the same thing. Yelling out "You goin' the wrong way!" while he waved his hand out the window, his warning so agitated he nearly wrecked. It struck them funny, the way his truck had jackknifed all over the road and they laughed low and nervous until Grace hit deep water and the truck swung wide, nearly plowing into a station wagon with a table tied upside down to its top.

"Lord God! Woman!" Even yelled, grabbing at the dash.

"You want to drive?" she yelled back.

"No."

"Then hush your mouth and quit makin' me nervous. It planed, is all. Just calm yourself down." She pushed in on the clutch and the gears made a terrible sound.

Canaan was in the middle, his arms around his bony knees. "Seems to me since we ain't in England, we ought to be riding on the right side of the road and not the left—" He pointed a finger over the dash.

"Left side of the road's higher up out of water—" Grace said in a snippy voice.

"Yeah, but—"

"You see any cars comin' our way?" she asked, reaching up to wipe away the fog from off the window.

"Well, no I sure don't—"

"Well, I tell you what—soon as I see a car comin', I'll move over to the other side. But for now, I know me two men who best keep their mouths shut!" She found her gear and the car steadied.

"Hush, Canaan. She's doin' fine—" Even said, speaking low, more for his own encouragement against terror than anything else. Where the rain was bad, her driving was worse.

"Lord have mercy, listen to you—you the one who screamed out 'Lord God Woman' just seconds ago and now you layin' it on his head—" Grace swerved and one tire went off the wrong side of the road. Up ahead Even saw the small bridge over what was normally a barely wet trickle of water. Brown water foamed white and rushed for the road.

"I ain't layin' it on nobody's head, Grace. I'm just trying to cooperate is all." He patted the dash. "You said for us to hush and that's what I'm doin'."

"Don't sound like you hushed to me—sounds like you still sittin' over there running your mouth big as you please." She managed to get the truck back to the road seconds before they hit the rail.

I am soon dead, Even thought. Headed to River Jordan and not nearly ready. Dear Lord—he prayed silently—I repent here and now of all heartless coursing with wayward women I didn't give a rat's ass about. I repent of all lies told in the middle of a Bull Gang brag at noon. I repent of wishing this one next to me dead, more than once, just to have a minute for my own thought to surface. And I repent of wishing the one sitting next to him tongueless for half an hour, for much the same reason. I repent of each and every sin, in the name of your only son—*"JeesusChristAlmighty!"* He screamed it out and threw an arm across Canaan's chest because Grace had hit the brakes too hard at a stop sign and the truck was spinning around in a circle.

"Hold on. Hold on. Just Plain Grace been here before—you hold on, now." Her hands were up off the wheel. Just letting it spin and jerk and travel where it wanted, like it was a ride at carnival. To his amazement it stopped back where it had started and headed forward again like nothing at all unusual had happened.

"You just sit tight and we be all right. You just sit tight—we be all right." She talked a rhyme to herself, grinding the gears, finally settling on what felt to him to be a wrong one since the truck jerked and refused to run smooth.

"You okay?" Canaan said out the side of his mouth. Quiet and grim. Sweat sagged under his eyes like a tiny string of pearls.

"No," Even said, just as low toward Canaan's ear. "Tell me something old and Greek. Some boring, confusin thing. Anything. I can't see shit in this rain and it's upsettin'."

"You say that true. Talk about not seeing things—now, Homer was a blind man. I ain't talkin' poor of vision, either. I'm talkin' blind as a bat blind—"

"Homer down at the meat market?" Grace put herself into their talk.

"No honey, another Homer I know. Somebody dead now." Canaan reached over and patted her knee, leaving his hand there longer than necessary in Even's opinion.

"Bats ain't really blind, you know," Grace said then, still riding on the wrong side of the road. "They send out noise and it paints a picture in their nose and they follow it to their food and their babies. So to say somebody's blind as a bat's really foolish and talkin' out the side of the brain that don't know shit."

Even leaned forward and looked at her. She was smiling underneath her hat. He could see her strong arms underneath whoever's shirt, those muscles cording up, and what he saw gave him momentary confidence in her appearance if not her abilities. Dead wrong and chauffeuring them to a sure death, she was still something to see. Canaan was watching her proud as a king rooster, his hand still on her leg.

"Anyhow," he continued. "Homer—the one who wrote the *Iliad*—"

"If he was a blind man, how'd he manage to write?" Grace interrupted.

Even snorted, seeing the humor in it.

"Well, I guess he had people sitting around and writing down what came out his mouth while he talked—"

"But you don't know this thing for sure. That this blind Homer man told stories and people took down his words and such." She put the truck in third and was taking her hands off the steering wheel while she talked.

They had gone a little over a mile by Even's estimation. He'd been watching the mechanics of driving and he was pretty sure he had the feel of it. Push in the left pedal to the floor. Find the gear. Let it out. Go forward. Finding the right gears seemed to be the thing of it.

"Grace, I'm pretty sure people took down his words," Canaan said.

"But you ain't sure. I mean, you ain't read somewhere that that's what happened in this case."

"No. I ain't read that, but I feel safe in sayin' that's what he did."

"How come you feel safe in saying somethin' if you ain't read it for sure?" Grace asked.

"'Cause that's the way things were done back then."

"You know this for a fact? You picked up a book somewhere and read that those blind folks back then carried on their business that way? By sittin' around and talkin' and just hopin' somebody's smart enough to pick up a pencil and write things down 'cause what they're sayin' just might be good enough to end up in a book?"

"They didn't have pencils back then," Even said from his side of the truck.

"No? So, how'd they write down those words of the blind man?" Grace asked, leaning round.

"With a stick in the mud," Even answered. "On a mud tablet is more like it."

Canaan looked at him, surprised.

"I ain't stupid, Canaan," Even said. "I had teachers, once."

Grace cleared her throat. "So if they wrote down this blind Homer man's words with a stick in the mud—then it sounds to me that to call someone a 'stick in the mud' is to call someone brilliant and smart enough to write down words fit for a book."

"In a sense—" But Canaan didn't seem sure anymore.

"Hmmm," Grace said. "Interestin'—tell me what this blind Homer man wrote, what'd he say good enough to make somebody pick up a stick and scribble in the mud and you stop long enough to notice?"

"I can't think of a damn thing worth repeatin'," Canaan snapped.

This one would argue with Christ and not blink an eye, was Even's first thought until he saw the corner of her mouth curve up and knew she was playing them like cards. He leaned forward and said, "I say it's rainin' outside, Grace. How 'bout you?"

She smiled a little broader. "Yeah, I'd say this sure enough is rain."

"To call this stuff rain is foolish and deceptive," Canaan said, put out with both of them. "More like sky and ocean traded off and once done, the ocean decided to pull the plug and be done with us. Rained like this back in 1912 and killed most everybody the other side of the river, once the Bouie and Leaf got done, that is," Canaan expounded. "Fools over in Hattiesburg, crazy for lumber, cut down all their trees and wore down their land. People east to Mobile still had farming on their minds, that's why they made it. I think I read over four hundred died in that great flood. Almost ended all talk of a rail hub up to Jackson."

"I think you should hush now, Canaan," Grace said while she leaned forward, struggling to see.

Even swallowed hard at the gray world ahead of him. There was no sense of bottom or top. Just a sense of being suspended in midair in the middle of a color nobody thought highly of. To his right, he could see water up to the lowest rail on a pasture he'd considered high land until then. He couldn't see out the left and was thankful for that small spot of blind. The wipers on the truck were set as high as they would go and totally worthless. Even tried to think on things religious in a summon of faith, but all he called up was Noah and the Ark and the punishing death of God's first disappointing go at creation. Shaking it off he tried someone newer, of a time closer to Christ, and drew up Moses, but he hung up on the Red Sea and the way it caved in on Pharaoh and killed his ass deader than whale shit. He gave up on things religious then and thought on work instead. Weighing two forms of death in his mind: water or fire. Which would be the darker? Up until then he'd thought fire the worst of the lot. But now he was no more sure of that than Canaan was sure of Homer's method of publishing. To be trapped in gray, not knowing which end was up, seemed worse than crisping to death underneath molten resin.

Grace blew the horn for an unknown reason, just saying out loud to the two, "Just makin' sure it works is all." Even heard it, weak and tinny, barely audible, such was the force of the rain. He was near out of breath with the probability Joody was facedown in water somewhere. Floating.

Her sticks catching on roots. Picking up dirt and moss. Trash catching up her nose and in her eyes and ears. Her hand minus the proper number of fingers, clutching for something. Anything. Anything at all.

"There it is! Right there! See the tree!"

The road was empty and Grace pulled over onto what seemed to be the last portion of decent shoulder and left the lights on. Even was already out the car.

"Where you goin'?" Grace put a hand to Canaan's arm.

"I ain't lettin' him find her dead on his own. And she's dead, too. They ain't no way she's not." Canaan was out the car then and headed round in front of the lights. He could see Even ahead of him, his pale blue shirt flapping like a cape.

"I'll just stay here and pray then," Grace said to no one in particular while she set the wipers back to slow and held on to the steering wheel.

We're not gonna make it. We're gonna die, ain't we? Joleb had learned he could think a conversation and she would answer. His tongue was nearly gone and he was afraid to use it for speech.

"Maybe. Maybe not. This here's a good rock, Joleb. See how it curves in and yet it's got itself a strong hangover ledge. A good place to stay out of the rain while we watch and see what happens."

How come you ain't scared?

"Life is life. Anything can happen—whatever happens is worth watchin' just 'cause it's happenin', even death, don't you think?"

He reached over and held her hand. Underneath her skin, she had veins that lay across bones like loose worms. He ran his finger across one and the movement soothed him.

"Death ain't a thing to fear, Joleb. It's livin' that's got most folks poleaxed." She looked around and reached a finger to the white mold inside the rock. "Milk dust," she said. "A good mold for cuts and slow healin' things." She put an arm around him and heard him wince. Broken rib, she thought, and felt up his side easy until she came to the one. She left her finger on it until she felt it grow warm. He was wrapped in her blanket, having lost his pants at some point over the course of the days. She had not asked him anything. Just worked on getting him well. He still talked funny and it'd take more than herbs to make his tongue proper again. But his leg wasn't broken and that was what had worried her the most. That he'd get laid up and drown inside his lungs from lack of movement. The broken rib was a sure problem, though. One that needed tending and soon. She cupped her hands and drank from the downpour, recalling how they'd had but a matter of minutes to break camp once it started. Minutes. She'd seen rain like this but once, and once had been enough.

"Wa gaa ya raaks," Joleb said.

"We sure did get my rocks." That and the dress he bought me once upon a time while I picked sweet wild onions. She would miss this world. Certain things about it.

I ain't ever seen water rise so fast. He looked wild-eyed down the hill.

"Oh, I have. It's always a scary thing, too. No matter how many times you seen it. Got such a force to it, man can't never think to own it. You remember that. Man can't own what ain't his. No matter how much he wants to." He pointed to a spot that was land a few minutes earlier and now seemed a lake. A roiling brown water lake determined to have them. It swirled up ugly and foamy and full of loose ground clutter.

"Don't look then. Look at the tree over there. See how big? I bet that tree's seen some things. All sorts of things in its great big life. There's a moon up there too, hiding behind all this storm. You ever sing a lunatic song out under a lunatic moon? No?"

We're gonna die, ain't we? He sent this thought to her while he sighed.

"Maybe. We just have to wait and see."

And suddenly he felt soothed again and at peace with his future. Like he'd been punished enough for everything he'd messed up and God was finally done with him.

Even's blue shirt was in front of him one instant and gone the next. Canaan played his light out through the wet and it looked as though sticks were falling from the sky. Straight gray sticks sent down from heaven. Felt almost that hard, too. Hitting all across the back of his shoulders and the top of his balding head like darning needles dumped out of a sky-high basket. "You, Even!" he yelled, and then his light went dead and he was left standing in the middle of a woods he had no clue of, underneath a fire hose of pain. Beating the light against his hand, he took one step forward and his legs went out from under him and he was sliding down the incline on his ass. "Yaaaaaaashiittt!" he yelled, his feet up in the air. His arms scrambling for handholds. "Eveeennnn—!" There was nothing there. Nothing but mud and more mud. He managed to turn to his side and see a short distance ahead, his side catching on roots that dug in and gouged. He thought he yelled again, but wasn't sure. I'm headed to death as sure as my name's Canaan. And I never will find out whose pants Grace is wearing. A log lay across the path in front of him and he shut his eyes and prepared to die.

When he hit it, the log let out a howling scream and Canaan realized he'd plowed into Even. The man had tried to stop his motion by holding onto the bulging root of some tree on one side and latching his legs around a rock on the other. Canaan put an end to his efforts as dam and in a heap of legs and arms and a tangle of feet they both went headfirst sliding toward the creek.

No time to think or pray, Even settled for yelling while he flew by things that had a name just days ago. Seeing trees all around, the tops of them flailing in the wind, lit up in blasts of lightning, he thought how high and mean everything looked from his low position. How blind the trees were to the torment of man. A root caught him in the ass and augered a gash in what felt to be his left cheek, ripping his pants and sending pain all the way up to the top of his head. Seeing a lump straight ahead that seemed to have the look of a sheared-off stump, Even curved his body to catch it, hoping it was heavy enough to stop them before they hit the water that he could see foaming less than a hundred feet beyond.

It was.

Joody's bag of rocks stopped them. Set down in the middle of the path they rammed into Even's chest, knocking the wind clean out of his lungs. Breathless and in pain he came to a stop at a point where he'd first seen her, months back—the giant pine with the velvet roots. Canaan was still on top of him, one leg riding his back, his arm looped between Even's legs like a queer boy going for a grab. Pushing him away, Even wrapped his arms around his chest and squeezed, looking for his lost breath, trying not to panic at the stars forming in his eyes.

Rolling off and over, a part of his brain thinking this was the best fun he'd had in all his sixty-three years of living, another part thinking at least he got fucked good and proper by an outstanding woman before he ended up drowned, Canaan crawled on his hands and knees, water washing mud off his face, finding himself eyeballing a row of feet. A woman's two dark ones dangled off a rock, as well as a pair of white ones with busted-up toes. Over the noise of the pouring down rain, he heard a woman say, "Well, here's our ride, Joleb. Seems we ain't gonna die, after all."

The ride back would eventually settle itself into a spot that would seem merely desperate and heroic and if not more than a little miraculous, at least lucky. But for a while yet, filled as it was with a large market of smells, it would live as a memory of pain and bleeding that spelled out suffering done by each one at various levels, in a wide variety of ways. Joleb crying out at every bump. Smelling like he'd crawled out of a sewer to find his way to the place by the creek. Grace so overcome with wanting to comfort and do for the boy, she nearly lost the truck a total of three times, all the while asking what measure of treatment Joody had used. Had she done this? No? And why not? Throwing out the odor of anxious sweat from her under-arms. A smell that reminded Even vaguely of rain-wet farm animals. Not too unpleasant if one was familiar with cows and coupling and the shear-ing of sheep. Canaan holding Joleb on his lap, not knowing where to put his large hands, seeing how the boy hurt all over and didn't have a place on him that wasn't raw skin and ooze. Ribs. Chest. Legs. Feet. The old man settled finally on the tray of Joleb's shoulders. His fingers wrapping around in order to brace him. Wrapped in a muddy blanket slick with the smell of the creek, Joleb leaned back and Even watched while Canaan pulled in breath through his mouth trying to trick his nose. In the middle of the misery Joody sat silent, facing him while he tried to ease himself off his ass, put some space to it, so at every bump and turn, his ass wouldn't feel seared. Her face was waist level, straight on with the zipper of his work pants. Her eyes steady looking up at him while her back curved and mold-ed itself under the dash and her legs folded up somewhere underneath that he couldn't see. He couldn't imagine where either, not with their long length and large feet. She was squatted down between him in a servant's pose and it disturbed him. If we die, I don't want you to be like that—

down there at my feet, he said. We ain't gonna die, Even, hush now, she answered in a strong voice that made him feel worn out inside and weepy. We made it this far, she said. You hold on now. You're just tired. Canaan's woman said then, Lord yes, I'd sure say he was tired. Just Plain Grace think you probably the tiredest man alive right now, and then she reached over and patted Joleb's leg as if a pat there would transfer over to Even's leg somehow. Transfer over to all of them. And in a strange way it did, for they all felt picked up and stretched out to the limit of their emotions. Lifted up to that place where crying felt right as rain and to not do it made one feel sin-like and dirty. Crying coming along like a gift. Like a dream of mercy and salvation and all those other things that seemed so out of reach earlier. So there inside that borrowed Ford truck while the rain beat down and they headed home, they cried with a sound like the wails of the Holy Rollers. Cried in rhythm with the worthless wipers slapping on glass like floppy shoes going nowhere. We made it! someone said. Maybe Canaan. Maybe Grace. Even wasn't sure. By God we made it! the voice said again and this time he knew it had come from Canaan. Someone else said Thank you, Jesus!—we sure did make it. Grace this time. Thank you, Jesus! that AME woman shouted again, but Joody didn't say anything at all. Just looked him straight in the eyes with those dark eyes of hers and Even read her. Read her clear as newborn glass. Out the age stick he judged to be her eleventh—the year of truth and not backing down and refusing to repent a thing—she said, Maybe God had a thing to do with this. Maybe not. But what I do know is this: you Even Grade, my sweet man, my only man, saved me sure as Jesus. Even read her words and shivered hard, having enough Lutheran left in him to fear wearing a shoe that didn't belong to him. One belonging to a man crucified and long gone from this place of rain and cryin', gone from this world with its large market of smells. Don't be afraid, she said then while they all cried in different ways for different reasons. Don't you dare be afraid of this praise I'm givin' you. You saved me sure as Jesus and I love you. And I won't repent of this, either. Take what else I got. Take my toes. Take all my fingers, it don't matter to me. Take it all 'til there ain't a side left to me. I won't repent. Not of this. And at that point, Even had shut his eyes and leaned back his head and listened to the rain beat down hard on the cab of the truck.

22

THINGS THAT FALL

J OLEB HEARD GRACE SINGING in the distance and thought he was gone up
to heaven. Gone clean up from the watery grave that swallowed the
campsite whole out by the Baby Black, and his glorified body set down outside some celestial place in a room designed for listening. A place where
the unredeemed could at least sit and hear good music while they pondered
the multitude of their sin.

> *There is a fountain filled with blood*
> *Drawn from Emanuel's veins*
> *And sinners plunged beneath the flood*
> *La la la de da la la*

Nope, I ain't in heaven after all, he reasoned. In heaven people would
sing the full song—know all the words concerning what got them there
without the confusion of *la de daa's* and such.

"Grace," he tried to say but only managed "Gaay—"

"That you, Joleb? You awake?" She came and stood over him.
Enormous. Bigger than ever. Dressed in funny men's clothes this time
instead of her usual belted cotton dress. "Gaay—" he said again.

"Hush, Joleb. Your tongue's all messed. You just hold yourself still and nod at what I say and I'll get it for you, okay?"

He pushed himself up or at least tried to, but his lower body wouldn't cooperate worth a damn.

"You need somethin' to drink. You think you could?"

He nodded because that had been what he'd wanted. That and to take a piss if he could ever find out where in the hell he was parked and what the direction to the bathroom might be. Without his glasses everything seemed fogged, but he saw the lumpy shape of boots over by the door and a small bookshelf with only two or three books in it.

"You stay still. You got a busted rib and about half a dozen other things wrong. None of them beyond healing, but that rib's the one we gotta watch. We waiting now for Mr. Mosley to get back from finding a phone, so we can get you moved from here and over to the hospital."

"Waa aah ee?" He looked up at her, her hands on her hips the way she used to study his mother's face when she jerked this way and that and made a nuisance of herself inside her wheelchair.

"Where you at? That what you askin'?"

He nodded his head up and down, hurting his tongue.

"You in Petal. On Bellrose in the Quarter over at Even Grade's house."

He frowned, wondering who the hell this Even Grade was and why in the world he was camped out with the coloreds on the wrong side of Petal.

"You sit still." She held up a hand and then pointed down at him. "I'll get your water now."

And then she was gone from the room. Disappeared out through a narrow doorway where he could see light shining down on table-shaped yellow. Just like heaven. I'm in colored heaven, he reasoned. A place where there ain't many books and folks only got water to drink and nobody knows all the words to the songs. Shit, but his head hurt like hell. He raised one hand and studied his nails. Caked with dirt, bloody, palms scraped raw like he'd been dragged down the highway facedown by the feet.

He felt down his legs, not recognizing the pants, wondering where his were, what happened to them, and who in the world took his off and put these things on. Loose and tan, old man's pants with an oversized safety pin working the zipper. Lord, it must be late. I should be home with Burris and

Dad eating oatmeal or French toast and helping Grace tend Ma.

Grace appeared with a glass of water and a straw.

"Here, try it regular first. Regular'll get you goin' and not get you used to bein' laid up and an invalid."

He assumed regular meant she wanted him to try drinking the way he'd always done it to avoid becoming spoiled. She put one hand behind his head and helped him lean up and put the glass to his mouth. His mouth wouldn't cooperate, though, and water ran down his chin. His tongue felt like a foreigner. A king-sized Polish sausage gone bad. Joleb shook the glass away.

"Well, try the straw then," she sighed, frowning down the way she used to do when Mary caught cold and had to be suctioned.

"Iaa aah maaa." I ain't Ma, he tried to say, but couldn't.

She pulled the paper off a red-and-white striped straw, the kind they used at Kress for sodas.

"Here we go, suck easy." He sucked easy, just like Grace ordered, and managed to get enough to wet his mouth, but that was about it. Once he was done she said, "There!" like he'd been a good boy and managed to do something special.

"Ahh gaah paaa." He pointed to his crotch. "Baaa!"

"Oh Lord—"

"Ahh gaah!"

"You ain't gonna like what I got to say here—but I could get you a bedpan you could go in, or even a towel to sit on and you could pee yourself. You got a busted rib and ain't got no business walkin'—"

"Naahh! Iaa ahh ah baabaa—"

"I know you ain't a baby, Joleb. Nobody ain't gonna think that, either. I could clean it up quick as you please, too."

"Naahh!"

She snorted through her nose and Joleb knew she was aggravated. "Okay, I'll get you there. Here, swing your legs around. Let's get yourself off the couch." He did, taking so long it was comical. "Okay, I'm gonna bend and I want you to put your arm around my neck and stand up, okay?" Joleb's arm went around her neck and he smelled lilac lotion and lima beans. When he went to put his foot down he screamed.

"Lord, God, it's broke. I was hopin' it weren't, but it is. You gotta hop easy, is all. Hop easy while I hold you."

Once inside the cubicle, sweat-drenched and shaking, Joleb clutched the sink while Grace stood behind him like she didn't intend to leave. He motioned her away with his hand. "Gowaa."

"Okay, but you ain't as big as you think you are—"

But I'm big enough not to want you here seeing my business, he said to himself.

"Actin' foolish, too. Act like I ain't never seen everything you got from week one of your bein' on this earth—"

She left, but kept the door cracked. Looking around while he fumbled with the pants, he saw everything was clean but small. There were rust spots in the sink and tub that had been scrubbed at and the toilet wore a rust border, too, but everything beyond it was spotless. Cracked linoleum of a type he'd never seen before was on the floor as well as a frayed blue rug. The mirror over the sink was missing a corner and the silvering was off in places and made him looked speckled and diseased.

He finished his business and finally managed to get the zipper to work, but only halfway this time—the safety pin stuck out crossways and worthless. Hopping over to the sink, he saw there was a new bar of Ivory soap on one side and a worn-down bar of Lava on the other. Joleb ran a finger over the Ivory, the act of tracing letters filled his nose, made it run. There was something large he should remember. Something important. He shut his eyes and traced. I-V-O-R-Y. He caught his nail inside the R, stalled. He had done something like this before—let his nail catch on the edge of a letter carved into something. The chained stopper went into the sink while he turned on the water. Picking up the white bar of soap, he set it to floating.

"Joleb? What you doin' in there?" The door opened all the way and Grace came in. "Why you doin' that? Now ain't the time to be worryin' about washin' your hands—"

The way the soap floated meant something, too. He pressed it to the bottom and it bounced back up. Did this two or three more times. "Whaa maa ie fooo?" He pointed to the soap—wanted to know why it was floating. Why it was the only soap that did. Once he found out the reason it might solve things; quiet that place inside that was telling him the carving of the letters and the buoyancy had essential meanings.

Grace turned off the water. "Say it one more time and let me listen." She studied his mirrored profile, pebbled and bleached.

"Whaa maaa iee fooo?" He pressed it under and it bounced back up. He did it again and looked at her, holding open his hands.

"You want to know why that soap floats?"

"Yaaa." He nodded his head up and down so hard his eyes hurt.

"Lord have mercy." Grace put a hand to his forehead, checking for a fever, and then she reached over and flushed the toilet. "I ain't got the answer to the soap, Joleb, but I know somebody who knows the answer to just about everything there is, at least to his way of thinkin', and as soon as he gets here we'll ask him. You come on now and leave that soap be." The mirror, even broken and speckled, sent back an image of worry while she took his arm.

Before he left he ran a finger over the towel hanging on the rod—lonely, threadbare, fray along the bottom—recalling how she had wanted him to pee himself while sitting on it. It seemed a stupid suggestion based on what he was seeing. Like pissing through a window screen at best, he reasoned.

"You all right?" she asked in a low voice while she held him around the waist.

"Yaaa maam." It took him longer than he'd imagined and wore him slap out to the point he felt near to fainting, but with her arm around him he finally made it back to the sofa. This sure is a tiny-ass place, he thought, exhausted, seeing a shut door to what looked to be the only other room in the house. It smells good, though, like Grace's cookin' is the only type cookin' ever done here. He breathed in deep as he could and wondered what day it was. What his dad was doing. If he was worried at all over things.

"Here, suck easy again," and she put the straw in his mouth. "You 'bout dehydrated seems to me."

The water was wonderful. Icy cold and sweet. The sofa was nice and felt good, too. Good and soft. Not like the one at home, tight with horsehair and springs. Always managing to feel gritty no matter how many times it got brushed off. His rear sank down in this one and there was stuffing on the arms. The whole thing was covered with a quilt that made him think of turkeys—all orange, yellow and red. Faded throughout with stitching that ran contrary to the pattern. He ran a hand along its surface and studied Grace, tried to map out the differences, because there were some. Her mussed-up hair for one. Something else besides, around her mouth. She looks sad, he realized. Sad and old. He felt ashamed that he'd become such a nuisance, and by God as soon as he figured out what he'd done to weigh so on people's minds and land him in colored heaven where rust ran amuck and nobody had their own clothes, he'd apologize proper.

A man came in then through the front door. A thin colored man older than Grace with a bald spot on the top of his head. He was wearing a pair of tiny square glasses on the end of his nose and while Grace held out the glass of water to Joleb, she turned to him and said, "Well?"

"I got through. Phone lines working down at the hardware store, most other places too, I guess." He looked at Joleb, his hands to his pockets. "You feelin' better now that you slept some?"

"Yaaaa," his head hurting too bad to nod this time.

"He ain't as good as he thinks he is what with that busted-up rib. I bet the foot's broke, too. I don't care what that other one in the back room says." The whole while she was talking, she was rubbing Joleb's good leg while the almost bald man frowned.

"Like I was sayin', I got through but we got to go across on the train. It'll be down from Meridian sometime around noon. Got some men to flag it to a stop and they said to have him ready and they'll ferry him across to a high spot in Hattiesburg. Can't tell exactly when, though. You know how trains is—thy God, Grace, the boy's pukin'!"

Joleb felt it coming up again and put out his hands in front of his face, in an effort to catch it but nothing was there, just awful dry heaves that hurt his sides and made him wish to be dead. He smelled the Ivory soap on his hands and it made him want to puke all the harder.

"My Lord, Joleb, what's wrong! Did that water make you sick?"

He was shaking his head from side to side, embarrassed and humiliated at himself for barfing like a baby. He put his soap-smelling finger under Grace's nose and said, "Sooob?"

"What the hell? Here—" The balding man had tossed her a towel from the kitchen and she was holding it to his head, wiping down his chin, dodging to avoid his finger. The towel smelled of grits and bacon and witch hazel.

"Sooab!" Joleb said.

"What's he sayin'?" the man asked, his voice suspicious.

"Joleb stop this. You stop this right now. Quit this crazy act."

Joleb made a small box of his hands and said, "Sooab! Whaa maaa iee fooo?" and Grace remembered what he'd been doing in front of Even's bathroom sink.

"Joleb, this is Canaan Mosley. The man I told you about—" She paused and turned to the man. "Canaan, Joleb here wants to know why Ivory soap floats."

He nodded, excited, studying the man wearing the glasses and the different seasons that crossed his face, the last one settling there winter-like in its confusion.

"You got any clue there?" Grace looked at Canaan, her voice exasperated. "On why that bar of white soap floats? 'Cause I told this one here you know just about everthing there was to know about just about everthing there is—"

"I think you give me too much credit on the knowin' of things, Grace."

Joleb looked back and forth from one to the other, his whole body trembling.

"Do you or don't you? I ain't got all day to sit here while you think on this thing, either." She rubbed at her head as if she had a headache.

"Seems to me the reason Ivory Soap floats is the same reason belonging to oil—it's lighter than water," Canaan answered, thinking the conversation as strange as one concerning Homer in the middle of a flood.

"There's your answer, Joleb, now swing your legs around and lay still."

"Like I was sayin' before we got off on the why of floatin' soap—I made those calls. Mr. Green's on his way here now. Said he'd call the authorities, too. And as for that other call. This is the last time I show up on the dark side of a matter. I felt foolish not knowing who I was callin', just sitting there waitin' for a voice on the other end of the line to say hello—"

"Did that voice say hello or not?"

"Yep. He said hello all right. And I told him what you said and that voice that I ain't got a clue of said he'll meet the ambulance at the Hattiesburg station. Which means we got to do what we got to do to get him at the crossin' in order to meet the train around noon. Decide who's goin' where and—thy God Grace, he's pukin' again!"

"Joleb—Lord, have mercy, there's blood here this time. Joleb, calm down now. You calm down. Joleb, look at me. Look here at Grace." To Canaan she said, "See if Even's got any ice left in the freezer. And if there is, wrap it in a cloth and bring it to me." She looked down at the cloth, at the stringing blood mixed with yellow bile, and folded it to a new place. "You be sweet now, we gonna get you to the hospital soon. Just be a sweet baby now."

Joleb shook his head, wanting her to quit serving up the brain-dead talk—the talk he'd been hearing for years through the walls and over the noise of running water in a back room.

A door opened then and through a haze of nearsightedness, Joleb saw a woman with antennas stuck in her head enter the room. A tall woman with scary cheekbones and arms like tree limbs. She put one hand on his knee and the other on Grace's shoulder and bent down and said, "I only got a partial read on this, but the biggest of it is—you keep mentioning the business of how we gonna get him to and from this place and this one's gonna puke up his guts. That's what I'm seein' here."

"He ain't got but a piece of ice left after the power bein' off for so long and all, but here it is," said Canaan as he came back into the middle of it. "Mornin', Judy."

Grace wrapped the ice in cloth and put it to his throat. She took another cloth and draped his face. Once the light was out of his eyes his head eased and Joleb felt sleepy again. Maybe I'll wake in the right place this time, he thought. Back on Stockwell Street with the redbirds and the yellow dining room walls and Burris sound asleep and snoring while Ma drools from her wheelchair.

Canaan stood smoking out on Even's front porch, making a quick list of hard damage. Even's porch steps were more gone than not. More shattered pine than stationary treads. What they used to be will be a memory come next week, he reasoned. Just a memory. Nothing more. And by the time next year rolls around, there'll be serious debate on whether or not there ever were steps leading up to Even Grade's. He smoked on.

Morning light came creeping on up, careening over the downed fence, its slats to the mud. Canaan's own personal portion was still standing in front of his place, but it wouldn't be long before it followed the collapse of his nearest neighbor's, what with the weight of leaning wood dragging urgent on the uprights. The same was true for the fence belonging to the house across the street. Just a meager portion was left white and stiff-up near the mailbox. Easy damage there, where the fences were concerned. Harder luck beyond, where Clorena's bright pink house was completely swept off its supports. The business of storm washing away its corner bolsters, leaving one pink corner sagging at a canterwalled angle. Canaan dipped his head to the right and wondered at it. Grace's goat had come loose from its leash and was roaming free, dragging a cast-off branch caught in its tether. Enjoying the new unlimited access to most yards in spite of it. "Worthless goat," Canaan said to his hands, which rested on the rail. His right one clenched up hard as a pine knot for a reason he couldn't determine. While he stood watching the goat's slow, happy progress, the beast raised its brown and white head and eyed him long and hard.

The door opened behind him and he turned and watched Even come forward on hobbled steps. He grunted the whole distance.

"I'd pull up your green chair for you and help you sit, but that seems a cruel form of courtesy," Canaan said, shaking out a cigarette and lighting it for him, instead. His fist relaxed. His breathing more regular, finally.

"You say that true," Even said with one last grunt. If not for Burris Green almost losing a toe when he was ten, Even knew he might yet be bleeding. Grace had learned suturing early on as a result and had sewn up his ass with catgut from an old guitar in her closet. After an overly long debate on the how to and why not of it, of course. Canaan and Joody standing in a corner, watching, faces fierce as wet cats. Once done, Joody bent to his ear and said, She's a six-sided woman, all right, but two sides are misfiring. I think she kept her hand to your naked ass 'bout one minute too long. Even, still embarrassed, looked over at Canaan, remembering the woman's hands and their slow, careful work.

"Clorena got a mess down there what with the tail of her house draggin' so." Canaan pointed with his cigarette. "Angles are hard things to get used to. Hard to tolerate much more than fifteen degrees or so inside a livin' area. Pots won't stay put and more times than not the shitter cracks and slides off its hole. Ain't gonna be much fun for her for a while." He'd lived with a severe angle a time or two and never intended to do it again.

There was movement inside the pink and Clorena's son Otil stood in his doorway stretching. Taking one step out in the middle of a wide yawn he fell flat to his face while they both watched. Jumping up, swearing, he turned to the house as if it had blind-kicked him in the back.

"Some folks ain't got the brain to be bothered by angles, I see," Canaan said.

"The fence is down." Even looked up and down the street. "But Lord, that worthless billboard is still standin' tall as ever and the goat's still roamin'." The goat was grazing underneath, the surplus leash and its limb clotted with trash. "Seems a wonder, sometimes, at what stands and falls round this place—"

"Not even God can kill that worthless piece-of-shit goat." Canaan spit over the rail.

Even squinted his eyes, thinking the man overly caustic after such a night of survival. "I think a pig is the noblest of all the animals," he said for no reason other than he'd woke smelling bacon and found himself thinking on the plight of pork and their route of travel through life.

Canaan looked at him as if he were crazed.

"One of the cleanest animals there is," Even continued. "Got sense enough to shit somewhere other than where it eats. Can't think of any other animal with that type of foresight. You?"

Canaan scratched at his balding head, his hand worrying him again. And his eyes. And the back of his neck, now that he thought on it. "No, not right off I can't. The one I saw in my dream had manners, too. Had the good sense to pull her parts together before speaking. Had the good sense to know when to keep her mouth shut as well." He shot a fierce look at the front door. At the quilt-covered feet he knew belonged to the boy.

We are speaking on something other than breakfast, Even thought. He sniffed the air still smelling bacon or maybe sausage, as well as the stink of turned-over mud. "Most folks hate the smell of manure. Cow. Horse. Pig. All of 'em. But I like it—" Even said, wondering if his brain had leaked out his ass overnight. He continued, regardless, "You can smell pigshit clear up to a quarter mile away. There's something noble in that—that an animal can throw out such a far-reachin' stink." He sniffed again. "I'd rather smell the odor of hog than this smell of sour, tossed-up mud."

"You say that true." Canaan was thoughtful for a moment and they both stood there quiet and easy. The goat was underneath the worthless sign. Turning in slow stupid circles, its line caught on something low. Canaan hopped down into a yard that used to be solid and picked up a heavy red clod, pitching it hard, coming close, but not enough. "There," he said, brushing his hands together, happy with his wasted effort. He climbed back up. "You say that true about smells. Smells are good. Ain't nothin' wrong with a good stink now and again to set a person right in his way of thinkin'."

It was delivered overly loud in Even's opinion.

"That gutted dream sow told me a sad thing that night she visited. Said I've tried to fix what ain't broke yet and in the process I've ignored the canyon in my soul. I took that to mean she was grieved at me because of my shortsightedness, and I spent a helluva time thinking on it before I came to and realized she was a dream and not human. Not God. Not nothin'. Just a dream of a pitiful pig is all." Canaan ran his hand over his question mark and looked square on at Even, waiting for a response, his eyes squinted up and testy.

"Did you know you can let a pig in the house and it won't shit?" Even said. "A dog'll drop waste ever chance it gets, but not a pig. Shows you how intelligent the one is as compared to the other. A sow won't mate with just any old boar, either. She's got to pick him out."

Canaan tested the weight of the rail and then leaned on it while he lit up another cigarette. "Sounds sad to me the boar ain't got a say in the whether or not of what he's to mount—"

"You ever meet a man who'd turn down a free ticket to course?"

"Not right off. But it don't mean it can't happen. Some men might think readin' and thinkin' a more profitable way to spend their nighttime hours. Don't mean he's no queerboy, either." He looked at Even hard.

Salt was beading on Even's top lip. Worried now, wishing he had ignored the broad smell that triggered this mouth gusher, he licked at his lips. A part of him knowing full well Canaan would have worked the conversation to this point regardless of topic. Be it religion. Weather. Medicine. He cut through and got to the heart of it. "How's Grace this mornin'?" Even asked, already knowing full well the answer.

"Mean as a snake and just about as fuckable."

"Shit, Canaan—"

"Thy God, you asked, Even Grade. Don't act like a baby on hearin' it."

"That's not what I expected to hear comin' back at me, is all."

"Well, sometimes we get a stomach full of what we ain't hungry for, don't we?"

Four teenagers sauntered around the corner, lazy in the heat, loud. Two girls. Two boys. All had sticks in their hands dragging at the mud. They waved and then went and stood in front of Clorena's tilted house, leaning their heads down as if the view made things right again.

Even cleared his throat. "Well, it ain't everday a woman comes along willin' to risk her life tryin' to save somebody she ain't never seen before—"

"Hell, Even! She just wanted to drive that great big truck! You saw how she was."

"Maybe. Maybe. But she drove it into a flash flood and I can't think of too many willin' to do that regardless of how bad they wanted to drive somethin' big."

"Hmmm," Canaan said, unconvinced.

"Then once there she winds up bringin' home somebody she'd given herself to believin' was dead—Joleb," Even said as a reminder.

"I ain't thick. I know his name."

"She sewed up my ass, too. In the middle of the dark."

"I think her sewing up your ass was the only part she enjoyed. She talked on it for most of an hour after you fell dead asleep. How good she made those neat little stitches. How she bet not even a doctor could do such good work. How your scar's gonna be good-lookin' enough to put on display. She stopped barely short of saying what a nice-shaped rear you wear. She wanted to say it, though. I could feel it." His fist was clenched again, knotted up round as a turtle on a rock.

The goat worked its way forward, dragging the snagged limb, raking up debris from off the road in the process. Doing a fine job, too, for such a sorry goat. Even licked salt from over his lip, the vision of pork gone now. Something heavier there instead and not so easy to get rid of.

"I'm too old to change, Even. Ain't got it in me to bend any more of myself in any more directions than I'm already goin'—and all the roast in the world ain't gonna make me change my mind on this one."

Even stood quiet, blowing smoke out his nose, sadder suddenly than he'd been in as long a while as he could remember.

"Too old to take up anything new." Canaan looked down at his arm, as if a newspaper should be folded up and quartered there waiting to be read.

"You seemed sure of things last night," Even said.

"Yep. I guess I did, didn't I? Seemed full up to my eyebrows with the new of it."

"Said God struck you with a thunderbolt, is how you called it—"

"I remember what I said." He tapped his ashes off the porch. "I ain't good at bein' a fetch and carry man, is all. Any minute now she's gonna up and send me down to Shasta to pick her out a dress to wear and clean underpants to step into. I ain't used to being spoke sharp to. I ain't used to not having time to read, or write, or fart in peace—"

"Ain't used to seeing a black woman coddle a white boy up close, either, I bet." Even looked straight ahead toward the storm-scabbed street.

"Or watching a woman I've seen all-night naked sew up another man's bare ass!" Canaan threw back in his face.

Even turned to him. Watched him smoke, knowing the old man would let the cigarette burn down 'til it was a nub, barely more than a small circle of ash, and then he'd spit it out, blow it to the dirt with the tip of his tongue.

"Look at me," Even said low.

"Nah, I ain't wantin' to right now."

"Well, whether you want to or not, you gonna listen—you're building a wall where there ain't no need of one. And it's a foolish thing to do, too."

"Maybe. Maybe not."

And then Canaan turned it, flipped the focus neat as a flapjack or a deck of cards, saying, "There's a circle in there on the couch that I ain't a part of, and a part of me is glad and another part wishes—another part wishes—hell, I don't know what part of me wishes for what. All I know is this—" He turned to Even, pointing his finger. "I ain't never fished in my life. Or drove a car or anything. I ain't never been to a museum or opera or picture show. I've read those things in books is all and because of that I fooled myself into believing I know a little bit about things I ain't got a clue of. I ain't never been outside the state of Mississippi—"

What was left of his cigarette was burning near his lip while he talked. Bobbing up and down throwing out confused circles of smoke that became circles inside of other circles. Seeing the design Even thought, That smoke's as clear a picture of this man's mind as I'm ever likely to see—

"—never seen any water that wasn't creek or river or swamp. Never went to school past the ninth grade. Never did anything other than clean up after folks—library, schools, office buildings. Nothing."

Even stood listening, wondering what words to call up, feeling thin as a rail when it came to advice on this issue. "Canaan, you the smartest man I ever met in my life. You know things. Not just facts, either, which any fool can know. You know things. The why and how-come of things—"

"I don't know shit about shit. The gutted sow knew as much and called me on it," he spit his nub over the rail. Even heard it sizzling in a puddle of wet.

"You said not five minutes back that pig was a dream, nothin' more—"

Canaan went, "Nahhh—" waving it away.

Even said then, "Fishin' ain't a hard thing to do, Canaan. Hell, you give a half-wit a pole and he can fish—"

"Not *her* way. *She's* got to stand barelegged in a stream and fish. *She's* got a fly rod and a tackle box. *She's* got a whole trunkload of things to teach me on that front. And this is just the beginning of what old Canaan ain't learned yet but just *gotta* know."

Even stood still knowing his bare ass and the woman's hands on it had never been the problem. What the problem *was* was another thing. He remembered back a ways, more than a year now since he first picked up "The Reality of the Negro" while its author chased a goat down the street. Remembered studying all that sea of red on white. The way it looked like it had been weighed and judged unworthy by someone who had a keen but limited eye for the value of things. Remembering those scribbles, Even caught sight of what might be working in the man. Just the edge of it. But it was enough to keep him quiet on it. Enough to make him reach for the man in much the same way he'd done when he'd come on him bleeding from a thrown-out bottle in the middle of a blazing hot summer day. While across the way Clorena's house sank another foot in the mud, sending the teenagers standing in front into fresh loud squeals, and while the worthless goat lumbered past hobbled heavy by dragged debris, Even laid his hand on a bone of the shoulder that felt like home and left it there.

"You black as me, but that's about it," Grace said finally.

"And I guess that ain't enough in your book," Joody answered.

"You right there, 'cause I ain't never been much for readin'."

Joleb was snoring, troubled-loud and fit-like on the couch while the two women sat in chairs on opposite sides of the room, neither looking in the other's direction. Just staring out at nothing fixed—maybe the morning light coming in through a window or maybe not. Just staring at nothing and everything all at once.

Joody slapped her knees and hooted, drawing the other's eyes to her. "I like you, Grace. I sure do. You a woman with a voice and that's a rare thing nowadays." She hooted again, softer because the boy had grunted, thrown his arm up over his head.

"You black as me, but that's all I said. Ain't no reason to start likin' me 'cause of what I said—it weren't meant as a nice thing. That thing I just said."

Joody shook at the shoulders, making noise with her sticks. "I think I like you even more now—"

"Well, don't. 'Cause we ain't never gonna be buddies—"

Joody bent at the waist, laughing so hard she had to wipe her eyes on the tail of Even's borrowed shirt. "Now I know why that one out there loves you more'n he loves Jesus." She slapped a hand over her mouth to quiet herself.

"I ain't never been much for love, neither—so you just stop this carrying on so 'cause it ain't gonna win me." Grace looked sideways to the hall that needed scrubbing. Turned her chair away from the woman and watched out her side vision the two men out on the porch talking low and smoking.

"When I was little I used to hate my bones," Joody said, her voice like low running water. "Wished for plump skin to cover it up. Got so bad I bruised myself sleepin', what with the way my knees bore into each other. Whew, Lord." She stood up and cracked her back. "My ma'am was bone-thin. My daddy had a little meat, but not much."

"You got a point to this?" Grace asked from a shadow.

"No. Just talk is all."

"Well, I ain't wantin' any of it, so you can hush now. Or else go on out back and talk to the trees or your rocks or some other thing. Just so long as you leave me alone."

"Whew, Lord! I see it now why that one out there loves you. See it clear as a bell—"

"A bell ain't clear at all. I ain't never seen one that weren't made of copper or some sort of steel. To say something's clear as a bell's showin' foolishness is all—" Grace heard a scrape and then a scuffling run. Turning, watching through Even's narrow kitchen opening, she saw the bony woman run out into the backyard laughing like a hyena.

"Lord have mercy on *all* our souls," Grace said, her head aching with a powerful ache.

"Seems to me you got a lot done on your own," Neva said in a silky voice. "Val, you should've called us last night, dear. Let us come on down and get you right then and there."

"The phones were down 'til this morning." She stood folding up Prizewinner into as small a bundle as the large Amish would allow, and once this was done, she set it on the couch with all the other stacks. She didn't own a suitcase. Never had.

"You know, you might be premature. Enid may surprise us and still show up."

"She called this morning from a place in New Mexico. She won't be showing." Val clamped down her mouth. Not wanting to think on, much less speak of, the three-minute conversation that had been so empty of so many things it crackled.

"New Mexico. That's novel." Neva sighed long and loud. "I had guessed this might come sooner or later. Later would have been better, of course—"

"Listen, if you're worried about me and my stuff taking up too much room, I guess I could leave some of it here 'til we decide things. Where I'm to go permanently, I mean." The oil was down in the lamp over the fireplace making her remember, and there was a melted candle on the table next to the kitchen doorway that was speaking to her. The place was clean, though. Cleaner than it'd been since Enid halfway showed up with her rollers and fingernail polish and her suitcase full of red underwear. Val walked over to the candle and took it out of its holder and slipped it into the pocket of her jeans. Jackson had stayed with her until 3 A.M. She had blown out the candle while he walked up the road to his house. "I can work out something else, if I have to."

"Don't be silly. You'll stay with us for as long as you please. Bea's all aflutter rearranging the guest room. Stripping sheets. Dusting. Busy as a beaver—" She laughed out loud. "She always wanted children, you know." Neva made a sour look with her mouth. "Not that you're a child. The bigger part of being a woman now, I'd say." She walked over to the picture of Bea's great-great-grandfather hanging inside an oval frame, the glass curving out in the ugly fashion of that time. "Did Enid say what to do with the car? Or was she too excited over the thought of touring Carlsbad Caverns to think on it?"

"She said I could have it. Said a man from Jackson bought it for her and that the ownership papers were in a tin box under her bed. Did you know that—that somebody else paid for it? 'Cause I didn't. I always thought she paid for it herself with the money from the beauty shop." She saw a sock under the couch. Jackson's.

"Sweetie, I'd hesitate to think your mother ever paid for a thing in her life—"

"Don't call her my mother. I never had a mother and you know it. The whole town knows it." Valuable went to the couch and scooped up the sock while Neva studied the picture. The sock was still wet in its thickest part, the part that covered his ankle. She stuffed it to the center of the middle stack, inside the pedal pushers she'd worn that night eons back when he'd blown smoke out his eye and picked the grass off her knees with his toes.

"Enid's problem is that she forgave herself too easily," Neva said.

Valuable turned to her, thinking it was a reasonably true statement, one based on clear evidence. Neva was still standing in front of the grim relative picture, tracing a finger down the nose. Her side to her, Valuable saw that the woman's nose twinned the man's in the oval frame, an astonishing similarity considering the wide margin of years and lack of blood between them.

"Did you know she ran off when she was thirteen?" She looked at Valuable. "No? Well, I guess that was something she pretended never happened. Luvenia was fit to be tied. "Neva walked over to a straight-backed chair and sat. "We found her down in Pascagoula livin' in a fish camp."

"Granny never said anything about that."

"Luvenia never said a lot of things she should've."

Another true statement. There was another drawer in her room where she kept her writing tools—pens, paper, ink—that she needed to go through, but Neva was being too curious. Valuable watched her pick up an ashtray then put it back down again. Watched her pick up a picture of Valuable as a baby, polish it with the tail of her shirt and then put it back down where it belonged. Where Enid was halfway at most things in life, this one had the tendency to pick. If I were to come to her with a splinter in my foot, I'd likely lose my leg, was Valuable's thought. And even without her grandmother there to correct her math, she knew it was true and reminded herself to be careful, very careful, around this one.

"We could put the house up for sale," Neva said, looking at her with a slight smile on her lips.

"No—"

"Or not," Neva said grinning, delighted, her teeth made white by the dark black of her hair.

Valuable picked up three stacks, including the one where Jackson's sock was hidden, and headed out the front door.

"Here, let me help you." The woman jumped up and opened the door then and Valuable went out, leaving Prizewinner still folded up on the couch, its stained center square exposed to the world.

The light was blinding after such a night of storm and wind. And the sky was such a deep blue it looked like it'd been done up by an overly ambitious painter trying hard to impress. Limbs were down, scattered in pieces all over the yard, busted up to the size of baseball bats. The mailbox was on its side, too. Sent there by the flash flood, she supposed.

"Looks to me like the earth moved in this part of town," Neva said, lifting one eyebrow. "Must have been a terrifying night, by the look of what's been left in pieces all over the yard."

Careful here. Be careful here. "It wasn't that bad. I slept through mostly."

"Mostly?" Neva winked at her while she opened the back door to her black Plymouth.

"Did it flood out your way?"

"No, believe it or not our bend of the river is higher up than Petal. Runnelstown climbs a bit in spite of things. A good choice of property; its only drawback being its ugly appearance. The Leaf won't crest for another week and we'll watch it daily. But I'm confident we'll be okay. Don't you worry about it." She patted Valuable's cheek.

"I'm not worried." Valuable had been looking up the hill toward the cemetery where Luvenia had slept through it all next to her long-dead father. Toward Jackson's house where he hadn't slept at all because he had been with her. Valuable felt a lump in her throat and a place in the center of her chest began to hurt as if pinched by hard fingers.

"I ought to clean out the perishables from the kitchen. I really have an hour or two more of work to do, so if you've got things you need to tend to, you could come back for me—" She had made him promise he'd stay away while she did this thing, knowing if he were there she wouldn't be able to do it at all. But she called back that promise now, missing him. Wanting him there, standing in the shade, waiting.

"Don't be silly. I'll help. That's what I'm here for. I don't want you here by yourself dealing with all these things that a young person shouldn't have to deal with." She smiled out in the sun, her teeth gleaming.

Valuable felt trapped somewhere cold without a coat. She looked at the sky, hating it. I'll look up at the sky from the River House and it'll be different. The sun will be a stranger—

"You know this could be the best thing that ever happened to you," Neva said in a voice so quiet Valuable almost believed she was sincere, that the cold woman knew how her heart was breaking.

"I've still got things to do, Aunt Neva—" Her throat was closing. I am dying here in slow pieces, she thought.

"Well, let's get to them, shall we? Two will make time fly. Get it done in half the time, just you wait and see." She tucked her arm through Valuable's and led her back across the yard and up the steps to the white house trimmed in blue at the corner of Hillcrest Loop.

Jackson had been watching for most of an hour. Just sitting next to a dripping culvert midways down the street and waiting, hidden behind a misplaced boxwood growing haphazard by the side of the road. He'd gauged the runoff through the concrete pipe and figured it had lessened in the past fifteen minutes to the point of fast trickle now. No longer a stream. Reaching, he let rainwater run into his cupped hand, the mud settling to the bottom of his palm in less than a minute. Where the sand along the bottom of the Baby Black Creek seemed silvery and full of possibilities, the sludge across his palm seemed dirty as old blood and just as limited.

Neva laughed aloud and Jackson looked up. Watched the two of them walk back into the house, arm in arm. There was a point five minutes earlier when he thought Val had seen him and he had held still, thinking if he'd been lucky enough for her to catch a glimpse of him through the brush, he'd best hold his place so her eyes could focus and see him fully. But she went on to study the trees and the dropped limbs all over the yard and what seemed to be either the sky or a cloud, and then she looked away and back at Neva, and Jackson knew she hadn't seen him at all. Freer to move but sad over it, he scratched his elbow and the spot under his neck where a yellow fly caught him two days back.

He patted his shirt, wishing for a cigarette. Something to calm him while he watched the too-fast progress she was making. Nervous over the empty yard with that large black car that looked of hearse. The water trickling steady out the pipe reminding him of last night's rain and other things.

"Come on, Val. Come on back out in the yard so I can see," his voice strangely calm and true to the way it'd always been. I should sound different, he thought. Empty. Drained of blood. He glanced down the street. Absent from the yard or not, it didn't really matter. Didn't matter a bit. He still saw her. Saw her fiddling with her hair while she looked the place over, top to bottom. Stopping and catching her bottom lip between her teeth while she thought long and hard over her list of things, making sure she hadn't forgotten something that might seem small to everybody else but was really big as a giant to her—something like Luvenia's scissors or her hand-colored pictures of horses.

They came back outdoors, Val loaded with Prizewinner and something else that looked like a handbag. Maybe one of Enid's. Neva moved fast and opened up the car door for her. Ran ahead and waited on her like Val was a princess or something. Good Neva. You go right ahead and open that door for Val. Your scales are gonna fall off and she'll see through you. Me and you both know that—

He inched out from the side of the boxwood to get a better look at her.

Lord! but she's pretty—

The sulphurs are orange now, he thought, seeing one block his view. Yellow just a month back when they were all over the woods like a happy plague. But this new crop's in now. Jerking around in the air like they're drunk, too. Bright orange as Halloween wax. Yellow just last month when they couldn't fly a straight line if their short life depended on it. All over the place. Up at the cemetery—

Val walked out to the mailbox and tried to lift it. Neva came over and helped and got the job done, but it still leaned and Jackson was glad.

He watched while Val brushed off her hands and Neva laughed hard about something in that booming man-like laugh of hers. But not Val. Val didn't crack a smile. Just walked to the car and opened the door. Looking over her shoulder in his direction she stood still as a statue and waited.

Neva bounded up to the front door and jiggled the knob. Tested it against entry. Clapping her hands together three times she shouted, "Done! River House here we come!" She jumped down three steps then and ran around to her side of the car. Happy as a clam. Happy as a bird come on a bug. Happy as a hunter come on a deer. Happy. So happy.

No. Not yet. Not yet—

An orange sulphur lit on his hand which was frozen on his knee, but he failed to notice. Three more batted next to his left ear, but they were pure nonsense and not worth considering.

Valuable stood still inside the shade the open car door made, one hand up over her eyes, looking. Stood still without moving a muscle while Neva cranked up the car and revved it like a racer.

His mouth was chalk.

His hands felt dead.

Val stood still. Her right hand over her eyes. Throwing a blue shadow that fell down her face like a silk scarf.

She sees me, Jackson realized. She sees me here beside the bush with this water running like dirty blood—

Overhead a kinglet darted for bugs. Catching its meal expertly in midair. Its hovering and flycatching nervous in application while it flitted in and out of the pinebreak, searching. The bird was pure foolishness and not worth noticing.

She sees me—

Does she?—

Yes, she sees me—

And judging this true and not imagined, he left his perch, unfolded himself from beside the boxwood and stood, jumping the ditch and walking to the center of the road where he raised his hand, palm out as if taking a pledge or oath. Raised it to the level of his face first and then higher up to its limit. Palm out. Fingers together. Reaching for the sky while he stood in the middle of the road and muddy water ran over his shoes.

She moved then and stood on the running board and her head lost its scarf. Broke into the light. He saw her hand raise up in a similar pledge. Stretched high to the limit of her arm. Her fingers together too, but not moving. As if to move them would turn it into a wave, which would turn it into good-bye.

Neva began the motion of backing out the drive and Val ducked into the car and pulled the door to. Her dark head disappearing first and then the hand she'd raised up, palm first, and then she was gone from his sight, all but the shape of her head in the front seat of a car that would always be a hearse, no matter its claim.

"She's goin' two miles away and it feels like a thousand," he said, and his voice was different this time and true to what he was feeling inside and he was glad.

The kinglet with a noise of chopped-up scream swooped down and caught an orange sulphur in its mouth and flew to the top of a pine to eat.

23

A PICTURE OF US ALL

L OUISE GREEN KNEW there were limits to things. She'd just never considered them pressing enough to study. Now this—

"You got any clue how he ended up over at the nigger's house?" her
brother asked. His eyes bloodshot from lack of sleep. His shirt undone
from neck to midchest.

She had parted her hair on a different side that morning for a reason
she couldn't remember anymore and the crossed hairs were hurting her; giving her a headache that ran from crown down to neck. "Grace said we're to
meet the train at noon. I told her we'd be over soon as we could get our
things together so you could talk to him first. See your son. You ready?"

"I asked you a simple question, dammit!" His hand went down hard
on the table and the sugar bowl lid went askew. "It seems to me you could
give me a simple enough answer—"

"No, Beryn," she sighed. "I haven't got a clue how this miraculous inci-
dent occurred. I got the phone call and relayed the message to you. So
there. You ready to go, or do you have some other territory you'd like to
cover?"

"I've got Mary's graveside service tomorrow afternoon—"

"That's tomorrow, Beryn. Today's here and we've got Joleb to consider." She had her purse in her hand—shiny yellow with a fake gold clasp—and was standing by the back door, ready to go.

"Seems to me a strange thing—I went over there the other night and he wasn't there then. Unless they lied, as most everybody knows they're inclined to do easy as breathin'. Rode up and down all over the place for most of an hour before I saw the goat—"

"Well Beryn, he's there now and waiting for his family. You know Grace doesn't lie—"

"How do you know a person don't lie? If they're good at it they never get found out."

Looking out she saw the lawn boy had left a ridge of grass standing. Just a narrow strip no more than two inches in width that was sticking up high as a cowlick in the center of all that green and it worried her. Set her teeth on edge at the boy's carelessness. And her own. That she'd hurriedly paid him his three dollars without checking behind his work.

"I don't know. I just don't know." Beryn turned his butter knife over and over while he sat slumped at the table.

Louise watched the light catch off his knife and throw itself all over the kitchen, finding her face on occasion, hurting her head.

"Grace told me plain as day the other night that she didn't have a clue where the boy was. That's what she said that very night. Up in my face she said it, too. Now, it seems strange to me he suddenly turns up resting on this man Grade's couch. Who'd she say had him?" The chair scraped against the floor when he stood, creased, unwrinkling himself like a badly folded shirt.

"I don't know any more than you do." She rubbed at her head. "He lives over on Bellrose. And he didn't 'have' the boy. You act as though they acquired him at auction, Beryn, or something even more ominous. This man—this Even Grade—found him out in the woods when he went to rescue a woman who would've drowned otherwise. Joleb too, had this man not made the trip. I may be speaking out of turn, but I'd say this has a good chance of making the paper." A picture of us all. A great big picture of us all—

Beryn reached down and turned the knife again and the glare hit her square in the eyes. Moving away from the limit of his aim she found the dark side of the fridge. "You don't want to go, do you? Don't want to see your only son."

He blushed, caught.

"Tell me this, Beryn—where'd this come from? This lack of feeling for Joleb?" She put her purse on the counter and moved across to a chair and sat. Seated at the table with Beryn standing beside her, she looked up the twin tunnels of his nose and saw that he needed to trim his nose hairs, had needed to trim them for a good many years in fact. She looked away feeling something kin to pity, but not quite. "Don't act like I'm the stupid one here, either, Beryn. You don't like the boy. You never have and I want to know why." Her hands folded patiently across her gray skirt, she waited, looking somewhere other than up.

Beryn strolled over to her blue metal canisters and lifted each lid. With his back almost to the limit of her observation, but not enough, he licked his forefinger, stuck it down deep into the sugar and licked it clean. Dump it soon as he leaves, Louise told herself. Dump it way out in the back of the yard for the ants and put in new. He walked to the sink then and turned on the water, letting it run constant, as if the wet movement would settle things between them.

"Well?" she said, impatient with his gimmicks.

"Ain't it obvious?" The water was still running.

"No. If it were obvious, I wouldn't be sitting here asking you about it when we'd be much better served to get ourselves into the car and head on over to Bellrose."

"Seems like you being a teacher and all, you ought to be smart enough to figure this thing out—" Ducking down and leaning on his elbow, he rested his head on his hand and watched the water. One hip jutted out angled and wooden-looking from inside his pants, as if a two-by-four was where leg should be. As if something sentimental had been attempted by a total idiot with a taste for prosthesis.

She removed her glasses and sighed. Rubbing the spot where the part was cross-haired and hurting. "Just pretend for a moment that I'm the stupid one here, then."

Beryn, brightening at the thought, said, "I'll tell you why I feel this way, if you'll tell me something—something I've been wanting to know for a while now."

His normal bland look was somewhere else. His eyes tuning up keen for the first time that Louise could remember in a long span of years. "Okay," she said, but it came out uneasy.

"The reason I feel different for the boy is that he's not mine. Never has been. It's that simple—"

Good Lord. He knows.

"I know he's my own flesh and blood, placed there by my own personal loins, but he ain't mine—"

Good Lord. He doesn't know.

"I remember how Mary cried out that night in childbirth," Beryn said then. "Fixed the queer name 'Joleb' to him and I remember how everybody, including you, hung on her last words and nailed it to the boy as if I didn't have a say in anything at all, other than placing him there inside her in the first place." He reached into his back pocket and pulled out his comb and put it to work. "And then by that second day when the doctor walked in and told us the truth of it—where we stood concerning Mary's recovering, what'd you do?" He sniffed his comb before putting it back to his pocket.

Louise looked away, disgusted.

"I'll tell you what you did—you ran out and hired a nigger wet nurse and you took my son out of my very own arms and you—" His voice cracked high, like rigid chalk breaking with a scream in the middle of a complicated word.

"Beryn, the baby needed milk—"

"There's cows out in every field! There's powdered milk that comes in boxes! Joleb didn't need his small baby mouth pressed onto black titty skin—" He trembled violently, his cuff links tap-dancing against the countertop while he pressed down his hands.

"You seemed approving at the time—"

"Who stopped long enough to ask? Who? Did you? Did anybody?" Beryn's shaking was alarming. Palsy runs back in this family, severe palsy that's crippling. This could be the beginning of it, she thought, fascinated by the movement.

"Did you ever once ask me how I felt on things?" Beryn reached over with one hand in an effort to still his shaking arm.

No. We didn't. We went straight to the father instead. A man of integrity who believed milk was milk and breast was breast and was thankful there was a wet, full one available to feed his son. She sat quietly, adrift in remorse, having built his dislike to another framework, one based on his suspecting the truth. But this! This narrow, bigoted, petty, bitter, irrational—she gave then, a teacher of English for fifteen years and counting, her mind as barren of proper descriptives as her womb.

"And there's my answer on why I can't take to the boy. It's through no fault of his and that makes me a little man, I realize." He wrapped his long arms around himself in a consoling hug, "But that's the truth of it."

"I must confess, I'm speechless, Beryn."

"Well, that's too bad, 'cause I've got some questions—"

"Shoot," she said, wishing for a gun. A small one with a big bore. Maybe a .38.

He held out one finger. "Now tell me this—why'd you rush to Grace and drag her into this? Why? You never hung out with coloreds. You never give 'em a second thought other than who's gonna cut your grass or clean your house. Yet you single-handedly found this one—with a full tit at that, too. How you'd do it? No—why'd you do it?"

Louise barely blinked. To judge any man, or woman, on any matter, the man or woman would have to be considered worthy to be judged. Would have to prove that he or she were capable of forward movement, toward good or evil. Regardless of eventual destination, there had to be an inclination somewhere inside to pick up one foot and lay it down and do the same, time and again. Beryn was nowhere and content to be. Stagnant-like and heavy, inert and immovable. Because of this she held her peace on the truth of it, saving that for someone more deserving. She lied with little effort. "We were trying to make it easy for you, Beryn," she said. "That's all. Just make it easier for you to deal with."

"Well, it was a disservice—"

"I realize that now. We were shortsighted in our approach—" Dear Lord, but my head hurts.

"As the near-blind." He tucked a hand under each armpit and said,

"You and all the rest can judge me a small man for thinking so, consider me brainless and small-minded from now 'til Jesus comes, but I'll not back down on the matter. I saw that baby put to her chest and my heart froze. Froze. You know how that feels? You have any idea how that knife cuts through a person?" He reached behind him and turned off the water.

Louise picked up the butter knife that was still on the table, catching and sending light to the base of his nose, exposing his hairs. "Yes. Yes, I do."

⌑

Joleb's head moved and his eyes opened, showing whites gone red now as he fought to focus, to bring it all in to where he was living, which was nowhere, just a place on a ledge inside a dead world where he was king.

"Gaaayy," he moaned.

"Good Lord, what in the world? And what's he doing with his face?" Louise was alarmed. The boy's appearance was worse than Burris's and his had been damn near a nightmare.

"He's sayin' 'Grace' is what he's saying and I ain't got a clue about the mouth and what it's doing."

"Dear Jesus!" Louise said.

"Have mercy," Grace said, wiping at her eyes.

"He'll heal just fine, but for his heart," Joody said, and both women turned to her and stared.

"Louise, this here's Judy, a friend of Even Grade's." Grace put her hand on Joleb's head, her eyes to his swollen mouth, which looked frog-like. "Louise Green is Joleb's aunt," she explained.

Louise ran her eyes over the black woman's sticks, trying to evaluate their purpose. Aware suddenly of her pause, she stuck out a hand and said, "Pleased to meet you." The woman's clasp inside her hand was strangely warm and loose.

"Like I said, he'll heal just fine, but for the heart," Joody said. "The heart's the problem, though. That and how he needs his daddy round to love him."

"Beryn is right outside. He's been sick with a flu or he'd be in here right this minute." Louise saw him out on the porch, leaving himself a wide margin between the two Negroes.

"That ain't the daddy I'm talking of—" Joody said.

"Judy, I think you need to hush now." Grace looked at the boy, who had moaned.

"No, I don't think so. When I need to hush I get a warning feeling near this stick," she pointed to a pale blue year with silver dots. "I ain't got it now, which means I ain't sayin' something that ain't already known." She smiled guilelessly.

"Who in the world *are* you?" Louise Green asked with genuine interest.

"Joolaa Graaa—" Joleb said from the couch, reliving a conversation he'd had with a man in a long black robe. "Who *are* you?" that man had asked inside a place lit up by candles.

Grace stood up, her hands to her hips, "You two want to talk—go off in the next room. You get the boy stirred up we never will get him on the you-know-what." She shooed them away as one would a dog or a goat or anything troublesome and underfoot. Once they moved to the kitchen Grace stared out the window at the three men on the porch, wondering how long it'd be before Mr. Beryn Green broke down, climbed off his nigger-hatin' high horse and spoke.

There was a salt mill on the table. And a knobby glass sugar bowl, just like in her house. Louise put her yellow purse to the cracked yellow table and it sat there like a slab of cheddar cheese. "Did Grace tell you about Joleb?" She couldn't imagine it, Grace was usually so reticent.

"The boy wears the truth like fuzz. Just like peach fuzz." Joody smacked her lips, wishing she had one.

This kitchen is warm. Warmer than any kitchen I've ever been in. It's a man's kitchen, though, what with the smell of cigarettes more lingering than beans or meat or dish soap. Louise watched her, thinking, She's but a tall bag of graceful bones in those overalls of hers. The black woman was fiddling with the coffee pot. Her long fingers put the parts in backward. Took them out again. Put them in upside down, the perking pole up high and leaning. A finger was missing on her right hand and Louise looked away out the back door to a yard full of pecan trees.

"Truth is loud sometimes. Fuzzy loud." Joody took the guts from the pot and set them aside. Filling the pot with water she turned it up and drank from its spout.

She may be a graceful bag of bones but this woman's confidence is somewhere other than the kitchen. "Here—show me where the grounds are and I'll perk up a pot." Louise watched her open and search through cabinets it was obvious she'd never seen before in her life. "Hold it there— open that one up again." This one "sees" fuzzy loud truth, but she's never perked coffee. What a wonder—

Joody put a finger to the side of her nose. "You a fine woman. Your hair's wrong, though, set as it is to the left of your nose rather than the right. You got large feet and broad hips, though."

"Coffee's not a hard thing to learn. You'll learn soon enough. And my mother was a large woman with large feet, I suppose that's the reason."

"You ain't never known a man, though. Ain't got no desire to, neither. Not yet."

Louise measured coffee. Well, she reads only partial because there had been that time in college when she'd almost, but not quite. "Not ever, my dear."

"We see about that."

Louise wondered if the woman's heritage was American Indian what with those cheekbones of hers. She noticed the sticks were multicolored but faded, their patterns orderly enough in a childish sort of way.

"Grace out there ain't decided she likes me yet—" She grinned, show-ing brilliant white teeth and blue gums. "She will one day. Just you wait and see. She's a fine woman, too. Drove that truck and saved us all. Sewed up Even Grade's ass good and proper. Loves that beat-up boy out there on the sofa though that love's settin' crossways of her man's throat out there on the porch."

"The man with the limp?" Thinking those old sticks look authorita-tive, somehow. Like something belonging to an ancient queen come ashore by mistake in a common land full of limits. Louise thought of a writing she'd favored during the early college years when she'd almost, but not quite. *She was a princess once, of an ancient house, reared in the cave of the wild north wind, her father—*

"No, the limpin' man's *my* man. That's Even Grade." Her chest puffed up like a bullfrog's. "That one's *my* man. And he ain't never limped 'til he rode down to the creek and rescued us and then he slid into a stump and got himself tore up over it." Joody leaned over and sniffed the coffee. Put her finger in the steam and then licked it like a child. "Ever now and again a man needs to be marked. 'Specially when they do something as sacred as saving somebody. Most boy babies have their rod's hood taken early on by the knife to break the manbody of its fear of pain. Even never lost his hood with his being an orphan and all and Deep Mother saw to the remedy by breaking open his rear with a stump—"

Louise was hypnotized; hypnotized by the sticks. As swollen in her tall and narrow heart by their mystery as one's foot might swell if stung by a dozen bees. They hang down chin level in front and longer in the back, she noticed, wondering how the woman slept and what she did when the hair grew long and away from her scalp. Wondering what she did to merit them. Who put them there. She never has to fool with a part, either. The coffee perked and gurgled in rhythm with the woman's lesson concerning foreskin and marking and pain. Louise wanted to touch the blue stick with silver dots. She wanted to roll it between her old-maid fingers. Who knows what this woman knows? What she's seen? Where she's been? How she managed to be?

She was a princess once . . . Well, how in the world had she landed in Petal?

Even looked at Canaan and Canaan looked right back. Their hands were in their pockets fingering loose change. Hidden. The movement missed by the man at the end of the porch who was pretending he was elsewhere. Wishing to God he was elsewhere, so ill at ease with the expended effort of pretending and wishing, he was pouring salt that dropped around his feet in curious patterns.

I have met hateful ones and swaggering ones and good ones and murdering ones. But never one of this brand, Even thought, at once curious and cautious, having heard of men so uncomfortable around coloreds they came near shitting themselves upon encounters, but never having met one up close within range of exhaled breath. August is done with us but for this, he thought, looking around his muck of a yard. The nervous white man standing on the porch a measly monument to the queerest August yet.

Thinking on sums and their strange totals, Even added Canaan's cold steadfast glare out onto mud that didn't bear consideration to mean he was insulted. The two of them having stood long enough in the presence of this Mr. Beryn Green without benefit of a "thank you for savin' my boy" or anything of the sort coming from the white man's mouth. There will be sport here of some sort, Even realized. He stood still as a post, his hands in his pockets stirring his loose change while he waited.

Mr. Green took a step forward and looked in the direction of Clorena's tilted pink house, lower now and fully in the mud on one side, sending the doorway at an angle that would prove a hard accommodation for entry or exit. He bent his bony head to the right in a solitary minute in study. He shook his head and blew air through his nose, thinking, You niggers—you give a nigger a two-by-four and he tries to build a tire. My, oh my. What he said out loud was this: "The owner didn't build that house that way on purpose, did he?" His voice sounded choppy as a three-year-old turned loose on a piano.

"She surely did." Canaan nodded his head.

Well here we go, thought Even Grade.

"Well, I never—" Beryn Green blew air again. Hard this time.

"There's a reason for it, though," said Canaan. "She's an off-balanced woman. Got one leg a foot longer than the other and she had the house built special to allow for it."

"Did it work?" Beryn leaned again, angled his head again and looked, thankful his limbs were equal and his house was rightly plumbed. Thinking, My, oh my.

"Mostly. For going frontways, that is. Not for backways, though. That's why we call her One-Way Woman." Canaan's hands were still in his pockets jingling change.

"Why's that?"

"'Cause she can't go but one way inside the house all the time. Has to go with the lean in order to allow for that overlong leg."

"Well, I'll be goddamn—" Beryn Green was hard at work thinking.

"If she goes in and forgets to fetch her mail out the box at the road, One-Way Woman's got to go clean out the back door and back round again just to get her bills."

"Why not take down the other side of the house? That way should she forget her mail, she could go both ways—" Beryn said with a smirk. Thinking, My, oh my, and These people vote now.

Canaan stared bug-eyed at the man. This almost ain't fun, this man is so dumb. He looked at him level. "Takin' it down on the other side would set her back where she started—with a level house that'd prove a trial to her overlong leg."

"Hmmm," was the suspicious sound that slid out of this Mr. Beryn Green.

"If we didn't have a near-to-dead boy in there, I'd take you over to meet her. She's contrary most times. Likes to bite black men for no reason. This one here—" He threw his thumb Even's way, "got ten stitches taken in his buttocks 'cause of her. Even Grade? Show him. Undo your pants now and show Mr. Green your ass."

Even fiddled with his belt.

"No. No now. You stop where you're at." Beryn Green held up his hand. Wanted no part of it, unsure as he was of the nigger passions and where their intentions might lead. "There ain't no need in that. It wouldn't be proper for him to expose himself out in the open and all."

"Hell, we expose ourselves daily round here. Dance naked round that goat wanderin' up thataways." Canaan pointed up the street. "You sure you don't want to see? 'Cause Even here don't mind. Even here likes to show his ass in public ever chance he gets. Don't you, Even?"

"You say that true," Even said. "Ever chance I get." He leaned over the rail and spit.

Canaan lit up a smoke. "Well, like I was saying, One-Way Woman's contrary most times, but she likes white folks. White men especially. Likes to take off her shoes and show off her sixteen toes."

This Mr. Green seemed to have the beginnings of palsy. Even listened to his cuff links rattle against the rail thinking, There is a reality here that he's too full of noise to ever work in the Hattiesburg Library.

"Nobody owns sixteen toes." Beryn looked around for his sister thinking, Witchcraft, and My, oh my and Holy shit all at once.

"That one does," Canaan said.

"Eight toes per foot, I suppose?" Beryn Green asked. A part of him knowing it couldn't possibly be true, but another part allowing it because he wanted it true.

"Nah—that'd be too easy for God. One-Way Woman's got five on one foot and eleven on the other."

"You're foolin' now. I can sense it. Both you boys are standin' here playin' with me and it ain't a nice thing, either, not with my son in there."

"Nah I ain't. I'll take you down and show you. She uses the eleven-toed foot as a rake. See how nice the street looks?" Canaan pointed.

Even shook his head. They'd freed the goat from his harness of refuse and dumped the raked-up trash to a center pile for burning later. Canaan pointed to the pile full of cans and paper and busted-up pieces of whatever.

"She hires out, too, every autumn when the leaves fall," Canaan said. "You want me to see if she'd come rake your yard with her foot?"

"I'd like to see my son, now—" Beryn held his hands still under his armpits. "There's not much time left before the train shows, I guess."

They had made three previous tries at getting him in the house. His vague excuses spelling out he'd never been inside a colored's domain and had no intention of breaking his record. Now this. Even watched Canaan step forward to the door. "Here you go, you go right on in." When the screen banged shut Canaan turned and said, "Serves that asshole right."

"You say that true," said Even Grade, his rear still sore and stiff but feeling remarkably better all of a sudden.

24

DANCE MUSIC

—

I T WAS HOT. Too hot too soon for two days after such a storm as two nights before.

Old folks quarreled and grumbled with young folks concerning it, seeing their young folks as too far inside the mercy margin of God to recognize a true mercy once it appeared. They ain't ever needed mercy, so how could they know the feel of it, more than one commented. And most, if not all, agreed.

"But for the train and what came across on it, there'd be no good thing to say about any of it! Not one single thing!" the old woman shouted to her granddaughter. "Teenagers!" she allowed next, to no one in particular, put out and pissed off with the girl's immediate near-blindness to God's gift and the lesson it dangled. "You think you know what you need!" this grandmother shouted one more time outside Hal's Music Store on the Hattiesburg side of the river. Her dress country-gone-to-city-but-once-a-month and not very good to look at, much less to wear while standing and hollering in the middle of the street. "You think 'cause I ain't got the money for a new record you can dance to, you've got need to sit down and cry and pout?"

To observers the two were like waddling geese. One young and running ahead and the other fat and old and needing a cane more than she needed to be heard. But getting neither.

"You read this paper here!" The old one shook it high in the air and a piece flew out the middle and sent her backtracking, her feet shuffling hard in worn-out flats, working the brick sidewalk hard as the hands that laid it there. Once done—once seeing it was nothing but a pharmacy flyer and nothing more—once on the waddle again, she caught up with the girl and yelled out again, "Read it, I say, and tell me straight on how piti- ful you are. How bad you need that new record to dance to. Do it! Go on girl, do it!" Yelling this out while shaking the paper in the sun, she drew a near crowd of Hattiesburgers who on notice of the old woman's dress and its not-very-good-to-look-at appearance knew she was coun- try-gone-to-city-but-once-a-month and turned their heads and put a rush to their steps.

"But Jesus, it's turned hot again, ain't it?" she said quick and quiet to a woman at her side walking too fast for casual, too fast to care about the heat. The old woman thinking the whole time the woman she'd spoken to—gone now and down the street—was someone she'd known once upon a time when she was young and thin and granddaughterless and didn't need a cane.

"You think you need a new record blaring loud and keeping me awake most of the night? I don't think so. Read about that poor Green boy the train brought over. Read about the only good thing to say about any of it. Go on, read. Read how he screamed so long and loud he's gone more'n halfway mad with it. Go on now, read it, girl. You girl! You ain't listening to word one I'm sayin', are you?" A pause while she looked both ways and crossed the street. Still waddling. Still yelling, "You think you got suffer- ing? We got a house and a bed and food in the cabinet," she was saying. "You got a brother at home workin' hard to help out your mama. What's that Green family got besides two fresh graves and a boy who'll end up in a loony bin? And still you want a record. Some loud music to keep your granny up all night!

"Lord, but it's hot! Too hot too soon for such a thing as two nights back. And humid as an armpit, too! Don't you think?" She said this to a city man who looked vaguely familiar. Like someone she'd known before she'd watched her seed split and produce this unruly granddaughter. Like someone she'd known back in the time of Roosevelt's first term, when her knees could still touch, before her burden of heavy fat crawled between them. The man hurried past, near running and holding to his hat.

"That poor boy spent days in the woods before being found," she yelled again with a flap of her arms. "Read it here. Came near dying and you want a record to dance to. You want your old granny to buy you a record—Well, I'll say this straight up. You read this story and I'll consider it. Sit down on the curb here while I catch my breath and fan some air up to my behind. Whew Lord! but it's a too-hot day. Too hot too soon for what we been through! Sit now and read. Read how young Joleb Green screamed his brother's name the whole way over the River Leaf. Read how he was still screamin' when they put him in the ambulance and carted him off. Read how he had to ride over on the very thing that killed his brother and then tell me how bad you want that record—how bad you want to dance."

25
LETTERS

JACKSON WALKED HOME from school missing the cotton. Missing the way it'd lie in drifts on the ground in clumps that looked like snow, but wasn't.

The big trucks should be parked out in the fields by now. Loud and throwing up oily black smoke. All those hired-on field hands should be hollering and singing, shootin' the shit while standing up to their thighs in all that white. And the machines—Lord, he missed them! The way they'd eat those rows in a too-hungry hurry, leaving a handful on each cotton plant. Not much, but still enough to remind anybody walking or riding by what had been planted and hoped on and prayed over and cussed at and finally harvested and taken in to market. The cotton should be in, Jackson thought. The leftovers of it should be scattered up and down every highway around here. Pieces of white stuck in fence barbs and low-hanging branches of the trees and in the swept-up saw grass that leans along the highways. The cotton should be a part of October. It just ain't right for me to see clean roads this time of year when I ought to be seeing white.

Wishing for this thing, he walked on up the hill, passing Val's blue-trimmed house with its bright red For Sale sign fresh in the ground. The mailbox still leaned, but not so much as the day before. He packed it a little with his foot every time he passed, determined he'd make it stand proper again. A job Neva hadn't been able to do. He glared at the real estate sign thinking, That sign's too fresh for this red-dust place. Too much like a brand-new pair of black shoes bought only for a funeral and nothing else. Remembering how Val had come flying down to his house in Enid's car (Val's car now) and wept all over his bed while he sat beside her, wondering where to put his hands. Where to let them rest that he wouldn't mind his mother walkin' in and seeing. He had settled on the crown of her head while her nose ran snot all over his beige Bronco Bill bedspread.

There should be cotton here, too. Blown clean up my street from the big trucks running loud up the county roads. Thinking on this and very little else, he passed the Hillcrest Cemetery to the right, and looking down saw his house at the bottom of the slope. White. Small. The magnolia trees with their fan-like leaves standing quiet along the boundaries the only things about the place that looked alive.

They were sitting across from each other, faced off and frosty as December— the way they'd been for months now—when Jackson came in from school and set his books down on the kitchen table.

"Take them to your room," Lucy said. "I'm tired of picking up after you."

"She means it, too, I tell you—" his father said. Falling in second to her words his new habit of late. A way of marking him as still a part of her. Not equal and to the side the way Jackson imagined a true marriage should be, but standing somewhere behind where he caught her words and made weak coward-like echoes. Jackson scooped up his books. Walking out he saw his dad's suspenders up on his shoulders and not down around his waist. Down being the only way Jackson had seen them once the man was done with work and quit of the shop for the day. Up meant something. He wasn't sure what it meant. But he was sure it meant something. His mother's head was tied back with a scarf and this probably meant something, too. Or maybe not. Since how she wore her hair was behind him now. That and how tired she was of picking up after him. And how sick to death she'd become of everything having to do with him since Burris Green was buried. Fine and good, he thought, walking out, but frowning on notice of the letter, opened and spread facedown on the kitchen table. He saw the envelope that belonged to the letter had an underside of pink.

Once in his room he sat on his bed and waited, smelling the onset of something. Feeling it grow out in the kitchen where his parents sat, one with his suspenders up, the other with a scarf in her hair. He steeled his face while he thought back on his short list, checked it twice. He'd been careful. They'd both been careful. Even Neva liked him now and had dropped her hard looks, what with the way he'd made himself sit in the parlor and play those dumb parlor games when he'd rather have been out-side in the dark, playing another sort of game entirely.

Muted voices floated back and he sat up hard and listened, and then he went and stood by the door as he'd never done in his life, fully convinced now that something was up. Something bigger than large. The voices were even and medium, too absent of all those things necessary to send a voice either up high enough or down deep enough to be understood. Just bland and unreadable and adult.

"Jackson!" his father yelled out from the kitchen. "This concerns you, boy. Come on in here."

You boy. He said, You boy, like I'm a nigger out cuttin' his grass and doing a sorry job of it, too. Walking in with a new casualness he'd learned since August—a flawless, insincere gait as hard to memorize as a half-worked speech in second period Speech class—he strolled into the kitchen and went to the fridge, poured up a glass of buttermilk.

"What's up?" Jackson said, shaking salt into the glass.

"A truckload of plenty—" His father drummed his fingers on that facedown letter. The one that came from the envelope with the pink under-side that spoke of woman and woman-related things. Things that could mean something or nothing at all. Same as his mother wearing a scarf could or could not mean something. Dad's suspenders being up means trouble and I know that. I know it because he's a man and a man is upfront with his trouble. But not a woman. A woman likes to bury hers and then dig it up loud and smelly as burnt toast. And a man is helpless to speak against it, or prepare for it, because it's woman-related and could mean anything. This not-knowing scared him sillier than being called You boy like a nigger by his dad, who was still drumming his fingers. Jackson trained his face to stay still, as well as his hands. His whole being forced calm like he'd come on a slinking, belly-to-ground dog showin' its teeth.

"I think you should sit, Jackson," John Henry said once he quit his drumming.

"I am sitting." A drink of buttermilk.

"You are? Well, you are at that, ain't you? Well, we've had some news here and it ain't good news and your mother here thinks you'll be distressed at it. Throw some kind of violent fit or something." He waved his hand in the air. "That's why she called me home from work an hour early to witness this."

Jackson took another drink, his heart so loud he could barely hear the words. Just a booming *kawhomp kawhomp kawhomp* thundering in his ears making his head hurt worse than any burnt-toast-smelling brand of headache.

"John Henry—" Lucy said and her tone was made of ice. Ice inside of ice inside of more ice. She could kill a ship, she's so cold, Jackson thought, listening.

"No now, you wanted me to do this thing and by God, I'm gonna do it. Brought me home an hour early just for this and by God if the boy's gonna throw a fit, I mean to see it. He won't, though. You'll see." He pointed his finger this time. Not at her, though. More like at the sugar bowl. He cleared his throat. His suspenders were still up, man-like and open, unlike her scarf, which floated behind her head, flashing every once in a while against faded brown hair.

Jackson drank deep and drummed his fingers on the table—pinky to ring to fuck to fore—and managed to look bored with it all while he sweated a river that ran clean down his back.

"Like I said, we've had some unexpected news—"

Well, here we go.

"—from Chamblee." And while his father squirmed Jackson relaxed. *He* was the one upset by what was face down. *He* was. It wasn't about Jackson or Val or what they'd done at all.

"Did Granny die?" Jackson hoped not because that would mean leaving Petal for a week at least, and that would be bad. Terribly bad.

"Lord no. That old woman'll live forever—" John Henry said while Lucy glared, the look jerking him back to where he needed to be quicker than lightning, as if she'd put her hands to the back of his drawers and pulled up hard. The tables have turned here, Jackson thought. Turned a while back, too, now that I think on it, and I wonder why?

"She took ill last winter, you know. Of course she's near to eighty-three and always felt poorly—though I doubted there was ever anything there true to it—" his father stammered out.

"The nurse has quit Peachtree," Lucy interrupted in a flat voice, look-ing hard at Jackson as if news of the nurse quitting would slay him dead to the floor. He stared right back and she looked away finally. "Gran has had another stroke. Or so the doctors think."

"Then why'd the nurse quit? Seems like she's needed now more'n ever."

"'Cause your grandmother threw her knitting at her and stabbed the woman in the temple with a crochet needle. It didn't kill her, thank the good Lord, just probed deep enough to leave it hanging under the skin. Not too much harm, but just enough to make her quit. I tell you, she threw it hard across the room. Twenty feet. How anybody sick can throw knitting twenty feet across the ro—" John Henry realized the error of his ways and pushed his chair back hard and stood, moving a safe distance toward the sink as if Lucy had something hidden in her lap that she intended to pull out and throw. Something that would leave itself dangling in a region lower than his head, too.

"So, she quit. They'll find another one." Fuck *me*, what total crap adults turn everything to. His heart was slowing to near normal, freeing up his face to be more animated and open and man-like, sending his thoughts somewhere other than women and their women-related things.

"They already have," Lucy said and smiled.

And Jackson knew. Knew without benefit of reading the facedown letter. Knew as cleanly as if he were seeing through a fresh-scrubbed window. Knew as well as if he were God and knew all there was to know about everything there is. He knew. But still he drummed his fingers and drank his buttermilk while his heart picked up the pace with its *kawhomp kawhomp kawhomp*, heavier now and darker and old-man–like. He kept his eyes fixed square on his mother's face. She squirmed, though. Twisted herself around in the kitchen chair as if her ass itched from poor hygiene.

"See Lucy? See what a silly worrier you've turned yourself into? Christ!" John Henry slid his suspenders off his shoulders with a pop and went to the fridge and rummaged for beer, off-duty and fully at home finally. "Make me come home early for this. Tell me I don't know my own son—" His voice came back small and brittle, buried as it was beside the cold bottle of milk.

"How long?" Jackson asked quietly, waiting patiently for the stab.

"How long *what*, Jackson?" His mother slumped to the side and played with the end to her scarf. Wrapped it round and round. Its silk tail limp as a man's failure.

"How long before you go?" he said, praying.

"*You?* Don't you mean *we*? We're going as a unit. A unit. *We* will be going by the first of November. Possibly sooner if the house sells as quickly as the real estate person believes. Once the house is sold, as well as your father's business, *we* will head out. There is no singular *you* who will be going. *We* will be going." She smiled then and it was a sad thing to see because it was such a dark and jagged exposition of her woman-like ways. A thesis, really. A library, actually. He'd never seen her look at him that way, never seen any mother look at her son that way, which meant he was part of a group of strangers who didn't like one another at all but were going somewhere to live together—as a unit—in a town he'd only visited once or twice in the past ten years. We. A unit. Going. Going. Gone.

"I must say, you're taking this better than I'd thought." But her smile said too much, spilled the beans. "Much better than I imagined."

I bet.

"If you want time to go tell Valuable, we'll allow it. Your father will even let you borrow the car for it, if that's what you want." She folded her hands over the facedown letter.

"The hell I will—" And then John Henry turned and saw her face and said, "Sure—I mean, I guess so, if that's what he wants to do. You got to be back before dark, though. I guess it'd be all right this once. So you can tell her in person, I mean. How is Val these days, anyhow?"

Jackson watched the man holding the bottle of beer and his heart sealed itself up inside his chest. I don't know these people. I don't know these people at all and I'm stuck with them. But his mouth said, "Fine. Val's just fine." He drained his glass and stood up then, an old man with an old beating heart. Gone from sixteen to sixty in thirty seconds flat. But his face was young and the same as it'd always been and his parents looked back at him the same as they'd done yesterday and the day before that and the day before that, and then they looked at each other in a way they'd only begun this past summer. "I'll see her tomorrow," Jackson said. "That's soon enough for this."

"Jackson, I'm sorry, but I've got no choice here."

I bet. I bet you're really sorry here, Ma. I bet you're so sorry you'll cry all night over this one. Both of us. You got both of us. Me and Dad. Got us by the balls this time—you and your woman-like, scarf-decorated, pink-enveloped "I'm sorry I've got no choice here" ways. He put his glass in the sink, rinsed it out, and then walked down the hall to his room. The letter was still facedown on the table. Face down and curled along the edges next to the envelope bearing pink.

"Where is she?" Neva asked, bored-sounding, which was a lie. The walnut paneling was in the process of being refinished in the library and they were sitting in the parlor, in strange chairs that felt stiff as new clothes.

"Up in the attic. She's got her head buried in that trunk and it keeps her busy I think, picking through all those old things up there—"

"Do you know this for sure?" Neva peered over glasses.

"Well, seeing how I'm not omnipotent, I can't be positive. But it's a safe guess. Honestly!" Bea turned back to her correspondence, picking up a recent letter from Enid, all sounds multiplying until the room seemed full of torn paper and rustling.

What'd I give for quiet and small and a room free of echo, Neva thought as she studied Bea's back, its fleshy, pale hump at the base of the neck new-formed, her jowls fleshy and white. Too much goose and not enough salad, she supposed.

"Do you think it's wise that she's up there?" Neva asked, her question sincere-sounding, which was another lie. "I mean, there are things up there that might upset her, what with her recent, limited circle of friends—"

"What in the world are you rambling on about?" Bea said. Her head bent over a letter.

"I'm not rambling on about anything—I mean, there are things up there that are best kept where they're at—buried deep in a trunk or a box or wherever the hell Luvenia stored that crap from the old place."

"Neva, please—"

"Please what? I just ask a simple question is all."

"You've never asked a simple question in all your life." Bea turned, her pen in her plump hand. The nib of it holding a blue-black tear ready to drop down to the Persian rug. "That's why I'm crazy for you." She smiled all the way up to her sweet blue eyes and Neva knew why she was with her inside these loud walls. The tear dropped and fell into a sea of cobalt blue where it blended true as if it belonged there.

"I hate this house, Bea—"

"I know, Sweet."

"All these dark rooms that nobody needs."

"I know. And it's set me to thinking—"

"Uhh ohh—"

"Now hear me out, Nev. Give it a chance." Bea's smile seemed confident, which was a lie. "I've thought recently of turning it into a country inn. A quiet getaway place—"

"Have you gone completely mad!" Neva came to her feet.

"No, it'd be a good source of income—"

"Which we sure as hell don't need!"

"We could entertain folks from Jackson or New Orleans or Atlanta. Open it up to the historical society and bill it as an inn with a past."

"This is Mississippi, Bea! The only history here is a bad one that nobody in their right mind would want to remember. We're on the river, too. A brown muddy river that's shaped like a bowel. You're mad. Completely. There is no way I'll stand for having people—total strangers—slip in and out of this place while we hold court and clean toilets. No way."

Bea was back to her letter. Bent low and reading, "I was just playing with the idea is all. I haven't set it to motion or anything like that." Her pen scratched on paper. "Valuable wanted to know where the shovel was kept, by the way. Maybe you could find it for her."

"Jobbing me out? Trying to find busywork for me now that I've shit-canned your inn idea?"

"No, you're just not your usual happy self is all and I thought a little activity would help."

"We have a child now, Bea. A living, breathing, miniature human female wandering around in all our things. Sticking her nose God knows where. Not a dog, mind you, or a cat—two things we could take to the pound or let out by the side of the road or tie up in a bag and toss in the river—but a child. I think this switch in routine is enough to irritate any-body."

"You love her, you and I both know it. Stop being so dramatic."

Ignored. That's what I am. Neva rose and went and stood behind Bea, reading over her shoulder, running a finger over her hump. She bent and rested her chin on her shoulder. "What's sweet Enid up to these days?"

"It seems she's married." Bea leaned back into Neva's neck.

"Nice. And while she honeymoons we get left to raise her child—"

"She said we could send her out if we wanted, and Valuable's not a child, Neva," Bea said.

"Oh, you're quite right there. Not a child at all. A young lady really. A beautiful young lady who plunders around up in the attic and oh, by the way, wants a shovel."

"Could you find it for her please? She's asked about it several times now."

"Aren't you a little bit curious about why she wants it?" Neva said.

"I would assume she wants to dig a hole or bury something. Maybe plant a rose bush."

"And this doesn't worry you?"

"Neva, you've always worried enough for both of us." She dipped in the pen again and turned, its nib pregnant and wet. "You know? Horses might be a thing to consider again. You were happiest doing dressage—those three-day events and all." Bea put the pen to paper and went back to her writing as if her only job in the world were throwing suggestions out over her shoulder every four or five minutes. Low yellow light cut into her, blossomed into a wide shadow that reached out and swallowed the couch with its tiny velvet pillows.

Her hands to the chair back, Neva said, "You think I've still got it? I mean with the horses?"

Three-day events. Three days gone from this place. Three days of small, quiet rooms.

"It's like sex and childbirth, hon. It's something you never forget."

And how should you know seeing how you never did one and hardly ever do the other, the whole while thinking, "three days away." Dressage was definitely a thought. And if I'm too old for competition—judging. Again, "three days away." Away from this drafty, loud house and if I know the face that's bent over that frivolous letter, a place soon to be filled with strangers looking for history. Slapping her legs, she said, "Horses might not be a bad idea after all."

"That's nice, dear." Bea was reading how Enid's handsome new husband once repossessed a houseboat and threw the occupant into a bayou full of alligators. Bea underlined the words. The man might just be an interesting asset to her mysterious inn idea.

"Well, I'm off to find the shovel. God knows, I think I'll sleep with one eye open tonight. Just in case it's something bigger than a rose bush she's wanting to plant."

"You're such a goose, Neva—such a dark person, really." Bea turned the envelope over looking for a return address. There wasn't one.

But the woman was gone, sidestepping out into the hall with only a cursory glance up the stairs toward the attic.

Grace stuck the letters down between her tits and walked out the door. The goat, grazing off to the side of the house, raised its head, its bells chime-like. Stepping down from the porch the woman stood with her hands to her hips searching the street for something, or so it seemed. She stood that way for a long minute then went walking out through the gate. The goat followed.

"You go on now—the man hates you. Hates your sorry guts." "Sorry guts" came out of her mouth like a lullaby sung easy and the animal wagged its tail. "You go on back inside that gate or I'll take off my shoe to you! Just Plain Grace'll do it, too. You know I will." The goat stood still in his tracks and cocked his head off to the side.

"Lord, but you a sorry goat after all, ain't you?"

Looking around, she saw the houses lining the street wore haloes of late-day sun. Seemed almost holy-like. Made that way by evening, which framed them, hid their massed centers of dark as well as their windows and doors, just showing off outlines that were pure false-gold and lit. The goat was steadfast in the center of it all, walking up and nudging Grace in the thigh like a stubborn angel, and she gave to it while she scratched out his head. "Well, you come on then. But if the man takes a newspaper to your sorry head, I ain't steppin' in this time. No sir, I ain't."

Even saw them coming and sat still on his porch wishing he had the broad magic to disappear, blend clean into the faded boards of his house unnoticed, like an old spider. He eased himself off his sore cheek and leaned to his side. The wound had grown back its center lumped and hard and with an even harder memory of the woman, for every time he saw her, either walking down the road or leaning on Canaan's porch in a full talk, his ass's memory spoke up and stung deep at a spot near where she did the last of her stitching.

And now here she comes. Walking straight on up the street with a stride that says business, loud as any of Joody's readings. The goat, too, with a gait that says, I'm lazy and she don't give a shit about it, neither. Its bell just a jingling. Sure to disturb Joody from whatever it was she did out back under the pecan trees while he sat quiet and waited and watched over her rocks, set in a wide circle in the center of his yard.

Joody's shrine honoring the night of near death was next to them. Set where the fence used to be. As homage, his ripped pants were stuck on a frame like that of a scarecrow, their busted rear facing the street for all the world's viewing. She'd buried a brick midways in the muck, next to his pants, in honor of the missing Mama Girl rock; a rock who'd screamed loud enough to warn her and Joleb that rain was on the way. Next to the shrine a pile of night wood was stacked inside the ring of rocks. Stacked in a particular order that she insisted on doing herself. Talking to the wood the whole while, he supposed. Those sticks having names and an order of burning, he imagined.

Once Joody was done with the business out back, there'd be a fire burning bright and people would come from all over just to see it burn.

She'd call out things, too, while she stood next to the flames and trembled. "Two of you thinking on one woman and she ain't having neither of you. She got herself a man up in Purvis, you both just too blind to know it!" or "You in the middle. You with the nose that got broke three years back. You got a toothache on the way come tomorrow, so what eatin' you want to do, you better get to!" And the crowd would stir and back up then, uneasy with a group read, not desiring their true thoughts spread to the dirt in front of neighbors. "Preacher man says you a witch-woman," one would call out, because one always did. "I ain't no witch. I ain't got no spells other than irritability," Joody would say right back, good-humored as always, slightly amused by the speculation. "You ain't ever seen a fire burn?" Even might call out, fed up with their watching and their words and with her for being so good-humored when it was his yard being clotted up and examined. And one would talk back, just one, mind you. Maybe the same one who had accused her of being a witch. "I seen a fire—I ain't no fool. I just ain't never seen a fire set to burn next to a scarecrow wearin' torn pants," or "I seen a fire. I just ain't ever seen a fire set inside such a fierce African-lookin' ring." And Even would call out again, "Well, go on back then to where life ain't fierce and your pants ain't torn and leave us be!" And then after they'd gotten their eyes overfull of news to take back to wherever it was they'd come from that wasn't Africa, they'd walk on down the road to their ordinary yards absent of strangeness. Walk on back to yards with plain autumn Mississippi grass and houses full of chairs. Walk on back to where Even Grade was, just three months ago.

Grace came through where the gate used to be. The fence was gone. Had been since the rain. But she made a point of walking through the absentee gate each and every time she visited. Her legs gleaming, made jewel-like and having a look to them of being oiled a little. Even thought she seemed all soft order next to the stacked-up wood and flapping pants.

"Evenin', Even Grade."

"Pretty near, I guess. I ain't looked at my watch in a while."

"Time ain't a big boy round here no more, is it?"

"You say that true." His voice was calm, sheltered.

She hauled herself to the porch, catching to a post. Even leaned and helped her with a hand cupping her elbow, holding the grunt inside. Once there she pulled up one of his yellow chairs. They were piled in a heap on his porch, crowded together like passengers on a bus. Joody thinking chairs set inside four walls ran too big a risk of breaking.

"We ain't got our fire goin' yet, I see. People ain't wandered up yet, either. She out back?"

He watched her steady, but saw no hint of criticism or any of those other things he'd been pricked with for two months now. His rear eased some and he sat more level with the green chair. "She's out back. It's her thinking time and I'm to stay put where I'm at and watch her rocks until she's done. She'll be here directly, I suppose." He looked steady away from the woman's legs, which was a hard thing to do, but something he managed.

"Most all women need airing out. Heavy thoughts kept in's about as bad a thing as a too-tight dress and not gettin' enough air to the behind." Her legs went out in front of her. "I got a word of thanks to give her." She patted her left breast as if the word were kept there. "She told me a good thing about somebody I knowed bein' in heaven and it gave me a measure a peace, and I mean to thank her for it." She looked at him and smiled.

Even didn't say anything. Just nodded his head, stunned her words sounded so opposite of a barbed wire fence.

She pulled a packet of letters from the top of her dress, leaving a gap between skin and cloth like the prow of a ship, a gap that made him look. He could see without trying to the beginning of things. Just the blue-brown cleavage line, but it was enough to make him sweat. Easy here, Even. Easy here, he told himself, You gettin' things up that ought to stay down—

She fanned herself with a letter while the goat hung its head over the porch, its nose level with Even's shoes, its head seeming bodiless. "I got me some mail," Grace said. "Lots of it, too." She patted the stack in her lap and he found himself wondering how they'd all managed to fit between her breasts.

"Seems like."

"Two at least from Grand Bay over in Alabama bottomland. These top two." She held the folded paper out like tall cards the necromancers used. "Grand Bay's all pecans. I got me a aunt there who's spent her life in the middle of pecan trees."

He pictured a woman perched high in a tree, living the life of squirrel or bird, and didn't stop long enough to consider it strange what with the angry-faced rocks staring back at him from across the yard that didn't have its fence, but still felt like it. He leaned back, put his tingling hands behind his head. "How you been doin', Grace?" His voice was low and steady, measured. He tried to grin at her.

"I been fine. Been doin' just fine, Even Grade. Got over to see Joleb yesterday and he's some better, I think. Got him up and movin' round now and his tongue's healed up good as ever. We walked all over the great big yard and he only cried once. So that's good, I think." She paused and slipped out of her shoes, wiggled her toes. The goat leaned forward and rested his head on her left foot and sighed as if tired. "Got me some mail, though."

Night was coming down fast and cold. Even crossed his arms, ready for Joody's fire now. "I ain't had any worthwhile mail in most of three years," he said. "And for the life of me, I can't even remember what that was."

"Well I got me some. Got me a whole stack from Canaan." She patted her lap.

"Good mail?" Canaan had been week-long moody and full of talk that didn't involve words, just gestures. All rude.

"You think he'd send me somethin' bad? Something mean and hard to read?"

Even thought back to that morning, Canaan's middle finger sent up the street to Otil, Clorena's worthless boy. He lied, "Nah—I don't think he'd send out bad, just something full of long words nobody but him understands."

"That what you think?" She was rubbing her foot over the head of the goat. The goat was close to being asleep, its lids halfway down over the brown orbs of its eyes, and Even found his own eyes growing heavy while he watched the woman's feet.

"You think he's just full of long words nobody likes?"

Even looked at her, wondering if he'd offended and not realized it because that was the weight to her tone, like one offended and hurt over something.

"Here, read this one—" she said. "Read this letter right here and see if it's just full of long words nobody likes." She reached down and got one from the bottom of the stack. He took it, noticing it was still warm from her lap. "Go on, read it. You'll see."

"Grace, it ain't none of my business—Lord, if I hurt you somehow, I didn't mean it."

She waved her hand. "I ain't hurt—I just want you to read it and see. Go ahead now, read it. Read what Canaan wrote to me."

Even opened it up, read the first three lines and folded it shut, embarrassed. Feeling like he'd seen Canaan's privates in midcoursing, or the condition of his bed sheets. "It ain't right to read his words—" he stammered.

"It ain't wrong if I give a person permission. Go on now, read." She was looking straight ahead at the rocks. He looked down and in disbelief saw the goat sucking the woman's big toe and felt shot through. Felt as trapped as when Enid tracked him down the green hedge fence. Only this time it's worse because I'm ready to leap over, he realized. Then—I am a sinner. A worthless sinner who's repented long and hard on this front and it still ain't enough to free me of this. Lord God Almighty. He read then, putting the paper at a level to block his eyes from goat and toe. His hand shaking.

"I don't hear you readin'—"

"You mean you want me to read it out loud?" He couldn't believe it.

"I sure do."

"I ain't never read another man's letters as long as I lived." The suckling goat forgotten.

"You read the *Hattiesburg American* and that's as big a stack of letters as I ever seen in my life. So don't be shy. Go on, read. I swear I think you the shyest man I ever met in all my life."

You don't know me at all, Even thought, and if you did you'd fly down from this porch and take the goat with you. If you knew what I was thinking, you'd run screaming into Clorena's tilted house. He scanned the letter again, unsure of where to begin. Finally settling at the beginning, which seemed as bad a place as any. "It's set here as some sort of rhyme—"

The face of all the world is changed, I think,
Since first I heard the footsteps of thy soul
Move still, oh, still, beside me, as they stole—

"Stole?" Grace sat bolt upright. "You think he thinks I stolt something from him? 'Cause he ain't been around in a day or two."

Even went on to the bottom of the letter noticing Canaan's flawless penmanship had been taken to a higher level than "The Reality of the Negro," which was plenty high enough. "It's a poem, Grace, by a woman I ain't ever heard of. Elizabeth Browning." There was a notation underneath in smaller cursive that he fumbled through and tried to finger. "It seems to me she was a Portuguese woman, maybe, 'cause that's where this is from."

"Go on, keep reading—you'll see he ain't just big words that nobody likes."

Even looked for his lost place in the rhyme. Read the previously line out loud again—

Move still, oh, still, beside me, as they stole
Betwixt me and the dreadful outer brink
Of obvious death, where I, who thought to sink—

She sat up again, "You think he's talkin' 'bout that night at the creek? That business about sinkin'? How we almost drowned—" Her eyes were wide open and he saw it, then. Saw the awful truth of it and why she had wandered up the road businesslike with letters between her tits. If she had ended up with Homer of the meat market, or the foreman down at Renfroe's Steel, it would've been a sweeter thing than this. And I led her here. Led her to this place where a man swims in words like he was born fish and not man. Swims in them like he expects everybody else in the world to do the same.

"It's a fine letter, Grace," Even said and she relaxed a little, leaning back in the chair while the goat nuzzled her toes. He folded it up and handed it to her, wondering how to make the offer. They need to be read to the woman, but please God, I ain't the one to do it. She needs to be read to, though, long and hard, and his thoughts seemed more on coursing than reading. "When Canaan gave you these letters, what'd you say?"

"I said, 'These is mighty nice letters, Canaan.'"

"And that's what you said each time he gave you one?"

"You think I'm a rude woman who don't know how to thank a person for a thing? That what you think of Just Plain Grace? 'Cause if you do—"

"That ain't what I'm thinking, Grace." No wonder Canaan's contrary, his heart and soul gone into something and it not being read. All those straight lines, all that measuring under low light a waste of his tired, weak eyes. Even cleared his throat, knowing God was as deaf to him concerning reading as He was concerning other things. He watched the goat at the woman's toe and knew that he'd have to do it. "I ain't had mail in so long," he said, "I just about forgot what it's like."

"It's a sad thing for a man not to get mail—"

"You say that true." Dear Lord, she's got a year's worth, it seems. A year's worth of news waiting.

"I sure got me some, though," Grace said, her alto voice cautious. "I think it's sad you ain't had no mail to read in so long a time—"

"Almost a year."

"I think a true Christian woman would share her mail, seeing how you ain't had none to read in so long a while."

"Seems like. You know any true Christian women around willin' to do that thing?" He watched her face and turned away. Gratitude being the last thing he'd ever wanted to find resting inside her golden brown eyes.

"They just a bunch a old letters—" she said while she ran a finger over the stack.

"Old's better than none." And he lifted her yoke of confusion and reached for the two on top. The two that had come in one single month from that place over in Alabama bottomland. That place called Grand Bay. Where her aunt lived high up in a pecan tree, like a squirrel, or a bird.

Val takes the letters; not reading yet; the actual reading will come later when she's down in her room and safe. She just takes them for now and lines them up by the dates. Spreads them out on the floor—all sixteen of them—looking to the top right corner to check their order. As best she can figure they begin their anonymous story July 2, 1940. She doesn't know who wrote them, but stuck as they were underneath a false bottom in a trunk shoved back and hidden, she knows they're important.

Light inside the attic is enough, but barely. It flows lukewarm and unlight-like, settling more similar to a thin fluid coating that barely enters the shadows, which have been permanent for years. Dark shapes standing like fixtures so much a part of shade for so long a time, what they are in full light would be foreign and unbelievable and Val knows this and ignores them.

The guts of the trunk are scattered on the attic floor. The diminishing light traces loose patterns across them. Done with dates, she places the albums tied in ribbon on top of the hatboxes. She takes the ivory dominoes and puts them back inside their wooden box. She takes the shoe box full of pictures, setting aside one or two with ratted edges, before putting it back into the trunk. Once these things are done, she pushes the trunk back to its spot underneath the painted-shut window and covers it with the sewing form. Leaning it as she had found it, like a falling, already dead, stiff body. The look of dead, gray body being the thing that drew her to the trunk in the first place. This done she walks like a spy through the narrow doorway set to the edge of the attic. She doesn't look back, either, the unlight-like light not being enough now to show her anything up there worth seeing.

26

SWANS

———————⚭———————

A T FIRST GLANCE she hadn't seen them, hidden as they were inside the workings of wood and metal and china. Hadn't seen the swans that seemed nowhere and everywhere at once, their twining necks always reaching. They swam along muted borders of rugs and along the rims of the china—their necks gold, their heads absent of eyes. They rose up out of the carved wood over the huge stone fireplaces where their mahogany tails would darken to purple inside the heat of burning logs. Swans lived on the porch, too, inside the iron scrollwork. Trapped in forty-five-degreed portions, their heads reaching out, always reaching out and through and around, as if struggling for air or life or recognition.

Jackson hated them. He had seen them at once and solidly hated them, but Valuable was yet to. Hate them, that is. She saw them more as a brass doorknob or a copper faucet. Simply ornamental. "They're just birds, Jackson, ignore them," Valuable would tell him, but he would stand and say, "They look like they belong in a funeral home to me—and what are those necks doing, anyhow?" and he would already be up and out of the library, or the parlor, or the dining room, or wherever he happened to be, for the

swans were everywhere. She would find him standing in the hall waiting for
her by the huge front door, its corners capped in brass, a pirate portal, but
still a way out. "We can go outside and sit on the porch if you want." Made
vaguely tired at the thought of running from birds when there were so many
other things to run from. And they would sit out there and he would relax
after a while. "I sure hate those prissy swans, Val. Jesus!" he would say, keeping his eyes level with the midsized trees in the yard's center in avoidance of
the birds trapped high up in metal. She would notice sweat beading over his
lip while she rocked, and a part of her would want to scold him for being
such a big baby about the River House decor—a thing she couldn't
change—and the other part of her, the biggest part of her, would want to
hold him for being so knowledgeable about the flagrant misuse of birds.

Midday on the previous Friday Valuable found herself roaming the garage
that hadn't held a car since World War II. The couple's black Plymouth
stayed at the side of the house, parked and ready on a circular brick drive,
leaving the garage empty but for lawnmowers and garden tools and a green
tractor that Neva used to bush-hog field grass to keep down the rats.
Shelves filled the back wall and high above the shelves were hung brightly
colored Japanese lanterns in blues and reds and yellows, and big-bulbed
outdoor Christmas lights and several wreaths of wound grapevine already
decorated for the various holidays—Thanksgiving, Christmas, Mardi
Gras, the Fourth of July. The holiday wall, she used to call it as a child.
One to pick from like the stuffed animal counter at the fair. The only holiday missing from the grease-smelling place being Easter, which made her
glad, thinking a stuffed rabbit hooked high and dangling would be grue-
some and something she'd not like to walk out of the sun and into dark
and see.

     To the right was a long worktable with a mounted vise and a table saw,
and a saw with narrow teeth that Neva called a band saw. When Valuable
was little she used to think it played music by Sousa while it worked the
planks and didn't find out until later that it made a screaming noise just
like all the others. The worktable was Neva's, crowded with equipment she
used expertly but quickly grew bored with. Valuable was tall enough now
to see the thick black cords feeding down through drilled holes set back of

each power tool, cords she used to think, when she was seven or eight years old, were snakes.

Underneath the table, set on hardwood pallets from the lumberyard, was the coffin with the gray satin lining. Valuable was so familiar with it she barely noticed it anymore. Thinking of it as little more than a very large oblong decoration used for Halloween. One too big to mount on the back wall by the Christmas lights. Made of mahogany that got polished once a year, it was dusty now and the lid was slightly off angle and out of square, as if it had been leaned against too hard by somebody who'd set it off its back hinge. Bea had it delivered years back as a surprise for Neva prior to Halloween, when the couple threw the biggest costume party south of Jackson. By invitation only, it lasted three days, culminating at midnight on October 31 with a ritualistic mock-Druid ceremony held in the broadest part of the backyard. It wouldn't be a yard by then, but a run-down cemetery with aboveground graves like those down in New Orleans. Valuable had never attended the party, Luvenia having considered the partygoers pagan. All those females doing what they did behind their masks against nature. But Valuable had always been allowed to help decorate the house and the yard before the guests arrived, her final job being to polish the coffin with paste wax that clabbered on the ends of her fingers and smelled good enough to eat.

She ran a finger over the dusty mahogany remembering the time Enid had put her in it when she was nine years old and shut down the lid, thinking it would be funny to see a child, alive and kicking, shut inside a thing for the dead. Neva had come up on the tractor then, jerked her out of the coffin and slapped Enid hard across the face, saying, "You ever do anything like this again, I'll kill you!" While Enid howled, Valuable got a ride on the big green tractor with the yellow deer on its side. Up and down and around the drive and out into the field across from River House. Picking up hay bales. Loading them onto a low wagon. Dropping them off in pyramids next to an orange sea of pumpkins. Neva had wrapped her arm around Valuable's stomach. Kissed the top of her head. Valuable picked up her shirttail and polished the side of the coffin, remembering how glad she was at the time that the half-state woman had been struck hard across the face and fallen down to the concrete like a drunk.

She looked around one more time and rubbed her back. It had been knotted all that day beginning at early morning, that's what had led her to roam inside the holiday garage—the feeling that her curse was on the way. Finding a shovel to bury the proof of it would be the thing to do ahead of time, but rakes in different sizes and a four-tine pitchfork and a hand-push tiller had been all there was by way of gardening implements. After walking around for another minute or so, her back burning, she'd left the garage and headed up to the house, shovelless.

Valuable brought her pillow down with her from her upstairs bedroom and put it in her chair. Walking in slow motion to the stove, which seemed larger and more steel-like than usual, she put on the skillet to heat and went to the fridge for eggs and bacon, but at the first smell of pork she grabbed for the counter. I'm sick with something. Really sick, too. Bea came in with the paper under her arm and sat down frumpy and wrinkled, cranky in her housecoat, morning being her least favorite time of the day.

"Neva put on coffee yet?" she asked.

"I don't think so." Valuable leaned her head on the open door of the fridge trying to decide if she really wanted to eat or maybe just lie down on the kitchen floor and die.

"Good lord, Val, what's wrong with you? You're white as a sheet—"

"I feel sick—" Bea got up and put a hand to Valuable's head, extending her hand forward and her rear back, away from the girl. "You don't have a fever, but Lord, you sure do look sick. Neva!" she called out, backing up some more, having always been afraid of severe contagions.

"My back hurts. Bad."

"Your back? Like your kidneys?" "Kidneys" came out high-pitched. Kidney ailments more frightening than contagions.

"I don't know what it's like. I just hurt. Maybe it's gas." She moved to her chair and sat against the pillow and felt somewhat better. Bea relaxed, gas being something she was well acquainted with.

Neva came in, a pencil stuck behind the ear. "James Malloy's got a bay gelding he's willing to—good Lord, Val, what's the matter with you?"

"She's sick," said Bea from across the room.

Neva put a hand to her forehead and Bea said, "She doesn't have a fever. I've already checked." Valuable went to lay her head down on her arms, but the act of leaning over hurt her back so bad she raised up again. "I feel faint—"

"Blood sugar, maybe. You need some juice." Neva went and opened up the fridge, but at the noise of the juice slopping into the glass, Valuable bolted to the back door, threw it open and puked off the back porch all over the hydrangea bush.

Standing there watching steam rise off blue she heard Bea gagging from inside the kitchen. Neva said, "Cut that shit out or get out of here!" Hearing the woman gag as she retreated made Valuable puke again. The weight of it bowed down the bush 'til it dragged the ground.

"Here, Val, here sweet—" It was Neva's voice behind her, coming through the fog of ringing ears. Those strong arms again, underneath and around her now while Val leaned heavy against her. "Here we go, now." Neva put a wet cloth to her head and wiped down her face, and Valuable was so grateful for her mouth to be wiped out she cried like a baby. "It's okay, sweetie. You've just got a bug is all." Her voice deep and nice. Valuable wished she could sound that way all the time, instead of hard and cold and carved out as the swans.

They went up the stairs, Valuable leaning into the woman, looking down at each carpet-covered tread, not able to see the woman's eyes, which would have scared her. Slow and steady up the long hall to the bathroom at its end. Once she was settled on the edge of the tub, Neva ran back down to the kitchen for juice and some crackers. Bea was standing with a hand-kerchief over her mouth by the stove. She waved it in front of her face every few seconds. Her teased and slept-on hair looking like a twice-runover wig.

"Is she better now?"

"She's done with puking for a while. I'll put her in the tub and let her soak and see if her back eases."

"What are we going to do about her?"

"About her? Lord, you act like this is perpetual," Neva said.

"I can't bear a sick child, Neva, you know that—"

"Well, short of murder, we don't have much choice in matters, do we?" And then she was out of the kitchen, its light diminishing with the sun higher now, the shape of Bea's mashed-up hair diffused and softened and steadied by shadows.

Upstairs, with Val leaning her head on her hands, Neva turned off the steamy water and tested it with her finger. "Here, Val. Sit up now and let me help." And she did. Looking at the aqua clawfoot tub the whole while, the feet not claws, but each a squat brass swan, his back burdened by the ceramic tub. "It's too heavy for the bird, Neva," Val said, pointing at a foot.

"I know that—don't look at it, then." She stripped the shirt up over the girl's head in one clean move. Val thinking, She's an honest-to-God lesbian and there's no blood between us and I should feel strange that she's doing this, but I don't. I don't feel stared at or anything. And Neva wasn't looking. Her eyes with their hard, fine points somewhere else other than teen tits and fuzzed crotch. Her hard eyes somewhere else entirely.

"Here now, stand up. Put your arms on my shoulders." And Valuable stood facing her, her back on fire while she felt her drawers being pushed down over her hips and then she felt a cool hand to her hot back, and a hand on her elbow as Neva helped her step into the tub.

"You soak now. You want some bath salts?" Neva was sitting on the toilet watching without seeing. Her eyes visualizing a blond almost-man sitting naked down by the creek. Her hard eyes seeing this almost-woman, this swan-like creature she'd held once and ridden on a tractor, astride the almost-man, sitting carefully like one would if seated on a horse for the very first time.

Val thought of the smell of bath salts and almost gagged again. "No thank you. This feels good, though. So good." And she leaned back her head into the high arch of the tub, holding her hand over her eyes.

Neva bent and picked up the discarded clothes, checking the crotch of Valuable's panties quickly, expertly. Her glance like that of hawk or eagle, predator birds having no choice in their creation or what they saw or felt or killed. She folded the panties across her lap, their pink color just fabric. "You rest, Sweet. I'm going for your robe." Angrier than she'd ever been in her fifty-two years, angry enough to take the banister between her bare teeth and gnaw it down to scattered shavings, angry enough to rip the crown molding down from the ceiling and hurl it like a spear into the heart of that almost-man, she threw open Val's door.

"Shit!" Neva checked the blameless crotch one more time to be sure before placing them on the bed, the blood inside her ears singing a song she'd never heard before. Steady Neva. Steady, here—and it settled her for a moment. Then, *If she doesn't bleed soon, I'll kill the little bastard, I swear. I should have done it after that romp by the creek. I should have done it then and buried his ass in the Halloween coffin.* She opened drawers and searched through clothing. Finding a robe, faded blue and knobby, threadbare and needful. "Shit! And here I wanted three days away! Shit!" She said it again while she kicked at the bed, the sharp, sluicing pain that traveled across her shin and up to her brain calming her, directing those eyes away from what her mind was seeing.

"Where are the goddamn panties—" The meager but ordered appearance of Valuable's clothing hurting her in places she didn't know she had. Making her feel stabbed all over. "Where are they?" Wondering if the girl had been running around drawerless and then seeing the only place she hadn't looked—a box slid underneath the bed. In it, on top of her pictures of horses, the girl's underwear. All three pairs. "Dear God. I bet Enid had three hundred and her not needing a one of them, seeing how they never stayed on past nine in the morning!" *Just what I need,* Neva thought. Knowing it meant going across the river and into a department store, two things she despised. With her ears roaring, she went back to the bathroom and sat on the toilet mother-like while Valuable soaked in the tub.

Thirty minutes later Valuable was better, sitting on the quilt reading, her legs tucked under her. She'd look up at the walls every now and again and look away, the pattern sickening, everything in the room moving and swimming like so many pale blue minnows in a small bowl of water. She finally found a spot on the floor that looked scuffed and still and she'd look at it regular when she needed to consider a sentence. Just a spot on the floor and no more. Just a spot three inches by one inch, and that was all.

She was finishing letter number fifteen. Her back was somewhat better and she'd thrown up only twice off the back porch, but she'd still not been cursed, or blessed, depending on whose version—Luvenia's or Joody's—seemed most appropriate. Cursed, she decided, glancing up at the wallpaper. Feeling weak and drowsy and almost bored, she read

through to the end. This one finished with a Scripture verse and some sort
of greeting:

> . . . *And the king of Babylon smote them because of their wickedness, and*
> *slew them at Riblah in the land of Hamath. So Judah was carried away out of*
> *their land. . . . His remembrance shall perish from the earth and he shall have no*
> *name in the street.*
>
> *The seed of Cain is cursed because the blood cried out from the ground. The*
> *nation writhes in agony over it and we, the failed ones who let the northern voice*
> *become ours, have but one path to travel. Remember this and remember me as I*
> *act out the sleeping arm of God. Fully awake now and raised to slay the dark*
> *seed of Cain.*

The only interesting thing about the letters so far was that they were
written by a killer. One who had no qualms about killing, either, seeing
how he thought he'd been hired on personally by God. I am not only the
daughter of a whore, but descended from a man who spilled blood. Part
of my heritage a southern Jack the Ripper with a drawl and bad teeth who
probably used words like "y'all" and "reckon" while he choked the life out
of folks. Covered in the quilt, Valuable felt detached and safe. The thought
of this killer-relative only partially disturbing.

She had wanted the letters to be between lovers. Secret lovers. But they
had turned out to be from an overly clinical person who liked to write
down what he'd done (killed them dead) and how he'd done it (hung 'em
up to think a while) while spouting sermon-like thoughts on why
he enjoyed killing so much (because God intended the just to inherit the
earth). This was a crazy person and I'm sure glad he's dead—and then
she stopped short and laid down letter number fifteen because she had no
proof anywhere that the person *was* dead. Now, why in the world did I
think he was dead? she asked herself. Because all these letters were hidden,
is why. But what does that have to do with him being alive or dead? Because
if he was alive he would want the letters back, it seems. What if he *is* alive,
just away killing in some other part of the country, and coming back for
the letters once he's done? Valuable shivered then, thrilled by the thought
of a killer creeping up the hall, climbing to the attic, taking out the con-
tents of the trunk, lifting out the false bottom, and finally reaching in—

She yawned terrifically, hungry finally, and opened up the final letter, thinking that once she was done reading she'd go down and try at breakfast again. It was nearly ten and Jackson had said he was coming over around eleven for a talk.

This one cried out once, that big-mouth boy did, and then, bless God, he came to himself and told me a joke. Vicksburg is sure different and this is the proof. He stood there, his neck inside a three-cord rope and says, You want a joke, boss? Never being one to pass one by, I said yes. How do you break a rooster from crowin' on the Sabbath, Boss? he says, all wild-eyed and loud, not bothered one bit by that three-cord rope. Tell it and be done with it, I says, and he looks at me square and says, You kill him Saturday night, that's what you do. Sounds true to me, I says and kicked the brace free and that's what we did. We killed that big-mouth boy while he laughed out loud. He bucked for three minutes and then he was done, as well he should be. Cain's seed is unruly. You cannot break a mule without pulling out the board. Hear your father's words: Time and again, Luvenia, you purt'near have to lay it to their head—

Valuable bent and vomited all over a carpet swan's neck.

27

TALK, LONG AND HARD

"CLAPTRAP," CANAAN SAID with conviction, the Saturday morning sun shining down on his shined-up shoes. "Ain't nothin but." He recrossed his legs and refolded his newspaper. The *Hattiesburg American,* barely two hours old, already having a look to it of a much folded map. One used by an insecure traveler afraid to trust his eyes.

"Sentiment's a fairy tale here in Mississippi," he said. "Ain't nothing but claptrap meant for white folks who got time to dream and write and pretend. Same as with those books on Greek statuary down at the library full of pictures of armless Venus and needle-dick David. White folks carved out by more white folks while black folks cart off the shavings, I suppose. More claptrap than this world needs, I tell you." He swatted a fly that wasn't there. Just wanting to hit down hard on something was Even's best guess. A pretend fly being as good a thing to hit down on as any of God's available creatures.

"I didn't know your sour outlook had found its way to books, Canaan." Even Grade turned to the side and tamped the pipe with one long finger. His face away, he lit it and felt the heat of the match wash back near to his eyebrows. Feeling ridiculous doing this thing but seeing Joody out front sweeping down her dirt, watching him, smiling sweet every other minute like a proud expectant mama, he did it anyhow. For her. The blend smells good, thank God. At least this is something.

She had worked more than a month on what was between his teeth. Digging and scraping late at night; hiding it behind her back when he'd walk up from work, wanting a kiss; sticking it between her legs so he couldn't see what it was when he'd grope her with his hands. During the month his guesswork concerning it had run a straight-string bead from carnal all the way to heavenly. It's a coursing toy, he'd think one minute, dismayed by his excitement. It's an icon to a supreme being, he'd think the next, alarmed by his disappointment. What it turned out to be was a hand-carved pipe done out of a solid piece of pecan. "I ain't never made a pipe before," she'd said, shy for once, holding it on the palm of her four-fingered hand, "and since I ain't never made one before, I give this one a name." And then she'd whispered it in his ear and he'd smiled though horrified by the look of it. His understanding blank on her reason for the name. He'd held the gift in his hand and wondered how he could rid himself of it discreetly, and then he'd shoved the thought from his head because she was reading him more and more of late. "I named it special," she'd said again, her face shortened by a smile, all her sticks dancing. "I know you did, Joody, and I thank you for it." Even had kissed a high cheekbone thinking, There is nothing straight, or ordinary, about this woman other than her internal framework.

She was raking the dirt. Making half-moon shapes that overlapped like shells dug from the ocean. She waved once and then went back to it. The wood of the pipe between his teeth was good-tasting with a flavor of roasted nut that lingered, and the stem was store-bought and easy on the mouth, but the image on the end was more embarrassing than any coursing toy he had ever imagined. Even looked up at the clear blue sky in avoidance of the hand-carved ass with its tiny scar.

Canaan was bristling and rustling, buried behind his paper. "I ain't soured on readin'. The words just seem as pointless now as—" He looked at Even, jumped as if poked with a hot cattle prod. "Thy God, that's some kinda pipe you got there, Even Grade," he said after a time of staring. The two of them were over on Canaan's porch for a change. Even's porch having become overburdened of chairs and rocks and hanging painted gourds full of dried-up beans.

"I'll have you know the stem of this pipe was store-bought," Even said between clenched teeth, his eyes still looking up at the sky but feeling Canaan's on him in a way that only a man stared at can feel.

"Thy God, I can see that."

"She walked all the way down to the hardware store and bought it, by herself." Even wondered over it, too, remembering how hard his purchase of paint had been and Clemens's loud-smelling and noisome teeth. Thinking Joody's tolerance was a wonder.

"I'd a bought a ticket to that conversation," Canaan said, his mouth open.

"You say that true."

"You got you some kinda pipe there—" Canaan's mouth said again, but his thoughts ran to, Lord God have mercy, she's carved him a squat naked man to suck on. A standin'-on-his-head-man with his short fat legs spread open wide, so's the smoke can come out his ass, too. He leaned around for a better look. "Lord have mercy, Even, she's carved his johnson complete. Exaggerated it, too." It dangled forward toward the upside-down chin of the upside-down head. Canaan tilted his head as far as it would go. "Thy God, Even. If you turn that thing upside down—it's got itself a woody!"

"Why you think I'm over here smoking on your porch and not down at the loading dock of the Feed and Seed?"

"I think you here 'cause you a smart man after all." And Canaan let it out then, long and loud. Laughing the way Even didn't dare, not with Joody watching him while her rocks grew ears and listened.

"She named it, too. Seeing how she ain't ever made a pipe before—" Even said between his teeth.

Canaan was choking. Bent double. His head down between his legs. His newspaper forgotten. Joody yelled out, concerned, "That smoke bothering you, Canaan Mosley?"

"Nah, Joody—it's fine smoke!" Even yelled back answering for him, still patting the man between the shoulders. "Canaan's just sitting here in a jealous fit over my pipe is all," and Joody grinned and folded her slim hands around the rake. "I'll carve you one too, Canaan, and then you'll both have fine smoke." And she turned and went back to her raking, the gourds shaking in the wind off Even's porch making a sound like rattles quickstolen off a snake.

Canaan sat up, wiping his eyes. Then he looked at Even again and it started up same as before. "You said she named that ugly thing?"

"Yep. Named it Mister Chuck Wagon for a reason I can't break open."

And Canaan whooped and hollered again. "Thy God, for a nine-fingered woman, she does a helluva lot of work!" He bent his head and howled again between his legs.

"You say that true, and they'll be busy come tonight carvin' you one, too," Even said, finally getting a good clean draw off the naked man, watching smoke float up like a good smellin' fart from between short, squat legs, determined once the laughin' stopped, to talk long and hard about the letters to Grace.

The field in front of the River House was low to the ground now. The gold-colored saw grass that seemed to stretch forever, whipped by wind and slammed down like a giant's hand, had smoothed it over in preparation of an afternoon nap. Valuable pulled up clusters, staring.

"There's not enough sides to me for this. Oh Jesus—" And the words were flat-toned and dead, worse than any fit of crying. "Oh Jesus," she said again, and Jackson pulled her to him and she came off her knees stiff as a frozen corpse, her hands still clutching the dead grass of October.

"Nothing's changed, Val. Nothing, you hear me? Nothing in this world has changed!" Chamblee, Georgia, looming like the poised head of an ax between them, changing everything. "You listen to me." He took her by the shoulders and pushed her up. "You look at me long and hard and judge what I'm sayin' here—" Her gray eyes bore into him and he felt carved out and empty. "I love you. Ain't nothing changed about that. And once school is out, I'll be back as sure as my name's Jackson McLain. We're getting married then, you hear me? Are you listening?"

"There's not enough of me for this. Not this." She put her face against his shirt then, breathed in hard against his buttons.

Jackson felt the wind blowing up under his jacket and the smell coming out of the pine-thick woods seemed more winter than fall. More December dead cold than easy October chill. Looking over his shoulder he saw Neva holding a death watch out on the porch. Rocking so easy it had to be a lie.

She hadn't wanted to let him in. Had stood there on the porch with her arms crossed against her too-white shirt. "Valuable's not feeling well," she'd said. But Jackson's hands had turned to fists by that time. Done at last with women and their woman-related things. Queerwoman or no, he was ready to fight her if he had to. Determined to kill the bitch if that's what it took to get past her and up those stairs.

"I am moving away to another state," he said between his teeth, "and she don't know and I've got to break it to her. Now you move to the side and let me through and I ain't askin' twice—"

Grinning, Neva backed away and let him pass. Jackson had run up the stairs, his mouth dry as Petal's dead cotton, his eyes wild with newfound resolve, wondering while he took the stairs two at a time if the woman behind him had any other shirts in the world besides white ones. Thinking blood red would be a good and fitting color for such a heartless, bloodless queer.

Valuable had been mopping at the ridiculous rug in her room, still in her robe. Her dark hair falling around her face, her face more pale than he'd ever seen it in his life.

"Get dressed, Val. We've got to talk." And he'd gone back down the stairs and stood trembling on the porch beside Neva, who was sitting in a rocker and smoking, her legs crossed just like a man's. Jackson looked straight ahead, studying the grass that was low-lying and quiet now, and waited. Wondered how to say the words.

"When are you leaving?" She sat up. Straw was in her hair and he reached out and lifted a piece from above her ear.

"The house has to sell. And Dad's got to find someone to take over his lease on the shop."

"That could take a while then?"

"Maybe." He watched Neva watching them from the porch and he raised his hand and saluted her with his middle finger. Without pause, she raised her hand and did the same. He smiled a bitter smile and thought, Well and good—so be it. "Maybe it won't sell at all," he said. "Who knows?"

"Oh, it'll sell. It'll sell quicker than any house in the world. It'll sell faster than lightning. Just you wait and see." She rubbed a small hand across her eyes. Her voice flat as the saw grass. I won't tell him now about my murdering great-grandfather, she thought. To tell him would be like the bloody things I have to bury (had to, she corrected herself) out in the yard. To tell him would be one more reason not to come back and he'll have enough of those. She grabbed at grass and pulled hard, the sound of its ripping up from the dirt fitting and proper.

"I can't do this thing, Val, if I can't know you'll be okay. I can't leave here if I think you'll be here getting sick over it."

"I can't promise anything, Jackson—oh Jesus." That dry sound again.

"Well, can you remember that it's not forever? Can you at least do that for me? Because I'm dying hard here—" And his voice cracked sharp as broken glass. As if his vocal cords and all their new almost-man sounds had been just a joke. Just a dream. She looked at him, her mouth opened up just a little, almost bird-like, and he shut his eyes to it. Shut them hard against the way they must look to some other entity looking down. The sun. A circling crow. Dust motes set drifting. Her with the clutched-up grass in her hands, him with his mouth sealed shut. The two of us trapped in dead gold, feeling the urgency of the earth. He felt her arms around him at the shoulders and then his back. Her hands flattened and hard as if the core of who he was were slipping out his spine and she had to stop it. And once he felt those hands there pressing in, stemming the flow of whatever it was that he felt was leaving him, freeing him from the urgency of earth not felt by sun or crow or dust motes drifting, he bent his head to his knees and allowed himself to cry.

28

THE REALITY OF CANAAN

CANAAN WALKS.

Up Bellrose and out past the forgotten, nameless sign that sounds less like thunder now. Sounds less like what it did two months back before the gourds and rocks and the nighttime fire settled in next door in his neighbor's yard. He walks as a man unaccustomed to walking walks. Stiff-legged. Hands jammed low into his pockets. His head down. His mind not caring where his legs take him or how long it takes them to get wherever it is they want to go. Walking hard thinking, Fool! What a foolish man I been! His shoes slicing through low grass and weeds alike. Walking. Thinking while he walks: She is the same. They are all the same.

He passes Main and Central, where the intersection splits the town into fourths, his feet up off the dirt stretch and onto the sidewalk. Carrying him past the boarded-up beauty shop and the hardware store bought out by Purina. Past the awninged barbershop where a man sits high up in the leather chair, draped in white, at the mercy of a man with scissors. Canaan looks down once and sees his bloodmark, still a stubborn stain on Petal's sidewalk, and then he walks on past, clearing the loading dock of the Feed and Seed, a place where his life held a seasoned order just two months back. A time in which he could, and a place where he was able to, read the *Hattiesburg American* inside a monumental peace. Not caring in the least if anybody else in this crusted Mississippi world was able to read or not.

He walks to where the highways join. Walks hard down one—he doesn't care which, seeing how all roads in and out of Petal lead nowhere. Up ahead he sees the gabled framework of the bridge breaking open the blue of the sky; changing it to dun-colored angles and brackets and equitable cubes. He walks forward thinking, This bridge breaks up the sky just like a woman. Just like that same woman years back did. Just like all women. Breaks it up. Steals the blue. He approaches the middle span between two places and watches dingy shade lay down a pattern. I should have sailed right on over with that green bottle, he thinks. Should have welcomed water into my lungs easy as a fish. He stands near the center of the bridge and wonders which is the worse of it: that she pretended to read and couldn't, or that Even Grade read his letters like a goddamn spy. Moving forward finally, seeing the creeping approach of land, he says to himself, "Both. Both are equally bad."

The bank is within spitting distance now. The river barely under him. Barely under the intrusive sound of his feet on metal girders. Those same steel fingers that dice up the sky before they dive into the water. The water underneath flowing past in layers queer and tea-toned, while deep inside some random shade of brown, fish slug along, whiskered and dreamless. A white bird, small and unspectacular, sits alone on the sandy bank then hops to a bleached log jutting out like a fingerbone. A flock of brown birds swoops down from a broadleaf and then gathers and leaves, gathers and leaves. Anxious and restless, their heads bob at the sound of feet walking, their eyes dart sideways, upward, searching for the sound before they gather and leave, gather and leave.

Canaan steals a look to the side. Just one look, quick and hard. This sorry river winds like a vision. Like a rainbow. Like a promise. Like hope. And then, "Fool . . . she could have . . . they are all . . ." He looks down again, done with wordthoughts and speculation, his feet and their work of beating down on the ground just fading echoes now against the sky-stealing girders. Below and to the side the brown birds quit their gathering and leaving and settle along the shoreline still as scattered stones in a grave-yard, their heads cocked up and listening for what's not there anymore.

"She is the same. They are all the same. . . ."

He finds himself walking slower once he passes Renfroe Salvage. The towering walls of near worthless metal climbing high and jagged and con-trary to any expression of nature he's ever seen. The streets seeming longer and longer. Stretching out like a ribbon unrolled in a fit of rage and then not put back up again. Left out and unfurled. Somebody's hard work. Still mad, but foggy on it and unable to finger what set him off in the first place, he passes Rices' Potato Chip Company and says to himself, Lord have mercy, I'm on Gordon Street. That's where I'm at. I've walked clear to Gordon Street from Bellrose. And then he sees the cubed-up boarding houses facing the place. All those small blocks of grassless yards, still dark and muddy-looking two months after rain. Clothes strung out on makeshift lines from floor to floor like so much messed-up kite string. The dark doors stand open exposing barely lit corners of ratty couches and strowed things. Chairs. Piles of laundry. Broken toys. He sees the tunnel-like openings into dark cave-like places where dark people live. Hears radio rubble. Nuisance noise. Thinks, I am a black man. This is my reality: dark and more dark. A naked boy baby with bulbed-out stomach and crying eyes strays back and forth like a dog. A spraddle-legged female breezes her-self with a funeral home fan. Careless. Her large legs spread. Her hiked-up skirt too high. Just more dark, Canaan says. Just more dark. Then, "Fool . . . she could have . . . they are all . . ."

By the time he reaches the Hattiesburg Library on Main, his lungs are given out and burning, his legs rubbery. I'll go inside and sit and read awhile, he thinks while he walks up the curving stairs. It's near three in the afternoon. I'll sit and read *The Abominable Book of Birds* to clear my mind. I'll sit still and read, just like the white folks do.

He pushes open the door to a warning. Nobody says he can't do it, but their eyes track him, hold up a hand to his sweaty black face saying he bet-ter reconsider. They look at one another and then they look to the lady behind the desk with the stamp and the pad and the blue ink that com-missioned her. Her eyes sayin', I like this stamp and pad and being able to say I'm the head librarian, but I don't like this. She fingers her necklace nervously, as if Canaan has walked into the place, his loose-skinned, blunt-ended johnson hanging clear out his unzipped pants.

He watches all the eyes, momentarily puzzled until he figures it out— Oh, he says to himself, I ain't supposed to be here. I *am* supposed to come creeping in to clean their shitty toilets four nights out of every six, but I *ain't* supposed to be in here otherwise, like normal folks. "The Reality of the Negro" says this sorta thing ain't allowed. Not here. Not now. He stands trembling, his legs tired, his nose smelling the odor of his Negro sweat—which up until then he thought smelled the same as everybody's else but which, wafting up to his nose, tells him this is just one more thing he's been foolish on. His eyes peer back at the bank of eyes tracking him heartless as a hound while he reasons, I am Negro and I ain't supposed to be here. Well, how do you like that?

Back outside to the afternoon heat, he goes down the steps and walks two blocks to the police station where he sits on a bench watching pigeons feed and scramble along the ground. He looks around at all the eyes looking elsewhere, at all the peaceful, it's okay to be here eyes that light on him like flies and then move on to something more interesting. I guess it's-okay-to-sit-here outside this police station on this bench in plain sight of all these policemen. I guess it's just fine to sit here and smell the stink of my own Negro sweat. I guess it's okay for old Canaan to do these things because everybody this side of the river Leaf knows here's where most of us niggers wind up at anyhow—

Canaan's school of thought is different now, settled to the forefront of his reasoning like bottle-birthed blood. He's not mad anymore because he is the same as everyone else. Even Grade. Clorena Gravis. Grace Johnson. Shebbie Sterns. James Evans. Willie Brackett. Emmit Till. Canaan is black. The woman's failure to read just more proof of what he was pretending he wasn't. His logic muddy as the river, but still a reality. Canaan blinks. Tired. Eyes burning inside all the bright. All he thinks while he studies pearlescent pigeons is this: I wish I knew how . . . I wish I knew . . . I ain't ever gonna, but I wish I knew how it felt—

(—*to be free.*)

29

THE OTHER SIDE OF THE FENCE

WHY, HE PICKS HIS WAY through here like he's familiar with famine, Joleb thought, watching.

He'd been sitting on the bench checking the man's progress. First he had climbed out of the dark car parked alongside the curb and then he had walked down the sidewalk on the other side of the tall green fence and then he had approached the gate where the guard stood with keys on a chain. Once he presented some type of paper, he was allowed to enter and make his way across to him, his shoes crunching on the sea of brown grass a small Japanese gardener fussed over night and day. Inside all that black Russ looks like a tall crow, he said to himself. Just like a tall crow looking for corn in the middle of famine. We're all dead here, Russ, he thought. There ain't no corn left here—

"How's today findin' you, Joleb?" Russ swooped down to the seat.

"Same as yesterday. Though I can't admit to it or I ain't never gonna get out of here." He picked at his gown with nervous fingers, his eyes large as an owl's behind his new glasses. Russ patted him on the knee and then crossed his legs like a woman, only he didn't look like a woman to

Joleb, but like a man with overly long legs he didn't know what to do with.

"We've got Oktoberfest comin' up at the parish. Lots of sausage and stuff. If you want to come, I bet I could spring you—"

"You're shitting me—"

Russ snorted. "No, I'm not. I bet they'd turn you loose for a day at least."

"I don't know." Outside thoughts made him nervous. Made his gut feel hot and thready. "It wouldn't mean I was turnin' Papist—"

"God forbid," Russ said, "what with Beryn being a Mason, and them hating Catholics so." He looked at Joleb steady smiling, one arm on the back of the iron bench, thinking, He's thinner than last week. Thinner and older around the eyes.

"How's Grace these days?" He had met her at Mary's graveside service and immediately fallen under her spell.

"In love, I think. That's all she talks on anyhow. Canaan this, Canaan that. She thinks this Mr. Mosley fella is slicker than shit." Joleb scratched his nose. "She told me the full story before anybody else, though, and I owe it to her to try to be happy for her. Owe her for a lot of things, so it seems." He looked at Russ. "You know the full story yet?"

"Most of it." Grace had told him her portion.

"Well, Grace may not know squat about readin', but she knows how to tell a person something."

"Yeah? How'd she break it to you?" Russ leaned forward, elbows to knees.

"She squared up her shoulders big as you please and spit it out. Same way she used to walk me up and down Hardy Street. Straight on with no nonsense." He began popping his fingers. "She had a baby girl that died and when I came along she thought I was an answer to prayer and she fed me from her chest." He looked straight at Russ and then his eyes went back out toward the fence. "Can you imagine that? Can you imagine that a colored woman would do that for a baby that wasn't hers?"

"I told you before—Grace being a part of your life is a real gift."

"It's more than that, Russ. Milk's personal. Aunt Louise told me that's why Beryn never liked me. 'Cause of the milk that come from Grace. She says he still don't know he ain't my daddy, not because she ain't tried to tell him, but because every time she tries, he just stares at her and keeps sayin', 'of course he's my son, Louise—he lives here.'" Joleb snorted and then stuck his hand in the bag and pulled out a peanut and thumped it out into the yard. "Hard to believe a man could be told the plain truth and still think otherwise," he said.

After meeting him, anything else would be unbelievable, Russ reasoned.

"Anyhoo—so much for Beryn." He slapped both hands down on his legs. "But I owe Grace. And I love her and all those times I found myself wishing she was my mama, I don't have to feel bad about them anymore, 'cause she fed me direct from her chest like she was my own flesh and blood. Milk's personal, Russ," he said again.

"Mr. Mosley said Grace didn't leave your side all that night," Russ said.

"That's nice, I guess. They all seemed nice for colored folks, even that one with sticks in her hair. I hardly remember any of it, though. Just waking up in a strange place, sore as hell. Not remembering's nice, I think." Joleb looked at the priest. "Did you know that Beryn is the stupidest man in all of Petal? Maybe even all of Mississippi?" He sat back without waiting for the answer. "I can say that now and not feel like I'm spittin' on his shoes. And it feels good. To know that he's stupid, I mean, and be able to live with it seeing how there's no blood between us." He threw a handful of peanuts to the pigeons. "Anyhoo—Grace is in love with this man Canaan and she's saved enough to live on for a while without working. She ain't ever goin' back to Stockwell Street, and I think this is good." Joleb emptied out the bag of peanuts to the ground and his feet were immediately mobbed by gray. "Beryn'll be lost without her, but he'd never admit to it what with his large fear of colored folks."

"Beryn will find his way, hopefully." He'll attach himself to that sister of his, was Russ's best guess. But that'll prove a challenge, too, what with the woman's hard as steel chassis. He unbuttoned the top button of his cassock.

"You Catholic preachers's got the right idea of it, though—stick with preaching and the blessing of those little wafers you feed folks and leave the sex and marryin' to the rest of the world."

"Well, it's not quite like that, Joleb—I mean we do espouse celibacy—"

Joleb pushed his glasses up off his nose, "What's that word mean? 'Espouse?' 'Cause it sounds varmint- or bird-related. Like a mouse or a grouse."

"It means, well, what I meant to say is this: We take a vow of celibacy, but not because we consider marriage less than ideal—"

"Marriage sucks donkey dick, Russ. You and I both know it. You're just spoutin' words, now."

Russ howled and slapped his legs and wished for a cigar to smoke. "Joleb, Joleb," he said, shaking his head, still laughing. "What's the world gonna do with you?"

"I hope not much else. I hope the world's about done, sir, 'cause a body can't stand much more of what the world's been doin'—" He reached down to the ground and picked up an overlooked peanut. "Aunt Louise is wearin' her hair down now. I ain't clear on what it means, but I know it means something. A man can get himself a new haircut and it don't mean anything other than he picked himself a bad barber. But a woman changin' her hair after a hundred years of up in a bun is headed down a new road. Beryn said she's developed a taste for a man finally. He thinks it's pure nonsense. I asked her about it the last time she visited, and she just says it's menopause, but I don't think that's it. You ever know a woman to change her hair and it not mean something?" He didn't wait for the answer. "Beryn says she's in love is all and once the man finds out she's cold as a witch's tit, she'll put her hair up in a bun again and get back on with the business of bein' mean as a snake."

Joleb's voice and its rhythms had a way of making Russ feel sleepy, like he was being sung to by a charm-clutching hillbilly. He shook himself alert. "In love? Louise Green?"

"Yes sir. At least that's what Beryn told me the last time he visited, which was a while back now that I think on it." He tried to cross his legs like the priest's, but it didn't feel right. He leaned forward instead, his elbows to his knees. "I'm gonna go live there for a while after I leave here, I think. I could go live with my father if I wanted to. He's offered, that is. Come close to beggin', almost. But I don't want to live there yet, seeing how I only met him three times now. We'll work into that, Grace says, but I just don't know—"

"Who's this man your aunt has met?" Russ asked, more curious on that front than Joleb's paternity.

"A George Willard out of Jackson. That's how she calls him, too. 'A George Willard out of Jackson,' just like that, like he's a piece of furniture, or maybe an appliance or a brand of turkey." He paused. "Runs the funeral home in Hattiesburg. A good business to be in, I guess, what with my track record on killin' folks—"

Russ didn't say anything. Just held himself still while he watched the aimless wandering of the pigeons bobbing across the brownish grass that was fully dead now. "So—you want to come to the parish festival or not? You could ask your friends to join you. Make a day of it."

"Yeah, that sounds nice. Jackson come by once. And I'd like to see Val. I never cared that much for her, but Jackson said she went lookin' for me when I was down at the creek. They might be nervous round those statues though, seein' how they're both Baptists." He looked at Russ.

"Well, ask them about it. See if they want to join you. I won't promise to drape a cloth over the Blessed Mother, but there'll be no strong-arm tactics as far as conversion, either." Russ smiled. "For anybody."

"Well, that's good seein' how I'm half Jew, now." Joleb leaned on his hand and looked sideways up at Russ. "I don't think that counts, though. With Jews, you're either all or nothing. A half Jew is like food done up half kosher—that's the hebe name for food, Russ—or a woman being half knocked-up. It just don't work. If you're halfway, you ain't Jewish, but something else. I don't know what, though. I ain't asked that particular question yet, but I'm sure there's a rule concerning it somewhere."

A young nurse with hair so red it looked fire-lit wheeled a man who looked to be in his mid-twenties to a spot next to a birdbath. The man was slumped over as if sleeping but with eyes wide open and looking straight ahead, like a seated somnambulist. "You see that man?" Joleb pointed to him. "The one by the birdbath?"

"Uh huh."

"He's here 'cause he thinks his pyloric valve ain't working."

"Pyloric valve?" Russ scrambled through his basic biology and still didn't have a clue. "I'm afraid I'm at a loss, Joleb. What's the pyloric valve?"

"Well, in a nutshell, and I'm not absolutely positive on this seein' how

I got the scoop from a man with the swearin' disease and I had to pick my information out through all his cusswords—kinda like digging at pecans—"

Russ felt his mouth fall open.

"Anyhoo—the pyloric valve is this tiny little valve and its only job in the whole wide world is to keep shit from backin' up into the stomach and possibly bein' puked out the mouth—" He slapped Russ's leg. "Imagine that, Russ—all that's keepin' our shit where it's suppose to be, a tiny little flap of skin."

"Joleb, I'm not a doctor, but I'm sure there's more—"

"Nah—I got it straight from somebody who's been here for years," Joleb continued. "Well, that guy over there by the birdbath is afraid his ain't workin'. And he can manage this fear most of the time, but every month or so they find him wanderin' round out in his yard over on Twenty-fourth Avenue, a belt tied tight around his waist and rubber stoppers up his ass to keep everything where it's at." Joleb sat back and laughed. "It ain't funny, but the guy with the swearin' disease, Tommy's his name—"

"Hold it, Joleb—what in the world is this swearing disease you keep mentioning?"

"Jeeze, Russ, pardon my rudeness, but for a man who's been to Rome, you ain't that bright. The swearin' disease afflicts people to the point they shout cusswords out at inappropriate times. Like when they're in church or the library or maybe at the picture show. They jerk sometimes, too. It's the swearing disease. Tommy's got it. Anyhoo, this Tommy says that that guy over there by the birdbath who's worried about his valve not workin', saves his poop in coffee cans, afraid that if it goes down the toilet, it'll slip back into our drinkin' water and he'll end up swallowin' it again. One fear's just about as bad as the other, don't you think?"

"Lord have mercy," Russ said, thinking he had enough special intentions from this place alone to fill a book.

"Ain't that the truth."

A breeze blew up Russ's sleeve, chilled his neck. Traffic moved slow and easy as if the cars were mindful of the building and the people trapped on the other side afflicted with the swearing disease, or afraid of their pyloric valves, or dealing with the belief that they were twice a murderer.

"You know—you've not asked me one single thing about that night and what happened," Joleb said as if he'd read the man's mind.

"Some things are best left to the phone booths, Joleb." Russ smiled and punched him in the side with an elbow. "You remember them, don't you?"

"I remember. The Sacred Heart hotline to God. It don't cost a dime, only a priest is the operator. All a body has to do is spill his guts all over that cold marble floor."

"It's not an unpleasant experience, Joleb."

"That's what the doctors say before they stick your ass with that great big needle, or turn on the juice and slap the paddle to your head." Joleb held out a hand to see if it was shaking. It wasn't and he exhaled a breath, as if relieved. "The funny thing is, I remember bein' afraid before they did it—shocked my ass, I mean. But other than that, I don't remember a damn thing about it."

"I think that's the point," Russ said. "You want to talk?" He leaned around and looked at the boy.

Joleb leaned his head to the side and thought on it. "No. But thanks for askin'." A man walking alone hooted once like an owl and then yelled out "Fucker! Fucker! Fucker!" the sound pitched high like a crow's call with the emphasis on the second syllable. "Ackkhhh!" he said as he walked fast toward the gate then keeled off at the last minute, veering to the right. His feet out to the front of him like his brain was low to the ground, buried in the toes of his house slippers.

"That's Tommy," Joleb said and then he grew quiet, watching the limited activity across the grounds, watching the cars running past, their speed as slow as suspended thoughts. "I loved her, you know—" Joleb said, looking straight ahead, thinking on Mary.

"I know you did, Joleb."

"I loved him, too—" Thinking on Burris, now.

"I know that, too."

"I just didn't love me, was the problem," Joleb said, thinking on Joleb finally, his eyes straight ahead, his hands not nervous anymore, his fingers linked together casual as a much older man might do. "Milk's personal, Russ. As personal as blood. I owe it to her to act like it."

"You owe it to you, too." Russ patted him on the back and left his
hand there, feeling the sharp bones running up the boy's spine, not thinking about time, or parish, or obligation, just staring out in a direction similar to Joleb's. On the near side of the fence was a waterless fountain with
a dusty boy holding a shouldered vase as its center font. Studying the stone
face covered with bird droppings that ran down like tears, Russ wondered
how long it had been since the fountain actually worked; since water had
actually found its way up and out and down. This place is Lenten-like and
dry as a desert, he reasoned. Dry as a valley full of old bones lacking the
good sense to know their time is over, but for the burying. Heavy with it,
he uncrossed his legs and leaned elbows to knees like Joleb. "The cars sure
go by slow here," Russ said. He looked to the right. "They pull into the
street and then catch themselves up and slow way down—"

"Like cars do when they make their way in a funeral procession
through town," Joleb said, matter-of-factly, his eyes steady and calm.

Russ thought on it while he watched and reasoned it true. Reasoned
that, like it or not, the people inside the tall green fence were dead now to
certain realities that plague the rest of the load-bearing world, and how,
like it or not, it was probably a small measure of grace worth considering.

30
VARIATIONS ON A THEME

L OUISE WAS POLISHING THE LAST SCONCE of her gas lamp when he
exited the house across the street. Dressed in black, a good suit, too,
by the look of the lines around his bulky shoulders, he bypassed his black
Pontiac and headed business-like across the street in her direction. Why, he
walks like a well-bred bulldog, she thought. One disqualified as showdog
because of overly large balls, she grinned, glad her hair was down and that
she was finally old enough and gray enough to think the truth and live with
it. Equally glad her womb was bone-dry and settled into its dependable
barrenness like a foot resting in well-worn leather. Early the previous
morning the ten-year-old boy across the street had blown himself up with
a bottle of gasoline, and a slow-moving train of casserole bearers had
cruised the curb all morning long. To be born is to die, she thought to herself then. To have one is to lose one, as well, I suppose. Louise turned her
back to George regardless of the cut of his suit, listening to his steps come
up the walk behind her while she worked the clouded glass gone burnt-
milk brown over summer.

"My hospitality is bankrupt, Mr. Willard—I'll bake a squash casserole, but I'll not have the wake for those people. Two in one's lifetime is enough for any individual," she said.

"I like your hair," he said to her back. Gray fell solid and opaque to her midback, silver and coarse. Like Christmas tinsel, the crinkled type.

"Flattery will not get the coffin inside my parlor, either."

"Well, ma'am, what *will* it get me?" he asked.

She turned, the polishing rag in her hand, and watched him rotate his handheld hat in his hands by its rim. His grin was too engaging, in her opinion. "I must say, Mr. Willard, if folks could see you now, they'd travel to Lucedale to get their burying done. You don't seem to have the appearance of a man fresh from the scene of profound grief."

"That's because the grieving couple intend to spring for the viewing stand with the slide-around panels." He set his hat to her porch rail. "The grieving father hasn't got an itch for that sentimental something constructed with his own two hands."

"Thank God for that at least."

"I agree, but I repeat the question, ma'am—what *will* flattery get me?"

"Not much around here. A cup of coffee, at most." She looked at him. "But oh I forgot—you are a man who doesn't drink coffee."

"That's true. That's very true." He ran a finger over his mustache. Thinking, It's also true this street is unlucky, statistically speaking. He rubbed his mustache again and grinned.

"So, that being the case, flattery is a waste of good breath." She turned her back to him again. The brown from the glass was gone and she watched his reflection appear in the space vacated by the rag. He was done with grinning, it seemed.

"Ten-year-old boys are a damn nuisance," he said and looked to the side, not bothered by most deaths, but bothered by this one. She had thought the exact same thing the morning before while she sipped coffee in between the screams of the siren. "All below the age of thirty are a nuisance, if you ask me." George Willard looked up and down the street.

"Well, no one has asked your opinion, so I think you can leave now. I'm sure you have work to do. Business to tend to in that little notebook of yours."

He put a leg up on the next highest riser. "You know, you've refused my dinner invitations three times now, and I'd like to know the reason for it. You don't look like a woman who is adverse to food." She turned, her mouth opened, and he held out a hand in advance rebuttal. "No offense intended. Skinny, too-thin women are as bad as ten-year-old boys. Nothing but a nuisance. Show me a woman who has no fear of a girdle and by God, I'll show you a woman." He swabbed his face with his handkerchief, his equilibrium restored. "So I ask again—why the refusal?"

"Maybe I don't want to go to dinner."

"No ma'am, that's not it. Like I said before, you have the framework that speaks of a woman who likes food."

"Maybe I don't want to go to dinner with you."

"Maybe. Maybe." He grinned while he shrugged out of his coat and folded it neatly across the porch rail next to his hat. "But I don't think so. I think it's something else, and I can't say that I've figured it out yet." He looked at her. "But I will."

Louise could hear the sound of a siren somewhere west. It rose and fell same as yesterday's, but instead of ending up screaming across from her front porch, this one faded. More cars pulled up behind the mortician's across the street and while Louise watched, people trundled in loaded down with cakes and huge jars of tea. She didn't recognize a single person.

"I wish somebody would explain why kids take to fire the way they do." October's heat was near bad as August. He wiped his forehead.

"Look over there, Mr. Willard, and tell me what you see." Louise had moved to the rail and stood leaning in, her stomach pressed to his jacket.

He saw those damn blue bottles set in every single window of the house was what he saw. Decorative blue bottles that had thrown shitty aquatic light all over his shoes while he made the final arrangements. It was a true wonder he had not sprouted gills by the time he was done. "I see a helluva lot of blue. For no good reason, either." Aroused, he mopped his face again, sweating over her stomach resting on his coat pocket.

She touched a finger to his arm and he froze. "Too much time cradled next to the same color makes a person mad. Plain mad. That kid craved red. Wouldn't you?"

He folded his handkerchief back into its neat square and put it away. Picking up his hat and coat, he turned and headed down the walk, calling out over his shoulder within plain earshot of all those strangers, "The same could be said for the color gray, Louise!" He was into his car then and gone, backing out of his crammed-in position like a man well accustomed to getting in and out of tight places.

"Dear Lord——" Louise said, running a finger around the neck of her gray sweater, unaware that she had spoken out loud.

After a week of tossing and turning and finally giving in and doing that thing that always made her blush the morning after but always helped her sleep immediately after, she called him at work and demanded he apologize for insulting her color. Gray. The presumed color of her womb. A color she could live with. He not only refused but ended up sitting across from her at her dining room table, negotiating the terms of their relationship.

"Very well, we are two sensible people. I think a contract is not out of line," Louise said finally, the weight of her letdown hair across her back suddenly burdensome. "Not a formal contract involving a circuit of lawyers with their hands held out for payment, but a written list of expectations clearly put, in order to know exactly where we stand."

They were in the gray-blue dining room. A color chosen because she'd read somewhere that grayed blue was said to increase the appetite while at the same time conferring a sense of urgency. They will eat heartily but quickly, she had told the decorator at the time, a short woman wearing mannish navy blue slacks and a nautical scarf, who nodded her head but warned herself never to accept a dinner invitation to the home of Louise Green.

"Are you agreed, then?" Louise looked across the table at the man not-so-recently out of Jackson, anxious to be done with this because she had instruments over her bed that needed dusting.

"My thoughts, exactly," George Willard said, running a finger over his mustache.

"That will be the first to go," Louise said, pointing to his upper lip with her pencil.

"Pardon?"

"I said, 'That will be the first to go.'" She pointed again with her pencil.

"The hell you talking about—"

"The growth of hair over your lip. It's unacceptable."

"The hell you say." George Willard put both his hands on the table, flat down, his stubby fingers spread like prostrate candles.

Her hands went down flat on mahogany, twinning his, the pencil trapped underneath. "Well, see? We are at an impasse already." They both had coffee in her fine china cups. His had not been touched since he was a man who never touched coffee, but hers was freshly creamed, the beige swirls turning like a monochromatic barber pole spinning in a colorless world.

George patted his hands on the table as if he were playing a piano flat-handed, going for noise instead of melody. "I have grown this mustache since the age of sixteen, ma'am—"

"Time enough to prove it can't be done," Louise said and sniffed. She was wearing gray with her yellow scarf as accent.

He continued as if he'd never heard her, "—and I'll not shave it now, or in the near future. I intend to go to my grave with it, in fact." He watched her write frantically on the paper, not at all alarmed by her notations. Thinking the whole while that her penmanship was remarkable. A true teacher's penmanship. A thing highly regarded. She wrote seven lines by his nearsighted guess, before looking up and across again.

"We'll move on and come back to that later. Number two. Are you Presbyterian?" She laid down the pencil and folded her sturdy Methodist hands.

"No ma'am, you can rest assured, I am not Presbyterian. I am lapsed-Mormon by way of a heartbroken grandfather, who's still on his knees in Jackson mourning my decision."

She stared at him, her mouth open without her knowing it. "And I suppose there are minion-like wives left back in Jackson breast-feeding your children?" Presbyterian having been the worst of her fears, what with their watered-down Lutheranisms and truncated creeds. Never imagining that this man not-so-recently out of Jackson, a place as far removed from Utah as Macedonia is from Meridian, Mississippi, could be a clodhopping follower of Joseph Smith.

He laughed out loud. "I have never considered the challenge of matrimony necessary. Not because of a lack of natural inclination, but because marriage held as much charm for me as a game of tennis. A game I hate, by the way. As much as I hate golf, I might add."

There will be years of hard work here to right his religious and recreational wrongs, Louise reasoned. She just so happened to love golf. "Number three." She was momentarily challenged but picked up her pencil again. "Do you snore?" She looked at him over her glasses.

"Tell me this, Louise—is this a regular test you give men? Or something you recently developed just for me?"

"Just answer the question, please."

"No—"

"Well, that's good then, because I cannot tolerate noise at night while I'm trying—"

"—I mean, no, I'm not going to answer any more of your foolish questions." He made a note in his notebook, slapped it shut and put it back in his pocket. Once this was done he patted his hands again on the table and smiled, watching her fingers. With those large hands of hers—I bet her ring finger is a full size bigger than mine.

"Well, I see no point in continuing." She lifted her cup and drank. It was almost five in the afternoon and she was done with this. Her beans were on the stove and she still had papers to grade, for God's sake. She glared. "I have lived alone for almost thirty—for several years now, here inside my house with my things, and to borrow an overused cliché, I am fast approaching the belief that what is not broken should not be fixed." She picked up the paper and folded it neatly in half.

"That's because you've lived with what *is* 'broke' for so long, you have no clue as to the joy a 'fixed' piece of machinery can bring." Another wink.

"The word should have been 'broken,' Mr. Willard. You said 'broke' and the word is incorrect. The correct word is 'broken,'" Louise said.

"The point is, you are not machinery, but you think like it and it's a damnable shame, too, because you are a stately woman. A stately woman."

"Like I said before—I see no advantage to this conversation."

"Well, that's a true pity, because short of you calling the law and having me removed bodily from the premises, I intend to sit here until a deal is struck." He pulled out a cigar, snipped off the end with cigar scissors from a small case inside his jacket and lit it up.

"I cannot tolerate smoke of any sort inside the house," she said while her hands played with the edges of the yellow paper.

She's nervous, George said to himself. Good. This is very good. He sucked on the end of the cigar—a large one he bought under the table from a Cajun out of Vicksburg—wetting it full in his mouth, pulling at the smoke, enjoying the taste of it while he smiled.

She pointed her pencil at him. "You imagine yourself as some sort of romantic figure, Mr. Willard. Some rogue horseman—"

"I hate horses, ma'am—they're as worthless as a boat. A man might as well take his money out back and burn it."

"Nevertheless, you imagine yourself some cavalier individual, and in truth you are as far from that possibility as a toad is from the White House—"

"Some say Eisenhower's resemblance to toad is quite remarkable—"

She raised one eyebrow because he seemed taller seated, his upper arms heavier. His virility compact and lethal. She could still remember the way his skin had felt underneath her finger when they stood out on the porch days back. "You are a small and rude man—"

"Rudeness I'll admit to. But rest assured, I am not small—" He blew smoke to the left side of her face and winked.

"You can leave now. I have supper to prepare." She put both hands down on the table and pushed back her chair and stood, her face so red it looked like a Chinese ornament against a hanging wall of gray silk.

He didn't stand up, but pushed himself back and turned to the side, his face to the wide window overlooking the lawn. "If you don't mind my asking—what's for dinner?" Roast? Round steak smothered in gravy? His stomach growled at the thought of it.

"Dried limas and tomatoes. And you are not invited."

"I hate limas. I ate one when I was seven and spent a week in bed. I hate limas almost as much as I hate stewed okra."

She leaned her stomach against the table and rubbed a hand over her eyes. "Is there anything in this world you do like?" Louise asked in a bored voice, wondering if she'd jotted the phone number to the police in back of the phone book, or if she would have to take the time to look it up.

"Besides you?"

She waved it away as one would shoo a fly and he shrugged.

"Sergei Rachmaninoff," George said then, quietly, suddenly serious.

"Beg pardon?" She felt weak.

"Rachmaninoff. Opus 43. Rhapsody on a Theme of Paganini, to be specific." George smoked, lost in the thought of it. "Variation Eighteen. *Andante cantabile.* Three minutes and fourteen seconds of the sweetest music this side of heaven." He would leave shortly and not try again for at least a week. He tapped his ashes into his hand, whipped temporarily but determined not to show it.

"Paganini—" She took her time with the syllables while she sat back down in the chair. Remembering November 7, 1934. Remembering Baltimore. Remembering the sixty-one-year-old composer seated at the piano. Remembering crying over the music. Her first time ever to do so.

"Yes, ma'am. Rachmaninoff. Played hard as steel. Played ferocious, as if life and limb depended on hitting that next chord—"

"Paganini—" Louise said again in a soft voice, thinking, The word, Mr. Willard, is 'ferociously' and I don't give a good damn.

"—the second entrance of strings is incredible. Played properly it's as powerful as a double portion of God's creation." He hummed the most familiar part. His favorite. (Her favorite.) Directing himself with his handheld cigar, his eyes shut, his head lifted. "La da da da daaaa, da daa da da da daaa . . ."

She listened, thinking, His voice is marvelous. A gentleman's tenor.

"Paganini." He looked at her square-on. "It's like standing on the inside of a glass globe and listening to a world one can't begin to touch—"

The sound of a car cranking up next door broke the spell drifting over their heads and she jumped.

"Well," she said, her mind feeling severed from where it had been seconds earlier. Severed as swiftly as one would snap the head off a shrimp. We've gone from boxing to a waltz and the man doesn't even know it, and it was a thought that disturbed her because it meant she had the momentary lead. She looked at the buffet, with its old silver. At the floors, their true wood showing through the same as always. She looked around the room at everything she had, and everything seemed at once an accurate picture of the state of her heart, what with its splinters and cold coats of wax and smell of old. Old. I am old now. Nothing but wax and wood and metal. I am old with nothing to break the momentum but menopause.

"Yes. Well." He patted his hands down on the table again, done with it.

A door slammed somewhere nearby and the voices of strangers who were not strangers to each other, just to Louise Green, rose and fell, unanswerable, indistinguishable. She heard laughter and the sound of shoes on street pavement, and then it drifted away, cloud-like. The grandfather clock chimed the half hour and she barely heard it, so heavy was the silence between them. Move, Louise. Do something, she told herself. Stand up. Rid yourself of this sudden feeling of being mislaid like last season's linen. Embarrassed, she stood, feeling an urgency to polish silver or wax wood or clean glass.

"I have made us a pecan pie, Mr. Willard. I'll put some cream on it and bring it back in." She reached for his cup of untouched coffee. "Would you like another cup?"

He just stared at her, smoking, a small grin up one corner of his mouth, encouraged suddenly while he thought to himself, I should have mentioned Rachmaninoff sooner. By God, I should have mentioned him last week. "Coffee, ma'am?" he said.

"Would you like some tea, then?"

"Yes, hot tea would be wonderful." He played the table again with his hands. He wanted to sing, but didn't dare. Music being too important to make sport of, to twist for his own convenience, or manipulate in any way, even for this one in her gray dress with that wonderful yellow scarf.

"You misunderstood—I was meaning iced tea with a sprig of mint, Mr. Willard. I hate hot tea. Hot tea is Leftist and un-American—"

"A cup of hot tea would be wonderful, Louise. With just a touch of cream to lighten it. One sugar, please." He put his hands behind his head and grinned like a bandit. She is a wonderful woman. A wonderful woman. Like an old tin of rum balls left in a china cabinet undiscovered for years. He watched her tall, compact body go through the swinging doors into the kitchen and knew immediately that come Christmas, they would be married.

31

COLD NOISE

JOODY WAS SITTING WAY BACK to the yard, Indian-like, alongside the mums that rattled now, what with October full in. Her back to the rustling stems of sunflower plants, dead too, but their dead stalks still hollering out like so many tall dead things that don't like being dead any more than they like watching their inky black seeds drop to the ground as fodder for the birds. She sat inside the cold noise of dead things, on hard ground packed down and frozen almost by last night's freeze. The spot next to her toe said a pig had died there once. Its belly slit. Its guts pulled out still steaming and piled high where the sunflower stems were hollerin' and carryin' on. The dirt said the sow didn't like it much either, what with her havin' a fresh litter to tend but that her not liking it one little bit hadn't stopped that knife from doing its work. Didn't stop those necessary entrails from being put out on the ground where they steamed high at first, and then no more high than the eventual green blades of the eventual green grass. The dirt trembled and talked a dead season about various things concerning what can actually be killed in a body, and Joody moved her foot, tired of listening to the wailings of pork. Having forgotten the boy's dream. And Canaan's vision. Having forgotten how imperative it is to listen to the dying words of anybody or anything inside the smallish realm of God's temporal world.

Joody's palms were up to the sky and her stars were overhead, shining, same as always. Venus is up, she thought. Bright as a gem. And it don't mean a thing no more. Not no more it don't. Joody bent her head to her feet and sniffed the earth, summoned some internal feeling. She stayed that way for a long minute then she sat up again. Gone now. Ain't no more either, she thought, and it don't mean nothin', as well. She flicked the fingers of her right hand, irritated with the stars and the stubborn moon and the trees and the dirt under her foot that wanted to talk. Missing wide open. Missing dark. Missing that creek-like blend of rot and birth that carried with it the easy side of hearing. She looked up in the direction of Venus and then she looked at the moon. "You always was a stubborn moon," she said. "Always kept your mouth shut when you should a been talkin', too. Just like a man." She shut her eyes and thought on the fire she'd burn later on and the voices that would call out to her from the street. "You let me lose one finger and that was enough, too." She shook her head and listened to her years rattle around her ears. The tiny wood clacking making her wish she could stand naked in clear, cold water. Stand there tall, her teats to the wind with not a care to her heart other than seeing the light coming down from the heavens. She licked her lips, thinking on the fire and the words she'd throw out to the people who'd come to see. Thinking on how the people were coming to Joody Two Sun, big as the moon now. Coming to Joody Two Sun with all their worries and concerns. Coming with ears tuned to listen, better than her foot, who was keen on ignoring the cold truth coming up at her from the stiff catch-hole of dirt—

None of the three saw it coming. Not even she, who summoned it while her years rattled. Not even Even Grade, who was standing at the back screen door watching, his quiet hands to his pockets. Not even Canaan Mosley, who was standing at his back door smoking a cigarette from behind a screen. Not even the woman in the house next to Canaan's who was at her back door, screen held to with her foot so she could empty out her slops. All any of them knew was that one minute Joody was up, crossed-legged, facing all those noisy weeds of autumn, and the next time they looked, she was flat to her back, her legs and arms splayed open like one struck down by a heavy hand, or by lightning, or maybe both.

This must be part of it, thought Even, who had shied away from her nightly ritual and now he knew why. Knew why he was happy to keep himself to the front of the house and facing the street while she did her business. He watched for one more minute and then he felt embarrassed for her, like he'd come on her in the middle of her tending her privates, and much as he'd like to stay and watch her pick herself up and brush herself off, he knew it wouldn't be proper.

Lord have mercy! thought Canaan, on seeing her flung hard to the ground, her arms spread open as one crucified to dirt. He hid behind his screen door and watched for movement, rubbed his eyes looking for the up and down motions accompanying breath. Assured she was still a part of the living he wondered over it, if her hitting the dirt was similar to those fits the Holy Rollers have where they moan and writhe and bark like dogs. He'd seen a preacher once who breathed on folks and they'd hit the ground, hard. One woman cracked her head open on a pew and lost her vision and the preacher got himself run out of town by the Methodists. This seemed different, though. Joody was alone, for one thing. Not another person in sight to whip her up to an emotional frenzy. She didn't appear to be hurt, either. In a coma, maybe. Possibly suffering from some internal injury, but wherever and whatever the state of her being, it existed outside the realm of physical pain. He eased open the door for a better look. I wonder if I might ought to go get Even? 'Cause it don't look right to me. Don't look like a woman at worship. Don't seem like a god of any sort would sling a woman down with such a heavy hand. He scratched at his head and then he turned away, thinking, If she's still flat down when I get done with shaving my face, I'll go get him. That's what I'll do. With one last look he killed the kitchen light and headed for the bathroom.

Canaan's neighbor emptying the bucket had seen more than either of the men, who had both blinked with inopportune timing. She'd seen the woman with a missing finger and sticks to her head sitting there in a nigger gal pose one minute and slung back hard like one in a harness the next, and while she watched what would be the topic of her conversation for months on end, she thought, Well now! and Good! God done chastised that one, finally! Saying while the wet ran down her steps and dripped to her grass, Yes, Lord! and too bad for you, you blasphemer, you witch, you friend of the serpent, known as Satan! 'Bout time somebody showed you the what for of this place called Petal. 'Bout time for sure somebody put you where you needed to be put three months back! Satisfied, she shut her door and made the sign against the evil eye, and while she did these things Venus climbed. As did the moon. Night shadows laid a mosaic across the prostrate woman that seemed at once familiar and strange. Two in one moved the light binocular, like an almost Trinity, like an almost painting, like a whole sea of almost things. Light moved. As did Venus. As did the moon. Again and again while leaves fell like dried-up skins in random patterns across the woman sprawled out. Tall dead stalks screamed their song while mums cried and rattled against the fence. Dirt ran in curious circles in and out and around the woman, a pattern that come tomorrow would be credited to ground slugs searching.

Thirty minutes later Canaan stood in his kitchen listening to the too quiet, hearing the hum of his refrigerator, its low motor noise soothing while the pilot light in his stove ticked off regular as a new clock. There was a drip from his sink that was steady too, leaving rust-colored proof of itself against what used to be white. Reality here is it ain't white no more, he thought to himself. Ain't been white in years and years, not since I been living here in fact. The floor creaked under his feet in rhythm with his breathing, and when he held himself still and listened he could hear the strain of the water heater warming off the back porch. He put his hands deep to his pockets thinking on these things without bothering to notice—the way a man thinks on a thing without really thinking on a thing.

The month previous he'd lifted "The Reality of the Negro" off the floor and moved it back to his table, covering up the spot left by the reckless ironing of a hard-core bachelor. His jar holding pencils and pens was back to the side of his thesis, set down where the candles had once dripped hot wax. The candles were gone now, hidden on the back shelf of a kitchen cabinet. I hope I can't find them, even if I need to, he had told himself when he put them there. I hope I don't ever remember where those candles is at even if I'm stranded in pitch black with a knife to my throat—

Before he'd stood and listened to the too quiet all around him, he'd been at his work again. Growing sick of writing after three lame words. All his current notations twisting themselves back into words he'd written months earlier when proving a point seemed inspirational and motivated. I am plagiarizing myself, he thought. And that's a damn shitty shame seeing how the words were sorry to begin with. He shoved the papers away and reached for *Antigone*. He'd bought the crisp new book off a dropout at Mississippi Southern who stood selling his textbooks curbside, hoping for bus fare back to Meridian. When he opened it the scrap of paper Even had given him months back fell out, still folded in two. Canaan spread it open and read out loud, "She was a princess once, of an ancient house, reared in the cave of the wild north wind, her father." He moved his finger up the page to what he'd decided was the same passage but a different translation. "She came of a race of ancient kings, her sire the offspring of gods. Reared in a distant country, among her fierce, northern father's tempests." Thumbing back through, enjoying the smell of the pages as well as the words flashing by, Canaan wondered over it all: how Even Grade had managed to cross-thread his dream with the words of Sophocles; how he'd managed to forget the coincidence until this very moment. "I never showed him this, neither," Canaan said. Bored suddenly with clandestine riddles, he folded the paper up and put it aside.

Moving around in the middle of the too quiet, Canaan went to the back door meaning to see if Joody was still sprawled out underneath the tree like someone fit-vexed. She wasn't. The moon was full, its shape hook-like and surrounded by stars, throwing enough light to showcase the left-over plants of summer waving in the breeze, but where the woman had been was smoothed over and empty, vacant as a near-memory.

Well, nothing to do but sit and hope for a fart, he thought while he studied the coffee pot. "Coffee'd be nice while I'm sittin' here with nothin' to do but play with myself," and then without warning he remembered where the candles were. Behind which door they sat and then he remembered why "The Reality of the Negro" had been moved to the floor in the first place and what he'd done first in the kitchen leaning against the table and then two more times later in the bedroom. He remembered her skin. The shape of her. The sound her feet made walking across his floor. The color of her eyes, more gold than brown. The feel of her earlobes between his fingers. Canaan remembered these things the way a man will remember something he wants to remember; he savored it. Played it back in consequential increments like a choice recording. And what he recalled washed away everything else that wasn't candle-related: his walk through to town, his anger (it seemed foolish and childlike now), his monthlong work over letters delivered up to Grace by the voice of Even Grade. All those things were covered over by remembering. Like a blanket over cold feet. Like a bandage over a scalp cut. Like moonlight over dead, loud pecan leaves.

He moved then, out of the kitchen and into the bedroom where he smoothed up his sloppy bed and put his old work shoes to the closet. He hung up the pants that had been on the floor for a week. Smelling man, smelling old, smelling his life come washing out from between his hung-up sweaty clothes. Reaching high up finding the primer resting next to a shoe box, he thumbed through to make sure it was true to expectations. He saw the dog and the cat and the silly blonde girl with the ball and then he shut the door. Shut the man-smell away and walked through his small living room and left, not bothering to lock the door. What's there to steal? he thought. Happier than he'd been in a month. Thinking on those candles and not those other things. Not his first wife with her folded-over arms. Not Even Grade, who knew more than a body had a right to know about the nature of man in general. Not Joody, who didn't know shit from Shinola 'bout anything other than carving up a naked man for a man to smoke or layin' in the dirt like a tired-out hound dog.

He went down his steps and ranged right in the direction of Clorena's tilted house. He could've gone left and got there quicker, but going that way meant going past Even Grade and he wasn't ready to do that yet. Not yet. Not after words were slung hard. His words, too. First things first, Canaan, my man, he told himself. First things first. Even Grade will be there when you find your way home. As he made the loop he looked back once and saw the man sitting in the green chair, alone on the porch, his elbows resting on his knees. If it hadn't been for the light of the moon he might have been just one more shadow that didn't mean a thing. Canaan saw the pyramid of wood and thought to himself, Now that's strange—seems like we ought to have a fire by now. Joody must not be done prayin' yet, and then he put it aside, not giving it another thought. Put the observation away in some drawer like a neatly folded map.

Even Grade watched him walk down the street in a direction obviously away, and said to himself, I might as well be living in a village full of women. A village full of women heavy-on with their monthly bleed. The gourds caught the wind and he didn't jump, as he'd done the first few times he'd heard them, thinking the sound too similar to snake to not be. Used to them now, he sat still as a wooden post. A couple walked past, looked furtively in his direction and then walked on a few steps. Even sighed heavily because instead of heading away, they were meandering their way back again, the man scratchin' out his head. "Ain't no fire yet, boss—" he called out while he looked at his wrist. The woman with him stuck her leg out and though underneath poor light Even judged her hips large enough to merit their own address.

"You see a fire? 'Cause I sure as hell don't," Even answered, the muscles along his face tightening.

"Nope, I ain't seein' no fire. I was just askin', though. They ain't no harm in askin'—" The man came forward a step and then the woman spoke from inside his shadow, his words apparently not enough to suit her. "We's askin' is all. Ain't no reason for you to get all stirred up over it. Ain't no reason I can see in you actin' that away over it—"

Why, her voice sounds like a peeping tree frog, Even thought. One from creekside in the middle of June. The gourd rattled over his head and he was still, his anger gone but for remnants hedging alongside his mouth.

"I got me a baby growin' inside, and I need a name," she called out.

"Hush Roue—hush up tellin' our business."

"Woman said she got the right name for it, is all. Woman over next to Renfroe's. Over near Gordon Street—"

"You hush now—I done tole you."

"I ain't hushin' and I done tole you if you tell me to hush one more time, I ain't—"

"Well, be quiet then. That ain't the same as me sayin' hush. Be quiet is all I'm sayin' and I'm sayin' it now, Be quiet and quit botherin' people."

Lord have mercy, Even thought, peering down at his feet.

"You, mister—you know when that fire be goin' up?" The man yelled it out, his arm around the woman's shoulder. Her leg was still out, indignant.

"No, I ain't got a clue."

"You know *if* they be a fire goin' up?"

"No, ain't got a clue on that, either."

"You don't know much then, do you?" he said, and his woman giggled frog-like until Even jumped off his porch and headed for them and then she quit her laughin' and ran off down the street. Her big butt taking her out ahead of her man by two easy strides.

Even walked back to the porch noticing the late hour, wondering for the first time where Joody was, wondering if she was still out under the pecan tree. She can't be—it's nearly nine, he reasoned. She can't be out there still. There's not a god up in heaven who'd expect such a thing seven days a week. Seeing the outlines of more evening walkers lookin' for a fire, he stood up and headed around the side of the house.

There was a light on in Grace's kitchen throwing weak yellow down onto her yard. It tangled with the dropped leaves and appeared dappled and shattered, like light playing unrehearsed on top of rough water. Canaan stood out by her gate and petted the goat while his thoughts ran headfirst to *Antigone.* A portion of it, rather. Namely Creon's words of warning to his son Haemon (called Harry by Canaan). *Better far be overthrown, if need be, by a man than to be called victim of a woman. . . .* Of course, Harry was pissed what with sweet Antigone due to be killed any second by his very own daddy. "Sounds to me like one man talking his way around a bad solution," Canaan said to himself, shelving the words more securely than the candles. Sick to death suddenly of everything associated with them. "Like one man's lame attempt at sayin' love ain't worth the price of an apology." He thought on Grace and tried to fit her inside some philosophical format. Tried to imagine her as Ismene or Eurydice, or some lowly singer in the chorus. And it wouldn't work. Her limbs were too unpredictable, her mouth too unbroken. He looked down at his hands petting the head of a goat and they looked travel-worn and bitter, gnarled due to lack of motion. A cripple's hands. Good for nothing. Frozen. The goat butted Canaan's thigh and the light of the moon bit into his legs, exposing him, and he looked away, not only from what he saw attached to his torso but from the Greeks and their predictable bureaucracy, their transparent temperaments. He looked away not with resentment but with expectation, as a man who after years of cold living has finally looked away from the very thing freezing him. Knowing that a man has no choice but to turn on what he's been eating once he sees his bones, once he sees the fruit of futile suckling. Canaan wiped his face. He had craved the sorrowful songs of the dead Greeks for so long. So very long. Craved it to the point of near-stupor. And now the only song playing like a fool's siren in his head, day in and day out, was "Amazing Grace, how sweet the sound that saved a wretch like me."

Canaan looked down at the goat. "I still like what ole Harry had to say to Creon, though. 'The man who thinks that he alone is wise, such a man brought to the proof is found but emptiness.' Emptiness. You hear that, goat? Empty as a beggar's pie safe. Empty as a lard can on Sunday. Empty, just plain empty." The goat wagged its sorry tail and blinked, wanting more. The bell jiggled and Canaan heard movement from the porch next door.

"Polecats slink better'n you and are a helluva lot quieter. She's in there, that one is." The voice was old female, two-toned, like the owner had smoked her whole life and done in the middle range of her vocals.

"I figured she might be," Canaan said, feeling foolish, wondering how much she'd heard.

"My guess is her lard can ain't empty neither. My guess is that lard can of hers is just what an old coot like you might be needin'—" She laughed and it rattled like seeds in a gourd, or stones in a can. (Or pebbles in a pig?)

"I was just talkin' to myself is all."

"I reckon that's 'cause nobody else round here'll listen." Canaan heard her spit to a cup. "I know who you is. Everbody round here knows who you is. Everbody round here knows you make as much sense as tits on a boar hog, too." She slapped at her legs. "Lordy, now I got the proof, too."

Feeling undone and foolish, as if those gods he'd just dismissed were upstairs laughing, Canaan took a backward step, unsure now. The goat's bells. Again those bells. Louder this time.

"You stand there long enough, the moon'll set and it'll be mornin'.

Then I reckon you can go on home and tell folks you dipped your wick in that lard can of hers whiles all the time you stood outside with that goat, watchin' the moon and yapping—"

"Ma'am, I am on my own business, here. I don't need no help."

"Seems to me you do, seein' how you standin' outside that gate like some gun-shy *Jee*hovah Witness." Cornered by a toothless crone, Canaan stepped through Grace's gate and went up to her porch. The goat followed, his feet loud and cloppy on the planks.

"You turn now and git—git from here. You ain't comin' in." He put his hand to the knob. Unlocked. He knocked then. If it'd been locked, he'd have turned and gone back home, knowing a locked door meant she was readying herself for bed. He pulled his watch up by its chain and looked. *Nine o'clock and here I stand with a book under my arm and a goat sniffin' my ass.* He knocked one more time, kicked back at the goat with a foot, and was turning to leave when she yelled out—

"You there! I got my head under! Come on in—"

He stepped inside and saw that not that much had changed. There was still the painting of Jesus and the twelve disciples eating their last supper, up on the wall. There were the same yellow crocheted arm rests on her couch. He heard the sound of water running and saw a shape out in the kitchen.

"It's me, Grace. Canaan."

"Well, come in then and sit."

"Come on in where?"

"In here in the kitchen. Lest you want to stand out there and talk from the living room. I do declare!"

He walked to the kitchen and found her washing her hair in the sink.

"You can sit, if you want. Or you can stand. I'll be done directly either way."

Canaan watched her hands, soaped up and sudsy to the wrist with white bubbles. She lathered twice and rinsed under the faucet and he watched her hands turn slick brown again. She was wearing a housedress covered in big blue and red and yellow flowers of a Hawaiian type, flowers big around as the head of a cabbage. He put the book to the table and crossed his legs, wishing he'd brought a smoke.

"I be done directly—"

"You take your time, Miss Johnson. What I got to say can wait 'til you're done. I ain't here on invitation, either. I should be, I guess, but I ain't." He intended to teach her to read. A lesson a night. He patted the book with his hand while he watched her red flowers.

Grace spoke to him, upside down, from under her arm, "Miss Johnson? What in the cryin'-out world? Why you here, Canaan? You here to plague me over something I ain't got a clue of again?" Her voice sounded strained.

Watching her peer under her arm made him uncomfortable. He could barely see the tip of her chin and her invisible eyes reminded him of thirty years back when he was married. When his wife had hid her flesh from him, pulled down the shades and made him wait until the moon disappeared behind a cloud to take him into herself. What was her name? Weren't married but six short months but seems like I ought to remember her name. Something that started with an *r*. Reba? No, Rena. Rena Brown out of Collins—

"I'm not here to bother you, Grace. That ain't it." Canaan watched her dip her hand into a jar of something and rub it through her hair, slow and steady. He looked around, sniffing, smelling turnips and corn bread and knew that's what she'd had for supper. He saw the coffee pot and knew that after she ate her turnips and corn bread, she'd had herself a cup of coffee. Probably sopped her leftover corn bread in raw honey, too. He saw her bent back curving over the counter and his eyes wished for her face while the rest of him wondered over her anatomy. There's her thigh. I see her hip under that red flower with palm-sized leaves. And there's something else, too. No? Well, she moved, I guess. He saw the calves of her legs, silky blue-brown, her bare feet, their plantar regions pinkish tan, and his thoughts went back to Rena Brown. Those brailled-out portions of hips and legs she served him. The way he'd felt his way through and across like a man in a tunnel, spilling his seed as hurriedly as a blind man tripping over a rock set middle of the road. Spilled it hard and fast and with absolute embarrassment. "I ain't here to worry you, Grace," he said again.

"If you ain't here to bother me, what you here for?"

Because though he has watched a decent age pass by, a man will sometimes still desire the world, was what he wanted to say. All he managed was, "We got some things to discuss, is all." It came out his mouth low, hesitant.

"Now you listen here—I ain't done nothin' to you! They ain't nothing to discuss! You the most confusin' man I ever knowed, nice one day, mean as a snake the next! A body can't know a shitworth of nothin' with you—can't know where in the world they stand from one minute to the next! And I'm just about to my limit with—" Her voice broke and her busy hands quit their work.

He stood then and went to her and bent down to her wet neck and said in a voice so low it felt like a stranger, "Shhh, you listen now, Grace, when I said I got things to say I didn't mean bad things, at least to me, they ain't." He looked at the book on the table and realized his foolishness. She would never agree to being taught, which meant she would never learn to read, which meant she would always be the blackest part of black, and even knowing these things, he still wanted her, wanted her more than ever. As surprised as if he'd been jumped by a thief in his own bathroom, he felt liberated by the knowledge, bulked up and strong, as if his heart had suddenly put on weight. Canaan put his hands to her head and felt her skull. Felt the water washing over his old bony fingers that were feeling younger by the minute. The water was cool wet, more than warm, and he wondered if she was chilled. "Shhh, now," he said, "I been mean and stupid. 'Bout as stupid as a man can get, too. It ain't been you, neither. Ain't none of it been your fault. Shhh, now. Hush now, Grace."

Canaan reached into the jar and smelled the juice of aloe and sweet oil while he rubbed it in her hair. Rubbed it easier than she had done while he watched the light lay itself to the ground like so much clutter below her window. Reaching behind him, he pulled the string to the kitchen bulb and watched the clutter disappear. Just dark and the occasional light from the night sky coming down through the trees and invading the bushes. Her head was still under the water and both hands were flat-palmed to the side of the sink. He felt her thigh next to his and he didn't know how to turn her to put her next to him because that's what he wanted. I'm the youngster here, he reasoned. I'm the fool who needs teachin', he told himself, recognizing the truth of it as clearly as he'd ever seen anything in his life.

"They ain't many who do, but you scare me, Canaan." Her voice came up from the sink, small-sounding and distant. Not like Grace's voice at all. Like another's voice.

"Shhh now. I ain't gonna scare you no more." His voice was low and sweet.

"They's things I can't begin to know 'bout you—"

"They don't matter now. They don't matter at all." And they didn't. He rubbed the oil in her head and then rinsed it clean. Reaching for a towel she'd put to the side, he put it to her head and turned off the water. Patting her head and wrapping it, clumsy and man-like, he turned her to him. All he could see was soft light off her lips while the cabbage flowers, the yellow ones, caught some portion of the moon and bathed her dark throat the color of gold.

"You remember what you said to me that first night? What you said after you got over bein' mad 'cause Even cooked up a roast and served me on the platter?" Grace had her leg up under the sheet. Canaan thought the pyramid was true to what every pyramid should be. He was smoking in the dark. Judging by the pink along the window, he guessed the time must be close to dawn.

"No, can't rightly say I do—I remember the night for sure, but your blue dress stole the words that went with it." He watched her sweet profile. When she talked she blinked her eyes together like drumbeats or bird's wings. Three accents for each of her words. She raised up on her elbow and the sheet fell away and he saw.

"You looked me square on and said all proud and stubborn, 'I'm a thinkin' man, Miss Johnson.'" He remembered it then. Remembered fumbling with his shirt, feeling hot and needful of air. She had been sitting at his table, her beautiful legs crossed. That royal blue dress of hers making a lie of every other color in the world. "That's right. That's what you said, 'I'm a thinkin man, Grace.'" She said it again.

"And what'd you say back?" He remembered while pressing a thumb over her nipple.

"Well, Just Plain Grace says big as you please, 'Well, Mr. Thinkin' Man, what you thinkin' 'bout now?'"

"And I said, 'I'm thinkin I've wasted too much time thinkin', is what I'm thinkin'.'"

They both laughed while the sheet fell away, Canaan feeling rejuvenated by the way it crumpled to the floor, like a frivolous shroud for the newly resurrected. "You ain't Just Plain Grace no more. I got my own name for you and there ain't nothing plain about it neither." He hummed a few bars. "You go to church—you know what it is, don't you?" He was embarrassed because of the poor quality of his singing voice.

"Just 'cause a person can't read don't mean they stupid." He heard the smile. Canaan patted her knee and studied the linear perfection of her legs while she sang the words in the dark.

32

THE SMELL OF A WISH

EVEN WALKED AROUND the house twice, finding himself standing next to where her fire should be. I talked it down and hated the blaze, but Lord God I'd give my left nut if it were here right this very minute! Bored by lack of entertainment, the people had wandered off and the street was empty. After kicking at a rock he went to the cinder blocks masquerading as steps and jumped to his porch. Calm now, Even! You calm yourself down! Time enough for panic later. Deaf to it he threw open the screen door and ran through the dark house to the bedroom, his sweat cold as ice. The door to the closet hit the wall so hard the picture of Jesus with his red heart pumpin' out of his chest went crooked and Even barely noticed, busy as he was feeling through the clothes, mumbling, "Busy as a blind boy bindin' books . . . Busy as a blind boy bindin' brooms. Busy, so busy." His hands said everything was the way it'd been earlier in the day, exactly the same, but for the missing yellow dress and Joody's new shoes—black high-top tennis shoes—and his knobby, brown knit sweater. "Holy Jesus! Holy Sweet Jesus! Holy Jesus!" Jesus with his red heart bursting was canted at a degree near forty-five, leaning and calm in spite of it, but Even didn't

notice because his own personal heart was near jumping out of his own
personal chest which felt fragile as glass. "Holy Jesus!" he said while he circled the house two more times in a run, like a dog in a panic put down in
a fresh yard full of unfamiliar smells.

Panting and weak, he found it underneath the pecan tree stickin' up
sweet to the ground next to a smoothed-out space in the cold October
dirt. There were marks to the ground similar to the curving lines of a
shell washed up from the ocean. Markings similar to what Joody made
with her rake when she worked the dirt outside her rings of rocks.
Through hard breath frosting under his nose he saw where she had been
knocked down flat, its center free of leaves as if she were still there, only
invisible. He saw her skull shape and where the age sticks had lined themselves up in tiny rows under its weight. Upright as a signpost, the stick
was in the space where her heart would've been. Her Year Eleven stick.
His favorite, with the tiny dots that looked like eyes. The same stick she'd
wrapped in her hair with a bloody hand in the year of being true and not
repenting.

"Well, there you go—she ain't ever been from round here anyhow," he
said, and then he bent and picked it up and put it in his pocket while he
walked away, wondering what to do.

While she walked, Joody sang those old songs she'd forgotten she knew.
Songs about mountains gone down flat and glad of it, too. Songs about
the desert ants of Arizona what ate a tribe of long-nosed, hateful Injins.
Songs about a woman gone to toad and then back out to woman again, and
how she preferred being toad because she could jump and croak and swim
and sing, all at once. She sang them all while she walked up the highway
noticing that the damage due to rain had all but disappeared. "Don't take
you long to right yourself, do it?" she said to a tree fresh down, its horizontal trunk already home for autumn fern, its dead limbs full of night
peepers singing like wind. "Don't take you long to figure yourself out, do
it? Bet you don't go round forgettin' who you is: that you a tree, no matter
what—standing, falling, split open by lightnin', no matter. You always a
tree, and ain't that a lesson?"

She walked on past the fork in the road feeling better, feeling more herself. "I been a thin woman, Mister Road. They's a thin woman walkin' 'long here on top your black back. A woman running on a sliver for three months now and her not even knowin' it. And, Lord have mercy, ain't that a lesson, too." The road was warm underneath her feet. She could feel the heat comin' up through the soles of her high-tops and it encouraged her. "Deep Mother, you was right." She pointed up to the sky with a long finger, pointed to the stars and the clouds drifting by slow, like floaty gauze. "You showin' me the way. You showin' me where to go, same as always! We been walkin' this way since we was born. Jes forgot is all. Jes forgot what for, is all."

Joody walked toward that spot between Eastabuchie and Moselle, looking for the wide rock next to a spraddled tree. The seasoned mark would lead her down to where she'd left a part of herself that hadn't ever really been hers to begin with, having already belonged to another. She hooted a laugh and a heavy old owl hoisted itself up out of the limb of a tree and flew off, its wingwork so slow it seemed in defiance of itself. Ah haa, there you are, she said to herself. She knew it'd take more than a rush of water to take down the pine tree forming up split, its unusual trunk similar to a man upside down on his head. Like Even's new pipe I carved out in honor of what led him down to the water. Like everything in orbit round every other thing there is. Ain't life a wonder? she thought, and then, And ain't that a lesson, too?

Neva woke, not due to moonlight, which was calmer and less glaring now that October was clouded over, but because of her dream. The dream involved sounds, loud knockings and clangings like a muffled bell to a firehouse was ringing a warning somewhere north of her. Valuable was there too, standing out in a wide open field where horses grazed. Their equine heads up suddenly, their nostrils flaring. "It's ringing, Neva, better go and see." Over Valuable's shoulder Neva could see the beginning of a stampede. She felt the tremor underneath her feet while dust off their hooves climbed high as the old magnolias and divots flew through the air like mortars. When she grabbed for Valuable to save her the girl disappeared to dust between her fingers and Neva screamed, sitting bolt upright in bed and immediately feeling under her, sure she had peed herself in a panic. All she felt was dry and all she could hear was snoring. Bea's. She reached out to make her roll over, thinking Bea's nose was a regular symphony nowadays. There's the bassoon. Now here comes the oboe—and then she heard it: the doorbell was ringing.

"Bea? Bea—" She shook Bea's arm.

"Wha—" Bea was still grogged over and Neva saw she had gone to bed with her glasses to her nose. Lifting them off and reaching over she set them next to the china figurines. "Bea. I've got to go check, somebody's at the door."

"They'll go away—stay put, hon, they'll go away. They always do—" Bea rolled over and Neva saw the reliable double white crease to her waist and touched it; ran a finger into the fold and left it there feeling flesh closing around it. I could put a pencil there and it'd stay put, I bet. Kissing her shoulder she said, "I'm going to check. Lord, it's fast on two A.M."

Going to the dresser she pulled out the Smith and Wesson and then stepped into her clothes. Glad she had a gun that she knew how to use. Glad she had something to do other than relive her dream. Dust. Val had turned to dust. Pink dust that scattered itself to the ground buried underneath the hooves of the horses. The bell was steady ringing. If it's Jackson, he's about to be dead as a knob and the thought of it made her grin. *Well, you see, officer, he was breaking in and I had no choice. You know how it happens. Two women—no three actually. Three women alone, who's to say what type of meanness he intended. Five shots? Why five shots? Well, you never can tell when they'll get back up again, can you? I mean, horny teenaged boys are as good at playin' possum as any possum I've ever seen round these parts.* The gun cocked, she went up the hall riding the wall sideways, her back to damask. She saw a tall, ghost-like shape through the panel and when she slid the brass eyepiece to the side and peered out she was absolutely amazed. "What the fuck?"

Joody had found her way to the house by following the new mark on her leg. Found it true as any given map drawn up by an experienced cartographer. Four gas lamps lit the walkway and this flickering quartet led her in when she rounded the curve to the road. Near the gate a bronze pickaninny was set between massive boxwoods, squatted down, holding out its rusted ring between its knees like a plea. Men ain't never lived here, Joody thought while she touched his ring. And they never will. Just women. Just painful women with shortened sides.

The house climbed up out of the dark like something from a hard dream. So tall its roof line disappeared into blue-black shadows that ate the trees. Joody fanned through her memory to see if she'd ever encountered such a ghostly sight, such a massive structure lit up by lights flickering on shiny brass posts. No, I guess I ain't. They ain't never been such a one as this. She waved to a cedar tree. She saw another up a ways, closer to the lights and felt encouraged. When she passed by she stripped a low limb of its thistles and put two of them in her mouth, chewing, drawing the mint up her nose. "Well, ain't you a sight, now," she said to the taller of the two trees, the stronger one, the one whose needles she was sucking.

At the second lamp she had shed her overalls and lifted the yellow dress over her head. Buttoning it up, the tiny black buttons feeling smooth and interesting to her fingers, the black alligator belt shiny in the night light of the lamp, she'd smoothed it down and then rolled her overalls to a lump and put them by a post. Stretching out her back because it'd been a pure job luggin' Mama Girl up from the creek, she heard pops fire off in all directions like the small reports from a handgun. A night bird of some sort lifted out from the top of the cedar tree at the noise and flew off, its head buried in the wind. Dragging her bag she went onto a porch of painted blue wood and looked the door's brass fixings over until she found the calling bell. After she mashed it long and hard, she stood to the side and waited, thinking, Well, ain't you a sight, you big old house. Ain't you a sad sight, now.

A pirate answered the door. A black-haired, wrinkled pirate holding a shiny gun leveled point-blank at Joody's stomach and for the first time since she'd struck out from Bellrose Street, Joody was startled.

"I ain't much for hellos myself, come the middle of night. But I can't say I ever pulled a weapon on one. Drove a raccoon away with a paring knife once, but he was a rude little thing. Strode in smellin' my beans, and I weren't in no mood to share." Joody stood, the bag in front of her, her face calm and untroubled in spite of what she was seeing. The gun was the least of it.

"We don't want any." Neva's eyes studied the bag.

Joody heard the voice and disliked it but looked at her steady. "I rung the bell 'cause I need to see Valuable Korner and I know this is where she's at. My leg told me so."

She lifted the skirt of the yellow dress and pointed to a mark near her knee and Neva thought to herself, So, this is the one. This is the crazy loon with sticks in her hair. But she stood still, the gun propped limb-like out from her center. "I got no reason to believe you know our business other than your mouth saying so. Only a fool would let somebody like you in at two in the mornin' and I'm no fool."

"Oh, that's the God's truth. Lord, you may be lots of things, but fool ain't one of them." Joody folded her arms and waited, studying her eyes. *I come on that crazy spotted girl outside El Dorado, Arkansas, who looked sweet as an angel, too. That light brown skin of hers. That silky hair, them blue eyes. Me just fourteen and starvin' for friends. Thinking that the time might be ripe for a traveling companion, especially one who looked just like an angel. Woke up on the third day with a knife to my throat and her jammin her fingers in my eyes fishin' for blood, too . . .* "I know you know me. That smell coming off the side of your neck says so. You don't know me personal, but you heard the girl talk on it." She spit out the cedar clippings to her hand and rubbed her palms together, drawing on their strength.

Neva kept the gun pointed gut-level, her eyes drawn irresistibly to the black woman's legs. "What do you want with her?" Her eyes were racing from face to legs and back again.

Joody sighed and studied the slope to Neva's nose, unimpressed with the pirate's weapon but worried by the guardianship line around her nostrils. "I could lie and make up something, but I ain't. Valuable's dying," she said. *. . .woke up with no breath to scream, either. Once I threw that angel girl off my belly, I straddled her and demanded what for. Eatin' solid as friends out the same can for two days straight and her trying to blind me with her knuckles. "I want your eyes," she'd said. "Got to have your black eyes. If I don't git your eyes, I'm gonna die!" was what she'd screamed right before I clubbed her into the unconscious world with a rock.* And now here I stand in the ass-end of Mississippi facing another.

"You're a liar, Valuable's asleep upstairs. She's not even sick." Neva could see the gas lamps behind her throwing shadows like horses. Dark horses running full throttle.

"You a hard woman with a plan, but they ain't no other place for the girl—right now." Joody made her point and stood still watching for blood. Satisfied there wouldn't be any, she continued, her dark eyes steady. "You don't see color neither, and that's a puzzle. You just see woman or man is all. Just woman or man. Mostly woman and that's a puzzle, too, seeing how that plan of yours destroys the best side a woman got. And ain't that a sorry lesson—"

Realizing there couldn't possibly be two like her in the world, Neva walked back into the house and put the gun on the table. It made a solid sound behind her that was pleasing. The barrel pointed greasily to the door and this pleased her, too. On her way back to the porch she tucked her shirt into her pants, gathering and smoothing the excess to two smooth tucks, military style, exactly as her father taught her. She pulled up a rocker. "Why'd you pick two A.M. to visit?" The rocker groaned under her, as if embarrassed by her lack of sensitivity.

"'Cause time ain't a big boy when somebody's sufferin' and that one is—I got something that belongs to her and I mean to give it to her. I should have 'fore now, but I got full of myself and stopped hearin'."

"Why is your hair like that?"

Joody watched the reflections of the gas lamps dance across the woman's black eyes and decided her questions were a game. A game like those white folks play where they move carved-out men all over a checkerboard. Well, two can play as well as one. "My ma'am would shame me, I've forgot myself here—my name's Joody Two Sun and my daddy was a Injin." She stuck out her hand and waited as a test. *You'll know,* Deep Mother had said to her. *You'll know what you need to know when she takes your hand. If she takes your hand.* Joody waited, not impatient or uncomfortable with the wait, just steady on, her eyes straight to the woman. Neva reached out finally and shook her hand and Joody read it all. All her plans. All her love. All her dark core waiting.

"The sticks now, please." Neva yawned terribly while she pointed to Joody's head.

"They mark my years." Joody's mouth was going dry.

"I see."

"No you don't, but that don't matter seeing how I'm here on account of Valuable." Joody could still taste the mint of the tree but it was wearing thin. Hold your spit then, she told herself. Hold it 'til we're done here, 'cause this one's heart is big as a bull. She managed to look settled and peaceful, glancing up once at the night sky looking for Taurus.

"I could get her, I suppose."

She's lying now, Joody realized. She'll change the subject next. "I'll be glad to wait."

"I've never had one of your race look me straight on." Neva changed the subject.

"I've never had one of your race expect me to," Joody said, her voice easy, but her heart pounding.

"I see. I see. Well, what do you have that belongs to Valuable?"

Joody hadn't been asked to sit but she was tired and her legs hurt. But instead of sitting next to the pirate woman, she moved back a ways and sat on the top step leading down to the walkway, a place where the breeze could wash her. "I got her rock," Joody said once she was leaning back on the post and comfortable.

"Her rock." Unbelievable.

"Her Mama Girl rock. I thought it was gone after the flood, but I went down to the creek and found it where it'd always sat. Right next to horse-head rock. I named it when I first got here, thinking it was meant to be mine. But it ain't mine. It belongs to her—has always belonged to her, especially now that she's carrying a boy child."

"—the hell you talkin' about!"

Joody waved a hand. "Ain't no point in lying, Pirate. I know you know. I wouldn'ta opened up my mouth if you didn't. But you know. Didn't know it was a boy, though; that was news. But it is. A sweet, towheaded boy baby. She'll need her totem now, 'cause she's dying of sadness, and the rock'll give her strength—"

"You're insane. I want you to leave now. Right this second—"

"I ain't goin' to, not until you agree to give it to her. If she don't get it, she ain't gonna make it through this thing." The gas quartet had led her into this black gulf and she wondered why. Why lead her in so willingly to a place of no resolution? She could see them out near the road, waving hopelessly. Such a large black cloud of a thing lives here. Such a large woman, too. A woman with a plan.

"I could shoot you and nobody would judge me over it."

"White folks been killin' black folks since the edge of forever. You won't, though, 'cause we got the same illness. And us havin' the same illness, it'd be like you was shootin' yourself and you ain't a fool."

"I'm not sick—"

"Yes ma'am, you is. Same as me. Sick with love over what's truly innocent 'cause what's innocent in us has nearly 'bout disappeared. You ain't seen innocent 'til you seen that one upstairs sleepin'. I thought I seen it once and it nearly 'bout dug out my eyes. So, yes ma'am, you sick same as me. Same as me."

The smell coming up off the river washed high and over, sweeping up from the muddy banks, carried by the wind over scrub and cedar, lifted up by some mulish gust and sent over the clay tiles of the house, to settle finally around the rockers and the gas lamps, wishing something—wishing anything. The smell was old, seasoned and dry with longing. An aging virgin's smell. Like the dried-up dust of a disfigured woman's parlor. Wishing, the smell said. Wishing for something, it pleaded. Wishing for anything at all. Neva ignored it, so used to the intractable odor of wet that it was nothing more to her than a smell that stayed forever. Insistent. Unwelcome. Like nobody's cat. Joody felt the breeze strum against her legs and her bony elbows and the high points of her cheeks—all those edges that wished for flesh. And once the music was done, the wishing done, the bones still cartilage-shaped angles that hurt even in their comfort, she sniffed high and hard and shut her eyes, still wishing.

"Ain't nothin' like the smell of a river at night," Joody said, feeling something stirring, some measure of indecision chipping away at the woman's way of thinking.

Neva saw the woman's face was calm, her eyes shut to the porch light and the smallish moths knocking themselves against pebbled glass globes. "I've grown so used to it, I hardly notice anymore."

"You too close then. You need to go back a ways and learn it all over, before it's too late—"

"Back a ways—"

"To a time before you knew it. Knew the river. Go back to when horses and stalls and pastures was all you knew. That time before you loved that

one upstairs but not what she's carrying. Go back a ways to that time of
loving women just like you, who loved you right back the way you wanted
to be loved. Go back now, girl, 'cause there ain't nothin' more healing in the
world than a river at night—"

"Unless it's a creek—" And Neva saw it again. Smelled the odor of old
and virgin-dry and saw them again at the Bogue Homa. Valuable. Sweetly
upright, one-pieced, one-fleshed and holy one instant, and then spread open
and changed the next. "Ahghhhh!" It came out Neva's mouth a loud scream
twinned to a wolf's howl or a mule's bray and then she felt hands con-
straining her arms, pressing her flesh to the wood of the rocker, pinning her
under an unwelcome weight. The Negro had sprung up amazingly agile for
one so tired. Sprung up high and hard, speaking low-urgent, "You got to
give it to get it!" She was speaking of mercy and Neva knew this.

"No!" Neva tried to pull away.

"You got no choice but to give up your foolishness—" Joody said, her
voice docile but fixed, her hands strong down.

"There's always a choice—" Neva's fingers were hooked to the chair,
bloodless.

"Before the doin' of a thing, there is. But once it's set, they ain't no
choice but to give to it! I know this better'n you!"

"You're a demon!" Neva hissed between her teeth.

"Maybe."

"No maybe to it. You're a thief, too!" Because the black woman wanted Valuable, Neva saw this now. Wanted her youth and her sweetness.
Wanted to suck it from her like candy on a pauper's tongue. "Thief! Git
from here! Git off my porch!"

"Now, that I ain't. I ain't never stole nothing in the whole of my life. I
wanted to once 'cause I was hungry, but I ain't never."

"Let me go!"

Joody's hands were still on the woman's arms and even bent like a tree
she was taller than Neva. Her feet planted on either side of those bare
white ones were in a pose so un-Negro, so unwoman, Neva was as close to
being frightened as she'd ever been in her life.

"You readin' me wrong and I see this now. See how large this thing is
with you. All I got to say to you is this: lest we both give up what we want

and let it be, she'll die before her time. If we don't behave ourselves, she'll never walk through this thing. I may not know much, but this much I do know. Now you read my hands and judge me true." And Joody shut her eyes and Neva felt a tingling along her arms that could have been because her blood was cut off by the woman's touch, but she didn't think so. Joody moved her hands and the force of it sent the woman rocking. She rocked that way for a while, the river all around them; the silence accommodating for once.

Neva kept her face to herself, remembering Val's stupor-like appearance for days now. Wondering how she'd not questioned it, been alarmed by it. She looked at the black woman who had put her face front-on to the post as if it were a breast, and thought of the gun, still cocked, inside on the table, and realized the foolishness of the weapon. What a fool, Neva, to think a bullet would stop this one. What a fool. The top of the cedar tree nodded in agreement. Joody put her right hand up to the post and Neva saw she only had four fingers. Good Lord!

"You say the rock'll help?" she said then, remembering Val's white face earlier in the day, and yesterday, and the day before that. Remembering how the principal at Runnelstown had called and said the girl was yet to attend one single class at the high school. Remembering how Val hadn't eaten a bite in more than three days, just laid up in that huge white bed like a curled-up puppy. Neva's feet were cold and hating the porch, missing the backside of Bea's warm, white legs.

"I don't know no more," Joody said, tired of the sadness and the certainty of what this one had in store. "The rock was hers, is all. To begin with. Named by Deep Mother through me, for her. Mama Girl. Girl Mama. And ain't that a sad lesson." The wind caught the top of the cedar tree and shook it hard, throwing down shadows that made the yard seem alive in the dark. More alive than the women on the porch. Without a backward glance Joody walked down the steps and out into the dark. The sound of the wind as stiff as its odor.

❧

After Even had found her age stick and knew that she'd be coming back— soon, or not so soon, the block of time concerning her return not so important as him knowing she'd be back—he set off walking down Bellrose, following the same path Canaan had taken a half hour earlier. Night was fully in on all the streets. Most houses with their quiet noise lit up in smallish places. Kitchens. Bedrooms. One or two porches. He smelled more than one garbage barrel out back burning, night being the best time to deal with refuse. Summer was different. Summer had a way of dealing with smells in its own sweet way—dew, rain, wind. Autumn was less gracious, more bullheaded, and the smell of the burn was still hovering sometimes when the sun broke through to morning. Once he was free of Shasta, Bellrose lost its charm and he found himself walking instead, in the direction of town, aware that his walking had focused his eye again to all life's edges. He had Joody's age stick in his pocket and he felt it now and again and the shape of it soothed him.

Petal at night was pretty much like Petal at day, he realized. Barren. Dusty. The only difference being the absence of people. But even their absence was ineffectual because of the constant feeling of void and lack of ancestry, or parentage. Like the town would be the same with or without the two-legged animals walkin' around in their overalls and straw hats, shopping. Passing the intersection he walked to Hillcrest Loop, remembering how he'd meant to visit the cemetery that day in August before being set off course by a red-gowned woman. Was it really that long ago? he wondered. The encounter similar in feel to last decade's work. Turning north he headed for the tombstones, the uphill climb feeling good to the shafts of his legs. Seeing the approach of the gate to Hillcrest Cemetery he thought, I bet I'm the only Negro willin' to visit a place of the dead at night, thinking on the tales he'd heard of haints and rootconjures gone awry and how victims of misfortune wandered along the plots at night, wailing. I'd give my eyeteeth to see one, he thought. Wondering how it'd look, this woeful proof of the hereafter, this midnight wanderer of Sheol. His head was down following the path that led back to the oldest part of the bonefill, a place where the markers were grayed and blackened, their dead gone there from fighting in that war between brothers. When to own one of Even's kind was worth any measure of killing. Stepping around a marble lamb on a slab, a haint stood up tall and blond, and Even screamed like a woman.

"Shit, Mr. Grade. I didn't mean to scare you!" Jackson grabbed for him.

Even put a hand to his chest and repented of ever wanting to see proof of the hereafter. "Lord, boy! Give me a minute, here." He bent down and tried to draw spit to his mouth, but failed at it.

"Shit, I'm sure sorry. I saw you comin' and debated on whether to let you pass by or not. I guess I came out on the wrong side of it."

He recognized the boy from the night at the creek. "Why you wanderin' round here at night?" Even asked. Curious in spite of his near heart attack.

"Same as you, I reckon. Ain't got nothin' better to do." Jackson had his hand on the stone marked Korner. "In truth, I was sittin' here wonderin' about that lamb over there. Wonderin' what killed that young-un underneath it."

"Lord have mercy." Even's heart was still thundering outside its normal range.

"Sorry I scared you." Jackson was quiet then, lifting his hand off the stone and tucking it under his arm, embarrassed.

"I like to read at the names and count off the years," Even said, pacing his breathing. "Night ain't the best time to do it, I guess." He rubbed at his chest.

"You think maybe you might know one of these dead folks?" Jackson said.

"Just hopin', is all."

"All our dead's buried over in Georgia. I hate that state."

"I been to Georgia once. There ain't much there but scrub and red dirt. Leastways the part I saw of it. Some say Stone Mountain's a wonder. Can't prove it by me, though. I saw country was all. Poor country marked off by rusted fences."

The boy was quiet. Just put his chin down to his chest. "You reckon there's a God, Mr. Grade? 'Cause I sure don't."

"Even. Seein' how you near killed me, call me Even." He spit finally, the water level to his mouth back where it should be, wonderin' where this was going. "Can't say I know one way or the other. Some days I'd bet my left nut on it. Other days I call myself a fool for ever believin' there was a chance at it." He pulled a pack of smokes from his pocket, shook one out for the boy and then lit them both off the strength of one match. "What's set you thinkin' on such?"

"The turn of things."

"That'll do it ever time." Even blew smoke through his nose. Wondered again where Joody had gone.

Jackson sat down on the long slab and scooted back against the headstone. He pointed with his lit cigarette. "I live down there in that white house with the big magnolia trees. At least I did. We're moving next week." Even was startled, remembering Valuable and the baby on the way and the way those two held to each other even when their flesh wasn't touching, remembering they were blood-kin.

Jackson looked up at the stars, all fixed and blanketed out against the black. "I been sitting here on Valuable's dead grandmother, Luvenia, tryin' to figure things out." He tapped his ashes to the side, away from her. "I was in the dry cleaners with my dad the day she croaked. I ain't never told Val about it and I was just wondering if maybe I ought to." He looked at Even. "After they took her away in the ambulance I looked around the store wondering what she'd seen that scared her so. 'Cause that's what happened. I wasn't but eight years old, but I knew it. She was standing there right as rain one minute, talking old lady quilt talk to the girl behind the counter, and the next minute she turned wide-eyed and green. Scared witless, was what she was. Anyhow, all I could see was this sign pinned up behind the counter on the wall over the calendar. A postcard of a man on a bucking horse was to the side of it, blocking one of the letters, but I managed to pick it out: *Not Responsible for Valuables*, it said. Only the *s* was blocked by the edge of the card. *Not Responsible for Valuable* was what Luvenia saw. I wasn't but eight and figured that out." Jackson looked at Even Grade. "You reckon I ought to tell Val?"

"I'd keep quiet on it—it might scare her," Even said, surprised at his speculation.

"You think?"

"Could be."

"You're probably right." Jackson looked at him steady and Even noticed the striking similarity to the girl's gray eyes. "You know, until that night we went looking for Joleb down by the creek I never thought one way or the other 'bout you nig—Negroes. My folks are suspicious of the colored. Scared almost, like most are here in Petal."

Even didn't know how to comment.

"I wasn't ever scared of Negroes. I just wasn't interested. Know what I mean?"

Even shrugged, feeling pretty much the same way about white folks.

"You got a family?"

He thought of Joody and Canaan. "Sorta. Enough of one to make me happy anyhow." Was it? Was it really enough?

"Valuable ain't got anybody. Not a single person in the world." Jackson snuffed out his smoke as proof.

"Well, that depends on how you look at it—"

"Oh, she's got those two crazy queers, I realize that, but that's not much to count on, is it?" The boy cleared his throat, embarrassed. "But she thinks highly of your girlfriend—"

Even couldn't help but smile to himself, the term girlfriend so foreign to what that woman was. Jackson went on, "If you could ask Miss Judy to keep an eye on her if she gets a chance to, I sure would appreciate it. I can't stand the thought of leaving with things . . . with things so unsettled for her."

"Well, that don't sound like too much to ask." Even squatted down on his haunches, imagining the pose to be the way a deal between men should be struck, thinking if he'd asked the same of any man he'd want the gaze eyeball to eyeball. "I hate to see anybody goin' through hard times, Jackson. Hate like hell to see—" anybody homeless, was what he was thinking, having lived under that low ceiling for way too long.

"You the only one who sees it that way. They sure as hell don't." Jackson nodded with his head in the direction of those magnolia trees.

"You want another smoke before I leave here?"

"Nah, one's enough for now." Jackson pushed himself up off the grave. "I got to go on home anyhow. That way you can study your markers in peace." He put his hands to his pockets and headed toward the cemetery's gate. He turned back once and said, hesitantly, as if the words ran a gamble on being judged foolish. "I keep thinking about Luvenia being scared shitless at reading that sign and I know just how she feels." He rubbed at his chest. "Ain't it a shame the body can't go where the heart lives." It was statement, not question. Jackson turned and walked through the gate and on down the hill.

Well, that's as true a thing as I'm ever likely to hear with both feet standing in a bonefill. Even looked out on all the shapes signifying living and breathing and then dying, their dimensions made ordinary by their common destination, and then turning he traveled the way the boy had gone. Done with walking. Tired finally. Ready and willing to wait for Joody's return.

He heard her stumbling through the house two hours later.

"Even? Even Grade?" she called to him, her feet hard on the floor, her hands out in front of her feeling for the bedpost.

"I'm here, Joody."

"Even?"

"I'm here, woman. Same as always. I always been here—"

She stumbled forward and fell on him. Fell in her yellow dress, her shoes to the bed, wet from the dew she'd collected jogging a shortcut through a field. A force had chased her. A looming force with far-reaching arms. Since Arizona she'd come out on the safe side of most things: mean niggers, mediocre Indians, crazy whites, rabid dogs and sharp-clawed cats. She'd outrun killer angels and well-intentioned Christians alike, but never anything like this. Never anything so unsolvable her six sides felt tinsel thin. "Hold me, please." She licked the underside of his neck, tasted his salt.

He already had his arms around her. "I am holding you."

"Not all of you is. Just a part. I need all of you to hold me."

And he shut his eyes and gave himself to her, wholly, with as much forgiveness and gentleness as he could manage, wrapping his bare legs around her marked-up ones plastered with grass. He felt her heart beating into his, the sweat of her walking speaking to him. He put his nose to her hair and breathed in hard, settling finally into relaxation in spite of things, as if all his parts were finally home.

33

HALLOWEEN

V ALUABLE'S FINGERS LOST THEIR BLOOD, hooked as they were around
the steering wheel of what used to be Enid's car. She wet her lips with
her tongue and glanced at her reflection in the rearview and then turned
the mirror facedown to the dash, where she'd not be threatened with that
temptation again. She tore down the highway, catching her right tire on a
shoulder's cusp and throwing a bank of glittering shale. Pale. Lord, she sure
felt pale.

After she'd left, Neva stood for fifteen minutes with her knees locked,
staring at the lit pumpkins flickering by the gate. She stayed that way
until Bea slapped her hard in the face to get her attention and to keep her
from fainting. "Bend your knees, Neva, or you're gonna spill. Bend them
now." Neva did, feeling blood rush up through her thighs and straight to
her head where stars exploded behind her eyes. The wind picked up and
whispered through the cedars with a whining sound, like that of crying.
Only the cedar trees mind her leaving, she thought to herself. Not Bea.
Not the monkeys or the ghosts or the witches or the clowns. Just the

trees. And me, of course. Always me. High up over Neva's head tree limbs waved feathery tops while men dressed up like women and women dressed down like men whooped and hollered in celebration of All Hallow's Eve.

"She disrupted our party. I'll not forgive her so soon for this one, I don't care what her problem is." Bea brushed the cracker crumbs off her Bo-Peep dress. The blue satin was tighter than last year's and her wig was losing its steam thanks to all those cranked-up fireplaces. Large synthetic curls fell down into her eyes like soggy sausages. "Folks will be scattering this gossip for years! Years!"

"I told you not to let her in the attic." Neva's sword was someplace in the living room with the ghouls and mummies and the men dressed like Las Vegas showgirls. "My sword's inside, I suppose. Beyond the goddamn cow." She fiddled with her empty scabbard while glancing to the porch. The black-and-white cow—he claimed to be a poet by day—was visiting from New Orleans. Decked out with a huge papier mâché head wearing marbles for eyes, it stood quoting Robert Louis Stevenson through a megaphone: *The friendly cow all red and white, I love with all my heart—She gives me cream with all her might, to eat with apple-tart.* Neva had been hearing that same line for fifteen minutes and was near to the point of pulling out the Smith and Wesson and blowing the bovine to hamburger heaven.

"It's too late to use it on her, she's miles away by now." Bea's crook was bent from where she'd taken a swing at the journalist.

"Use what?"

"The sword, that's what you were asking about, isn't it? Your goddamn sword?"

"Shut up, Bea." And then Neva caught herself. The woman had nearly fainted from embarrassment. "I'm sorry. What she did was unexpected is all. It's still Halloween and we've spent a fortune. Let's not ruin things."

"Let's not ruin things! Let's not ruin things! Oh, rest assured it's ruined. Only thing left to do now is open up our veins. The crowd's got a taste for it, too. I'm sure they'd like to watch." Bea pulled off her wig and tossed it to the ground. Grappling with her staff, she hoisted an armful of blue satin and made her way up the steps like a busted ship heading for port. "By the way, the reporter's with the *Times-Picayune.* A charming young man. My guess is he's about to win the Pulitzer." She blew Neva a kiss over her shoulder and then she was gone.

"Fuck you, Bea." Neva unfastened her regalia and let it drop to her ankles. Before it had landed properly, she was halfway to the garage. Fumbling inside her pirate pants for the keys, all she could wonder about was where the girl had gone.

Jackson had kissed her good-bye underneath the knobby magnolia while she pulled at his T-shirt. That's what she remembered. One scratchy dry kiss under boat-sized emerald leaves. He wouldn't tell her exactly what time he was leaving for Georgia because he suspected she would follow and he was right. He'd stood there trying to get her hands to behave themselves and failing at it.

"Val, please! This is hard enough—"

"Hard enough? How? You're the one leaving! Packed and ready to go. You're not even crying over it!" It was the second time she had been near hysteria. The first time had been when the men in the suits came to her house and told her Luvenia was dead. Jackson had looked around and grabbed at her restless hands because the man in the catering truck was smirking in their direction.

"Valuable, listen to me." She watched him lick his desert lips. "I want you to have a good time tonight. Try to, anyhow. Forget we're leaving. Just pretend it's a day just like yesterday, or the day before that."

She'd slapped him then. Hard on the face, which surprised her. She walked off, stumbly. Her feet begged her to stop their forward motion and pivot to see if he was following, but she couldn't. All she managed was her hand to her hair in a move meant to be casual, but instead sadly desperate, for she found herself clutching thick shanks and pulling. Wishing for pain. Wishing for some pinch or pang or prick, other than the one who was leaving her. Jackson's hand caught at her waist when she was up near the carved-out pumpkins decorating the wide front steps. Their candles were already lit, as were two-thirds of the out-of-town guests. Drunken shouts sailed from all the windows clean out to the river's edge where the faux tombstones were leaning. A shame, too, considering there was a real cemetery not two hundred feet away where the dead slept through with boring half-baked dreams, anxious, she was sure, for entertainment. If I were dead, I wouldn't mind the revelry, she thought. I'd welcome a shouting drunk, even a homosexual one. The pumpkins sat squat-red and steamy against the early night-blue sky. Red and pitiful. Their rinds shriveled and puckered like sores slow healing. Three of them glared out from wilted eyes. "I love you, Val," he said to her hair while he uncoiled her fingers. Kissed her knuckles. Sweetly this time. "I love you. I can't leave you like this. Not fighting . . ."

Pivoted finally, she was kissed in plain view of the Cuisine Extraordinaire truck, Jackson's lips parted like a pumpkin's; his eyes nonglaring and sweet, but lit up by fear.

"He knew. He knew me better than anybody, too." Valuable downshifted and studied the highway. Meridian was north. She knew that much. Knew it was above and to the east of Hattiesburg, like most good places in Mississippi, she supposed. If I stay on this road, I'll find him. Find his car because I heard him say they were going through Meridian. So, I'll find Meridian and then I'll go east through Alabama, all the way to Chamblee, Georgia. Or was it Chamblain? Shit! I wish I'd listened better! Clutching the steering wheel, she flew through the night, imagining herself a bird. A falcon, maybe. One soaring. Eyes beaded in focus. Captured by some covert crust of wind. An eagle, possibly. A young loner on fledgling flight searching out some vector point from which to watch *gray meanness plait long finger shadows*. . . . Valuable reached for the radio and found Perry Como, hating herself. Seeing herself not as predator bird layered in dignity and purpose, but as a simple, mean-spirited, purple-winged crow.

The miles went by in the dark. Foggy miles, too, which seemed fitting for Halloween. Valuable wiped her face on her sleeve and smelled her sweat. Nervous sweat. Scared sweat. Goat sweat. Christ, I stink, and it's a strange stink, too. A different stink from a regular working-in-the-garden stink. What? What is it? She wiped her face again, careful to keep her hands to the wheel and smelled it: mothballs and age, death and decay, and she remembered. Remembered how she'd found it a month back hidden in the attic and been horrified by it. Remembered how the kiss from Jackson had been such a closed and final door, it killed her common sense as surely as slicing off her braid had killed hope creekside. Stumbling upstairs through a Halloween party brimming with as much bizarre entertainment as a body could imagine, she'd pulled the shroud from underneath her bed and put her fingers through the slits. Death had lived there, death she was a part of because she loved the killer's daughter, death that lived in her by reason of spilled seed from a chuck wagon. The garment was so stiff-heavy it tore her skin when she slid it over her head. Tore the skin of her nose clean off. "Good," she said to the dumb Mama Girl rock. "It's about time I bleed."

She was stricken. Dying. She had been since the flood. She read her near extinction in the mirror's reflection. She counted off expiration signs wide-eyed and with near boredom. Like the half-concerned might casually thumb through a downed oak's age rings. Jackson is leaving me, was one ring. Jackson is leaving me, was another. Jackson is leaving me: rings four, seventeen, ninety-two, and three million. All the way up the increments of imagination, the equation was the same. He was leaving and so there was nothing. No rock. No moon. No meaning. No call for propriety. Nothing. So, reason discarded like last Easter's shoes, she dressed in her great-grandfather's Klan outfit and made her way down the stairs, moving through the throng like a child inside a tent. Like tent-covered Luvenia outside on the peeling platform wondering over the stars, she supposed. Through the eye slits she saw the black trombone player wipe his face and sit down hard in a chair and study his feet. The black cook barbecuing baby ribs dropped a side to the floor and picked it up again. Put it back on the rack. The blank-faced crowd grew silent in waves that started with their eyes. By the time a dropped pin could be heard, Valuable was done, the first part of the letter delivered up through scattering speech running away from her. The court jester with the notebook got the finish, though. The bell on the end of his satin cap jingled with her last sentence:

"'We killed that big-mouth boy while he laughed out loud. He bucked for three minutes and then he was done, as well he should be. Cain's seed is unruly. You cannot break a mule without pulling out the board. Hear your father's words: Time and again, Luvenia, you purt'near have to lay it to their head!'"

Neva got to her first and grabbed her hard. "You act like this is hot news around here! You act like this is our fault!" She was fending off Bea with her free hand. The party was asphyxiated but listening. Like spirits skilled in stenography.

"You act like that makes it right." Valuable could barely speak, her teeth were chattering so badly. Neva jerked the hood from off her head, ripped the garment up over her shoulders while the man sitting on the stairs called out, "Is Luvenia spelled with a *u*?" Bea swung her crook at him and decapitated the hall tree instead.

Neva shook her like a rag doll. "You've embarrassed the hell out of us!"

"We're not a normal family, Neva—it's foolish to expect us to behave as one." She copied Neva's words while grabbing at her sword, pulling it free with a slicing sound. For about half a second the throng gave a postmortem sigh of expectation, as if they were about to witness with their very own eyes the cocktail story of the lifetime.

"I'm not expecting normal, Valuable. I'm expecting decent. Seems you should know the difference." Neva jerked the sword out of Valuable's trembling hands and threw it to the floor. A werewolf and a monkey jumped out of the way of the clatter.

"Oh Jackson, oh Jackson, oh Jackson." She sang it with the wind, a little high and sharp. Too girl-like to be considered serious singing. A sign up ahead said Columbia, 55 miles, and she knew she'd gone the wrong way. Taken a wrong turn somewhere and headed west instead of east. Zigged when she should have zagged. Maybe when I pulled out of Hillcrest Loop after seeing his empty house. Maybe that was it. Maybe because seeing his house made it real. Empty and clean, not a speck of dust anywhere. The grass was even cut, and I remember how he hated doing that. October's grass? Who in their right mind would cut October's grass? She flipped on the radio and almost landed in a ditch. She snapped it back off again, unhappy with the selection. "Holy shit! Holy shit! What have I done . . ." Slowing finally and doing a wobbly, desperate three-point turn, she headed back in the direction she'd come, realizing there was only one place left for her to go.

"Joleb?" The silver was gone from her. Her shirt damp and plain gray again, made that way by late fog and sweat. "Joleb?"

"Jeeze, Val, what in the hell you doin' here?"

"Joleb Green?" She put out a hand and touched the front of his shirt and felt his ribs. Completely and totally confused by seeing his face answer her knock.

"Joleb—you Joleb!" Valuable heard a black woman's voice call this out from behind him.

"What!? Christ! I got everbody under the sun calling for me at once." He pushed his glasses up on his nose and grinned. "Come on in here. We're out of candy, though."

"Candy?" She felt stupid. Struck dumb as a moron all of a sudden. She pushed at the goat, which had followed her up the steps. Joleb kicked at it, his boot catching the bell and making it jingle and Val felt bad because it was the goat that led her to the house in the first place—the way she'd seen it standing sentry by a partial fence next to a ring of rocks. Those rocks and the animal a signpost of sorts, leading to the woman with sticks in her hair. The only person in the world left for her. She had guessed the wrong house, though. "Get now!" Joleb kicked at it again while he pulled her into the small house.

"We outta candy." A black woman was standing in the kitchen door-way, her hands to her hips. Her eyes winked dark-angry, and Val didn't blame her one bit, either, considering the late hour. Gosh, she's pretty, Valuable thought, never having seen such long legs on a woman. Never, not even attached to a white movie star in one of those Hollywood magazines. Those legs go forever, she thought, and then she realized she was staring and looked away.

Grace watched her. Sized her situation up in ten seconds flat. Homeless and needing something. And from what Even Grade said, one in the oven, too. She noticed the way the girl clutched at her own personal elbows like those bony triangles were all there was to her stability.

"She ain't here for candy, Grace," Joleb spoke for her. "Gosh, Val, what you doin' out at this hour?" He had both hands to her shoulders, looking her face over like he'd never seen it before in his life. She flinched, her shoulders still sore from where Neva had grabbed her and shaken her 'til her teeth rattled like loose bones. "Jackson came by this afternoon to say good-bye. . . . Shit, I'm sorry—" he said, seeing Val's face.

"You watch your mouth or I'll whip your tail quicker than Jesus." Grace watched the girl's face. Ain't she pitiful standing there in a size six shoe. Nobody to tell her how to take care of herself. How to cut that flipped-out hair.

"She fed me from her chest," Joleb said, smiling while he picked Valuable's ice-cold hands. "Milk's personal," he added.

The black woman rushed him and Valuable stepped back, thinking Joleb was about to be struck in the mouth. But Joleb just stood there grinning while the woman hissed in his ear, "I done tole you we ain't gonna have any more of that titty talk! I ain't gonna tell you again about it either! You keep talkin' that way Canaan gonna forget all my braggin' about how good you been doin' and have me take you back and park your skinny ass inside the gate." She nodded at Val and headed back into the kitchen.

"She loves me," Joleb said, beaming.

"I can tell," Val said, realizing Joleb had gone insane. Or is it me? More confused by the elements working inside the tiny, cramped house than the stampeding party she'd left back at the river. "Do you live here?"

"Nah! I'm just got out for a trial run. To see if I go loony again. I got my pills in there on the table next to that pile of papers." He pointed to where the woman had gone. "That's where Canaan does his studyin'. He's at work now over at the library. He don't know if he likes me yet, but Grace thinks he's just about the smartest—"

"I think a boy I raised from shitty diapers done forgot ever bit of what I taught him—" The woman stuck her head around the doorframe and Joleb stopped to consider. "Oh," he said, snapping his fingers. "Valuable—this is Grace Johnson. Grace—this is Valuable Korner. Grace, her and Jackson's the ones who came lookin' for me that night I got lost." He beamed again.

"How do." The woman had a rag over one arm and a frying pan in the other.

"Pleased to meet you, ma'am."

"I heard Next Door Joody talkin' 'bout you."

Valuable said nothing. Just stood quietly with her hands in front of her.

Grace watched the girl, thinking, Dear Sweet Lord Jesus, we got trouble wearing a child-size dress and a size-six shoe standing here sweet as a baby chicken, too. And ain't that a shame. She threw her towel up over her shoulder. "Next Door Joody said you managed to get borned all by yourself and got left right off by your mama and look at you now—sweet, pretty." And pregnant, Grace thought.

"I got left, too," Joleb said. "Ain't that right, Grace?"

"Lord God, you was a sweet baby—" She had gone back into the kitchen for another pot.

"But I got left, though. Ma had a stroke and left, soon as she named me." He leaned in and whispered, his eyes on the kitchen doorway the whole while, "Joleb is short for Joe Lieberstein. Ma was trying to say 'Go get Joe Lieb—' and everybody in the room thought she was saying 'Call it Joleb.'" He pushed his glasses up again and adjusted his shirt, looking down to see if his buttons were all lined up.

"God has his ways, Joleb. Ain't I always told you that? God has his ways." Grace yelled this while drying a big, beat-up stockpot. Val thought the pot seemed large enough to hold an entire cow.

"Her baby died and I got the milk. Milk's personal." Joleb was shaky. He looked at his hand and then put it in his pocket.

"Joleb—I ain't sayin' it again!" Grace's head appeared in the doorway, her fine-tuned ears picking up the titty talk.

Joleb smiled. Val looked from one to the other and added it up: these two love each other. High as the moon. Thick as syrup. Like a mother and son. Joleb moved to the couch and sat, sprawling back like he was worn slap out. He put his head to his hand.

"Valuable, why aren't you home?" His voice sounded old as ages, and she looked away because his hand was shaking again.

"I guess because I don't have one. Anymore." She spoke before thinking and was immediately sorry because the woman had appeared in the doorway like a dark, domestic Holy Ghost. Listening. Moving. Spreading her calico wings while she dried a metal colander.

"Well, I got three," Joleb said.

"Three?" She sat beside him and he gave his shoulder to her the way she supposed a brother might.

"Homes." He blew breath out, like the business of having three homes was the most exhausting business in the world. "I got the place over on Stockwell, with Beryn. But he ain't my real daddy. And I got my Aunt Louise's place over on Eighth, but she's about to get married to a short mortician who gives me the creeps. You think you could live with some-body who handles the dead all day long? I don't. Lord." He looked at her and she shook her head, not as an answer, but because she was totally bewildered. He continued. "And I got my real dad's Spanish-lookin' place over in Hattiesburg. Three." He looked at her. "I ain't braggin', though. I guess it might sound like it—"

"Sounds like a brag to me—" Grace said from the kitchen. "Sounds like a rude boy in there talkin', to me!"

"Your real dad?" She looked at her thumbnail and picked at a dry edge, made it bleed.

He spoke in a whisper: "He's a Jew. Grace don't like me telling folks that right off 'cause she said it's rude to say right off 'My daddy's a Jew.' To blurt it out before I say who my daddy is and all. Like the big news is he's a Jew and not that he's my daddy. Which, since I never had a clue of him 'til that time—" His hand was worse and he glared at it, "—'til all that stuff happened, I personally think it don't really matter what I say about him, since I don't really know him at all. Yet." He took his glasses off and rubbed his eyes. "I guess I sound pretty crazy, don't I?" His voice was old again. And tired.

Valuable reached over and patted his knee. "It's really good to see you, Joleb. I'm glad you were here. And I'm glad you've got so many places to live."

Grace came into the room and stood with her arms crossed, looking at the two of them sitting on the couch. We got a big load of trouble here, she thought to herself, wishing she had a pair of decent scissors so she could trim up the girl's hair. Val couldn't help noticing how Grace was so much prettier than Joody, but harder, more intimidating than Neva even, who never really intimidated Val at all, just the rest of the actual, known world. Standing up, she smoothed down her shirt, which was drying out finally. "Actually, I didn't know how late it was. I needed to talk to Miss Joody and I saw the goat and thought she lived here."

"She's next door at Even Grade's place," Grace said.

"I've got her overalls out in the car," she said, wiping a hand across her nose, embarrassed that she smelled of mothballs and was sitting in a stranger's house making people feel sorry for her. She rubbed her arms remembering how Neva had tried to make her stay. Remembering how Bea was brandishing her crook in wide circles. Scaring the pigs and monkeys and especially the caterers.

Grace was watching her. "They ain't got a light on, but I heard her talk of you and I guess if you had a need to talk to her, she's already aware of it. Probably out gatherin' wood right this second to build herself a fire." The woman's nostrils went wide.

"Well," Valuable said. Missing Jackson. The thought of his dry kiss swimming up large as the ocean and swallowing her. She stood up determined to leave before she cried. Grace was back in the kitchen and Valuable was glad, wanting to leave before she saw any more evidence of that thick love between these two. "Joleb?"

He had followed her to the door. "Yeah?"

"Will you be here tomorrow?"

"Probably." He yawned wide and she felt the catch of it. "Come back over and see me, okay?"

"Sure." She saw how thin he'd become. And he was already thin to begin with.

He smiled at her and stuck out his hand like a grown-up and she remembered how she'd bought him a Nehi once in the middle of a blazing hot summer day and how he'd jerked it away without even saying thanks. It was a hard thought she had while she shook his hand in return, but it helped her get off the porch without crying. Maybe that's it, she thought while she walked across the yard. Maybe if I think of all those slung, hateful words, this ocean won't swallow me. Maybe that's what I've got to do.

"—It's your house, Even Grade. You say the word and I'll agree to it. I plied thee my troth and I ain't goin back on it. You wearin' it in your pocket right this second, as proof." Her year eleven strand was yet to be wound back up.

Her leaving that stick out in the yard for him to find and him picking it up and carrying it around in his pants being some sort of symbolic marriage. She touched her one loose strand of hair. "I plied. You say. I'll do—"

I bet, he thought, but he hid the thought, or at least he thought he did.

They hadn't been asleep. Joody had been up on one elbow explaining the origin of root conjures. How their magic had been stolen from the moon by a crippled but crafty bird. Working her way up to one for curing warts as well as farts, a severe case of gas having led him up the root conjure path in the first place. Then there was the knock at the door, hesitant, urgent-sounding in its hesitancy, and he had pulled on his pants and walked bare-footed to the door, opening it up to find the white girl, her hair all sweaty and plastered to her head, standing on the porch biting at her nails. Joody's overalls—worn and frayed round the hem—were draped over her arm. He didn't stop to wonder. Didn't stop for a second. Just stepped aside for the homecoming that he imagined would involve crying and hugging, and once that was done, more crying and hugging. And he had been right. Lord God, he'd been right. Well, here we go, he thought while moving on heavy feet to the kitchen.

"Valuable? Look at you!" Joody was encased. Those spindly teenaged arms circling giving her the appearance of a scared-shitless baby bat attached to a tree.

Even Grade made up coffee and watched and tried hard not to listen. The sound of coffee perking more preferable to what was brewing in the living room. Just listen to that, Even Grade. Coffee likes a man. Coffee has but one course—down and out to water again. His reasoning seeing an uneasy parallel between the two: man and coffee and their inevitable desti-nations. His belief caught in the cross hairs of late that when it comes to the doings of woman, man is little more than witless in his decisions. He stirred at his cup letting the spoon knock against cheap cracked china; he was unusually loud with the sugar lid, letting it miss its rounded ledge. The icebox kicked into its rollicking cycle and he didn't have to try so hard to make noise so he wouldn't hear their talk. Leaning back into his chair, his legs stretched and crossed under his table, he waited.

A few minutes later, this:

"—you say and I'll do. It's your place. It ain't mine and if you say no, I'll send her away this very night. You got my stick right there in your pants."

He looked at her and found her face a total blank, smoothed over like burned skin free of signals. Whatever she wanted him to say or do, it wasn't riding there between her eyes for him to see.

"Tell me what's goin' on," he said and leaned his head to his hand. And she did, jumping murky details the way a horse jumps a fence.

"Do her people know where she's at?" he asked.

"I don't know. She didn't say, she was crying—"

"Does this mean the police are out lookin' for her?"

"I ain't asked that either—"

"How long she planning on stayin'?"

"That too—"

"You mean you didn't ask or you don't know?"

"Either one'll do for an answer, I guess—"

"Joody, I've kept quiet on a lot 'cause after considering, it seemed the thing to do. But I got to say this—"

"Well, go on, say it. You got my stick." And she folded her hands on the table and watched him, unusually patient, he thought, which made him immediately suspicious. Her fingers were steepled the way she used to hold them back at the creek, back during those days when she would search out his face and say, "Ain't nothing even or halfway straight in this world. Who give you such a name?"

"It ain't a black-and-white thing," he held up his hand for emphasis, "but I think we got a case of bail-out happening here—"

"Bail-out?"

"They in trouble and who they callin'? Their folks?"

"They?"

"White folks."

"I thought you said it weren't a black or white thing."

"Well, that's true. That's what I said—"

"Then who's this 'they' you talking on?"

"Okay. Forget that. What I'm sayin' here is this—" She stared at Even from across the table. "We got trouble in there on the couch and I'm tired is all. Tired of tryin' to fix what other people's broke." He wanted to look at her but found his gaze drawn to the sugar bowl instead. "I got me a mess with Canaan 'cause I interfered . . . tried to fix him up with somebody—" He cleared his throat, digging up more examples of his meddling. "Tried to ease Grace's mind by readin' that pack of mail to her. Had to break it to Canaan she couldn't read all those letters he'd been bending over night after night. That was one more time I stuck my nose where it shouldn't a gone. Now we got that girl's car sittin' out there in our front yard and how long you think before the police come sniffin' around lookin' for the nigger who stole it? How you think Clorena and the rest of the street's gonna feel wakin' up and seein' a white girl comin' out our house? It's bad enough we got a fire big enough to roast a damn cow blazing up every night but Sunday, but now this. And I tell you what, it seems lately every time I try to smooth things over, I get a fresh pile—"

"You got blocked wind, don't you, Even?"

He was poleaxed. Completely.

She snorted through her nose. "It's that wind wantin' to go south talkin', 'cause the Even Grade I know wouldn't sit here like a wet-assed baby whining while a girl who feels she ain't got nowhere else in the world to go is fallin' asleep right now on the couch." She reached over and patted his hand and smiled. "I got a root mix in a jar outside the house. I'll make it up and you'll blow your wind past those piles of yours so quick, they never even know it." She smiled and got up and went out the back door.

Still stunned he looked through the opening and saw the girl sound asleep on the quilted couch, stretched out on her side against leaf-colored shades of orange, her legs curled up, one hand under her head. From the kitchen he could hear her snoring, soft as a hummingbird, and he thought of the boy out in the cemetery in the middle of the night, the boy who jumped up from beside a lamb on a slab and near scared the shit out of him. The boy off in another state now while his pregnant girl is sleeping like a worn-out orphan in the middle of niggerville. And then he remembered how that boy'd said out in the dark, while moonlit shapes held watch all around them, Ain't it a shame the body can't go where the heart wants, and Even sighed. Not so loud Joody would hear because being called a wet-assed baby once was enough for any man's lifetime; the sigh just loud enough for him.

"Well, at least she got her overalls back," he said to his empty coffee cup, and then he stood up and made for bed. Washed out the coffee pot. Checked the pilot light in the oven. Pulled the string. Sent the kitchen into dark. He felt a hand at his elbow and jumped. She'd come back in through the door, quiet as a snake.

"I got it now. You put this on your tongue." She opened his hand and sprinkled a powder to his palm that smelled of toadstools and ground-up hemp. "Lick it clean and that wind'll break free and you'll feel better." She stood in the dark in front of him, her expectations as full and readable as her earlier face had been blank. She's put too much trust in me, he thought. Put too much confidence in my temperament, he reasoned. He licked his palm then, and walking through they headed for bed, the living room dark, the house quiet and still but for the hummingbird snoring on the couch.

He had been a reasonably adequate doctor for so long, most in the region had forgotten he'd been a less than remarkable man first. Doctors in the South being something other than man or son or brother or friend or classmate or student or liar or coward. Merited or not, Southern women—and men, for that matter—seemed to put an inordinate amount of confidence in one who owned a shingle. Once the square was fixed to the side of the house, the past evidence of less-than-noble living became as useful as a fossil. It became dust. It became dust on top of dust. It became a speck of useless nothing that nobody wanted to remember anymore. Like leftover candle wax high up on a mantle. Dr. H was no exception to the rule. His full name was there on the front of his brown house in plain sight for anyone to read, but no one bothered reading it anymore. They just went straight on up his steps, crossed his wide porch with its cement pots holding low ivy, and on through a door opening to brisk summer-sounding bells. Dr. H was a good doctor, most thought. His house/office was comfortably positioned in the suburbs, away from the two hospitals, the yard dotted with ornate bird feeders and seasonal plants. Patients walked through and sat and forgot, momentarily, their fear of cancer or colitis. Their migraines disappeared into designated plots heavy with Fancy Ruffled and Pink Standard caladiums.

But there were nightfeet that skipped the front entranceway, following the path that led to the side of the house instead. Finding the stoop with the heavy paneled door, hands feeling along its surface because that side of the house was never lit up, and then knocking once they'd felt around long enough. After the knock they stood waiting underneath the shade of a beautiful bougainvillea that grew trained over a white slatted trellis like a bride would use.

Neva found the path and tapped three times. She didn't bother standing under the trellis because the trellis with its bougainvillea was for frivolous weak individuals who couldn't decide how to come to the point of a problem. The trellis was for individuals like Bea, who'd taken to her bed since Halloween and was yet to come out from under the covers.

The door opened and she stepped into dark and followed his waddling suspendered form down a hall to his study. She knew he'd not want any talking done until he was inside and the door shut, since his live-in house-keeper had a tendency to talk while she felt up the cabbages and collards at the Hattiesburg curb market.

The door shut and she sat down hard in a curved leather chair that faced his heavy desk. She smelled things that reminded her of her father. Dust. Cherry-blend tobacco. Good bourbon. More dust.

"Ah Neva. Always a privilege." He was yet to look at her. His eyes fumbling with various papers on his desk, instead. Journals of some sort, which she found encouraging. "I can always count on you to interrupt my sleep, if nothing else."

"Cut the shit, Mack." His name was not Mack, it was Michael, but she'd been calling him Mack since he'd set her younger brother's broken arm when they were both in their teens.

He stopped his fumbling and rested his hands on his stomach. His girth was wider than it'd been the previous summer when a friend of hers from Purvis had needed him. He turned in his swivel wooden chair and looked out the window, his meaty arms cascading over wood.

A streetlight illuminated the yard—the tall pine trees, the rounded shrubs, the bird feeders on poles. Through the window Neva saw a man tumbling past, his leashed dog hell-bent on relief, both heads down in the cold November wind. The doctor reached over and pulled the venetian blinds shut, turning the notch of the desk lamp up a degree.

"What can I do for you, Neva?"

"Nothing illegal."

"Well, that's a relief." He laughed a laugh and she smelled mouthwash and smirked. Surely he didn't think—

"Enid's daughter is pregnant," she said, coming to the point, "and I've arranged a private adoption with a couple down in New Orleans."

"So why come to me?"

"Because she needs looking after."

He drummed his fingers over his leather desk blotter. "She doesn't have a doctor?"

"As far as I know, other than a case of measles, she's never been sick. Even if she had been, with Enid as a mother, who's to say—"

"How old is she?"

"Fifteen."

"Who's the father?"

"A boy who lives in another state and let's leave it at that."

He ran a pudgy finger down the edge of a paper and she saw that his nails were neat and clipped and recently manicured, his cuticles pushed back to the proper level. "Fifteen is really young to—are you sure adoption is the answer? There are places I know where reputable men—"

"No." She looked square at him and then she looked around, studied his pipe in its pipestand, his decanter of brandy, his books on the bookcase, their titles predictable. Lord, even our subtleties are obvious.

"Just can't seem to get clear of those Catholic roots, can you?" he said finally, and then he covered it with, "I suppose looking after the girl shouldn't be a problem. Vitamins? The occasional pelvic exam, I suppose? A midnight home delivery?"

She clenched her teeth and looked at his manicured fingers again. "Other than the midnight delivery, you've pretty much called it."

"Well, actually, I don't see why we couldn't have had this conversation in the light of day, Neva. There's nothing here that merits all this skulking around, really—" He reached over and straightened the picture of his nephew's confirmation. "When you called, I thought it was some other matter."

"Like what?"

"Oh, I don't know. A body to bury, maybe. Something gone awry at that brouhaha of yours we're still reading about in the *Times-Picayune*."

She crossed her legs. "Just good doctoring is all."

He bent and laughed out loud. "I see—sought out at midnight."

"Look, Mack. There's an edge to this—Valuable's her name, by the way. Valuable Korner. Strange you haven't asked that yet. Anyway—" She waved her hand, dismissing her comment. "Valuable doesn't know about the adoption. Hell, she doesn't even know she's pregnant yet. I'm just running interference before the fact as usual."

"Sounds more like after the fact to me—"

She looked at his sagging yellowed skin, his paunch, his old man appearance poured into obviously expensive clothes. "I can't control the world, Mack. Just River House."

"And all these things that this girl doesn't know, this business of adoption and pregnancy, these are things you're going to handle in your own charming way?"

"I intend to inform her she's pregnant as soon as she makes an appearance. She ran off three days ago. Halloween night—that brouhaha you charmingly made reference to—but I know where's she staying." Neva had driven around in a panic that first night. Going to the cemetery. Jackson's empty house. The blue-and-white house on Hillcrest. Kamper Zoo. At some point near 4 A.M., she'd seen the car parked in front of a small house in the Quarter.

He put up his hand. "Enough, please. I don't think I want to hear any more."

"She's not to know of the adoption, though. Not a word of it."

"And that's where I come in." He looked at her. "There will be an extra fee, of course," he said as he leaned into the light. She saw that he'd gone to a comb-over. His lobes had dropped too, gravity the final victor over all of us, she thought. Hunched as he was he seemed loose-fleshed and breasty enough to need a bra. She found herself sitting up straighter.

"Then, we understand each other?"

"As much as anybody in Mississippi can, I suppose." And then he opened his venetian blinds again and turned in his chair. When Neva left his office, his face was still to the side, his eyes still watching his street.

Even Grade woke early for a Saturday. Woke up startled and sweaty after a hard dream of hard work, his muscles sore, like he'd done sixty miles in a push-car and all of that uphill. Jackson was there inside his dream and he'd left him looking startled and ghost-like, his white boy's voice coming up out of a sea of tombstones standing quiet against the moon, *Ain't it a shame*—and then Even's waking-up ears heard it: the long and drawn out *zz zzzinng*, as if the sounds were made through a nose pinched shut in an effort to sound like a mosquito. *Ain't it a shame*—This is where he stood inside the thought on waking to the sound.

"The only thing a shame round here is a body can't sleep worth a damn—" he said, rolling out of bed wishing for one more hour, or maybe half that, to sleep. Wishing he had the white man's leisure of waking up slower than the sun, which he beat by more than an hour every single work-day, five days a week. Slower than the sun, which he never saw except sinking, him being underneath those pipes by the time it rose proper. He pulled on his pants and heard the noise again: *zz zzzinng*.

Like a sleepwalker, and that being what he nearly was, he went to the sink intending to make coffee and saw that it'd been done. Well, I'll be damn, he thought, and then he saw the small spoon and realized Valuable had made up the coffee. Not Joody, who didn't believe in the concept of measuring things.

"Why?" Joody had asked for the tenth time, six days back when he doled it into the perking cup.

"Why what?"

"Why you bein' so careful with measuring those things?"

"Because I like my coffee to taste the same each time. Each morning," was his answer.

"What if you ain't found the true flavor of the bean yet 'cause you been measurin' and not givin' the bean a chance to talk for itself?" And he

had given in to her, standing stranded in that spot where all answers would
be counted foolish and unsportsmanlike and like he wasn't willin' to give
the bean a chance. Giving in to her because she had been standing there,
his too-big pants rolled up to her knees, those sad tattoos running down
her legs like so many cracks in marble.

Even had given up trying to teach coffee, having more of a gift for
making it himself and not complaining about it than standing guard while
Joody measured with a spoon. He poured up a cup and noticed it poured
up perfect. Just the right color and smell to it.

He went to the door and stood leaning against its frame, his cup resting in the palm of his hand, and saw the girl sitting, her legs in their flow-
eredy pants dangling over the edge of his porch. Her arms around themselves because the morning air was chilly and the clothes she was wearing
were apparently the only clothes she owned.

The girl didn't talk much, just moved through their presence like one
accustomed to shadows. Acknowledging Joody's talk concerning the magic
of certain November spiders with nods of her head and vague hand
motions. As he watched those signals he had to give the girl credit, having
thought to himself that Joody's ramblings had more the sound of distrac-
tion at their core than information.

In the middle of one delivered up her second night of staying, a
lengthy, animated lesson concerning the hardworking daddy longlegs spider and how Deep Mother had sent it to earth as a special female warning
against the laziness of the male, Even had interrupted and asked Valuable
about her family, whether or not somebody back home might be worrying.
She'd said in less words than ten that if they'd been worried, she expected
they would've come that first night. And he had hushed on it, seeing the
sad truth in her reasoning. Joody had looked at him, nodding with her head
toward the back of the house, and said, "There's a full pound of salt out
in the kitchen, should you need more of it—" the rest of her thought—*to
heap on her sores*—served up silent. That was night before last while supper
cooked. Beans and collards and some of Val's coldwater corn bread. The
best corn bread Even had ever tasted in all of his life.

He studied the back of her head, seeing it beginning to part off from
lack of washing and sniffed, relieved to just smell dirt, his place, dead

leaves and the brittle smell of rusted-out roof. Glad to smell these things, not wishing to catch a whiff of the girl's drawers. Three days away. Mercy.

"Valuable—the coffee's good. Thank you." He knew she'd shrug up her shoulders and be embarrassed and he wasn't disappointed.

"You're welcome, Mr. Even," she said and he flinched, the putting together of Mister to Even making him think on a child's primitive learning tool. A ruler. A gauge. Something an adult would draw out in a crayon and attach a cartoon nose to in order to set down a lesson concerning the straightedge. Three days now, he thought shaking his head, and then he dismissed it, because while he'd seen strange things since August, the strangest yet was Canaan Mosley out fishing in the yard.

"That's mighty good, Canaan! You just 'bout hit this rock here." Joody yelled this out and clapped her hands. Valuable laughed and clapped, too.

"Try again, Mr. Mosley. Try one more time. You just about got it." Valuable swung her legs out and in, her shoes dragging dirt in between.

"You think?" Canaan said while reeling in the line.

Even looked at the back of the girl's dark shiny hair. At Joody's sticks turning all glittery in the sun. At Canaan's brown fuzz looking dusty as a sponge. Seeing broad examples, he wondered if shine was something that sought out a woman and chose to ignore a man, like so many other things that sought out man and skipped the female entirely. Like reason.

"I'm standin' here watchin'—now you reel it in good and do it again and see if it don't get better. Go on now, reel it in! You'll see!" Joody yelled.

Even walked forward and put his hand to the post. Valuable looked up and smiled a shy smile. "I appreciate you lettin' me hang around," she said.

"You ain't been a problem," he said. Watching her sitting there swinging her legs, he wondered on his mother. If she'd found herself living off of others. Wandering from porch front to porch front. Adjusting herself to shadows while he squirmed inside her belly.

"You a handsome man, Even Grade," Joody called out and whistled a wolfcall through her fingers, expertly. "You 'bout the most handsome man there is!" She whistled loud again and grinned. "Watch this now—and you Canaan blow that thought out through your nose and get shed of it!" Canaan shook his head and chuckled while he reeled.

"You 'bout ready, Joody?" Canaan's tongue was out to the corner where

a cigarette usually parked. Even watched him examine his feather for damage, blow it free of clutter, and then in defiance of his awkwardness, he
threw back his arm and sent the line sailing out in a perfect arc that flew
high before it fell and hit the dust with a thud.

"You hit it right on again, Canaan! Right on the mark, Canaan Man!"
Joody clapped her hands and jumped up and down three times and
Valuable laughed out loud and tried to whistle. "Grace gonna be so proud
of you—just you wait," Joody yelled.

Even chuckled and shook his head, happy for a reason he couldn't dis-
tinguish other than at that moment of Canaan's near-perfect cast, all
seemed right with the world, as right as a thing can be what with a white
girl camped out in the middle of the Quarter with no plans of leaving.

34

THE TRUTH OF THINGS

O VER A HELPING OF OYSTER DRESSING, Valuable had learned Luvenia's mystery husband had died underneath a tractor. "He was hay-milling on a slope and the damn thing bucked," Neva said, fork-slicing a purple stack of pickled beets. "Married sixteen years. Just long enough to get your mother, Enid." Bea had offered this, wiping her mouth down with her napkin. A turkey leg was to the side of her plate, huge and knobby with brown-gold scales slicked with grease. "Takes a total fool and a real run of bad luck to get killed by a tractor," Neva said, pushing away her plate. Valuable isolated the oysters to the side of her plate and wondered how in the world anybody could get killed by a John Deere. Ground hollows or no, those heavy cross-furrowed tires seemed like wide insurance to her. Too broad to roll. Constant, but for the bumps. As safe as rolling rubber life preservers for the land-bound.

Two weeks into operating the hay cutter, Valuable found a rut and reconsidered.

The tractor righted itself but not before throwing her sideways onto a tire well, almost breaking her elbow. She had the good sense to keep her foot to the clutch and throw it into neutral. She had the further good sense to disengage the blade while she checked herself out. Standing eye-level with a crowd of workmen, Neva, who had led her down the path of hay-making, cheered and whistled. Shouting through her tubed hands from across the road: "You're a natural, Val! A natural! Are you okay? You sure?"

The gold grass of autumn was underneath her. Dead. Chopped to pieces the size of toothpicks. Laid down and bare, the exposed rats scattered, insulted yet fearless. She killed fourteen the first day and spent an hour into dusk burying them. Slicing through wet ground with her foot to a shovel again. Delighted to have something to bury. She gave in to it a week later because her legs were sore, leaving the dead to rot peacefully. Necessary fodder, she reasoned, for the buzzards. They appeared high up in blue, drifting near-motionless. Like black fluted holes in a sky punched through by dark fingers.

Bush-hogging while pregnant gave her a feeling of accomplishment. Of power. Of recourse. She listened to the *swish swish swish* of the blade behind her and wondered how many other pregnant fifteen-year-olds had done the same. Had mowed down a field of barn grass and Texas millet, broom sedge and meadow cat's tail. Had attached the hay rake to the back of a John Deere and left ochre piles to cure. Had operated the baler. Had watched compact squares of hay appear behind them like magic. This is better than school, she told herself. If I fail at being a mother, I can at least do highway work. She laughed out loud for the first time since Neva had told her. Since that first humiliating trip to the old overweight doctor. The sound of her laughter blended with the *swish swish swish*, reaching all the way over to the woman with the skill saw.

"She's come a long way from crying on the steps," Bea said.

The workmen were unloading lumber from off the big truck. Yellow-new and sweet, the sound of it crashing down to faded palettes seemed full of possibilities. Neva measured twice, cut once. Her arms were cording up, turning ropy again, the way they'd been years ago. Sawdust powdered her shirt, clumped in her sweat.

"It still won't work, though. You'll never get away with it."

"You know what she told me? She said Luvenia told her she couldn't get pregnant unless she was bleeding when she did the marriage act thing. Can you believe that? She actually called fucking the 'marriage act thing.' Said she told her this when she was seven. Christ! What I wouldn't give to have that woman in front of me for seven minutes. Just long enough to kill her myself. Slow. With a crowbar, maybe. Val said that's why she didn't think she was pregnant. 'Cause she wasn't on the rag when—" Neva stalled, couldn't say the words.

Bea gave her a sideways look. She'd taken up smoking and twin tubes of gray escaped her nostrils. "If men had to fuck in the middle of blood, the world would've died a long time ago."

"Exactly."

"What'd Dr. H say?"

"He said sometime in mid-May, give or take a week."

"The horse season. Wonderful timing." Bea dropped her cigarette to a bucket of water where it sizzled. "It still won't work. You're insane for trying it."

"You're her blood relative for God's sake—" Neva pointed her pencil at Bea, "and you're the one with the disappearing act every single time there's a decision to be made. So don't you stand there and preach to me about what will or won't work. Where were you when it came time to tell her? Where were you when she climbed up on that table?" Neva and Valuable had gone into the chrome and crisp-noisy room, an apprehensive delegation of two. Both hating those blunt-nailed fingers, but for different reasons. "Go back inside and do what you do best, make up a shopping list."

Bea brushed a handful of shavings onto the new floor of the barn, having lived with the woman long enough to know the art of ignoring her. She snagged her fresh manicure against a two-by-twelve. "If there is no adoptive couple waiting in New Orleans, what exactly do you intend to do with the baby? Knock it in the head and throw it in the river?"

"Believe me, I considered that option." Neva was talking around a pencil stuck in her mouth.

"You're gonna trip up here."

"I don't think so."

Bea walked over to the new gate and pushed, watched it swing slow and easy until it touched the new sweet-smelling wall. "You haven't answered my question. About what you're going to do with it." Valuable was on the back track of the field. Bea could barely hear the noise of the diesel.

"You locate Enid yet?"

"The last letter I wrote came back. She's moved on it seems—"

"To answer your question, I intend to give the baby to the Brothers in Bay St. Louis."

"Catholics? You've got to be joking!"

"You got a better plan, Bea? 'Cause I'm ready to hear it." She spit into the dirt like a man. Sawdust everywhere. The smell of it grand. "An adoption here, even a private one, would ruin her. People would know and still be talking on it twenty years from where we're standing. Right now they think she's out of town with her mother. You come up with some other plan and I'll listen."

Bea noticed that Neva was starting to gray. A late bloomer, too, what with her being in her fifties. "What're you gonna do? Sedate Val while you steal her baby? Tie her up and put her in the attic?" She waved her arms around. "And then sleep with both eyes open once she finds out the thing is gone?"

"Val will see the reasonableness of adoption by that point." Horses will help. Give a girl a horse and she can get over anything. If not a horse, then a brand-new tractor. Neva looked across the field and saw her, a tiny moving dot controlling whirling blades.

"If Valuable gets wind of this, she'll run away. She will never in a million years stand for it. Not after the way she pined for her daddy all those years. Not after the way she never really had a mother—"

"If it comes down to that, if she gets difficult, I'll tell her the truth."

"And what truth is that exactly?"

"That Jackson is actually her half-brother."

"You don't have any limits, do you?" Bea pulled off her cowboy hat. Holding it in her mouth by the brim, she retied the floral scarf over her honey-blond hair.

"No, I guess I don't." Neva scored the wood with a pencil, measured again to be sure the stall opening was correct. There was a man coming from Lucedale to lay out the tack room in a week.

"She loves you, this is going to kill her."

"She'll pout for a while and then she'll recover. We've already seen proof enough of that." Val made the circle honking the flat-sounding horn and waving. Neva waved back.

"This is different and you know it."

Neva looked at the woman, Bea's show of concern comical. "I don't know what I paid for that outfit you're wearing, but it looks like shit." She grinned when she said it.

"Fuck you, Neva." Bea walked off. Her steps small and angry inside new cowboy boots that were killing her feet.

Neva lined up the skill saw. Measure twice, cut once. It always worked for her.

35

KINSMEN

"I 'VE NEVER SEEN A GIRL NAKED, you know. I especially never seen a pregnant girl naked—"

"And that's not likely to change anytime soon, either."

"No? I'll give you twenty dollars."

Valuable looked at him. They were up in the attic, the diminishing light cosmetic and kind. From where she stood, he seemed less Joleb-like, more pulled together. This place is a castle, he'd told her the first time he visited—the day after Christmas—weeks before she showed him the attic. Jesus, Val. Seems like some Viking ought to be totin' in a dead moose any second now! was his comment on seeing the giant fireplaces.

"You don't have twenty dollars anyway." Two things were out in front of her: a dress with a high, old-fashioned collar, and her stomach. She put a hand to both and found her stomach sweeter.

"Would you if I did?"

"Not in a million years."

"How about thirty dollars?"

"No."

She'd cleared out a space the size of a small office and they were sitting in the last of the light. The trunk positioned under the window. Stacks and stacks of dusty, falling-apart books concerning theology and mystagogy and homiletics to the side of them. Books Catholic in theme, which seemed a mystery in itself what with Neva and Bea's agnostic inclinations. Two weeks earlier she'd modeled the Klan outfit, slipping it over her head and sidestepping around dress forms and rusted-out bed frames and three-legged chairs. A short fat killer, was how she looked. One with female hands. She had told Joleb all of it. Explained that her great-grandfather had been a bona fide murderer who killed coloreds for no reason other than their pigmentation. She did all those things trying to buy her some space, drive him away, make her seem undesirable as a friend, but it had had the opposite effect. God, Val, I think you were a saint in a previous life, he'd said. Lord. You mean you wore this thing downstairs at a party? Christ! What'd they do? I bet they shit bricks. I bet they're still shittin' bricks. Lord! She had looked at him steady, saying, "I made an ass of myself, is all." Meaning every word of it.

"Does it move yet?" His eyes to her stomach.

"All the livelong day."

"Will you let me feel?"

She looked at him. His glasses were new ones with light brown frames instead of black and he'd lost his Buddy Holly look and just seemed book-wormish now, which was deceptive. School as forgotten and necessary as a baby tooth for both of them. "Maybe."

"Don't you think you ought to be tellin' Jackson?"

"I told you not to ever say his name."

"I know you did, but Val, just because a guy's quit writing and callin', don't mean he's stopped—" He watched her stiffen up, look to the window once and then back down again at her stomach.

"Joleb, don't make me sorry I've told you things. Please," she said. Her hands were to her stomach as if it had ears and were listening.

He kept quiet. At least for thirty seconds. "Since you won't let me see you naked and you won't listen to me about Jackson, can I at least stay for dinner?"

"If you'll behave." She slid back; leaned against his knees, her stomach large in front of her. He put up a hand as if to touch her hair, leaving it there for what seemed to him a great while, and then he reached to the side and picked up a book, blowing along its edges, sending dust motes scattering into leftover light, like panicked snow. "These things sure are stinky." It was olive green. A book on the typography of Christ. The initials R.L.L. were stamped on the title page in blue. "You think anybody ever bothered to read this shit?"

She had, had even found the theory concerning the kinsman redeemer poetic and applicable, but the time allowed before admitting to it was the same amount of time it'd take for Joleb to see her naked. A million years.

"Somebody must have." She was still watching the window when Joleb picked up another book. *Theorum Magisterum.* The same initials were on the inside of its cover: R.L.L. "You can stay for supper, but you've got to call your dad." She scooted up because her back was hurting again. No matter how she moved a hand cupped her heart, pressed in like a vise.

Joleb held himself as still as possible, feeling her backbones, all their knobs, against his shins. Not wanting her to move. Not wanting to jostle her or do something that would make her move her back from off his legs. "I will. I'll call him," he said. Done with saying "Which one?" like it was some smart-ass silly joke. His dad owned the biggest department store in Hattiesburg. Another up in Jackson. Two more in Louisiana. His dad was Jewish and all of Petal knew it, thanks to Joleb who had come out the other side of a train's death trestle with a newfound belief in loud honesty.

"We're having roast turkey and greens." Her voice distant and tired. Remembering the fish that came up out of Lake Shelby like a writhing rainbow. Sheeted with wet, gleaming. A floppy two-pound surprise. Grace and Canaan had whooped down the bank while Even helped her land it. Put a hand to her back while she reeled. Fetched it from off the bank when she slung it there, screaming. His hands stable. Sure. A father's hands. "I hope you like collards." She didn't used to, but did now.

"That's nice," he said, not wanting to move, not wanting her to move, thinking the feel of her warm back against his legs was as sweet a thing as he'd ever been given a chance to feel.

His legs behind her like a sports chair, she felt the baby move a great walloping move and almost reached around for Joleb's hand, but didn't. Pearl was hers now and that's how she chose to keep it. Nobody but Even Grade and the old doctor who smelled nice, but wasn't, had touched her stomach, felt it move. Pearl. A name sent by Deep Mother back in August. A name designed by the moon. A name that could withstand anything. Anything, at all. The baby shifted and she sucked in a breath. She felt Joleb's legs, wondered over his stillness what with his natural body language belonging to that of the nervous Chihuahua family. Outside the window was the downside of day, its slice of gray sky and one or two clouds drifting past.

Even saw Canaan sitting on the platform of the loading dock and pulled into a parking spot and turned off his truck. The door screamed when opened— a built-in motivation that limited his stops and starts, the front edge of the truck having been wrecked and then pulled back out, the realignment resisting the improvement, voicing it every time the handle was pulled.

"Miss that walk, do you? You think that river's losing its color now that Even Grade ain't stoppin' and considering it every day?" It was more statement than question. Canaan's newspaper rattled like dried leaves and there was a wax bread wrapper floating off toward a gutter. Even watched it while Canaan talked. "Got yourself a 'forty Ford and you still got to stop and see what's goin' on before you head to Bellrose." He looked over the top of newsprint and grinned.

"You say that true."

Canaan stuck his paper under his arm and handed Even a Coke. Feeling it cool against his hand, Even thought, Why this could be back last summer but for the cool April weather and Canaan's marriage and the move coming up tomorrow to Grand Bay and the girl.

"That's a fine truck you got there, Even Grade. Door screams like a runover goose, but it's a real fine truck." Canaan's truck was newer and nicer and they both knew it. But Canaan's was also in full possession of Grace now, the old man having yet to learn to drive. He eyed Even's ticking in the heat. "You sure you don't mind helpin' in the move?"

"I've said as much. You ready to spend life down in the land of pecans?" He pronounced it "peecans."

"As ready as any man can be for anything that involves a woman."

"Ain't that the God's truth."

The street seems smaller, Even realized. Smaller and more cluttered than last summer. He put a hand to his chest and scratched against his shirt. It had been two months now of married life and Canaan seemed as settled and happy as an old possum. The mummy look to his eyes gone. Something else resting on his question-marked brow. Something akin to astonishment, maybe. "How's married life?"

"Like a trip to the zoo ever day of the year." Canaan smiled.

"Just think, Canaan, this time last year we was single men."

"Thy God, that's a fact—"

"Not a care in the world—" Even said, noticing the rusty water tower standing tall near the cusp of town. Town council was fulfilling its promise to paint. The jacked-up scaffolding looked like whale-sized polio braces.

"—other than how long to wear those socks before washin' them out." Canaan crossed his legs.

"Or how many days left to eat on that roast pork—"

"Just a year ago we weren't even considering a truck." They both watched Clemens come out of the hardware store and put up a white sign announcing tomorrow's fifty percent markdown on fertilizer. At the bottom in bold Kelly green: "Easter Sail!" Even Grade wondered one more time how one so ignorant of the basics of spelling had managed to buy a store. "Or a teat."

"And now look at us—"

"Full up with both."

Canaan shook his newspaper. "How's the girl?" he asked. Seeing an advertisement at the bottom of the page. *Clemens' Feed & Seed. Fertilizer. Easter Sail.* He shook his head.

"She's due in three weeks. Things should settle then." Even gave a side glance and then looked away, tensed up.

"You a foolish man if you think that."

"How so?"

"You dug in now. Christmastime, the girl was just a solid nuisance showin' up on weekends. Come January things thawed and Lord, if you didn't start thinking you needed to drive by the River House to check on things. Come the spring it's fishing ever weekend we got sun. You and Joody. Both of you. Bad as missionaries—" Canaan spit in the dust. "Last I heard you two was ready to 'dopt each other. Lord, it's like—" He looked around for a suitable example, his eyes seeing the misspelled sign on legs and moving on. "It's like—"

"Grace and Joleb?" Even finished his Coke and set the bottle on its side, spun it once. Clemens came back outside and took off his glasses and rubbed at them with his shirt. He put his hands to his pockets and pretended to study the sidewalk. Finally he walked over and folded up the sign, eyeing the two suspiciously as if they'd been plotting thievery. "You ever seen such a man as that one?" Even nodded with his head. "Mean as a snake and can't spell worth a lick."

The light was easy all round. Spring-like. Soft night with what was left of day reflecting up off the pavement in mauve shadows. Even smelled charcoal somewhere close. Meat put to barbecuing on a grill.

"Seems a sad reality that now we got permission to sit in the front of the bus, we both got trucks to drive." Canaan pointed to a column. "Folks in Alabama ain't keen on it, though. They got police dogs in Birmingham ready to chomp. Says right here a Negro got strung up by the neck, his faced blowed off with a shotgun, but the death certificate pronounced him dead of heart attack." Canaan wet his finger and turned a page. "'Course there's a argument to be said on the truth of it. I reckon I'd come close to having an infarction with two barrels trained on my head."

"Maybe you two should stay put where you're at—"

"She's got her heart set on Grand Bay what with her aunt ailing and that great big ole house of hers just sitting there waitin'. Ain't nothing there but stretches of worthless land, that I can see. Ain't a library anywhere to be found. But lord have mercy at the pecan trees."

"How you gonna spend your time?"

"Fishin'." He looked over his glasses at Even and shook out his paper. He was yet to catch one. Gabled the end of his pole with bigger and more shinier contraptions each time out. Last go round, the time Valuable caught the three-pound trout, Canaan looked like he was fishing with a Christmas tree. "Shame you got your feet dug in here."

Even put his hand in his pocket and felt her stick. Ran his fingers over it, thinking of his cluttered-up porch, his gourds, the noise, the looming potentiality of emptiness, the way it was swimming up in front of him like a long, dark hall.

"You heard from Pascagoula yet?" Canaan asked.

"Nah—I guess I ain't goin' to. I guess most shipyards are full of pipe fitters waitin' to hire on."

"We ain't joined at the hip, you know. Ain't nothing wrote down nowhere that says ole Canaan can't move to a new state by himself." He sounded irritated and Even knew the man was upset. That he'd been seeing the four of them making the change together.

"I know that. Grace has found herself with a large-roomed house, but odds say we'd come close to blows, sooner or later—" Even looked at him, remembering how he'd looked standing underneath an awning dripping blood. "I'd be lying, though, if I said I was happy about this. Be lying through my teeth."

"—Says here folks outside Birmingham set out to lynch an NAACP fellow down from Memphis for leading a voter registration drive—" Canaan wouldn't look at him.

"You go on and read then and pretend you ain't listenin'. But I'm talkin' true and I want you to know it."

"Says here we got rain comin' tomorrow."

"Soon as supper's done we'll be over to help you finish with the packin'."

"Don't matter one way or t'other to me. Long as we get there before that white girl of yours drops that baby of hers out her bottom."

"She ain't what you think—"

"I heard that before—"

"Well, she ain't. I promised the boy I'd see to her is all—"

"You foolin' yourself, Even Grade. Grace says she saw you feelin' that girl's stomach back in March and I swore she was lying. I said the Even Grade I knew wouldn't come close to doing such a damn-fool thing as laying his Negro hands on a white girl's belly." He looked at Even's face. "Now I see by that look your face is wearin' she was telling me true all along. Did myself out of two nights' worth of fuckin' over it, too." He shook his head and clucked. "I swear to high God, ever single one of you is acting like Valuable's carrying the Messiah. She ain't nothin' but a white girl who got herself knocked up proper is all—"

Even Grade's hands turned to fists. Easy, Even, this is an old man's last discourse, he told himself. Let him go because this is the last of it—

"And you—you got yourself a case of orphanitis, is all. Walkin' around wondering over similarities. Looking at her stomach and her situation, wondering about your own personal mama. I think it's a damn shame, too. You act like you're responsible somehow and that's a white girl's lie—"

"She's never once asked me for a goddamn thing! You're talking foolishness—" Even felt the anger up around his throat now.

"Oh, she ain't asked for it, but she's sure soaking it up, ain't she? Hangin' on all your words like you her daddy. You both got it. Both of you is eat up with orphanitis—"

"You like that word, do you?" Thinking, It's a pity the last Petal sees of Even Grade and Canaan Mosley will be the two of us thrashing around on the loading dock of the Feed and Seed. And then he felt it leave him. He watched the old man rub his finger and thumb together. Watched the way his foot was rocking back and forth and he knew the man was ill-suited for farewell. That the word was clogging up between them like a knob in the throat.

"You sit here and read, but I'm beat." Even stood and heard the rustle behind him as he headed to his truck. Knew without seeing it that Canaan had turned the paper to a new page; was reading. But for coming close to flogging solid the best friend I ever had in my life, it could be last summer, he thought while he drove away. It could almost be last summer again.

"How'd you make that thing?" Joleb pointed to the fluted green mound in the center of the table. He'd eaten out of the River House fridge regular enough, but this was his first time at a sit-down.

"Why, congealed salad's really easy enough. Anybody with the ability to read can just follow the directions." Bea unfurled her napkin and it made a snapping sound. Her new ring glittered on her fat finger.

"Lord." Joleb stabbed the green mound with his fork and a grape came free of the Jell-O with a pop. "Grace cooked plain all those years and now I got kosher to deal with. It's a wonder my digestive track's not revolted and strangled my pyloric." They all just looked at him. Neva, Bea and Valuable, who continued eating her turkey, ravenous in her eight month. Her taste buds having found smoked meat their favorite.

Joleb cut into his turkey without a care in the world while he rummaged for an easygoing topic. "You folks find it difficult being queer?" He looked around, genuine interest all over his face.

Neva raised one eyebrow. Bea cinched up one corner of her mouth like it'd been hooked, fish-like. Valuable bit into her meat.

Joleb continued, "'Cause it'd seem difficult to me what with Hattiesburg being in the middle of the Bible Belt and all." He picked up his fork and directed it to Neva. "Did you know most guys think they're queer at one time or another?" He put his fork on his plate and spooned gravy onto his greens with the big silver spoon. Valuable copied him, the look of it appetizing. "My shrink told me that. Said all guys go through what he calls a halfway period of homosexuality when they're in about the fifth grade or so. Some go through it later. Lord—" He looked up to the ceiling, having stumbled on a thought. "I swear there was a time when all I could think on was Jackson. I hated Val here—" He nodded to her with his head. She smiled and sprinkled hot vinegar on her greens. "I never thought I was queer, though. Just thought I was crazy. Which, turns out, I was. So—" he beamed all the way round, "you folks find it difficult or not? Or is it something you'd rather not talk about in front of an unmarried knocked-up girl and all."

Neva looked at Bea's new ring, at all that flash, her compensatory gift in lieu of the brand-new barn, which had gone five thousand over estimate. Then she looked at Joleb, trying to remember if she'd ever met anyone able to offend so many in such a short amount of time.

"To answer your question, Joleb, sometimes it's difficult. People stare, and once you walk past, you know you're being laughed at. I've always known people round here don't like me, so yes, I guess it's hard at times." She looked him square on. "The same degree of difficulty, I would imagine, a crazy person finds." She smiled.

"Lord, you said a mouthful there. 'Cause it's hard as hell most times." He drank noisily from his glass of iced tea. "This is sure great salad, ma'am," he said to Bea, who still had her mouth opened.

"Thank you." She finally managed to bring her lips together.

"How's your father?" Neva asked, buttering her roll.

"Same as always. Quiet. Works a lot in his library. It's full of books, you know." He raked at his greens and then he looked to the ceiling again, tagged by another thought. "I like to go into Lieberstein's and go up to the counter and stare at the saleswomen. It makes 'em nervous as hell. Cosmetics. Luggage. Women's wear. Any of them." He looked at Val and noticed she was helping herself to more turkey. "Once they're all watching, I lean in like I'm looking at something inside the glass cases—a watch or one of those alligator billfolds—and then I lick the counter with my tongue." He smiled like he thought it was a grand idea.

"Joleb, that's rude!" Val said, shocked.

"You think?"

"You better believe I think. You've been foolish enough. If you don't straighten up you won't ever get to see a girl naked. No matter how much money you offer them." She wiped her mouth, pointed to his mouth with her napkin and he did the same.

"Lord. I never thought of that." He looked down at his plate.

"And how'd you think that made your father feel—all that licking of the counter and embarrassing him in front of people he has to work around every day? How do you think he likes it when somebody comes up and says, 'Say, Joe, didn't I see your bastard son licking the counter over in cosmetics?'"

"I guess he wouldn't like it one little bit," Joleb said, thinking Val had taken to slinging the word "bastard" around much too frequently. As if she were trying to get herself used to hearing the word since she was about to have one.

"I bet if Grace'd been there, she'd have whipped you quick as Jesus. Slapped you silly. Open-handed. Hard as she could. You ought to be ashamed of yourself!"

"Lord, Val, Russ over at Sacred Heart said the same." He was looking at her like she'd suddenly sprouted credibility. "Said I had the makings of being a perfect Catholic what with my preoccupation with guilt coupled with my lack of motivation to do anything about it." The words were obviously not Joleb's and everybody at the table knew it.

Neva held her coffee cup up midway in the air, poised between table and mouth.

Bea said, "Excuse me, Joleb, are you talking about Father Landry?"

"No ma'am, that ain't his name—"

"Who, then?"

"Russ. A guy named Russ. Big tall guy. Kinda looks like a crow what with that long black thing he wears and he's got brown hair that's kinda thinnin' right here." He pointed to his temple area. "He smokes cigars and swears like a sailor. At least when he's back in the kitchen eatin'."

"Then I'm correct. Father Russell Landry." Bea licked her lips.

Joleb looked stunned. As if the man having a last name had never entered his mind. He shrugged then. Over it. "You're not goin' to tell Grace I've been licking those counters, are you?"

"She'd whip your tail and you know it." Val appeared thoughtful.

"I know. That's why I'm askin'."

"No. Only if you keep acting like an idiot." And then she went at the greens again, looking around at the group. "He's not a fool. Most of this is put-on, you know."

Joleb looked at her, confused. Wondering what she meant. What he was putting on. As far as he could tell, he'd tried to be a good guest. To find dinner conversation that would be interesting and inclusive to everyone because both Russ and his father had told him he needed to improve his manners as well as learn not to blurt things out. He watched Val pour gravy on the greens. "Lord, Val—you've not only got a belly like one, you've turned to a pig."

Neva lit a cigarette, her movements slow and deliberate, careful. Bea watched her, licking at her lips, and there was something working in her eyes that was just between the two of them. Behind gray smoke Neva said, "Val knows Grace firsthand now, Joleb. You best hush concerning her eating habits or she'll have Grace nail you, how'd you put it? quicker than Jesus." Her mouth was done up in either a smile or a grimace and Joleb thought, If that's a smile, she ought not to, 'cause it's fierce and unattractive, even for a lesbian, and he felt pleased with himself for thinking the thought and not blurting it out and made a note to remember his keeping his mouth shut so he could tell both Father Russ and his father Joe Lieberstein about it later.

Valuable moved to a rocker and sat, patiently, her face tranquil. She put her hands underneath her belly and held her baby and Neva looked away, out toward the hard-flanked horses grazing in the field. Valuable could feel its head, or maybe its shoulders. Sometimes at night she watched tiny tumbling feet raise hills across her belly. Neva pulled the rocker closer so she wouldn't have to strain to talk or listen and for a few minutes their motion was tandem and harmonious.

"Is something wrong that I don't know about?" This from Val, who was rubbing her stomach, feeling its knobs. Guessing at them.

"I hate to leave you here to handle things. You're really too big to be feeding them by yourself." Neva watched the gray mare nip at another and then tear off across the pasture, divots flying up from her feet, her tail straight up like a flag.

"I've done it before. It'll be fine." Val reached out and took the woman's hand and sighed. The wind picked up and Neva felt the odd mix of winter leaving and spring's approach. Breathing deep, Val hooked her little finger between Neva's third and fourth digit while Neva watched the yard, the new barn, the purple color that night had become. When she squinted her eyes she could almost pretend the far trees were mountains and she wondered if most in the low South craved summits and peaks the way she did. Neva watched Val's stomach heave upward, the movement of Jackson's baby, and she looked away from it.

"They'll be turned out by the time we leave. All you have to do is dump the feed in the evening and open the stall doors. They'll run right at it. Mr. Grade said he would come over Sunday morning and turn them out. I still hate to leave it to you." The gray mare seemed to have a sweet disposition. But still. "You're so close to term and all."

"I'll be with folks. Even Grade will help me, so you won't worry. Bea said you've been needing three days away for a really long time."

True. But why? From whom? "We're leaving at four A.M. That's awful early for you to get up. We should be in Memphis by midafternoon. I'll call and leave you the number." Neva fumbled with her cigarette case. Managed to put one to her mouth and light it, one-handed.

"I hope you're not foolin' about liking them—" There was a question to it.

"Who?"

"Joody and Even. Them."

"Oh." Neva thought a moment, shaped her words. "I do like them. More than I thought I would, anyway. Joody's staying the weekend at my invitation. I wouldn't do that if I didn't like her." It beat the girl driving back and forth through the colored part of town. At least River House was set off the road away from loud-mouthed eyes. Folks in Petal had been blabbing about one thing or the other since Halloween.

Val looked at her trying to read her face but all she saw was Neva, unreadable, dependable, older than she was months back. "Joody'll be here in a little while I guess. Soon as Even gets off work and can bring her—" She unhooked her finger from Neva's hand.

"What time will you be back from Grand Bay?" Neva had cut back the cedars. Their behind-her-back whispering squelched, finally. She could see the gas lamp through the feathered branches flickering . . . flickering . . . flickering.

"I'm not sure."

"I'd prefer you were back before dark so I can call and check. If I call and nobody answers, I'll make myself sick worrying." Neva looked at her, the girl's stomach a bulwark between them.

Valuable sighed and leaned back her head and then she picked up Neva's hand and said, "Here. Feel this." Through the shirt Neva felt bumps and soft elbow-like angles moving underneath skin. Val moved her hand to her belly button and Neva felt a wide shape. A shoulder? A rump? Val moved her hand lower and Neva felt what she thought must be the head. "Lord, Val, how do you stand it?" She broke to a sweat and her heart rate increased. Her hand was glued to belly, the feel of the baby burning her.

"At first I was mad. And then I got scared. But now I'm just glad. It moves all the time. Like a fish. I've decided to name it Pearl. Girl or boy, it'll be Pearl." She shut her eyes and smiled. "That Doctor H is horrible, you know. He tries to be nice but there is something about him—something to him that's metal-like and sharp. Like those instruments he keeps in that special cabinet in his office. He makes me nervous—"

"If he hurts you, I'll kill him—"

"He won't." Val patted at her hand. "He won't hurt me. The baby will. But not the doctor."

"The baby?" Neva croaked.

"Getting out. That'll hurt like hell. Joody says it will but that I'll forget it once it's over and the baby's at the breast. But it won't be the doctor's fault. And Jackson can't hurt me either. He can't take this baby. I won't let him—"

"Jackson?" Neva was confused.

"I won't let him take it just because I'm a bastard myself and my mother's run away. Or because my great-grandfather was a killer. Any of those things. I won't let him. I'd kill him first before I let him." She let go of Neva's hand and brushed her hair up off the back of her neck and looked at the woman. "Pearl is mine. All mine. I don't know what kind of sorry woman would leave a baby in the middle of a bed. I don't know about Enid or what kind of female it takes to do such a horrible thing. All I know is I'm not one."

Neva felt subtle movement underneath her fingers. Small flutterings, miniature applause. She felt hills and ridges shifting to valleys around Val's belly button and looked down. Saw her hand was still on Val's stomach, unprodded. "I know you're not, Val. I know you'd never do such a thing." She moved her hand and looked at night, fully in now. At the dark spreading into one solid purple shadow. At the horses wandering in, their tails swishing, swishing, swishing. But I am, she said to herself. I'm that kind of female, and for the first time since any of this began, she was sad.

"It seems a heavy world tonight, don't it?" Joody and Neva were standing out beside the family cemetery. "Heavier than most. Wind's vagrant, too. Got its shoes off tonight—"

"Somewhat." Neva looked eastward and saw in amazement that Val had cut down a small pine tree at some point during her gestational period. A small pine that had apparently bothered her for some reason. "Lord, the girl cut down a tree." Neva pointed to it and Joody turned back to the house and looked up. "It was blocking something she wanted to see—" Joody pointed to a high, small window, "from there. That girl's truly named and don't but a few know it, and ain't that a pity."

Neva looked around the yard and tried to imagine a swing set or maybe a slide or even a small yard pool, and couldn't. She looked over at the barn and tried to imagine giving up three days away and judging and the smell of horses in exchange for diapers and baby food, and couldn't.

"I ain't never seen such a large animal dwelling," Joody said.

"It's too big." And it was. Its size monumental and awesome. A flaunt against the backdrop of nothingness. The wind picked up and it was a hot wind.

"Big as an ark, almost." Joody looked at the moon, at the ghost clouds drifting over it. "Good Friday's on its way." She squatted herself on the ground and picked at the grass. Neva was left standing, determined not to follow Joody's postural lead. Determined to make her body do what she wanted it to for a change. Part of being wood, she told herself, is to behave like it. To stand, fall, rot, burn. All those things are part of it. And this tree chooses to stand. She held her elbows with her hands.

"I had the gardener come and Val sent him home," Neva said. The gate to the cemetery was stiff and cold. It gave a resistant squeak underneath her fingers and then swung inward. "She told him the caladiums couldn't go down in the dirt 'til six o'clock Good Friday morning."

"You can't lay that to me."

"Yes, ma'am, I bet I can." Neva looked back at her while treading on the bones belonging to Cyril Korner, who'd died a tortured death of cancer to the bowel. "You've got your finger in more than one pot and you know it." Neva looked at her crouched down in the dark, but the look was low-mild in its appraisal. "Not that it's a bad thing, but it's there. Stirring. Always stirring." She breathed deeply, saw Even and Valuable inside the yellow barn examining the hay that Val had brought full circle. The equality of their silhouettes misleading.

"How come some Korners are here and those two belonging to the girl are at Hillcrest?" Joody was moving through the cemetery. Touching headstones. Patting them like they'd done well for themselves.

"There was a feud way back over something. Somebody felt cheated. Land, I suppose. Oil leases up in Purvis, I think Bea said." Next to Cyril was Richard Benjamin Korner and next to him lay Eunice, the wife. The grass was neatly clipped and Valuable had put flowers on one or two of them. Neva knew she would rotate the homage to someone else the following Sunday. Her actions sporadic, ritualistic and disturbing.

"You gonna lay here too?"

"I'll take cremation any day of the year, I think."

"Fire's a comfort, then?"

"More so than wet, dark dirt."

"I think I agree."

Neva laughed. "Well, that's a first! You agreeing with me over something."

"Now that you shiftin', I agree with you more than you realize. I find myself confused by it, too."

"Why? Because I'm queer?"

Joody hooted like a tired owl. "Lord, no. Not that business. I guess lovin' women must be the easiest thing in the world to do. To love somebody we know so well. To love a body same as ours. Lovin' a man's hard. What with all their contrariness and bullheadedness and their wide-open blind spots. Loving a woman would be easy, it seems—"

"Not as easy as you think—"

"You been with that one a long while." It was a statement.

"More than twenty years." Neva moved to the fence line and looked south through the dark, in the direction of the river that she couldn't see but was there—so ugly in its sluggishness she thanked a God she didn't believe in for the trees. "She loved me—saw through me even when I put up a fight. I guess she put up with my moods and that was something back then." She looked back at Joody and light fell to the black woman's mouth and teeth. Niblets of pearl disappearing into dark. "I haven't always been the charming person you see standing before you—"

Joody laughed again, the sound delightful, and Neva grinned in spite of herself.

"Neva, you're a pure gift. You like to think your womanhood's gone to leather, but it ain't."

"Whatever—"

"You like to think you give all you got to give, but there's a load ever bit big as that there barn waitin' to do. You don't want to, though."

"I'll not do it."

"You're her kinsman. You got no choice."

"There's always a choice."

Joody walked over to her and stood so close their shoulders touched. She felt the heat of a white shoulder, her controlled breathing. "Tell me this—do you miss the fluid?" Joody turned to her.

"What fluid?"

"Man's emission. His fluid. Does your body miss it?" Joody had one strand blowing loose. Like a fern frond tangled in sticks.

"I never had any use for any part of a man—"

"You was a daddy's girl, though."

"I'll not speak of him."

"You love your brother, too."

"Him either."

The wind picked up, lifting their shirts easy, and they both thought the wind surprisingly warm for April. Joody studied the other woman's folded-up arms. The way she held to them with leather palms and then she put a hand to her.

"Get your hands off me."

"Then you listen. I ain't ever felt such a sense of something coming and like what I do each and ever second is gonna make a difference." Joody quit pulling at Neva's wrist but left her hand on the woman's arm, her fingers spread open like a starfish. Night blended skin, blurred their pigment. "Only thing left to say is this—be sure."

"Be sure?" It came out high, incredulous.

"Be sure this plan of yours is the thing to do—"

Neva looked down because her eyes had filled. Suddenly. Unexpectedly. Wet exploded from her stomach region, spilling salt that trailed across middle-aged breasts, turned them silver.

"You a hard woman, being easy ain't easy," and then Joody patted her arm and walked away, quiet as a spectre through the gate of the cemetery. Neva stared at her feet, watching dust disappear off her boots. Watching the leather shine up, the benefit of dropped wet. Feeling the unaccustomed restraint of a tightened-up throat. Feeling the cumbersome weight of freedom around her neck like a three-cord rope. Thinking the whole while, You better be sure, Neva. You better damn well be sure—

36
PEARL

⸙

VALUABLE FOUND A ROAD in Grand Bay, Alabama, that was a wonder. A pure wonder. She'd seen it on a day the previous month when they'd gone fishing in the bayou and she had wanted to stop right then and there, but there hadn't been time because Grace had to get back to her aunt (all the Negroes pronounced it "ont") who was feeling poorly. It was a leveled-out dirt road and whether or not someone lived down at the end of it didn't matter. It was the road itself and how it presented itself to the world that held her. Long and narrow, with tall, thick bordering trees on both sides that touched at their tops, it seemed tunnel-like and diminishing. At the end of it was light, as if the trees had suddenly run headlong into a pasture or field or some type of opening, their shade eclipsed by openness and possibilities. Valuable had Joleb drive her past it four times. Grace and Canaan's new house was about two miles beyond the road. And knowing they were there unloading things from off the truck while she drove back and forth, studying the road from different angles, seemed a comfort. Like she had a place to go where she knew people once she was done puzzling this thing out.

"Lord, Val, you seen enough yet?" Joleb fiddled with the radio, found Patsy Cline.

"One more time. Just once more and that'll be enough."

He went down about a quarter of a mile and turned around. Dust washed up behind him. "I said I was gonna help. I promised Grace and she's already gonna have my ass—I'll do this once more and then we're goin' on."

They approached it from the south and he slowed while she looked. Turning herself around in her seat so she could see. He noticed her pretzel-like position, sighed once, put the car in reverse and backed up so she could see straight down without twisting herself around so.

I have never seen such a pretty sight, she said to herself. Not wanting to open her mouth and ruin it by speaking on it to Joleb, who was fiddling with the radio again trying to find a station. She looked at the road. Studied it the way a person studies a painting in a museum. Watched it reach for that spot of light at the end. The only color to it, the greens being so muted by shade they appeared almost colorless. The road seeming like something. A lesson maybe. A sermon possibly. Or somebody. And then it hit her. It reminds me of Even Grade. That's what it is. This road seems a picture of the man. "I'm done now, Joleb." She put her hand to his arm, the puzzle solved.

"Well, Christ, it's about fuckin' time—"

"Don't use that word around Pearl." She put a hand to her stomach and held her baby.

"Lord, Val. You act like your stomach's got ears." He headed back to Highway 188 and turned left. Once there it was a doglegged shot to the intersection of Dawes and Grand Bay–Wilmer Road. The house sat behind the Mobile County Co-Op. A sprawling four-bedroom house with a porch on three sides, a tin roof that hadn't turned red yet and a kitchen the size of any of the houses in the Quarter. It was a country house with a yard that went on forever set down in the middle of a grove of pecan trees.

When they pulled up the goat was roaming, the truck was empty and Even and Canaan were standing out in the shade, smoking.

"Somebody's got near perfect timing," Canaan snorted.

"It's her fault. She had me goin' back and forth looking at a damn dirt road for nearly an hour."

Valuable climbed out of the car, her movements cumbersome yet magnificent, her back steady hurting, her hand to her lower stomach holding her baby as if her hand were a gate. Canaan watched from across the yard irritated that every time he looked at her he felt pity clot up in his throat. Even watched and thought, Maternal—that's as clear a picture of a maternal as I'm ever likely to see. And then he was ashamed of himself for staring and not offering to help. She was wearing overalls with the side grabs undone. Neva had given her one of her shirts. A large white one that was rolled up at the sleeves making her arms look child-like and stunted. She looked at Even. "Where's Aunt Persia?"

"Inside banging her cane on the floor. She was asking for you. Expectin' you in before now to say howdy." He looked at his watch and it was a paternal statement. Canaan shook his head. Grimaced like one with a bad taste in his mouth.

"I figured she would, but I had to see that road again. It's a true wonder and there's not many of those left." She climbed the broad steps, carefully because she couldn't see her feet and her back burned. She looked over her shoulder. "It's your road, you know. Can't think of a more perfect way to describe you than that road back there." She ducked her head, embarrassed, and went inside.

Canaan and Even and Joleb stood outside in the big front yard and looked at each other. Canaan opened up his mouth to speak and then shut it again while the wind picked up and jabbered through the newborn leaves of the trees.

Aunt ("Ont") Persia sat in the corner most of the time clutching her cane. It was carved in the shape of a grasshopper flying like a racehorse, and like the road with the light at its end, Valuable thought it completely wonderful. Persia said very little, just interjecting her words into conversations that had no relevance. Earlier Grace and Joody were talking religion and Persia called out, "Ding dong, but don't he have a big way to him!" Grace said, "What's that, Ont Persia? What you speaking on?" and Persia shouted, "Africa!" Then, "Music Box!" and then she banged her cane to the floor and clamped her gums down, her mouth turning to a thin line that divided her face in half. She was nearly blind and had been near death for close to twenty years.

Her body was like an empty container that used to hold something inestimably good, and because of that Valuable liked to sit by her and hold her hand and listen to her nonsense talk. "Tallyboy!" she yelled while she picked up Valuable's hand and gave it an old, dry kiss to the palm.

"Tallyboy's in heaven, Ontie," Grace said back to her. "Joody told me so." The two women were unboxing things at the table. Mason jars. Beans. Canaan's books. Joody was unusually quiet. "I think she lied, though, 'cause he was as full of the devil as any man can get and not burn clean up while standin'."

Valuable was sitting in a comfortable chair, her feet up on a small stool. "Laughin' man!" Persia shouted, banging down her cane.

"You right there, Ont Persia. Full of the devil, though."

Valuable leaned forward suddenly, her back tight as well as her stomach. It didn't hurt though, just made her feel compressed every few minutes like she was being squeezed from the bottom up.

"Devil or no, Tallyboy made me laugh," Grace said. "Made me laugh so hard I'd come close to peein' myself no matter where I was at. Church. Work. Choir. He took pleasure in makin' me laugh where I ought not to, too." She took her hands out of a box and set a large ledger down, its edges brown and curled.

"Damn foolish men!" Persia shouted. Then, "Jesus saves!"

Grace looked over at Valuable. "You ain't the only girl who found herself in a fix." Valuable wondered momentarily what she meant and then the baby kicked and she knew. She put a hand low to her belly and covered his ears.

Grace talked on, "—was a small man with a great big mouth. Spread himself all over Greene, Forrest and half a dozen other counties. Just Plain Grace had to have him, though. Had to have that big, ole mouth of his runnin' night and day, so full of jokes and laughin' I hardly knew myself from one minute to the next. His mouth so full of shit, grass grew tall under ever step he took."

"Knocked you up!" Persia shouted.

"That he did."

"Were you happy?" Valuable asked from her spot next to Persia. Happiness more important now than anything.

"I thought I was." The way it came out of Grace's mouth sounded new. As if the thought had run crossways with reality and separated off toward a new way of thinking. "I used to get mad as hell at him. Told him that if he wanted to run around and come back smelling of whores he could get himself out of here and away from me. Me and his baby what was growin' in my belly by that time. Before the document between us, but not much before. He did right by me at least that way—"

Joody was watching the exchange. Her eyes going from Grace to Valuable and back again. Her body completely still. Her sticks hanging like chimes inside an airless house.

"—He tried for a while. Came back and made good and then he'd up and disappear. It'd got so that I didn't worry, 'cause he always came back. But for that last time. Weren't until after two days of solid praying, I knew something was wrong—"

"What happened?" Valuable said, sitting up. Joody sat still as a rock. Her mouth parted like a crack in a stone. Her bones burning up from her feet.

"I buried him and my baby girl on the same day." Grace looked at Valuable. "The shock of learning what happened to him brought on the birth, but she was too little. Breathed for an hour was all." Grace was stand-ing by an empty box. She turned it upside down and thumped it three times, done with it. Dust and pieces of cardboard fell out and landed white, like dirty salt. "I sat there and listened to the preacher, or tried to, but all I could think was how they found him strung up in a tree outside Vicksburg—"

Valuable watched Grace slide forward toward her. First she saw her eyes, large as fiery twin planets, and then she saw those marvelous, terrible, capable hands, wide as the Leaf River.

"—'bout near crazy. My milk was wetting my dress. My baby's milk. Me sitting there thinking of that rope nearly slicing off his head, my baby tucked in there with him to the crook of his arm. Ont Persia was there and some of Tallyboy's people. The folks I worked for then—the old Liebersteins. Only thing that kept me from screaming was that foolish joke he used to tell. The dumb-ass joke about how to make a rooster quiet on the Sabbath—"

"Kill it Sat'day night!" Persia yelled while she banged her cane to bring down the house.

Valuable felt Grace's sorrow on her neck, eating her. Tearing at her skin. Sorrow's breath fell and singed her solid through so there was nothing left but char. Nothing left at all worth anything to anybody. Nothing left for Pearl or Jackson or Neva or Even. She felt her stomach wrapping around her then, hard as a brick, vise-like, determined. It didn't hurt. It just squeezed and squeezed and the squeezing put her breath back into her body, made her heart beat again. The all-embracing constriction around her middle moved her eyes off of Grace and back to the carved-out grasshopper cane and the woman who may have been worth something once upon a time, but was now little more than a shouting shell. Valuable sat there shaking uncontrollably. Set down hard on the hard stool of sorrow, the words floated up like bubbles from a drowning child: *Brief. Girlhood is brief. Summer is brief. Love is brief. Life is brief.*

Even Grade had the letter in his pocket, crisp new and full of potential. He was yet to mention it, though, even though Pascagoula was little more than a stone's throw from Grand Bay and a trip over there to put his name on the list would be considered expedient and convenient. But the business of Valuable and her baby had cemented his feet; had become more of a weight than he'd realized. Not a burdensome weight, though, but one wearing a color that stopped his forward motion. Like a stop sign or a traffic light or the lights on a police car. He didn't need to make a box of his hands to see it, either. He saw it in the way she stood and walked and sat and talked. He saw it swelling out of her in portions equal to her belly. Even Grade bent forward and felt the scratch of the letter in his pocket, knowing it was a consideration that would have to wait.

Canaan drank from his jar of tea and handed it up to Even who drank deep and passed it on to Joleb who slurped loud as a horse. The three of them had been sitting that way, halfway listening to the inside woman-talk, resting up from unloading the beds and the cartons and the mattresses. The three of them—drinking, resting, listening, breathing each other's smell of sweat. Sitting that way with their hands dangling between their legs. Even looked out over the lay of the land while gnats swarmed. Such a flat-level place. Named after a bay that's nowhere in sight.

"Here you go." He felt cool wet on his shoulder, droplets from the communal glass, and he reached and took it from Joleb and set it on the steps. A truck finally moved past at a crawl, its bed loaded with the strewn guts of a tractor. Somebody's hard work, Even thought. The screen door slammed and steps approached from around the side porch and all three men came to attention.

"Joleb, I need you to take me back—"

"Now? Christ, Val, we just got here—" He saw her face and stopped short. Even saw her face, too, and jumped to his feet. "You sick, Valuable?"

"No sir. I'm not sick."

"Is it the baby then?"

"No sir. It's nothing really, except that I remembered some things Neva asked me to do and I need to get back and do them—"

"They won't be home until Sunday. Can't it wait?" Joleb wiped his glasses on his shirt.

"Joleb, please." She had her hand to her stomach and Even was struck by her low-riding fingers, barely above pubis, childlike, too tiny to hold such a thing in place. He heard pieces of conversation coming through the screens of the house and he wondered at Grace (that mouth of hers), at Joody (that mouth of hers), at Persia (that mouth of hers). Valuable's become a victim of something female here, was his thought. Something's happened that's not of her making and whoever did it should be skinned first and shot later once they were naked under a broiling sun.

She went down the steps to the car, slowly, magnificently, terribly. Like a small barge. One hand to her belly. One outstretched like the new-blind.

"Valuable—" She had opened the door. Joleb had gone back inside to say good-bye to Grace. "We gonna get through this thing. You know that."

She turned, one hand on the door, the other on her stomach. "Even—"

He waited, seeing his own reflection in the orbs of her eyes and then he put a hand to her belly and felt its stricture. She put her cold hand on top of his. He read her then and it was loud as a scream—*SORRYSOSOR-RYHELPMEOHEVENOHEVENOHEVEN*—

"Jesus, girl, what's become of you? I can't let you go from here! Not like this—"

She looked away, both of them hearing the slam of the screen door. In one movement they took back their hands like novice thieves. "I just need rest is all."

"I'll take you then."

"No. You stay and stop by later. Bring Joody, then. We're only two hours away—"

Grace walked out to the car wiping her hands to her apron, concern in her eyes. "You all right?"

"Just tired is all." Valuable couldn't look at her. Joody was behind Grace. Persia was on the porch, towering over Canaan who was standing on the steps. "Bring me a geetar!" Persia shouted and banged her cane. Canaan reached behind and took the cane and said, "You hush now!"

"Valuable, if it was that talk of my baby dying—"

"It wasn't that."

Joody separated herself from the group and stood out in the center of the yard, post-like in the sun. Like a marker of sorts. The way her mother had looked when she fell inside her shadow. Valuable looked at her, saw some strong peaceful something in her eyes, some calm knowing, and settled. Joleb climbed in the car and with little more than a wave they pulled out and headed back to Petal.

Joleb wasn't sure what he had expected of the day.

But it wasn't this.

He stood frozen in the doorway, watching.

Valuable was flat on her back, but he knew it was a temporary position. She would stay there for thirty seconds and then she would roll to her side and whimper and then she'd go to her other side and yell and then she'd get up on her knees and scream bloody murder and then she'd go onto her back again.

"Lord, Val, I got to go for the doctor!"

"No! Don't leave me—Jesus!" There was a phone downstairs he had suddenly remembered seeing.

"Just five minutes, Val! Just long enough to get to the phone! I swear it. Just long enough to call the doctor—"

"Go then——" It came out guttural and jagged, like vocals from a busted box.

"Who is he? Who's the doctor?"

"Doctor somebody——" She flipped herself and got up on her knees.
"Doctor H— Oh Jesus! Oh JEEESUS!"

"Doctor who?! Tell me! What's his last name?" He was shouting over
her, crying without realizing it. Fogging his glasses. "Talk to me, Val! Tell
me who he is!"

"I don't know. Don't know——" She turned herself again and climbed
off the bed, clutching the bedpost. "Help me take off my pants! Help me!
Hurry!"

"Why you want to take off your pants?"

"Do it, Joleb! Get over here and help me! Hurry up!"

Swallowing hard, he worked at the grabs, shimmied the overalls over
quaking hips, watched them fall in a clump to her feet. He looked at the
crotch and saw wet and colored; saw she'd peed herself and maybe bled a
little. "You pissed your pants, Val——"

"Help me, Joleb! JEEESUS!"

"Help you what! Quit screaming—what do you want me to do?" He
was wringing his hands.

"Take them. Get them off of me!" She had tried to kick away the overalls and couldn't. She could feel the wet of them against her ankles. The
bed was soaked pink. "I've got to hold to the post. Help me."

She meant her large underdrawers, and while he worked his hands into
the waistband and slid them down, he looked to the side toward her bookcase reading titles. *Treasure Island. Huckleberry Finn. Light in August.* He could
smell her. The way her sweat had mixed with something metallic and sharp.
Wet was running down her legs, which were shaking seizure-like. "There
now, Val. Here we go——" He put an arm around her, terrified. "Step out
now. Come on, you can do it." She did and then she screamed and put her
face to the post. Her legs were spread and he saw more water coming out.

"JOLEB!——"

"I'm here, Val. I'm right here. I ain't goin' nowhere. Lord, you really had
to go, didn't you?"

With one arm around her he sat her on the edge of the bed, saw its

large wet pink center and ran to her quilt, flapping it in the air 'til it floated down and covered up the pink. He heard the snap of it and thought of
a sail whipped by wind on a boat leaving white-ribbon wakes that moved
away. Wishing the whole while he were on that boat and headed out of
there.

"Jeeesus!" Valuable grabbed him by the shirt, pulling him forward until
their noses touched.

He put his hands to either side of her and pushed away. "Valuable,
now you listen. Listen to me, okay? I want you to calm down and listen—"
He made the words soft slow and to his amazement she settled. Pillows. By
God she needs pillows. He plumped up the ones she had and looked
around for more, the accumulation of pillows seen as a short-term answer
for her suffering. He saw two more on the couch at the end of the bed and
fetched them up.

"Here now. Slide up. Slide up here—" He helped her scoot up to the
end of the bed. "Now all this thrashing around is making it worse, Val—"
She was bare-assed and hideous. Christ! Only a lesbian could tolerate
seeing this. And where's a lesbian when you really need one? Up in Memphis
at a fuckin' horse show! He laughed at how ridiculous it all was. The absur-
dity of being stuck here in this great big house with Val sick and all. She
looked up and smiled with him. A break in the torture coming finally.

She had been fine up until Richton. Just saying her stomach felt funny.
Tensing up every few minutes. You think it's the baby coming? he had asked
a dozen times and she'd said no, that it didn't hurt at all. Just felt strange
and binding. Here, feel, she'd said once and he'd reached over, careful to
keep his eyes on the road, and what he'd felt was as hard as a brick. Lord!
Don't that hurt? But she'd said, Not a bit. Not one little bit. . . .

"Okay, see? See how being calm is helping?"

She nodded her head because she couldn't talk.

"You ever seen a dog whelp out?" Joleb pulled at the low end of the
top sheet, jerked it free from the end of the bed. Valuable was shaking her
head. "You ain't? Well, I sure have. And while they're sick and trying to get
those things out, they breathe fast and shallow-like. Like this." He panted
for about ten seconds, motioning with his hands for her to join him and

she tried to copy him and then she laughed a croupy laugh because it all seemed so silly.

"I know it sounds silly but I want you to try that. Try that and see if it don't help—" He spread the sheet over her knees so he wouldn't have to look at her anymore. Feeling so sorry and sad she looked so horrible down there. Joleb swiped at his face, glad she hadn't taken him up on his offer of twenty dollars up in the attic. Was that yesterday? Was it really? he wondered.

Another pain hit her and she rolled at the sheet, wadding and winding. She ended up exposed, the sheet a white tube across her belly.

"Pant, Val. Pant like I showed you." He saw more gush and he sat on the edge of her bed listening to the sound of her moaning wail. Curious over its foreign sound. She could be Zorba the Greek and it wouldn't make any difference, his knees were knocking while he listened, terrified. He strained his ears to pick up familiar strands of it. Thanking his lucky stars the whole while he'd been born dicked and scrotumed and udderless. He watched while she propped herself up on her elbows and panted, moaning while inspecting the space between her legs in a way both anticipatory and dreadful.

"Easy now. Easy now, Val. Hold now." He was patting her knee regular as a metronome while he looked out a window. "I got to call somebody. As soon as this one ends I'm going downstairs and I'm going to call the operator and tell her what's happening and see if she can get somebody over here. But I'll wait 'til this one's over, okay? You think you're having the baby? You think that's what this is all about?" She rolled her eyes, their whites showing at crescent angles. Her eyes full of terror while she breathed as best she could like a dog.

He droned on. His hillbilly cadence both soothing and annoying as hell. Soft words he didn't know he had. She interrupted him. "Help me— oh Jesus—with it." He looked and caught her pulling at her shirt. Her fingers would go to a button and then back to the rolled-up sheet. At least her knees were together and he was thankful for that. "Help me, please." He worked the buttons through with fingers that wouldn't quit shaking and then helped her lean up so he could take it off. "This too?" The back fastener of her brassiere was cutting into her skin. At her nod he fiddled with the clasps, pulling her forward, smelling wet hair, the tang to it. He saw her back bones rising to the surface of her skin in between her panting breaths.

"Lord! Who makes these things? It sure ain't a man 'cause a man could figure out a way to get out of it better than this." He finally got it free and threw it across the room. "Here—you sit still and I'll find you a loose shirt." He saw one over a chair. A soft T-shirt that looked like a man's. Neva's, he decided. She's as close to a man as one ever gets round this place. Joleb pulled it over her head, helping work one arm in at a time, seeing her large breasts, thinking, Well, the top of her's not near as bad as the lower half, but it still ain't worth twenty dollars—

"You think you'll be okay while I go call somebody?" She nodded. So tired. Thinking, Now that wasn't so bad. Why was I carrying on so? I'll just sleep for a while. She had the tubed-up sheet across her stomach and was holding to it and Joleb thought it looked somehow nautical. Like something that might be cute attached to an anchor-shaped pillow.

"Bring me some water—" she said.

"Okay, I'll get you some water. And you just lay still, okay? Quit that thrashing around business because that makes it worse—"

"Okay," she said, thinking, I can't say anything else. Okay is okay but anything else is too much because I'm tired. So sleepy.

He looked at his watch. Four o'clock. They had left Grand Bay at around two and as best he could figure, all hell broke loose around three-thirty.

"Gosh, Val, I wish you'd told me you were hurting. Lord." And then he left the room, looking back once and seeing her with her eyes shut, glad she was finally sleeping, glad having babies took such an awful long time because that meant someone would be here before the king-sized, big daddy problem of getting the thing out of her reared its ugly little head.

"How fast you goin'?" Grace leaned across Joody and looked. "Sign says one thing but they ain't nobody round that I can see. I think you could go a little bit faster and it wouldn't hurt a bit!" He slowed to go round a curve, his lips clamped shut, just about fed up to the limit with her and her inconsistencies.

"Oh, Lord—Oh Lord have mercy!" Grace bent her head to her lap like she was sniffin' at her knees—she would do this thing about every five miles—and he wanted to slap her hard and be done with it. He would have, too, if Joody hadn't been between them. But then again he wanted to slap that one, too. The way she'd stood out in the center of the yard like a post for nearly an hour before she'd said word one about any of it. Grace back in the kitchen stirring up potato salad like she didn't have a care in the world. The old fool Persia banging her cane like some damn idiot. Women! All of them. Foolish as geese. As easy to herd along a course as a cat.

"Yeah, you pray hard, Grace. You pray hard your words can be undone—"

"Even—" This from Joody.

"And you shut up too, woman! You just keep your female mouth buttoned up tight! I just about had it with all of you!" He slammed a fist to the steering wheel.

"Oh Lord—" Grace began rocking then. Rocking back and forth and mumbling like the tongue talkers. "Helobo shelobo—"

"You quit that nonsense or I'm puttin' you in the back—"

"I was waitin', trying to hear what Deep Mother was saying. That ain't foolish, Even—" Joody said.

"You hush about this Deep Mother! You stood there knowing something was wrong and you didn't say a word on it! Just stood there—"

"I stood there because it was right to stand there—"

"—The hell you say! Who in their right mind stands around listening for something when the truth is plain as the fuckin' nose on a face? Who?" Both women stared, never having heard that particular swear come out his mouth. They'd never heard him shout, either. "Nobody! We got a heart for a reason! We got a brain for a reason! You still sitting here waitin' for a voice. You just got a suspicion something's wrong. Just a suspicion and it's enough to get me tearing down the road just to check."

"You the one who jumped in the truck like he'd been shot—" Joody put her hands around her knees.

That was true. He had. Leaving Canaan standing on the porch, a napkin in his hand, potato salad on his face.

"You sitting here yellin' at us because you're scared is all. Ain't no point in trying to deny it, either." Grace wiped at her eyes.

He felt the truth of it nail him. But there was something else. There was the look in her eyes. The way he couldn't sit still after she left. "I know it. You're saying the truth now, and I know it," he said. He drove past Richton and turned left. Ignoring the speed limit. Nine more miles is all, he told himself. Nine more miles and we'll be there.

Halfway down the stairs he heard the scream. Running back up he found her pulling at her knees, yelling to bring down the house, "There's something down there, Joleb! Something down there! I feel it!"

He went and looked and sure enough there was. Something black and wet. "Lord have mercy, Val—"

"What?"

"It's coming out!"

"I got to go to the bathroom. Number two. I can't stop myself from pushing—"

"Hell, go ahead. I'll clean it up. Don't you worry. But Lord—"

She pulled at her knees and yelled and he told himself, I forgot Burris and all that business at the trestle. Folks told me about it, but I still can't remember. But this—this is fixed. I'll never forget this. Pushing his glasses up, he got on his knees at the foot of the bed, wondering where he should put his hands. All he could see was black. A black something that would come out and then go back in a little. Just a wad of black. "Something's trying to come out—"

"Don't you think I know that! AAAHH!" she yelled again.

"Well, okay, but you can't see it, so I thought I'd tell you—"

"Catch it, Joleb. Don't let it fall on its head." Her face was bleached white as a bone. "I'm real tired," she said.

"I know you are, but Lord, hang on, here it comes—" He saw her stomach was solid again and now the black had a brow and a nose. It was like watching something take shape out of river mud. He put his hand to her privates and worked his fingers underneath it and thought how like a softball the wet round black thing seemed. Like trying to dislodge a softball from a drainpipe. That's what this is like. A softball stuck in a drain. "Okay, Val, here it is! Here it comes now! Oh Lordy! Lordy! Its head is out now— Val? Val, you listening?" Her face seemed fixed to a wide-open stare.

The baby came out nose up, its head flopping back into Joleb's hand. Such tiny features, too. Squinted eyes. Tiny nose and mouth. A mouth like Val's, he thought. Like a baby bird's mouth. Tiny and sweet. The shoulders delivered next, rotating themselves around until the whole thing popped out and gave a squeal. "Hot damn, it's a boy! It's a boy baby!" He wanted to shout and dance. Glad there was another boy in the room to take away the feeling of being outnumbered. He caught it up and realized he should've found something to wrap it up in because it was slimy as hell. Wet and slippery as a seven-pound catfish.

"I'm cold, Joleb." Her face was the color of chalk and she couldn't seem to lift her hands. He worked one free from its hold on the sheet and put the baby inside the crook of her arm. "Lord, Val, you got yourself a boy." It was crying soft like a cat. Snorting little snotty sounds. Honking, almost, and he laughed. And then he cried and clapped his hands together. "Hot damn—ain't you a picture, little man!" He ran around to the side of the bed and helped her turn her face and look at it because she seemed frozen. "See it, Val—see what you got."

"Where, Joleb? Where is it?"

"Why it's right here, silly—can't you feel it?" He dislodged her other hand and put it on the baby's head and she sighed and said, "There you are, sweet baby. There you are—" Her teeth were chattering, "Cold. I'm cold, Joleb," she said.

"Here you go." He reached down and pulled at Prizewinner and covered her lower half up with it, trying not to look. There was a green, noodle-looking cord still attached to the baby, but there was no way in hell he was going to mess with it. That's somebody else's job. It ain't mine. No way. Not that. "Now, ain't you something—"

"Sweet baby Pearl." She kissed him, or tried to, but her lips missed. The baby mewed like a kitten and waved angry fists around in the air. She was pulling at the front of her shirt with hands that wouldn't quit shaking, try-ing to get it up. Joleb helped her, leaving bloody handprints all over the white T-shirt. The baby latched on to her tit like he smelled it. Sucking hard like he was starving to death. Joleb stared, fascinated at the tiny mouth against skin. At the sucking motions building inside its cheeks. Seeing him-self and Grace. Seeing all the babies in the world. Seeing his basic theory come alive. The baby lost the nipple and bumped around, blind as a bat, bumping and bumping and bumping 'til he found it again and latched on. Val's hands were patting it, white-blue hands trembling. She looked up, her lips moved but he couldn't hear. He bent to her and heard her whisper, "Milk's personal." He patted her hand, noticed Val was trying to smile at him, in the wrong direction though, like she still thought he was standing at the foot of the bed.

"You bet it is," he said, picking up the baby's miniature foot. Val was sleeping. Her lips to the baby's head. What a mess we got here, he thought, wondering where to begin the cleanup. Deciding to call the operator and tell her to get the police over here if nothing else, and let them do it. Val was giving off hard shudders when he eased off the bed.

He was standing in the doorway looking back at her thinking it was the prettiest thing he'd ever seen in his life, that her giving that baby milk would set it on the right course of living, when he heard the door slam downstairs, and the sound of feet running up the stairs.

He met Even Grade at the entrance to the hall, the man's eyes all over his blood-printed shirt. "Valuable's had herself a boy. She was cold and I covered her up so she could rest. There's a pure-d mess in there though."

The women ran past him and Even heard the mewly newborn cry. He put a hand to the top of Joleb's head. "You did good," he thought he said but he wasn't sure. He walked down the long hall to the room, noticing it seemed to stretch forever. There's a bathroom at the end of this one, too, I bet. Just like those Lutherans had. Now ain't that a coincidence? His hand was to the doorframe when he heard the flapping sound as the women jerked back the quilt covering her, their sudden intake of brittle breath. Like mannequins they all stood there staring. Arms frozen. Mouths open breathing metallic air. Even Grade looked down and away, noticing the swans hooked into the rug under the bed were swimming in a deep, new ruby sea.

Grace spent the two and a half hours roaming the River House kitchen as if she were its final, rightful owner. Pulling open cabinets with a queen's authority, she found cans of evaporated milk, mixed them with water and Karo syrup. This done she poured the sweet blend into small glass bottles Even had found up in Valuable's bedroom. His scaredy-cat eyes desperate to see anything other than what the man in the white coat was doing to the girl's body. Glass is good, he told himself. Glass baby bottles even better. Look at those, Even, over by the Mama Girl rock and you'll get through this thing. Clear, short glass bottles, six of them, next to four fragile baby garments made of old vintage lace and spotted satin streamers. He had lifted the top one to his nose and smelled old or maybe attic, one or the other. His hands too large to handle it, he juggled the bottles instead and walked clinking down the stairs to Grace.

Standing back against a wall he watched her work. Stove top to sink and back again. Her feet out of her shoes while the metal tongs in her hand pinched rings and rubber nipples, lifted out the steaming glass bottles by their necks. All her capable kitchen sounds multiplying. A spoon going into the sink sounded like a gunshot. A lid set to a pot had the report of a cannon.

The doctor came in and stood and repeated his diagnosis three times as if they were brain-dead or stupid. Once he said, "You people want to write this down?" and before Even could go for a pencil, he shook his head and went to the kitchen phone and called the mortician. "An hour tops," he said when he turned. Even was holding a pencil, poised for instructions. The fat doctor looked at it and waved it away. "Just tell Neva to call me," he said. "I forgot how hard it is for you people to cipher." He took his coat and left. A good thing, too, what with Grace reaching for the knife.

She went back to the noise then, louder than before, and Even retreated, a shell-shocked enemy. Joleb was on the landing, the boy sitting timberlike and pale as one shot through. Even sat down hard, winded and old, his hand on Joleb's knee.

"I ain't gonna start thinkin' I killed her," Joleb said in a low voice, lifting his own hand and looking at it, satisfied it was steady.

"That's good, 'cause you didn't. You saved that baby and that's what Val would've wanted." Even moved his hand off the boy's knee, and leaned on his hands and studied the plush carpet, hating the color of it.

"I might still kill Jackson, though," Joleb said, deaf to encouragement. They both jumped at some large clamor and crash coming up from the kitchen. "I might yet kill him."

"That wouldn't change a thing—" Meaning the girl would still be dead as a knob.

"I realize that. I may be crazy, but I ain't stupid." He ran a hand under his nose and then wiped it on his pants. "Killing him won't change a thing, but I bet it'd make me feel a helluva lot better."

"Maybe for a while, but then it'd pass and you'd feel worse." Even felt a knot in his throat for he had suddenly seen a picture of Valuable's face the first time she caught a fish. The girl's belly was already large but she'd screamed like a three-year-old while the fish flopped on the ground. There were other things he remembered about her, too. Shy confidence. Blooming hope. Possibilities. He swallowed hard against them. "I ain't ever killed. But I've found myself wantin' to." He could've said that wanting to was as bad internally as doing it, what with the way it ate at the gut and took up whole rooms inside the heart, but he didn't. Sick of his thoughts and his dribbled-out, sparse words, as well as the crashing sounds coming out of the kitchen.

"Men ain't supposed to cry, are they?"

Even didn't know what to say, so he put an arm about the boy. Joleb cleared his throat and popped his knuckles.

"There's a place she used to stand up in the attic. A place by this small window where the river looks almost pretty—" He wiped at his nose again, his voice cracking. "She would stand there and the light would hit her and she would look so pretty. And I wanted to say that to her. I wanted to tell her that she was pretty even though she'd gotten herself knocked up and all. That even her big belly hadn't made her ugly." Even pressed his arm tighter around Joleb's shoulder. "I wanted to, but I didn't. And now she's dead and she don't know how pretty I thought she was—" He leaned his head to his knees and cried.

"It's okay. It's gonna be okay—" Even patted him on the back. They were still sitting huddled together an hour later when a car pulled up the drive. The car lights came shining through the leaded door panels and spilled up the stairs, illuminating their legs.

Pulling in the drive, the lights of the car exposing all the vehicles, Neva said to herself, "Well, thank God she listened to me and stayed put instead of going off to Grand Bay—" She had left Bea in a huff up in Memphis. Told her simply that she had to go for cigarettes. Once she hit the highway she headed for home pulling an empty trailer, struck since Batesville with a horrible vision of Valuable trampled by the horses. The window was rolled down and Neva heard the crunch first of gravel and then the hum of tires. Car lights ahead of her, like a standard, she felt the noose loosening, felt silly for being afraid, worried now over what Bea must be thinking. What she would have to buy to soothe her ruffled feathers. The lights illumined pillars, swung wide arches into the porch. Then she saw them. Saw the legs first—Joody at the end of the porch and the other one, Grace Something or Other, sitting in a rocker—but there was no sign of Valuable, no sign of her anywhere, and Neva knew.

Pulling past them to the slot at the side, she got out and walked around to the porch. Grace stood up and the chair rocked. Neva moved away, holding up a hand because she saw the woman's mouth open up. "Don't," she said and shook her head. She pointing a finger to Joody. "Don't. Don't either of you say anything. Not yet. Don't say the words." The baby wailed and she shut her eyes, walked away from the house. "Tell Mr. Grade I'll be in the barn." She had both hands over her ears the whole while she was walking, but she could still hear the baby.

He found her leaning her head against a stall and there was a pile of leather goods—straps, harnesses, leads—blocking his path. He walked around them until he was face to face, knowing what she wanted. "The doctor said she bled to death," he said, his voice tired. "Said there was a tear—"

"Wait—" She looked to the side, took deep gulping breaths. He waited, listening to the sound of horses. The ticking of the hooded lights. The sound of wind against high girders and tin. When he reasoned it was time to continue, he said, "She never told anybody she was hurtin'. And Joleb said that as far as he could tell she didn't start goin' into it hard 'til around four o'clock. He told the doctor she wouldn't let him leave her to call—"

"Wait—" Neva moved away from him, put her head against the stall. "Joleb did his best—"

"How in the hell does something like—"

"The doctor said it was a miracle the baby made it because most don't—"

"Shut up. Just shut up." She put her hands over her ears.

He leaned back against the wall and waited. The women were up in the room cleaning things. Joleb's Aunt Louise had followed the mortician in and picked up Joleb, who seemed terribly sad but not undone. Before Joleb left to go, they let him hold the baby while the doctor and the women worked over Valuable, getting her ready.

Neva walked over to the bales of hay and jerked one down from above head level. Loose straw scattered, some settling in her hair. Sitting down and looking at her feet she said, "I want you to listen and I want you to listen good." He couldn't see her eyes. A horse leaned over and nuzzled at his head and he swatted it back. "You go in there and you get that baby and you get rid of it—"

"I ain't gonna do it."

"You do it, or I'll throw it in the river. You get it and take it away and I don't care where it goes. There will be a funeral and she's to be buried along with this. I'll not have her talked about on top of all . . . on top of this. But you hear me true—if you don't take it, it'll be dead five minutes after you leave."

"You're crazy—"

"You're damn straight on that one, Mr. Grade. Now you've got some choices in this—it's not like we don't have choices—"

He listened, appalled.

"—there's the Brothers of the Sacred Heart in Bay St. Louis. I can draw you a map. All you have to do is ring the bell and hand it to them. Tell them you found it out beside the road. Tell them anything you want. They're famous for not asking questions."

"Just hand it over? That's what you expect of me? To leave it on some damn steps to cry—" His voice cracked.

She shrugged. "Raise it yourself then. Give it to Grace, this family owes her one now that I think of it—"

The horses were restless, unfamiliar with his smell, he supposed. There was still blood to his shirt from where he'd held back Joleb. Stiff splotches turning to brown, smeared up and down. One place above his belt that looked to be a thumbprint.

"I don't give a rat's ass about the details," Neva said. "But I want that baby gone before I leave this barn. So you go back up to the house and you tell those two women to do what they've got to do to decide. Throw the bones. Dance a jig. Kill a cat. I don't care. But you go right now and I don't ever want to see any of you again."

Neva didn't watch them drive off. She heard the sounds of departure the same as she'd heard the sound of the hearse leaving thirty minutes earlier. Right before it carried her away, its lights on, the motor running, the short mortician had stood before Neva and said, It's our business, you know. She'd looked at him puzzled, What? What business is that? The man put a notebook in his pocket, his head still down. Confidentiality, he'd said, kicking at gravel. And she'd answered, Oh that. Yes, well that's good I suppose. Finished finally, his package retrieved, he'd driven off and she hadn't looked then, either. Just stood inside the barn and listened. And it was the same with the coloreds. She heard the shifting of transmission. The building whine of a motor. Heard everything she needed to hear. Then she went to the stalls and freed the horses. Slapping their rears. Done with them. They ran out into the black-green pasture, confused, glad to be out of their stalls, but anxious. The garage door was stubborn, but she'd managed it. She shut it back a few minutes later. The cans of diesel were heavy and the liquid sloshed when she dumped it next to the hay. When she struck the match and tossed it to the ground and walked out, not bothering to run, she knew heat was up her back but all she felt was tired. Later, while she watched the sonofabitch barn blaze up to the sky, throwing offshoots that ignited the garage and set it on fire, too, she prayed the vagrant wind would pick up and carry flames over to the River House. Burn it down, too. Once and for all. But the wind quieted itself instead. While she watched the blue leap of flame she thought on the sudden stillness and chalked it up to the fact that every being with power and ability to answer her prayers was deaf to her.

37

BAY ST. LOUIS

———————

HIS MEMORIES WERE LOUD AND CLINGY AS VINES, and if not for the railroad running steady alongside the truck, he reasoned their noise might have driven him to some extreme point, similar to that of Joody's.

They followed the tracks for most of the way into Alabama. Catching up with a southbound train near Richton and advancing steady on it until at one point it seemed train and truck were motionless, locked frozen inside a landscape that moved all around them. Silos, tall and ghostly, paraded past. Then a barn and small farmhouse. And then the truck picked up speed and passed the train, its whistle blowing out behind them with a sound that plummeted, like a diminishing scream from the far side of a cliff.

I am man born of woman—he hung on this inward ladder rung of a thought while he felt the baby sleeping in the crook of his arm—*And here, finally, is the proof.* Even looked down and saw a stream of milk running, pooling along the folds of the baby's neck like snow white blood. Moving in a way to avoid waking him, he reached into his back pocket and fetched out his handkerchief and with careful, careful movements he wiped at the milk. Sopped it up. Put his hand to the bleeding. He wet the corner of the handkerchief with his spit and cleaned the baby's face, noticing the sharp contrast in color between his fingers and infant skin. Sly as a grandma, he picked the infant up under the arms and put him to his shoulder again and patted at his back, feeling the baby come up reflexed and humped, pulling his knees to his belly while he made tiny little squealy noises.

While he patted at the baby's back, Even watched the landscape known as George County, Mississippi, slide past. Little more than a wasteland of scragged-out pine and near swamp, in his opinion. An opinion Canaan would share, he was sure, what with Canaan being male and wide open to true reason. A land consisting of haphazard farmers with the meager boast of three cows and four chickens. Maybe a pig or two. But no brood sow. The land seemed too poor, too barren, too unacquainted with the elements of surplus for that. A fog was rolling in from the south, hovering midway up the trunks of the trees, gathering inside the low pockets of marshland. Instead of feeling the impulse to warn Grace concerning its hazards, he sat back and relaxed, remembering all of her capabilities. Her surefootedness. The noisy proof of her abilities while she rummaged in the kitchen.

"I'll get Canaan to ride with me to Bay St. Louis," Even said, jumping at his words, thinking for an instant that he'd shouted.

"He ain't goin'. I ain't lettin' him have a hand in you givin' away that baby," Grace said.

"I'll go by myself then," Even said. There was an uneasy quiet. Then, "You two act like I got a choice in this. And that's a pitiful shame in my book considering all we gone through." The infant burped and Even relaxed and shut his eyes, rocked by the truck. With his eyes still shut, he stuck a finger into the back of the large diaper, feeling dry. His hand steady patting. Confident in his decision.

Joody could see the top of her head in the rearview mirror and the view spoke words from her earliest age sticks, those hollow, faded years when her breath was hers and nobody else's; years unbrushed, unstirred by reading, uncut and pure, like a thick forest never threatened by scythe. She watched Even's hands on the baby and a hot, sharp edge of something fluttered inside her chest. Something besides regret. Something that felt akin to humiliation. She saw his large fingers to the baby's back and wanted them. Needed them. On her back. Under her armpit. Inside her mouth. I would kill for one finger, she thought, and it was a hot, bristly desire that made her weak. She sent him her thought/need on an easy-to-read silver platter and it came right back to her, unopened, refused. While she watched, his head nodded once, twice, his eyes closing down and heavy while his fingers stayed locked in the baby's garment.

Joody put an unconscious hand to Grace's knee and jerked it back, reading her. Feeling muscles to bone to marrow to blood. Seeing links as strong as a circle of rocks. Borders turning and spinning round a shape that was growing. Why, this one has a seed! A female, bearing a name uncommon! Old Canaan's wood still able to sprout after all. Joody shut her eyes and Grace muttered something like, Lord God, if Jesus don't love a U-turn! and then gave out one blasting trumpet sob, not unlike that of a swan.

The read had cut like a mirror inside a ruin. Like something full of brag over the rotting frames of leftovers. I can read but I can't have. The girl had for half a minute and then she didn't. Grace gonna have again after all these years. Sad and foggy with riddles, her buckboard logic worn clean out, Joody felt like crying. I'm tired of this. Tired of knowing. I've had my fill. Careful not to bump and wake the baby, she went at her years while she watched the fog resting like scattered pox. Some areas contaminated and others clear. Just like life.

"—the hell you doing!" Grace had jerked herself up straight as a pole. Even turned to see Joody unwinding her hair.

"Leave me alone—"

"I ain't either! I got my hands crammed full of everything there is, and here you go! Lord yes, here you go!"

"You just keep on driving—I ain't hurtin' nobody."

"Joody—it ain't the time to be turning crazy. Not now. Not with a fog rolling in." Even said this, low and quiet to keep from waking up the baby. As a reply she reached across his stomach and threw out a handful of sticks. They banged against the side of the truck as they flew out into the night.

"Lord, woman!"

"You hush, too. Your words ain't nothin' right now. I ain't nothin'. All those years of reading other people's news ain't worth the spit inside a goose. I'm sick of it!" Her hair was partially out and blowing wild. She threw three more sticks out the window. Her younger, happier years, he supposed, seeing how they came from the top of her head. "I'm finished with listenin'. Others' stories and sad business. Others' good news. Everybody got something but Joody Two Sun. Ain't no news for her! She got to stand out in the sun 'til it swallow her whole! Just like Ma'am! I ain't listenin' no more to a single thing that comes out anybody's mouth." Her hands were busy with the last of a group of sticks near the back of her skull. In Even's opinion the woman seemed all electrified hair and hard bones.

"Joody, don't——" Grace had put her hand on the woman's leg and was patting it.

"Don't what? What is it exactly that you ain't wantin' me to do? Unwind my hair? Rant and rave?" She threw another handful of sticks out the window.

"That'd do for a start." There was humor to her voice and Even counted her as foolish as a blind man walking straight for a hole. Joody ripped out one stubborn stick and it came out weighted by bloody scalp. Well, there's your answer, Grace, he reasoned. I bet you lose that humor now.

"It ain't your fault and you know it," Grace said, her voice still steady. "It ain't nobody's fault. You heard what that doctor said——"

"I heard Deep Mother whisper everything was gonna be all right, too. Been whisperin' that for months! Words carry about as much weight with me right now as a cupful of dried-up chicken shit!"

"You ain't hearin' me, Joody—it wouldn't have made any difference if you'd been there at all. You could've stood over her tall as Jesus and it wouldn't have meant a thing. Just been one more shadow is all. Just one more body in the room throwing off a shadow and breathin'."

"Oh Jesus. Oh sweet Jesus. I knew—I knew——" Joody remembered the girl looking up at her across that sweet fire and saying, "I believe in you." She remembered the touch of her own personal hand to Grace's knee and feeling the flutter of jealousy. How she had wondered where her news was. Where it was hiding itself. She remembered all these things.

"What'd you know? That they were brother and sister? From what I hear everbody in Petal knew that."

"I knew before——"

"And you think you should've opened up your mouth and said something? Well, let me tell you about folks—you can light a fire and talk to a pig all you want, but it don't mean nothin'. People is people. You make yourself too big."

"She's grievin' is all—" and her grief is six-sided. Even didn't finish, his mouth gone dry as a desert. He saw her back in the sand of Arizona, thrown down and spread open and small. Unrepentant. Proud. Knowing. She's a voice with no one talking back, he reasoned. The bearer of news and the owner of a dusty mailbox. He cleared his throat. "She's so sad she's got to throw part of herself away because of it."

"And there you sit ready to throw away that girl's baby—I guess you so sad you got to toss out something, too!" Grace dismissed him, put a hand to Joody's arm. "You throwin' away your years for nothin', woman! All those years spent with your mama. All those years you spent by yourself, making do. Throwing it all away and it's for nothing!"

"It ain't for nothin'. It's because . . . because . . ."

"She ain't got any mail—" Even said, wishing himself dead or at least out of the truck, realizing the second the words were out of his mouth that he had exposed her; left her drawerless in the middle of a windstorm.

Joody turned to him and stared, her mouth open. Her eyes saying, Hush, Even! Don't tattletale my selfish grief, while her hair, kinked and crinkly and a whole lot longer than he'd ever realized, whipped his lips, caught in his eyes, tangled in her mouth. "She believed in me—she told me so." It came out as a whisper and he knew she was speaking only in part of Valuable. That the largest part of what she was saying was "Joody believed in Joody, and that believing made Joody feel special." He saw himself inside the curved orb of her eyes and he nodded, putting his right hand to her knee with all fingers down the inside of her leg, but his smallest. She laid her hand on top of his, her missing digit replaced by his own, underneath. I love you, he said with his eyes, and she blinked once, her salt sliding down alongside her nose that had always reminded him of Africa. The baby stirred and he bumped it with his free arm. His hand still to Joody.

Grace, grieving single-mindedly, said with hard finality, "You think you the only one she believed in? She believed in all of us, especially that one right over there!" She pointed her finger at the baby. It wasn't until an hour later when they were pulling up at the house in Grand Bay that Even summed up the angles of the conversation and began to suspect the finger had been pointed at him. And that her words had been an indictment.

Canaan, with Persia clutching his elbow, watched the truck come to a dusty stop. Grace stepped out and then Joody, and Canaan's first thoughts on seeing Joody's head was, Thy God! If she don't look like Electra, undone and grieving! The wind picked up and sounded through the trees, and from where he stood the woman seemed all wild-flying hair and hard-edged bones; her nose up, she sniffed the air like a hound.

Pursia tugged at his arm and yelled out, "Jesus wept!"

"And you'll weep too, if you don't hush it up!" Canaan jerked his arm free and walked down the steps saying to everyone and no one in particular, "The old fool's been yelling out and banging that damn cane of hers all day long! Don't you ever leave me alone with her again—"

"Honor thy father and mother!" Persia yelled.

"You ain't either one and I swear, I'm gonna take that cane and break—" And then he saw Even climb out of the truck and what he was holding, and he hushed.

"Thy God—" He paused, waiting for something. Anything. Some word to set things right again. Grace walked forward, her arms crossed pinions over her chest, her head down. "You go with him and you might as well keep on goin'—" and then she took Persia's arm and led her away. "Where's the girl? Where's that Valuable?" Persia was asking. Joody was still out in the center of the yard, her back to the rest, her feet planted in the same spot as earlier in the day—around lunchtime, Canaan figured. Even Grade met him at the steps. "I was gonna ask you to go with me. But that'd be too much."

"First off—" Canaan was holding up his hand. "Where's the girl?"

"They can tell you—I ain't got the heart right now. I got to get on the road anyhow."

"Did you steal that baby?"

"Do I look like a fool, Canaan?"

"Somewhat."

"Neva gave it to me to dispose of—"

"Thy God!"

From the center of the yard: "Lord God sure do love a U-turn. Just ask Grace. Just you go and ask Grace," Joody said. The alternating winds scattering her words. Breaking them apart.

"Jesus H. God, will somebody please tell me what's goin' on here?"

"Valuable's dead," Even said, and then he walked up the steps to the house. The screen door had a black metal peacock on it and he jerked it open by the neck, heard the sound of a hinge that needed oiling. Grace was at the dining room table, one elbow propped up holding her head. Persia had the other hand held to her lap and her face was working loose, her lower jaw disengaging from its hinges. A woman's comfort, he thought, the way they cry so easy. All of them. Young. Old. Middle-aged. This ancient one here with her sad loose skin. Go ahead then. You women weep and cry and carry on while I do the hard work. The manwork that falls to all men who are men by birth but have no earthly clue by whom or where from, or how they happened to be—

The baby was quiet inside his arm. Breathing fast inside some soft pleasant dream, he supposed. His tiny, casually clasped hands resting over his fragile chest, his fingers pink and open and trusting in their linkage. Even looked down and thought, This is a blind man's arm holding the blind to come. Holding one whose seeing newborn eyes are gonna be put out before he's had a chance to see. Made blind by one already blind who found himself inside a world he ain't got a clue of—

Even walked past the women and went through to the kitchen and made up coffee. One-handed. Measuring. Placing. Pouring. Setting it to the stove. Striking a match. Finding a thermos under the sink and washing it out. Doing all these things expertly while he held a baby inside his arm, next to the casing bones of his chest. Man bones that hurt and ached and wanted to cry but couldn't. His grief harder than they imagined. Harder than he imagined. His sadness so cold, it burned all the way down to his toes. Not just for the girl, though. Her sweetness enough to spend a lifetime crying over, for sure. That was there, true. But this deep, ripping grief working steady at his seams, breaking his bones, was for him. For Even Grade. For Even Grade, who wanted some taste of history, or knowing, to replace what he knew for sure of Memphis with its large gray, low-ceiling world. And ain't this something? he said to himself. Ain't this salt put to the sore? I got to do it again and they don't know it. That Persia out there—she don't know it. That Joody out there careening in the wind— she's already forgot. That Grace in there leaning on her hand underneath a yellow light—she ain't got a clue, either. None of them know. They've for- gotten Even Grade and who he is or who he thinks he is, but ain't sure of. They grieve like women who know. Like women who own knowing years. Like people viewing the proof of themselves the same way they look at a pair of shoes stuck back in the closet, shoes they can pull out and polish any old time they want. It's the one who ain't got the shoes or the knowing proof of one's own self, who burns with the wanting. I got to pick myself up inside my very own arms and carry my own self across a cold yard and put my own self down, sleeping and unknowing, on the steps. I got to walk away and leave my own self there alone. Again. I got to be the arms and legs and body that does it, too. I can't blame my mother this time. Nobody to blame but me. And still these weeping women don't know—

He sat in a kitchen chair, exhausted. One large hand over the baby's chest. Feeling its up and down movements. The heartbeats. Wondering over it. Wondering how his mother did it. How many minutes it took her to do it. How many times she considered some other option before doing it.

Canaan walked in, his owlish face quiet and empty, his mouth fresh out of words. His question-mark brow smooth as a never-plowed field. He saw the coffee was done, but judged by Even's face that the man was way past the wanting of it. Moving quietly (like a man not used to moving quietly, which means he made more noise in his quietness than he would have walk- ing normally), Canaan poured hot coffee into the thermos. Cursing the squeaks underneath his shoes, he reached over the table and picked up the sugar bowl. He looked at Even's face again and frowned, thinking, This one here's got to give himself away again. That's why he's got that hand to that chest. It's his chest he's holding. Not that baby's—

Dropping four snow white cubes into black, he shook his head and said, "I ain't lettin' you go by yourself, Even Grade."

"I'll manage."

"I'm sure you would, but that ain't the point." Canaan went and stood behind Even and Even sensed the man's presence and prayed he wouldn't touch him. If he touches me, I'll come undone. The Reality of Even Grade being that he'll fly apart, wilder than Joody—

The baby stuck out its legs and grunted and Even felt warm underneath his hand and laughed, of all things. Canaan snorted, his hands resting on the back of the chair. "The world can burn down around our feet, but there ain't no stoppin' the power of the bowel."

"There's diapers in the truck—"

"I'll get them."

"I'm gonna use Persia's room for this—"

"I'll be right there."

While he waited, Even ran the tap until the water warmed, soaking a cloth he found under the sink. Outside the kitchen window the pecan trees seemed like an army of top-heavy soldiers. Acres and acres of them. A thousand dried-up arms waving in defeat, reaching to heaven for mercy. Stop this, he told himself. The world is not a poem or something extraordinary to be considered. The world's the world. Ain't no use considering it any other way. He looked around at Persia's kitchen, thinking the room already had the look of Grace. The pot holders. The way she stacked things. The way she kept the bread bowl on top of the stove with the rising towel over it, spread open and honest, green and dusty with flour. It's hard to believe Persia ever had a claim to this place, Even thought.

"I got to make peace with these women and then I got to give you away, little man, and I want you to be big about it, as big as I got to be while I make this hard peace. These things don't have to be bad things, either," he told the baby, but the baby slept through, its sleep cushioned and censored by not-knowing. The only one who seemed pinched by the words was the one who spoke them: Even Grade.

Joody was easy—Even put his face alongside her neck and said low, "We all grieving over large things, love. Lots of great big things that go way back. Loss, mainly." She cupped his face with her hands and while her hair whipped him, she kissed him and said, "I love you, Even Grade." She didn't say, "I trust you," and he was glad, trust being a too-hard thing to live up to. Love seemed to rest on a lower rung. He looked over at Canaan, who was standing by the steps holding the baby stiff-armed and cautious, like the infant was porcupine and not human. Grace was there, reaching over once and smoothing down the blanket. She looked at Even and shot him with her eyes, and he knew Canaan's woman was going to be harder.

Patting Joody's arm, he walked over and with open intentions hugged her in plain view of Canaan. Even smelled her hair and her neck, he felt the curves and they felt familiar and sweet as he had imagined. Next to her ear he said, "I ain't trying to hurt anybody, least of all you—" As pliable as concrete, she stood there, her neck canted upward because of his height, on her toes because she didn't want her face at his chest. Even pressed easy and said, "If you got to hate somebody, hate me then, not Canaan. He's a good man. Solid—" He broke then and cried, the only time he had ever cried in front of another, loud and hard like her sob back in the truck. Grace put her arms around his waist then, and said in her low and husky voice, "Well, okay then, Even Grade. Well, okay. I guess you think you doing the right thing." When he took the baby from Canaan and walked hurriedly toward the truck, all Even could think was, Sweet Jesus—those arms weren't at all like my mother's.

They rode through the towns blistered. Each burned by things unspoken. To ease it, Canaan thought on poisonous plants. Noxious greenery. Deceptive and deadly things that are oftentimes if not beautiful, at least inordinately interesting. Hemlock. Pokeweed. Black nightshade and jimson. Sheep laurel and monkshood. The lush and lethal death camas. He held the baby and thought of foxglove and henbane and wondered how many humans had actually died of it. Their degree of pain. His thoughts on Death. Large-lettered and carved in bas-relief. Painted in a color considered outstanding. Red, he decided. Red, trimmed in lacquer black and Chinese gold. He put his bony hand to the baby's blond head and sighed.

Even Grade drove over Bayou Casotte, not commenting on the waterway, thinking instead how silver the moon seemed, hating its commonplace beauty and the regularity of its movement. It seemed they were following it. Chasing it. Heading west with a hunger for silver. It played large and luminous across the water and the marshes, touching the tips of shag and bitterweed, gripping the tall stems of swaying cattails.

He drove through Pascagoula and Moss Point, and while he poured up coffee from the thermos he saw the approach of the Singing River. Seeing the sign Canaan said, "You hear music? 'Cause I sure don't." His sudden vocals sending the baby's arms up-flying in alarm, like the infant had found himself inside a dream of falling.

"Nope. Don't hear a thing," Even said, Canaan's question already gone flying out the window behind him like three of Joody's years. He looked at Canaan's hand on the baby's head and said, "Joleb Green said she named the baby Pearl, you know."

Canaan looked at the baby and then looked at the moon. "Well, they'll give him another, I reckon," and that was all he had to say on it, but Even watched him run his fingers over the baby's skull in consolation.

The moon ahead and the water to both sides, Even drove as one herded toward a course prearranged. Canaan, immersed in his own quiet world, seemed in agreement. The silence large between them. As heavy as the baby was light. As large as the gulf water to the side. They passed Ocean Springs and Biloxi and Gulfport. The lights of Canaan's truck the only lights visible for miles other than the spotlights beaming on Beauvoir. They moved through Pass Christian and Even saw the approach of the bridge. A sign said: St. Stanislaus, Next Paved Left After the Bridge. Another sign said: You Are About to Cross the Beautiful Bay of St. Louis.

The tide was coming in and the water rippled, in-moving and trilled. Canaan sniffed the sea breeze coming in the open windows, thinking the smell of it freshly different from the moldy, cold, wet smell of the river. He licked his lips and tasted salt and looked up at the full moon and then back down at its silvery reflection on the water. While he watched, patterns erupted on the barely moving surface like renegade fish breaking the rules and turning to birds. A light at the end of the bridge flagged a sign with an orange arrow. The sign said St. Stanislaus Academy. Brothers of the Sacred Heart. The arrow pointed left, toward a cove. The words "1 mile" were printed in Day-Glo orange.

Even saw the color of the sign and it came back in a flood. Without knowing that he did it, he put his nose to his armpit and smelled, thinking the old way. Hearing the old words. Wondering if he had taken on an odor again—

The Lutherans had fingers that pinched like teeth, but the white boys were worse—the way they took things and did things and forced things. The smell of boy-urine underneath every motive in spite of vicious scrubbing. Citford Industrial Soap in the bright orange tin. Bought bulk, the tan squares wore down to slivers that turned to gray, gooey mush that sat on fingers like cold grease. Eight years old, his hand to a faucet, a white hand stopping it. Cornered. Water. Not water. Water. Not water. Face to the tile, standing naked first while water beaded pearl-like on fingers. Bent over later, the water forgotten. The orange tin to the floor, crashing like a cymbal while he kicked and screamed. Fearful of water, he avoided the room at the end of the hall. Licked his palms at night and rubbed at his underarms. Tried not to sweat. Tried not to get dirty. For months this, until a wide-aproned woman scrubbed him. Behind the ears. His privates. Hard fingers deep at his crevices, as a lesson. Tearing at his ears and neck skin in front of sixteen younger boys—this too as a lesson. Down in the steel kitchen while he stood naked in a tub of barely warm water that turned dirty brown after twenty seconds. She only had to do it once with the other boys laughing and the attendant standing lazy in the doorway, scratching his head and grinning. Just once and it was enough. He learned to fight the following day. Using teeth and claws that left marks as proof. He won back his safe perimeter and eventually his self-respect, but he never got over his fear of carrying an odor—

Even slowed down and made the turn. Passed the sign. Done with orange, finally.

"You don't have to do this, you know," Canaan said.

"Do what?"

"Give yourself away again," and then he cleared his throat, embarrassed.

Even slowed to make the narrow street, noticing the small businesses, closet-sized and quaint. Stores with a rich seaside look to them that seemed queer for coastal Mississippi. "He's a white baby. I'm a black man."

"There are worse things to lose a shirt over than that—"

Even looked at him, wondering if the man had gone crazy.

"Don't look at me like I'm witless—you know good and well what I'm speaking of." The baby had his fist around Canaan's finger.

"I ain't the daddy."

"But you know who is, and that's a gift—"

"He's white."

"I reckon he'll tan, come summer."

A pier that stretched to a point of disappearance marched off to the left while to the right, a gray statue of the Virgin Mother greeted the truck with broad stone arms. Lights, only two or three, were shining in a solid brick structure set far back on the lawn. Somewhere there were wind chimes calling out major notes, sweet and clear. Large and fresh-smelling, with its face to the ocean, the place had nothing obviously fierce, or unreasonably cold, or unwelcoming about it. And to Even Grade's line of reasoning, it seemed as far from the bleak, grassless yards of the Lutheran home as anything inside God's world could actually be. In a place like this, not knowing where you come from ain't so important. Not knowing could become a background noise, nothing more. The breeze seemed to carry peace with it and Even calmed. The wind chimes again, welcoming almost. Even Grade looked around and judged the place promising with nothing to fear—either for him or the boy—and with that firmly stamped in his mind, he turned the truck around and headed back to Alabama.

38

JACKSON

"To tell you the truth, I don't know what the big deal is." Joleb accidentally switched on the wipers. Licking his lips, he switched them off again, looking once to the side.

"I know you don't, that's why we're having this little talk." George Willard patted his coat, felt around for his notebook. Louise said he carried an inordinate compulsion for its presence. You love that thing more than me, she'd said that morning, her one-sided, almost-lascivious grin turning him on fast as lightning. Never, sweet Louise. Never. Come over here and sit in my lap and I'll prove it. She had replied, Take that thing out of your pocket and I will. Better yet, come clean out of your clothes, Mr. Willard, and I'll kiss you good and proper, her grin broader, making him hard. He had shed his clothes in less than a minute. "Properly," he had said, hopping on one foot, dancing with a black sock. "The word's 'properly'"—

"Did Beryn tell you to talk to me, or Joe?" Joleb shifted gears and noticed his speed. Thirty-five miles an hour. Perfect.

"Neither one."

"Louise, then. It had to be Aunt Louise." Joleb passed over the bridge to the Baby Black and barely looked at the water. Water's water, he told himself. It ain't personal like milk. His eyes to the road, he took that extra measure of carefulness, considering the cargo fragile as eggs, but a helluva lot more expensive. Its value priceless, for more than one reason. A speed zone was coming up and he kept his movements relaxed. Hands at ten and two. Bracketed by woods, he reminded himself to not slam on the brakes, no matter what, not even if a spastic deer were to spring out to the center of the highway. He wanted to wipe his nose but didn't, what with this being his first real job and all, and what with his sharp-eyed boss watching every single move he made.

George looked at him and grinned, impressed with the kid. Kid, hell. Near strapping adult. With an inborn natural gift for mortuary, too. Joleb had helped two weeks past with a teenaged victim of electrocution—a girl fried in the bathtub while tuning to a new station on her plugged-in radio. Helped with the whole process—the transport as well as the preparation of the corpse—only stopping once to say, "Lord have mercy, Mr. Willard, what a mess. And ain't it a shame, too, 'cause there ain't a song on the radio worth listening to right now, except maybe 'Heartbreak Hotel.'"

Joleb felt him watching him and downshifted expertly, slowing to a fluid smooth stop at the railroad crossing. Easing off the clutch he picked up speed again, and best of all, the monument never budged. Didn't give an inch. Just sat there covered up in a moving quilt like it was sleeping.

"You ain't saying much, so I guess it was Aunt Louise."

"Louise is concerned about your nomadic tendencies, that much is correct. And I'll not say anything else about it."

"Man, oh man—" Joleb had used his key, was all. Used his own personal key and gone to the couch in the living room where the record player was, not wanting to make those hall boards squeak by walking the distance to his bedroom.

George grinned and snipped the end off his cigar, amused by it all. The whole business having a voyeur's edge of satisfaction. "You can't keep hopping from house to house, is the point. People have to settle to a routine, know what to expect and when to expect you. That way they can plan. You've been putting it off because it's more fun this way."

"I tell you what, Mr. Willard, I've seen enough naked females to last me a lifetime." He pushed his glasses up on his nose and turned on the signal as well as putting out his hand. Four miles to River House.

"Your aunt has no clue, Joleb, that you were there on the couch and that you possibly could have witnessed the whole business. I think we best leave her standing on that side of assumption."

"The lights were off, thank God." Joleb had still seen tree-trunk legs running up to wide ass as well as that shank of gray hair halfway down her back when she came in the room and put on a record.

"Yes, the Lord is certainly merciful," George said, thinking, And so was she. He'd cried mercy three times that he could remember. Once while standing out in the hall underneath a deer head wearing seven points.

"I swear I shut my eyes, Mr. Willard. I had no desire to see her in the altogether."

"I'm sure you didn't."

"I've seen enough of women in the altogether."

"I'm sure you have." George drew deep on his cigar and smiled. "But a body needs regularity, Joleb, and I'm not talking bowels." He chuckled to himself. "You were a week early and I had no clue you were on the sofa 'til Joe called and I went looking. Of course you were a week off with Beryn as well, so between all the phone calls that night, we got very little sleep. I'll just say once more that you've got three families who want you and it's time to make up your mind."

"Man oh man—"

"Choices, my boy. The world is full of choices."

Neva heard the bell and put one finger to the drapery, opening its seam like a wound. But for his new trappings—the shiny loud car out in the drive—Jackson seemed the same. Maybe half an inch taller, but no more than that. He had yellow roses done up with a white ribbon riding in the crook of his arm. The flowers were about three months too late in her opinion. "Bea?" The wound closed and light disappeared.

Bea was humped in her chair, reading in the dark. Rummaging for words through the shadows. She called out, "Ahah! The word was 'elongated,' Nevé. Imagine that! 'Elongated.' I thought yesterday it was 'electrocute.'" A new hobby of late, her reading in the dark as well as calling Neva by her given French name: Nevé. A family name worn by females for six generations. French for coarsely granular snow from which glaciers are formed. Looking up, Bea's eyes softened. "What is it, sweet?"

"Jackson's here."

Rising like a woman hinged haphazardly, Bea moved to her. "Do you think he'll go away?"

"He's going around back now. Around the side of the house. He brought her flowers, too. Yellow ones. That's them propped up on the porch rail." The two women tracked his progress from inside limited borders, like neutralized animals, once feared, but toothless and fenced now. Shards of light fell and cut across the floors, dissecting objects unaccustomed to exposure. A crushed brass umbrella stand. The busted hall tree. Scattered books and overflowing ashtrays. Boxes of bulbs brought up from the basement sprouting anemic green. They watched from a refrigerator's tall shadow his casual prowl through the cemetery, his eventual stroll out the gate and into the bank of woods where he bent and picked up an abandoned sweater Neva had forgotten about.

"Somebody's timing is impeccable." Bea blew her nose on a tissue, a small flame erupting from her heart.

"Yes, isn't it? Makes me think there might be a God after all." Neva was blinking rapidly, her lips halfway opened to a smile.

Jackson heard the sound of a truck and hesitated before walking out of the woods. He was holding in his hand a mildewed gold sweater he'd found wet and soggy on the ground next to a rusted-out saw leaning on a stump. The place was in a shambles. Lord! As if River House had been used to stage a battle of some sort, what with charred ribs of the garage up and pointing to the sky. After mashing at the front bell until his finger turned cold and blue, he'd peered through and seen an umbrella stand on its side, its center crushed and bent (as if stomped). Three umbrellas lay scattered at the base of the stairs (as if thrown there). Everything dark. Just random background glimmers near the doorways, like pieces of copper clouds were floating in from far-off distant black. Putting Valuable's yellow "I'm sorry I quit writing" roses on the porch, he'd headed around back, passing under a magnolia tree streaked in red, puzzled by it until he looked up and saw a can of paint had been blown there from the heat of the fire. I kissed Val under that very tree, he thought to himself and looked away, the once white now bleeding blossom making him nervous. Those phone calls around Easter making him nervous, too. Neva's voice once. Then Bea's. Both voices followed by the cold sound of the receiver being replaced. Six phone calls all one-way and six-worded. Jackson saying, each time more politely than before, "Could I speak to Val, please—"

"You see that car!"

"I see it! I'm clear! You watch me through the posts, will ya—"

Voices. One of which sounded an awful lot like Joleb's, but for the life of him, Jackson couldn't figure out why Joleb would be all the way out in Runnelstown when he was supposed to be locked up safe in the loony bin in Hattiesburg. The other voice, he didn't recognize.

"—gate's open, Joe! Take it slow now! You got it! Just back it in! Slow now! Watch out for that car! Steady—"

Listening while the truck crunched on gravel and the strange voice called out directions, Jackson came fully out of the woods with the gold sweater in his hand just in time to see a large gray truck make its way around the back edge of the house. It straightened once and then curved to Jackson's right, headed for the cemetery while carefully maneuvering between the remaining post of the burned-out garage. Jackson felt the texture of the wet sweater in his hand and let it fall heavy to the ground. It landed in a pile of soggy raked-up smelly carnations, the stink of rot making him want to puke.

Throwing up a hand, planning on yelling out a proper greeting to Joleb who was driving, Jackson watched in disbelief as the truck made a sudden wide turn, its rear accelerating in his direction. Right before plowing him down, the truck slammed to a stop and its back door flew open, hitting Jackson square in the chest, knocking the breath clean out of his body.

Vaulting out like a madman, Joleb caught Jackson by the front of his shirt and slung him sideways onto the pile of rotting flowers, screaming the whole while, "You murdering bastard, I'll kill you for sure! I'll kill you!" Fighting like a giant toddler, kicking as well as punching, clawing, ripping at hair and clothes, Joleb lunged toward Jackson's neck with the solid hope of biting through to the jugular. His hands slippery and wet, he looked down through a haze and saw red all over the place. Jackson's face. Shirt. The knuckles of his fist. I'm winning! By God! For the first time in my life, I'm winning—

Jackson, more startled than hurt, tried to buck him off. "You idiot! Get off me now!"

"I'll kill you!" Joleb hit him hard with a glancing blow over the eyes and Jackson saw red both ways. Rearing up he tossed Joleb off as one near weightless and scrambled over, grabbing him by the neck in a stranglehold. He would have snuffed him into unconsciousness and then left him witless on the ground to settle down, if he hadn't been pulled off by the short man.

"Cut this shit out right this very minute!"

Jackson tottered to a safe position where he could stand back, winded and bleeding and disappointed as hell at such a pissant welcome. Red ran down his shirt and dripped off his ear, which felt ripped. He bent and spit and saw more red. "Christ, Joleb, what in the world set you off!"

"You killed her, you rotten bastard!" Joleb grubbed along the ground for his glasses.

"I ain't killed anybody!"

"Joleb, we have work to do." George, grabbing the back of Joleb's shirt, jerked him up like a puppy. "You get your ass up and check the cargo! You can carry on like this on your own time. I'll not have it here, though. Not while you're on the clock!"

Still spitting and wiping himself off, Jackson looked up and saw an audience on the back porch of the River House. Two crows were standing in the shadows—one dusty blond and wearing a black scarf, the other with dark hair going gray and blowing free. Droop-shouldered and old, they appeared skinny and frail, their wings clipped. Linked by their elbows, they walked down the steps and across the yard toward the truck. Jackson wiped his mouth and looked at the still-opened door, wondering where Val was and why she hadn't come on out to see about him.

"Mr. Willard," the blond crow said. She looked at Jackson once, then looked away.

"Miss Moore. Miss Gondst." George had tossed his jacket to the truck seat. "I apologize for the skirmish here—"

"There's no need—" Bea said the words while the other just stared out in the direction of the tree that had stopped the truck.

"My God, that tree she cut down—" Neva said, her words gouted whispers.

"—saved this one here's life," George said. Glad of it, too, what with a homicide a huge slug to chug in a fledgling business. "If she'd cut that tree down proper to the ground, we'd be calling for my other vehicle right about now." The truck was still running, blowing smoke, its bumper pinioned against pine.

Neva looked at Jackson and a light of some sort swam up into her dark eyes and then blinked out. Jackson had seen a lot of women go from good looking to bad, more than his share in his family alone, but he had never seen such a transformation as this. These two looked like they hadn't eaten in months. Neva's cheeks were hollowed out and Bea actually had a waist again.

George Willard's notebook was flapping on the ground and Joleb walked over and picked it up for him. "You can hold my pay until the damage is paid for and then you can fire me. It was worth it, though. And I ain't sorry I did it."

George took the notebook and threw it up in the air, fit-like. The pages flew open, tissue-thin as worthless wings. "We'll discuss this on the ride back." He turned, hiding his face in an effort to hide the truth. Hell's bells, he admired the kid for what he'd done. For raising a fist in a claim for justice. There was something of his stalwart aunt to him after all.

Jackson stood looking from one to the other and back to the truck, which was still running and edging backward. At the faces of the women. A slight smile to Bea's face, like she'd just witnessed something that had pleased her. Neva's empty and expressionless, which scared him more than Joleb trying to kill him with the truck. "Where's Valuable?" he croaked out.

"She's right here, buddy boy—" Joleb wiped his bloody nose on his sleeve. His eyes filling up in spite of things.

"I think you men should finish your work first," Neva interrupted. "We've already settled this account. He can find Valuable later. She's not going anywhere."

Joleb looked at the truck. With a shrug he brushed a brown carnation off his shirtsleeves, picked at dead grass stuck to his pants, then went forward on slow feet. The rear end messed up enough to make a terrible grinding sound, but not enough to keep it from being operational, the truck jerked once and then drove as intended. When he had it where he wanted it, he looked over at George.

"I apologize for the delay—" George said, pulling out his handkerchief and wiping his balding head, not liking the nasty turn here. Thinking, What a sour smell this affair has. "It was done last week and I should have—"

"Nonsense. Last week would've been too soon. Today's perfect. Don't you think so, Bea?" Neva said this and George Willard felt cold.

"Perfect," Bea said, but the sound was hesitant, like a bird's cough.

Joleb, uneasy, watched them in triune truck mirrors, remembering things. Number One in capital letters: she had loved him; still loved him. He sensed Valuable's restraining finger on his shoulder, her voice whispering in his ear, *Wait a minute, Joleb. Wait a minute here.* Number Two in letters just as big: whatever Jackson had done, she would have forgiven him. Her voice whispered again, *You're right, Joleb. I would have forgiven him, because I love him. You're absolutely right about that.* She'd never really gone down into the ground at all, in Joleb's opinion. At least not that part of her that still cared about Jackson McLain, that had kissed Jackson McLain's baby with bloodless lips. Joleb ran his hands down the front of his legs and wished he'd remembered these things before he'd ever started this mess.

George slid out a lift-and-pulley–type affair and with one or two adjustments it became an A-frame hoist. Chains beat against metal, their racket fierce as five thousand hammers.

Jackson saw the sign on the side of the truck then. Willard Monument Works. He saw through the solid rain of swinging chains a covered object in the back. A gray padded quilt was tucked around all its edges. He saw this Mr. Willard fellow give a sideways look at Joleb, who was still fidgeting. He saw the faces of the women gleaming beaded salt full of expectation. As if it had sprung out their pores while they waited in some last-chance prayer line. Jackson saw the tamped-down ground, sprinkled by dead flowers and pebbled in spots by rain. A trough here. A gully there. A serious washout up near one end of the mound. One she would be terribly offended by because it would make her feel exposed and uncared for, and she wouldn't want that. She would hate the sinkhole because it said nobody had bothered to see to her after the storm and make sure she was okay. She had wanted to go off somewhere by herself and decompose back to humus, in private, so the neglect of others would be less obvious. She had wanted to wander off into the middle of the woods and die silently by a tree, and here was the reason. Yes, she would be terribly offended by that washout there. She would wish that he would walk over and rummage through the ashes of the garage until he located the shovel and fixed it—

Jackson's knowing was like night breathing, or night swallowing. There all along. Just hidden. She. Valuable. Her face to the east. Her bones set to the dark. Her hands—where were her hands? Folded on her stomach? Resting underneath her head like she'd been caught napping? Where? Proof was milling around in gnatlike circles. The women and their peculiar clothing. Black, but not bossy black like before. True black. Mourners' black. Black as the back side of the heart, black. Joleb. His words. His murderous rage. His bent-up glasses, tilted and repositioned to his face. The flowers. Heaped and smelly. She'd hate that, too, that somebody hadn't done away with them before their shame showed. That all their wilted edges and dried-up leaves were left open to prying, alive eyes.

She. She. She. Oh God— "You LIE! YOU ARE ALL FUCKING LIARS!!" Jackson screamed this out to no one in particular, since no one in particular had said a single word. He ran to the back of the truck and with a sound like wind slapping in a sail, ripped off the covering.

Jackson retreated three steps, bent at the waist and vomited while the unaffected, accustomed now to loss, watched the nonessential elements of the River House play in the wind. Birds. Dust. Ashes. Petals of flowers. Still breathing hard, his hands brushing at his knees while he studied his ruined loafers, Jackson stumbled aimless as a drunk, wiping his mouth on his sleeve. The words out in front of him, as well as behind, tattooed to his forehead and heart like some essential proverb:

VALUABLE KORNER
"MOTHER OF PEARL"
OCTOBER 19, 1941—APRIL 13, 1957
Finally at rest in her Father's arms

While water gushed out the hose, Joleb told him about it. The others moved around him like sluggish ants and Jackson thought, Why, they've all got an urge to garden all of a sudden, and ain't that strange? Joleb talked steady while he worked at the faucet stopping a leak. Neva had put a raggedy apron on over her black and gone for a hand spade. Bea was wearing a beat-up straw hat over her black scarf. The red wheelbarrow was parked by the cemetery fence catching her handfuls of dead flowers. Gardeners inspired by the new marble ornament, Jackson supposed, and looked away from the pink.

The leak stopped, Joleb wandered over and sat on the steps beside him. He felt like Val might expect him to put his arm around Jackson, or maybe pat him on the leg or something. Some show of comfort. But Joleb couldn't, thinking it might be offensive right at the moment considering how he had tried to kill him a half hour earlier. Neva came out the back door with a box in her hands—a wooden slatted box of bulbs, their pinkish green tips an inch up in sawdust.

"How?" Jackson asked.

"I just told you how. She died having a baby. Your baby." Joleb drank from the hose and then tossed it aside.

"But how?"

"She bled to death."

"How?" he asked again. Joleb blew out his air and looked down at his hands like, Boy, oh boy, we got us a one-word Indian, here!

"How?" Jackson asked Neva this time, believing her viciousness would make her the most forthright with the information.

"We've told you how. There's nothing more to say." Neva looked up while she pulled on plaid gardening gloves. She picked out a mushy bulb and culled it to the side. Joleb looked at her and glared, suddenly remembering why he hated her so much. Hated all women, for that matter. Well, except for Grace and his Aunt Louise and Joody and maybe that crazy cane-banging Persia. And, of course, Valuable. He would always love Valuable.

Jackson's hands were shaking like one palsied, and Joleb looked away, troubled. "She died having the baby, Jackson." He spoke slowly, spacing out his words as if speaking to a retard. Water gushed over by the camellia bushes, the hose writhing along the grass like a snake.

"How?" Jackson asked again and put a restraining hand to his eyes because they felt like they were about to shoot across the yard.

Joleb remembered feeling the same way when he was in the hospital. All those holes and spaces that needed filling up. He understood what Jackson wanted. "You want to know the whole story, don't you? Everything."

Jackson nodded, flooded suddenly by relief at being understood. Amazed it had turned out to be the moron who finally did the understanding.

"About a week before Easter, we were coming home in the car from Grand Bay, and she thought she was having bathroom cramps. By the time I got her upstairs and in the bed, the baby was almost here, only we didn't know that's what was happening. If I had known that I would have taken her straight to the hospital. She thought she had to go to the bathroom was all. So I didn't worry too much. When she started hurting really bad, she wouldn't let me leave her to go to the phone. Just kept screaming for me to stand there and help her with this, or help her with that and I did. She was pulling at her clothes, saying they were hurting her so I helped her get undressed—" He took a deep breath, thinking back to everything.

Neva was still as a pole over by the faucet, listening. Hearing things she'd wondered about for months now, hanging up on words "screaming" and "hurt."

"—she had wet the bed, bad, so I put the quilt down on top of it for her, so she wouldn't have to feel it, so maybe she would be more comfortable or something. And then she was cold because she didn't have her clothes on, so I got her a clean sheet to cover up with—" He took off his glasses and played with them. Bent the earpiece back and forth. "We both finally figured out what was going on and I headed downstairs to call the doctor. When I was halfway down she yelled for me, and when I got up there it—the baby—was already coming out—"

Neva's back was to him, her hand with the tool, extended. The other hand over her chest while her eyes shut down to steady her breathing.

"—she had a baby boy right here, up in her room. Something happened, I can't remember what the doctor called it, but something happened to her insides that made her bleed to death. He said that the same thing would've happened even if she'd gone to the hospital."

Jackson realized his heart was moving his body while he sat on the steps. The edge of the porch advanced and retreated, advanced, retreated. Bricks seemed to breathe from his side vision.

"Why didn't you tell me?" Jackson stood up, done with Joleb. The question Neva's, who stood statue-like watching the yard work. The fresh sod too green against the century-old St. Augustine. Two days of solid rain had done the damage, and once she'd seen it, she'd called right away, knowing the monument would be delivered as soon as the weather permitted, knowing Valuable deserved far more than a washout around her toes. A crew of six men, implements in hand, had made an appearance fifteen minutes after the boy puked on the lawn. Neva bent over her box of bulbs again, Val's schedule of putting them to the ground on Good Friday sidetracked by Valuable herself.

"Why didn't you tell me? She had the number. She could've called me, or told me something—" Jackson looked at Neva while Joleb stood, brushed his hands to his pants and watched George fool with the truck.

"You quit writing to her," Neva said bluntly.

"I was . . ." What? Busy? True. But not too busy. Never too busy for this.

"Because she stopped getting letters, she asked us not to say anything. Toward the end she was afraid you'd try to take the baby. She was plagued with various . . ." What? Irrational concerns? True. But none worth exposing in order to reestablish a broken connection. "We thought it best, is all. Now, leave me alone."

"Where's the baby?"

"The baby died," Joleb said matter-of-factly, waiting for Neva to turn around and declare him a liar or maybe even slap him in the face. She didn't do a thing. Just stood there watching the workers.

Neva sighed, slightly puzzled but not enough to contradict. He'd been so brutally honest with all the other details the lie seemed out of place and unnecessary.

The hood slammed to the truck and Joleb looked over at George and judged his distance. Pushing his glasses up on his nose he said quickly, "Valuable named the baby Pearl and he only lived a few minutes. We buried the baby with her because we thought that was what she'd want."

"Joleb! You Joleb! We got more work back at the shop——" George Willard shut the back doors with a bang. Joleb watched his aunt's husband climb into the driver's seat and crank it up, assume his position as vehicle operator. Well, I guess I'm fired, he thought. Guess I get to sit in the other side going home and twiddle my thumbs and not worry a bit about being so careful. Relieved suddenly he turned to Jackson, glad he'd kept his mouth shut about Pearl was being raised by the coloreds.

"Jackson, I'm sorry I tried to run you down. If I had it to do over, I hope I'd not do the same thing. I can't say that I wouldn't, but I hope I'd at least take my time and think it through."

Jackson looked at him while his hands shook violently between his knees. Joleb put his hand on his shoulder and whispered, "Used to, when I couldn't get mine to quit shaking, I'd sit on them. Sometimes that helps." He walked off whistling toward the truck while watching Negro feet bearing down hard on shovels. Valuable would like the way they fixed her up. All those flowers and that pink marble headstone. She'd like the baby being in Grand Bay, too. He'd been there and seen the whole business for himself. Seen them all hovering over that pink-white baby like he was a living and breathing ten-pound pearl.

Joleb picked up George's notebook from off the ground and thumbed through it. Every single page was nothing but doodles and lines and arrows going this way and that. Total foolishness. He climbed in, tossing the notebook to George, who caught it and slipped it back into his shirt pocket. "That notebook makes her crazy, you know," Joleb said. "Makes her crazy as hell."

"I've told her the truth about it, but she imagines the worst."

"She thinks you keep other women's phone numbers in there. Maybe their body dimensions and shoe size." His Aunt Louise having turned talkative over morning oatmeal, which made him squirm, too. Joleb craned his neck to see out the back. Watching for Jackson's car.

"Does she really, now?" George pulled out a cigar, snipped off the end and lit it up, all the while shifting gears and dodging yard debris. Joleb was impressed.

"Why don't you just pull it out and show it to her?"

"Because a sagacious man holds his cards to his chest." George Willard, not-so-recently-out-of-Jackson, winked at Joleb and then pulled out on the highway, grinning while he worked his way through the gears.

Joleb had no idea what 'sagacious' meant, but he sure as hell intended to look it up as soon as he found a dictionary.

Jackson stood up and his handkerchief dropped to the ground. It had been stuck to his head to stop his bleeding, and he'd forgotten.

"You really should see a doctor about that." Neva glanced at him once.

Jackson picked up his mop rag and shoved it to his pocket. "Something's wrong here. I don't know what it is, but something just don't feel right about this whole thing."

"I think it might be that we've had time to adjust to this and you've walked into it fresh—"

"No, that ain't it—"

"Well, I tell you what, as soon as you figure it out, you come back and see me and explain it. None of us is going anywhere. Hell, nobody this side of the Leaf has ever gone anywhere." She picked up her box of bulbs and headed off in the direction of Bea. Jackson looked over at the yard men and one of them caught his eye and threw up a companionable hand. They were sitting on their asses, wiping their sweat and talking. One began to sing the refrain of a familiar-sounding church song. Jackson heard the baritone, low and deep, following him while he walked around the house, headed to his car. Shaken. Every fixed marker he'd ever trusted in rubbed out, blown clean off the map. The voices bellowed out the chorus behind him while magnolia leaves clattered overhead.

In the sweet, by and by, we shall meet on that beautiful shore
In the sweet, by and by, we shall meet on that beautiful shore . . .

Eleven hours later, when he pulled up in his drive on Peachtree Street in Chamblee, Georgia, Jackson could still hear the black men singing.

39

R.L.L.

———————

NEVA BREATHED IN DEEP, her eyes cool for the first time in months. Their actual orbs bathed in something not so cold as ice, but almost. He sat beside her. His long legs stretched out. Those black shoes of his shiny. She saw the kneeler in front of her, standard brown leather, old and cracked. Behind her, the cutout railings of the choir loft that had always reminded her of *Heidi.* Neva breathed in deep and smelled inexpensive cologne.

"If you're expecting those classic words, 'Bless me, Father, for I have sinned,' you're wasting your time."

"How are you, you hard old queer?" The priest kissed her soundly, genuinely, on the cheek and grappled with her shoulder, determined to hold her. She gave to it finally and laid a head to his chest and he breathed in her smell, that familiar mixture of all things highly polished. Leather. Brass. Marble. Hard things involving elbow grease. The base of the altar showed the beloved disciple leaning on Christ, but he was too much of a cynic to comment, even to himself, on the similarity. "I'm waiting on an answer. How've you been, Nevé?" He had always loved her given name. Like a desperate prayer sent aloft from an iceberg, he always thought.

"You're determined to make this hard on me, aren't you, Louis?" She had always called him Louis instead of Russ.

"No harder than you deserve."

"I suppose you want me to haul ass and make my way to the confessional and pour out my heart?"

"No. Just close in the distance is all. Come see me more than once a decade. Maybe write to Dad once in a while is all."

"He's forgotten me."

"He's eighty-two, but he's not forgotten. Not by a long shot."

"Well, he should."

"I won't let him." He kissed her hard again and she relaxed, leaning back on his arm while watching ceiling shepherds, pastel and flaked. One of the ancient popes was missing his eye. "It's been fifteen years, Nevé. Time enough for anything to pass."

"To be my younger brother, you always have been a pompous know-it-all ass."

"Just confident, my dear. Just confident."

"In what?"

"In knowing you'd show up one day, needing me to listen. Needing, if not redemption, at least restoration. You burned down a barn, after all, or so the story goes. Buried a sweet nonrelative you had grown uncharacteristically attached to." Russ patted her hand. "I think you need me. Finally."

"I think you overestimate my quest for inner peace, Louis—"

"No—it's there." Russell Landry watched a candle sputter and blink and then burn on brighter than ever. "Just waiting to surface, Nevé. Like most things."

Epilogue
GRAND BAY, ALABAMA

1961

E VEN GRADE STOOD IN THE CENTER of the bridge and considered the
season. Knowing without looking through his hands or pondering on
a rock or praying to the heavens that like the earth, turned over fresh and
waiting for the sun, April would always signal for him the beginning of
things. That he would always look forward to that month and miss it when
it was gone and be struck the whole while by remembering. That he would
always see April as if it were the end of a walk up a long dark hall, or the
light at the end of a stretch of dirt road.

Grand Bay was different. Quieter. Slower in speculation. A community of little more than a hundred, most too busy coddling cash crops of cotton and soybeans to take time to notice a man standing center of a bridge.
There were more trucks than cars here, just like back in Petal. But after four
years of consideration, Even had judged the standard of the tractor higher in Grand Bay than in Mississippi. He was yet to see the bones of one
drifting to dust underneath somebody's little-used overhang. He was yet to
see the actual Grand Bay, as well. Folks talked about it and claimed it was
back there somewhere hidden behind the reeds and the water oaks, but its

only proof of existence came at night when Even caught a whiff of brack-
ish water.

He settled for the reality of the Escatawpa River, instead.

South, off of Highway 416 in the direction of Hurley, Mississippi,
the Escatawpa ran a natural border between the Cotton and Magnolia
States, and in those early days after the long trip to Bay St. Louis he would
stand and study the water, his eyes casting for secrets. Farmers would pass
him and honk and he'd wave. One or two would stop to ask if he were okay
and if he needed anything, anything at all, and he'd answer back, I'm fine,
just lookin', is all, and they'd drive off, not made curious in the least by a
black man standing tall and still in the middle of nowhere.

Even shifted his weight and looked down by his foot and saw something more dull than shiny, somebody's nickel, and then he looked at the
water again, remembering how he used to stand one foot in Petal, the other
in Hattiesburg. And now here I stand, one foot in Alabama, the other in
Mississippi. And he reasoned it symbolic somehow, a statement concerning personal growth, and a broader scope.

Pearl squirmed. "I want Sophy," he said. The voice a perfect mix of the
two—a husky thread that had belonged to Valuable, the low harmonic tone
that was clearly Jackson's.

"She'll be here in a minute." Even patted his leg.

"How long a minute?" Pearl didn't trust minutes. They could turn to
hours before he knew it.

"A medium-sized minute," Even said, and Pearl settled, his legs dangling over Even's shoulders, his chin resting on the top of Even's head while
he sucked his thumb. He mumbled around it, "How come Sophy gets a
cake, too?"

"Because she's a year younger than you are and when you get a cake she
wants one, too." Even shifted his weight, his hands to the boy's tennis
shoes. He could feel the toe nearly to the end and realized he'd be needing
a new pair in a week or two.

"I'm older than Sophy?" Pearl peered around and looked into Even's
eyes, genuinely surprised. He had both hands to Even's cheeks, the still-wet
thumb of his right hand mashing Even's eyebrow.

"I thought you knew that, son. You're four and she's three."

"Are you sure?" He still had his hands to Even's cheeks.

"Yes, I'm sure." Even wondered what little Miss Sophocles Marie had been up to this time. Barely three and ruling the world. The Grand Enfant of Grand Bay. Some year's Pecan Queen, he was certain.

Pearl's gray eyes were upside down, his gaze as serious as his tone. "Daddy, Sophy don't know that. She says she's older than me and don't have to listen to a word I say. Not even when I say, 'Don't you get in that road, Sophy!'" He pointed his finger for emphasis.

"Were you tryin' to boss her again?" Even watched gray eyes disappear. An emerald green like that of peacock feathers was springing up along the banks of the river and he'd brought the boy to see. "Girls don't like to be bossed, Pearl. I told you that." Even Grade made a box of his hands and peered through, careful of tennis shoes swinging.

"Do boys?"

"Nope, boys don't like it either."

"Does Joody?"

"Never, ever."

"What about Canaan?"

"Not him either," Even snorted—leave it to Grace and Canaan's daughter to lead this one down a course of no resolution.

"Do you?"

"No. Nobody likes to be bossed. But somebody's got to work. Some folks will work without a boss, but not everybody. That's why there are bosses in the world."

"I think Grace is all of usses boss." Pearl put his thumb back into his mouth, satisfied with his evaluation.

Canaan pulled up and parked. Before the two adults could grab her, Sophy reached over and blasted the air with the horn and Even and Pearl nearly jumped out of their skin. Joody climbed out, the girl riding on her hip.

Tennis shoes drummed on his shoulders. "I want Sophy." Even lifted him over his head and the boy ran whooping like an Indian. Dressed in cobalt blue, the little girl was the pint-sized image of Grace. When she saw Pearl running up the highway she bucked like a horse and yelled out, "Pearl!"

"She ain't got her shoes on, Canaan," Joody warned, her arms tight, but not too tight, around the squirming three-year-old.

"I got them here. Right here in my hand. If I ain't too old for this business, I don't know who is," he grumbled, black patent leather shoes in his hands, small white socks tucked in each, while his daughter threw back her head and viewed Pearl upside down.

"I tell you what, we ain't in the truck five seconds before she starts pulling off her clothes—" Canaan said. "This best be a habit I can break or this one ain't ever leaving the house without me or her mother!"

"You say that true. Where's Grace?" Even said, watching Joody kiss the girl underneath her neck, making her squeal. With the child to her hip, one leg of her overalls rode up and he could see the markings running down her leg disappear into a white tennis shoe.

"She's back home with Joleb and Persia. Joleb's a grown man now, Even. Just you wait and see. He says he's goin' to the Philippines in three weeks." Joody handed over the child and stretched her arms to the sky, popping out her back. She ran a hand over her head and Even wondered if she missed those years she threw out the window. With her hair short as velvet, the full light of the sun gave it a color of pewter. The Velveteen Rabbit, Canaan called her. Sheared close to the scalp, it suited her. Gave her a look as alien to Alabama as a pineapple plant on Mars.

Sophy's shoes to her feet, she ran to Even and hugged his knees. A brand-new stick to her hair gleamed in the sun. Three months early, too. Grace, uncharacteristically silent on it, allowed Joody this ritual. That, and her storytelling of Good King Nez and his tribe of red-faced rocks. "She wore you down, I see." Even ran his finger over Sophy's new blue stick. "How long'd it take?"

"'Bout five minutes of steady whining." This from Canaan.

Pearl was rolling down the embankment that ran headlong into a white beach where they picnicked during the summer. When he reached the bottom he threw back his head and howled like a wolf. His arms were out and his shirt halfway off when Even whistled, loud and long. "Not today, Pearl!"

"Not for just a minute?" The boy pouted, his shirt still up, his belly button showing.

"No sir, it's still too cold. We got to wait a while."

Sophy was sitting beside the road pulling off her shoes again, already ten steps ahead of him.

"Sophy Mosley, if you pull those shoes off one more time I'm gonna whip you quicker than Jesus," Canaan yelled, while he went running to the blue. "Don't you pull those off—"

"But, Daddy—"

"No, ma'am. You ain't gonna do it. You'll catch pneumonia."

"What's pneumonia?" She had her shoes off and in her hand. The socks tucked in neatly. She looked at Even and grinned.

"It's a bad fever," Canaan said.

"What's a fever?" She had dropped her shoes and was reaching around behind her searching for buttons.

Pearl had scrambled back up the hill, huffing and puffing, grass in his hair. "Pneumonia means you're too sick to get any cake. Don't it, Daddy?"

Even looked from one to the other. "That's right. Too sick for cake. But that's okay, we'll give Joleb Sophy's piece." He winked at Joody.

"But Joleb eats like a pig—Mama said so." Her lower lip began to quiver.

"That's Parris Island's problem now." Canaan opened the truck door and deposited his daughter on the seat, rearranging her blue dress. Large dark fingers to tiny pearl buttons. "Got himself an official Gyrene haircut. Ugliest shape to a head you ever seen in your life!" Canaan buckled the patent leather shoes, looking at his daughter. "What you cryin' for?"

"'Cause Joleb's gonna eat my cake! Uncle Even said so!" She wailed loud enough to bring down the house while Pearl grinned. Even looked from one to the other, felt Joody come up and rest her chin on his shoulder, listened to her voice whisper in his ear, "Mister Canaan man just buckled those babydoll shoes in less than thirty seconds. Not bad for a man who still can't catch a fish." Even nodded, watching. She said, "I think you two about the most special men I ever met in my life—"

"You met a lot of men in your life, Miss Joody Two Sun?" Even pulled her to him.

"I met me a few." She was acting shy and he loved it. She knew he loved it.

"A few?" This soft in her ear while Sophy screamed.

"One or two."

"Well, now, I think we better go down there and sit by the water and talk about this." He grinned while he watched Pearl climb up into Canaan's truck and huddle by Sophy. Pearl took her thumb and tried to put it to her mouth to shut up her crying. She screamed louder.

"Sophy, you hush it right now!" Canaan straightened her dress out and rolled his eyes while the girl cried harder. "I'm taking these two home. Jesus H. God, if it ain't one thing, it's another!" But he was smiling.

Even saw the tiny scar shaped like a question mark over the man's eyebrow, and it seemed like it had always been there. He tried to remember how he had looked before a hurled bottle birthed it, but couldn't.

"You go on—we'll be there in a minute." He had his finger in the side loop of Joody's overalls, tugging.

Pearl leaned up, concerned. "How long a minute?"

"A medium-sized minute," Even said, and the boy leaned back, satisfied.

Waving them on, standing and watching until they made the turn and headed for home, Even took her hand and walked her down the embankment to the sand. Slipping out of their shoes, they stood ankle-deep in water the color of ten-minute tea and smiled.

ACKNOWLEDGMENTS

I WOULD LIKE TO THANK several people for their support during the writing of *Mother of Pearl*. My father and mother played a part in the book's beginning without their being aware of it. I am forever in their debt. My father drew the figurative map that enabled me to find my way back to Petal, Mississippi. Pointed out where my great-grandmother Luvenia was buried, that quiet spot up on Hillcrest Loop where the story seemed to rise up out of the ground like so much smoke. His and my mother's shared memories eliminated time-consuming U-turns that might have proved discouraging.

In due season my husband took this map and faithfully navigated through the Mississippi underbrush. Helped me find the water. And once it was found—once I actually stood on that bridge and imagined—he provided the necessary environment that made the actual writing possible.

My agent, Wendy Weil, has been as generous with her enthusiasm as her thoughtful advice. She's made it feel as though New York were right up the street from my front porch in Grand Bay, Alabama. I consider this a marvelous gift. Emily Forland, who after a long summer of reading, pulled the manuscript out of a tall stack and gave it a future; I am happily in her debt. Martha Levin's thoughtful, sensitive, enthusiastic editing brought the book to what it should be, what it was designed to be all along.

Finally, to my friends Mary Gerhardt and Judy Sheppard—you read it, believed in it, held your breath while I waited. I look forward to repayment in a similar way.

ABOUT THE AUTHOR

MELINDA HAYNES grew up in Hattiesburg, Mississippi. A painter for most of her life, she now writes full-time from her home in Grand Bay, Alabama, where she lives with her husband, Ray, and an adopted greyhound, Elaine. *Mother of Pearl* is her first novel.